# Desert Rose

## Peter Chandler

Desert Rose

No part of this book may be copied, transmitted by any means, or stored in any retrieval system, without the expressed or written consent of the author.

Cover design and photo by Lou Ramos and Karen Iglinsky

ISBN-10: 1481906704
ISBN-13: 978-1481906708

# Acknowledgements

Thanks and appreciation goes to the members of the Johnson County Writers Club for their encouragement and knowledge. Without them, and my wife's insistence, I would have never pursued my dream.

Everything has beauty,

but not everyone sees it

Confucius

# Prologue

The *John Deere*, looking more like a prehistoric monster in the fading light of day than a backhoe, took another bite out of Southwest Texas' sun baked soil.

With narrowed eyes, Cody watched as the operator brought its squealing jaw back up, swung it to the side, and then vomited the load onto a waiting vinyl tarp, one of several that had been spread out like picnic blankets in a city park.

Like a scene out of an old west movie, several hand held screens then sifted through the dirt as if panning for gold in the Sierra Madre Mountains of Southern California.

With a hint of pity in his eyes, Billy, standing next to him with his arms crossed in front of his barrel shaped chest, took them off the proceedings for a brief moment and gave him back the sketch. He gestured over his shoulder towards one of the department's Ford Expeditions and said, "You know, I kind'a feel sorry for him."

Cody looked at him with deep furrowed brows. "You've got to be kidding? Why?"

"All those years spent in the dark, of being lied to and deceived, and then learning the answers may be right here under his feet. That had to be hard on him. I don't know if I could've handled that myself."

"Yeah, well let's not forget the most important thing here, lieutenant. Olivia's the one who has to grow up with all this baggage."

Upon hearing those words, Billy got closer to him, looking around; making sure no one else was within listening range. "What about that thing inside the barn?" he asked. "Will it take care of yours?"

Finding closure there was the last thing on Cody's mind, and certainly the last thing he had expected to find. He had thought about that, and whether he could actually prove that what he had seen was indeed the end of the riddle; the end of his nightmares, and the end of his twelve months long search.

"We'll just have to wait and see," he told Billy, shifting his eyes to the Expedition while running the back of his right index finger across his thick mustache. After a few seconds of silence, he said, "I'll be right back."

At the sight of him approaching, Deputy Jones lifted the crime scene tape as high as he could so the thirty six year old, six foot, four inch, Pecos County sheriff could pass by. The four deputies, huddled by the passenger's side of the Expedition, parted as if he was Moses and they were the Red Sea. In the back seat, mostly hidden from view by the looming darkness and the tinted window, sat a handcuffed figure with his face buried between his knees. Before Cody eyed him, he cocked an ear towards the howl of a Prairie Tenor staking his claim on a piece of the vast territory, warning all other Coyote's, except the females of course, to stay away.

Concerned about his long time friend, Billy approached and noticed him staring at the distant mountain.

"You know something, lieutenant," Cody said, "We just might have it all wrong."

"About what?"

"The coyote."

# 1

Olivia's eyes flew open at the seismic tremor of the walls. Facing the bedroom door, she lifted her head off the pillow and stared at the sliver of light sneaking through the bottom. She listened. It was the *other* daddy; the one who would come home in the middle of the night slamming the door behind him, looking and smelling like a New York City Sanitation Department worker who had finished his route then stopped at the local bar to wipe out all memories of the day.

In reality, though, he had either fallen as he staggered home drunk, or wound up in some trash laden alley after certain bill collectors had paid him a visit.

How could this daddy be so different from the other? How could this be the same one who would tip toe into her bedroom and plant a powder puff kiss on her cheek. How could he be the one who would treat her mommy like a queen? How could they be one and the same?

It didn't matter that she was only four years old. She knew her daddies. She knew them from the beginning—just as she knew the difference between night and day, good and evil.

Unfortunately, the administrators and teachers at PS 205 on Southern Blvd didn't. They only suspected.

"She's such a bright little girl," the kindergarten teacher said on Francis' last visit to Olivia's school. "I'll never understand why she keeps falling and bumping into things at home. She doesn't do it here."

"I guess she's just a little more careful here," Francis said. "You know how kids are. They don't want the others to make fun of them and laugh."

"I suppose you're right. Anyway, I'm sorry you had to come in today, but we just needed to know what was going on. We'll just keep an eye on her to make sure it doesn't happen here."

"Thank you, Ms. Pennyworth. And I'll try to watch her more closely at home, I promise."

At home that night, the first clap of thunder came from her daddy's mouth after her mommy told him there was no money to spare. That all she had was a few dollars to buy groceries come Friday.

As the voices grew louder, the natural curiosity of a child took over. She got out of bed and went to the door. She opened it just enough to peek out and confirm her suspicion. Then she ran back, jumped into her bed, and then pulled the cover over her head so that not even the nightlight would sneak in. She wrapped herself around teddy bear and waited for the storm to pass.

She heard but didn't see the two legs being kicked away, leaving the coffee table listing starboard like a sinking barge. She heard but didn't see the ceramic lamp spread out on the floor like pieces of a jigsaw puzzle. And she heard but didn't see the second hand curio cabinet, its shelves looking like collapsed bleacher seats.

The rampage continued even in the master bedroom where he emptied then splintered the dresser draws against the wall. He attempted to set the subsequent pile of wood, paper, and clothing on fire, but was too drunk to even light the match.

After a while, her ears had enough. Unafraid of goblins, monsters, or the boogeyman, she grabbed teddy, jumped out of bed, and then ran to the darkness. There she sheltered herself and, like one yet to witness the evils of the world, assumed the fetal position. In the breathing silence, she felt the rapid thumping of her heart and the warm tears flowing down her cheeks. She pinched her eyes shut, then rocked back and forth mumbling, "Stop, don't stop, stop, don't stop, stop, don't stop."

Outside her storm shelter, Tony was busy knocking out several of her mother's teeth and blackening her left eye. When she tried to get away, he pummeled the back of her head with a half empty beer bottle until it shattered. Blood and beer blinded her as it flowed freely down her face. She fell back against the wall, painting it with a swath of crimson as she slithered to the trash littered floor. Through mangled lips she tried to calm the storm but couldn't. It kept pelting her with punches that felt like baseball size hail. By the time he was through, her face looked like a medium rare hamburger that had been doused with ketchup then trampled on.

Through lips foaming like a mad dog, he cursed her bloodied face and screamed for her to get up. When she didn't move fast enough, he grabbed her by the hair, ripping strands off her moistened scalp as he lifted her up. Then he twisted her arm behind her back.

Olivia's eyes flew open again, not at the bone-chilling scream that had penetrated her sanctuary, but the eerie silence that followed. She lifted her head from between her knees, pushed herself up off the floor and opened the door.

# 2

"I have read the affidavits, the settlement agreement, and the final decree," the Judge said. "And...."

DEA agent, Robert W. Albrecht, smartly dressed in one of his best *Calvin Klein* suits, glanced at his *Cartier* watch, then looked over his shoulder towards the right side of the gallery where New York socialite, Nancy Brewer, knowing she had finally opened Amber's eyes, sat with a smirk of satisfaction on her face. The leech sitting next to his attorney was about to be permanently extracted from his third marriage.

"...since, in the opinion of this court, the stipulations as written were found warranted," the Judge continued, picking up the gavel, "Absolute Divorce Decree, Case No.CV77-1040 is hereby...."

When the gavel came down, the five foot nine, two hundred and thirty pound, Robert, peered at his mother-in-law thru slanted, slate-gray eyes. Then, with his left arm inconspicuously close to his chest, he cocked his thumb and pointed the index finger straight at her. *Pop...Pop...Pop.*

"...granted. This court is now adjourned."

It was a scene played out in real life on June 8, 2002, and in his mind as he drove to work exactly two years later to the date. He considered the former day one of the most damaging of his life, just as the United States Drug Enforcement Agency considered January, 16, 2003, theirs. The events of that day were so damaging that after Tony D'Angelo's body was discovered, those who were involved in the investigation knew better than to discuss the outcome among themselves, let alone anyone outside the agency.

What they didn't know then was that Tony's untimely death impacted Robert's life more than anyone could have ever imagined. As a result, he was more than willing to talk about it as soon as Carlos Badillo's whereabouts would come to light.

To his surprise, the opportunity to do just that came on the day after headquarters received a call from the Dallas, Texas field office.

When he arrived at the Arlington, Virginia headquarters, he started the day off with his usual stop by the large box of donuts conveniently located next to the coffee pot. Once he filled the Styrofoam cup and picked out his jelly filled fix, he proceeded down the hallway towards his cubicle stuffing his chubby face and carefully sipping the hot brew. Halfway there, an agent, who had just come out of the department chief's office, walked past him and said, "Good morning," then startled him by finishing it off with, "you're just in time."

Just as he was about to take another bite, Robert stopped and turned around. "For what?"

With a smirk on his face, the agent glanced back over his shoulder and flipped a thumb towards the door at the end of the hallway. "He wants to see you right away."

"What's up?"

"He wouldn't say. You'd better get in there."

Robert wolfed the rest of the donut, gushed what was left of the coffee, and then slam dunked the cup into the trashcan. After wiping his mouth and hands, he brushed the white powdered sugar off the front of his navy blue, suit, and then stuffed the napkin into his pocket. At the chief's door, he made a feeble attempt to flatten the creases on the jacket with the palms of his hands then knocked.

"Come in."

He opened the door and prudently stuck his head in. "Did you want to see me?"

"Yes. Close the door behind you and pull up a chair." Without looking up, the chief pointed to one against the wall to his left.

Chief Weatherford was a six foot, two inch ogre who tipped the scales around two hundred and eighty pounds. He had short-cropped white hair, a round face with a ruddy complexion, and gunmetal blue eyes. The minute Robert sat down he stopped scanning the paper work in his hands and looked him straight in the eye. "We got word your man crossed the border and is back in the states."

"Carlos?"

"Yes. He was spotted on the international bridge by one of our Mexican counterparts. Unfortunately, the agent couldn't make a move without blowing his cover or stirring up an international ruckus on the bridge. All he could do was get in touch with one of our stateside agents working at the crossing."

"Tell me we got him."

Weatherford put the papers down, leaned back in his chair, and then reluctantly said, "No. As luck would have it the agent lost him somewhere on our side of the bridge before backup could get there."

"How in the world did that happen?"

"Easy!" Weatherford said in disgust. "He picked the morning rush hour to make his move. In case you don't know, that's when the Mexican labor horde comes across."

"That makes the score two to nothing, doesn't it?"

"He's not only a thorn on our side, Robert, he's also one of the most cunning we've faced in a long time. Unless we keep track of him, we'll never find it. We'll lose the game for sure."

"Wait a minute. As far as we know his territory was the east coast. What's he doing in Texas?"

"Apparently he knows something we don't."

"He must've gotten some kind of a lead then, otherwise he wouldn't take a chance coming back here—not after what he did."

"My thoughts exactly." Weatherford paused. "Anyway, this increases our chances to nail him and get back what we lost." He paused for a brief moment with a sly grin then continued, "And since it happened under your watch, guess who's going to have the honor of doing just that."

"Me?"

"Yes, you."

"I don't get it. Did you forget what happened the last time?"

"Not at all. Believe me this is not my doing. The request came straight from the top."

"You mean____"

6

"Yes. For some unknown reason he's willing to take another chance on you. I have my orders and now you have yours."

Robert didn't have a clue. The assignment had his name written on it from the day Carlos disappeared. They were just waiting for the right time to let him have it.

Regardless, the last thing he needed now was to get too emotional about it and perhaps ruin his chances for an early retirement. He had to stay calm, professional and, above all, surprised. With tempered emotions, he took hold of the Windsor knot and slipped it up snug to his collar as if preparing for a formal banquet. Then, with a casual aura about him, he leaned forward in his chair. "So when do I leave?"

"You'll report to the Dallas field office tomorrow afternoon. All the arrangements have been made. Everything you need to get the job done will be on your desk before noon. The bottom line here is that we find out whether he has it or knows where it is. Needless to say, the information we glean stays within this office and the deputy director's."

"What about help. I'm sure Dallas knows I couldn't possibly work this on my own."

"The agents they'll assign to you will be given false information on the case. You and you alone will know what's really going down. Stay in Dallas until you know for sure where Carlos is. We have people around the southwest keeping their eyes and ears open. The minute you hear something, no matter where he turns up, you get there fast. Do I make myself clear?"

"Yes, sir."

Weatherford leaned forward in his chair and set his arms on the desk. He glanced at the clock on the wall to his left. "You'd better get going," he said, his steely eyes seemingly penetrating Robert's. "The clock is ticking."

Just then the phone rang. He picked it up, cupped the receiver with his other hand and motioned towards the door.

Robert got up off his chair and headed towards it. As he turned the knob, the deep, gruff voice stopped him cold. "Robert."

He looked back over his shoulder, hoping they hadn't changed their minds. "Yes, sir?"

"I'm sure you know what'll happen if you mess up this time."

"Yes, sir."

"Good luck."

"Thanks."

Out in the hallway, he balled his fist and breathed a sigh of relief as he recalls the time he and a friend had lunch on the corner of Manhattan's 96th Street and 3rd Avenue.

"Did you get it?" Robert asked him.

"New *Cadillac*. Not bad. Uncle Sam must be paying good money these days."

Robert brushed the bread crumbs off his lap then gave Tony D'Angelo a slant eye look. "Never mind that. Just answer the question."

"Okay! Okay! Don't get your cogliones in an uproar. The last thing you wanna do is spill mayonnaise on that fancy cashmere coat of yours. Your old lady might not like that, you know."

"For your information, there is no old lady."

"What's the matter? Didn't she like your taste in clothes?"

"That's none of your business." He took another bite out of the Pastrami sandwich, then, as not to spill a drop on the driver's side of the leather bench seat, took a careful sip of the hot coffee. "Now let's get down to ours."

"Sure. Word is there's a big shipment coming across the border sometime next week. If everything works out okay, it should be up here three or four days from now."

"Listen punk. You'd better be right. I went through a lot of trouble to get you back out on the streets for this. Double-cross me and you can kiss the plea deal, your pretty little wife, *and* your kid goodbye. You sure won't have to worry about paying back any of your debts, either."

Ignoring the threat, Tony took another bite out of his baloney sandwich, chewed for a couple of seconds, then said, "Yeah, yeah. Don't worry, I'll get it."

"You'd better."

"I'll call ya as soon as I hear anything." With his eyes fixed on Robert's, he opened the passenger side door. "In the meantime, tell Uncle Sam to keep his pants on." He stepped out of the car and eyed every alley, nook, and cranny on the block, making sure the grim reaper wouldn't spoil his day. He tossed the sandwich wrapper and empty coffee cup on the sidewalk then walked past the front of the car to cross the street.

Robert rolled down his window and hollered, "Hey!"

Halfway across, Tony stopped and turned around, ignoring the vehicles let loose by the green traffic light a block away. "What?"

"Lay off the booze, you hear."

"Yes, mother."

Robert smiled.

"Judging from the smile on your face you must've finally gotten that promotion," the agent walking past him in the hallway said.

"Huh?" He paused to get his bearings back. "Better yet my friend," he said, a sly grin forming. "Better yet."

Twenty years of loyalty, awards, and accomplishments, did nothing to bring him closer to the allusive promotion. As a result, he was no longer concerned with it. Before being rudely awakened by the agent, he saw the light of redemption. He saw a future that could never be provided by civil service. He saw the golden calf that had crossed the border to give him back what he had lost.

After giving Robert enough time to get to his work station, Weatherford got on his secure hot line and dialed another secure line. When someone had picked up on the other end, he immediately said, "The minnow has crossed the Rio Grande."

"When?"

"Yesterday."

"Why wasn't I told?"

"They said you were up on Capitol Hill testifying at a hearing. Besides, you've waited this long, one more day isn't going to hurt you."

"I suppose you're right. Has the fisherman been informed?"

"He's on his way."

"Good. Let's hope he doesn't let the big one get away this time. We'll take it from here."

"He's all yours. Keep me posted."

Weatherford hung up.

# 3

"The temperature around the Persian Basin for Thursday, June 24, 2004 is expected to be above the century mark with wind gusts from the southwest at around thirty to forty miles per hour," the meteorologist said.

After fumbling in the dark for several seconds, Cody silenced the pre-dawn chatter with one slap to the snooze button on top of the radio. He un-hitched one eye and peeked at the clock's red LED numbers. It read 3:10 am.

The extreme heat wasn't unusual for the southwest portion of the state, especially around the Chihuahuan Desert that extends from Mexico all the way into parts of Texas, Arizona, and New Mexico. About the only thing that had changed from day to day during that summer were the wind gusts. And on that particular day, the forecast turned out to be exactly what the meteorologist predicted.

Although he had spent only three days training at the El Paso Intelligence Center, he was more than ready to get back home to Fort Stockton—a much smaller city with a population of around 7,800. It wasn't that he didn't consider what he had learned at the Drug Enforcement Agency's center necessary in light of the increase in drug trafficking, but the sooner he could get back to familiar territory, the better he liked it. And in order to get there without facing the rising sun as he drove east on Texas' Interstate Highway 10, he had to rise and beat it by at least three hours, taking into account unscheduled pit stops along the way.

Reluctantly, he slid his knuckles up the wall behind the headboard and turned on the lamp.

After showering, he put on his triple X white, western style shirt, his full cut *Wrangler* jeans, and his Ostrich skin cowboy boots. He took the 45 caliber out of the nightstand drawer and stuffed into his overnight case. Then, before going down to the lobby, he scanned the room to make sure nothing was left behind.

Before leaving the motel parking lot, he took the pistol out of his case and shoved it into the glove compartment of his Dodge Ram pickup. Then he drove through the barren streets of the Texas border city until he pulled into the empty parking lot of a Circle K convenience store on the city's eastern outskirts.

The middle aged store clerk, mesmerized by the pre-dawn news coming out of Iraq, didn't even bother to take his eyes off the small television at the sound of the little bells hanging over the doorway, or Cody's "Mornin". He just lifted his arm up slightly and casually waved as if he had known him forever.

Cody shook his head then walked directly back to the percolators where he filled his lungs with the aroma of fresh coffee. A large cup, sans cream and sweetener, was just what he needed to jump start his day. The next order of business was breakfast. At the frozen food case, he spent several minutes pondering his choices. It had been awhile since he had any so he settled for a couple of egg, bacon, and cheese burritos.

As he waited for them to finish heating in the microwave, the doorbells announced the entrance of two young males between the age of sixteen and seventeen. One a heavily tanned Hispanic in a black T-shirt and Olive drab shorts, the other a Caucasian whose thin face was still battling with the dreaded teen acne. He wore a cotton T-shirt that may have been white at one time, and jeans that would have made a 60's hippy proud to own. Both of them wore rolled up black, knitted cotton caps.

Neither could see Cody behind the various soda and coffee dispensing machines set up on counters behind the microwave.

The Hispanic went to the checkout counter while his companion, knowing there was at least one more person besides the clerk inside the store, went from aisle to aisle like a *Wall Mart* wearied husband anxiously searching for his wife.

In the meantime, the microwave's beeper drew Cody's attention back to the Burritos. After dressing them with his favorite picante sauce, he placed his breakfast into one of those folding type cardboard carry out trays then headed towards the cash register.

On the way there, an uneasy feeling crept over him when the Hispanic's eyes nearly popped out of their sockets on spotting him. Then a spike of adrenalin kicked in when he looked past the young man's shoulder towards the storefront window. Out there, behind the wheel of an oil burning vehicle, sat another young man whose eyes were swaying from side to side like a couple of synchronized pendulums. It was enough to make him focus on the make, model, and year, and then the physical details of the two inside the store. With all that firmly in mind, he continued his journey to the register.

His instincts, however, were revved even further when they avoided his scrutiny by wandering over to a rack and picking up copies of a women's magazine. That in itself wasn't unusual, except one of them was holding his upside down. Occasionally they would sneak a peek over the top edge of the magazines to check on his whereabouts.

It had been quite a while since he had seen the obvious tactic. He was eleven years old at the time. That's when he and his twelve year old friend, Clayton sashayed into a convenience store with the notion to help themselves to some candy.

Having been eyed suspiciously by the storekeeper, they too resorted to the same tactic over at the magazine rack. The only difference was their choice of comic books.

Needless to say, they didn't get away with it. Cody paid dearly once the county sheriff paid his parents a visit. After that, his brief life of crime came to a screeching halt.

Two other events had impacted his life back then. The first was when Clayton gave him his first cigarette. After he turned as green as the grass under his feet and regurgitated that morning's breakfast, he never let one touch his lips again. The second was when Clayton picked up a neighborhood cat and, like a doting mother with a newborn baby, lovingly cradled it in his arms.

"What're you going to do, rock him to sleep?" Cody asked, jokingly.

"Want to hear a siren?"

"Siren?"

Without batting an eye, Clayton wrung the poor critter's neck as if it was a hand towel that had just been taken out of a bucket of water. The cat hissed, kicked, and clawed before letting out a scream that sounded like a fire engine on its way to a major fire.

After the bone crunching sound and subsequent silence, Clayton threw it down and gave it the coup de grace with the heel of his right boot.

It was Cody's first look at death, his first encounter with outright murder, and the first meaningless smile to come across his face.

There were several more incidents, far worse than one could imagine. But what bothered Cody the most was the sparkle in Clayton's dark brown beady eyes, the tremors of his stout body, and the bulge at the front of his pants after each one of them. Although raised on a farm, Cody had no idea what the latter was all about until years later when he became well versed on criminal profile and psychology.

Not long after those displays of viciousness, their friendship waned and they eventually parted ways. Since then there had been times when he had questioned whether or not Clayton's behavior was responsible for his career choice—one that gave him the opportunity to make up for past indifferences and help stop such travesties at any cost.

"Five dollars and ten cents," the store clerk said.

"Huh?… Oh. Sorry."

The clerk took the six dollars and, with eyes finally fixed on the young men, cautiously opened the register and handed him the change. Before Cody could stuff it into his pocket, the two men walked out, jumped into the vehicle, and immediately took off.

Cody shifted his look from them to the clerk. "What d'ya you think?" he nodded towards the parking lot, probing to see just how much attention the clerk had paid to what had just happened.

"I don't know."

"How about dialing the local authorities for me?"

The clerk found the non-emergency number on a list taped to the counter. He dialed it then handed Cody the receiver.

After identifying himself, Cody gave the operator the information he had stored away plus their heading. He put icing on the cake by telling them the vehicle had only one working taillight and a valve-knocking engine.

"They'll take care of the rest," he said after hanging up. "Just save the surveillance tape from that camera up there. You never know if and when they might need it."

Back in his truck, he popped the lid off the coffee cup then stuck Katelyn's favorite *Vince Gill* CD into the player. Halfway through the melodious love song, he leaned forward and with his elbows resting on the steering wheel cradled his face between his thumb and forefinger.

It had been a little over a year since it happened. Still, the chilling sensation of her long, slender fingers kneading his forest of thick hair would occasionally surface. He wondered if the feeling would ever go away. Would he really want it to? He shook the thought off, just as he had done whenever the one person who turned their lives upside down flashed wide screen on his mind, and then pulled out onto the highway.

The long drive home was uneventful until he got close to Fort Stockton. That's when he decided to monitor his two-way radio. Within minutes, *Garth Brook's* voice mingled with the crackling transmission to Lieutenant, Billy Parker, whose radio call sign was "six zero two".

He and Billy Parker, a Native American with weather beaten skin, high cheekbones, and light brown eyes, had been friends ever since they attended Texas A&M University in College Station. About the only physical change on Cody since their days at the Lower Rio Grande Valley Regional Police Academy was the recent birthing of gray in his bushy, dark brown eyebrows, hair, and mustache. He didn't exactly care for the oncoming aging factor but it did complement the slight tan painted by time out on the range. As for Billy, the most noticeable changes were the receding tide of black hair, the weight gain, and the missing lock Cody thought looked more like a pig's tail than that of a pony. He lowered the volume of the CD player then cocked his right ear towards the radio.

"We just received several calls from citizens heading north on 385 from Marathon," the dispatcher said. "They claim there's some kind of flickering light beam in an area west of the highway. One said it nearly blinded him as he glanced at it through his driver's side window. Another thinks it might be some sort of distress signal."

"What's their ten twenty?" Billy asked.

"About thirty miles south of the interstate. They say it's coming from somewhere near the northern tip of the Glass Mountains."

Billy acknowledged the transmission with the standard, "Ten four," then proceeded to the location.

Cody, in the meantime, recalled that the area mentioned was an undulating stage of fine sandy loam with props of rock outcrops, sparse grass, and a cast of scrub brush, cacti, alligator juniper, and Mesquite trees. And that various breeds of cattle, including the ever present Brahman bulls with their distinctive humps, large ears, and bag like folds under their neck, were serving time behind the miles of barbwire, which were stretched along both sides of highway 385.

Once in a while a dust devil, spinning towards oblivion, or a tumble weed rolling towards its final destination, would get into the act, joining the livestock in bringing life to the normally static scene.

The area also included part of a large cattle ranch owned by Kyle Wesley. He wondered if perhaps there were illegal aliens or drug runners making their way up north through his property. As he got closer to Fort Stockton, his mind drifted back to the family's trip to Marfa, Texas. He took them there in the summer of 2000 to prove once and for all that the sightings of those mysterious lights in the desert were just individual imaginations brought on by the UFO phenomenon and Marfa's proximity to Roswell, New Mexico. But to his dismay, Tammie, who was sitting on top of his broad shoulders with her arms firmly wrapped around his thick neck, let go one hand and pointed them out as soon as the sun disappeared over the horizon.

"Over there, daddy, look," she screamed, with the white rays around the dark blue iris' gleaming like the lights in their sight. "Look, they're going up and down and around. They're blinking on and off."

Needless to say, his brows lifted pretty high that night also. His mouth didn't exactly stay shut either. "Well, I'll be___"

"Maybe now you'll believe," Katelyn said, with the teeth gleaming smile of a Cheshire cat.

Believe? Maybe. But according to his watch, the orange glow of the sun's awakening would have already blanketed the desert, enhancing its color and those of the various stratums of the mountain. It had to be something other than mysterious lights appearing out of nowhere in the darkness.

After rubbing his chin for a few seconds, he decided to join Billy in checking it out. A half hour of his time, he thought, wouldn't exactly hurt his plans. Besides, if it turned out to be drug runners, Billy would more than likely call for backup anyway. And it sounded like he was the closest one to Billy at the time.

He picked up the radio microphone and clicked the transmit button. "Control, this is six zero one. I'm about ten miles west of the 290 interchange. I'll meet six zero two at his location." The dispatcher, recognizing Cody's deep drawl, acknowledged, "Ten four ... Six zero two, do you copy?"

"I copy."

"What's it doing?" Cody asked.

"It seems to be blinking on and off," Billy responded.

"How far do you think the source is?"

"I'd say about three quarters of a mile or so from where I'm standing."

"Just keep an eye on it. I should be there in a couple of minutes."

# 4

The twenty four mile long mountain range—with its highest elevations reaching over 5,700 feet above sea level—was off to his right as he drove south. To his left stood the weather beaten windmills, once the lifeblood of the early pioneers who had occupied the time worn farmhouses just outside of Fort Stockton; which back then was named St. Gall.

On arrival at Billy's location, he pulled up behind the Expedition parked on the right side of the road. Through the dust and insect splattered windshield he spotted Billy leaning slightly forward, tan shirt flapping, hat pulled down in front, peering at the light through his binoculars.

He got out of the pickup and stretched, loosening the kinks born out of the two hundred and seventy mile drive. The terrain in front of him consisted of multicolored gravel, rocks, and vestiges of Buffalo grass. The wide open sky above had wispy clouds far and few in between, rushing northeastward as if they too were trying to avoid the rising sun.

When finished, he jammed the *Stetson* down on his head then sauntered over to join his deputy.

"I thought you'd be in your office right about now," he said.

"I would have but some of Tom Caleb's steers got out last night."

"Again?"

"Yep. This time they were strolling down the middle of the highway. I'm guessing they found another break in the fence somewhere."

"How many times is this now?"

Billy lowered the binoculars and flared three fanned fingers at him.

"If I remember correctly he lost one during the last great escape," Cody said. "Is he missing any this time?"

"Don't know yet. This call came in just as Tom's boys started rounding them up." He paused for a moment then shot a low brow gaze over Cody's shoulder towards the bed of the pickup.

"Speaking of one short, where's Diablo?"

"He's at the kennel."

"So, did you warn them?"

A grin formed once he figured out what Billy was talking about. After nursing Diablo back from injuries inflicted by an abusive owner, he donated the German Sheppard to a Dallas K-9 unit where he lived up to the Spanish word for Devil. The reputation didn't exactly diminish after his retirement and eventual return to Cody.

"Yep." He swapped the grin for a more serious look and turned his attention to the situation at hand. "So what do we have out there?"

Billy shrugged his shoulders and, with deep furrowed brows, said, "Hard to tell. The wind started to pick up just as I got here. I'm guessing it's a piece of glass, a mirror, or some kind of metal object. Here, take a look. Let me know what you think."

Before he could grab the binoculars from Billy's outstretched hand, he heard the rumbling of a muffler. It got louder as a 1985 decaying, Chevrolet pickup towing a cattle trailer rattled from the south. When it reached their location, the driver, his graying T-shirt and straw cowboy hat barely visible through the dust covered windows, pulled off the highway and parked across from Cody's pickup.

"Looks like we have company."

"Jack Bauer," Billy said. "If I'm not mistaken, he recently got a warning citation for that muffler."

"Doesn't he own a small farm somewhere around here?"

"No. His mother's farmhouse is about fifteen miles west of I-10. Not far from the other side of the mountain, as a matter of fact." He nodded towards Jack. "From what I've heard, he's been living there all his life."

"He must've been down around Marathon."

"Looks that way," Billy said. "Let's just see what he has to say." He walked out from behind the passenger side of the Expedition and waited for Jack to come out.

When the tall, lanky bachelor did, he moseyed to the back of the trailer. As he checked the locks on the gate, his eyes met Billy's gaze.

"Make a delivery this morning, Jack?" Billy asked.

"Maybe... Maybe not."

"Sounds to me like he doesn't want to talk about it."

"One things for sure," Billy said over his right shoulder. "He hasn't changed much since the last time we met. I guess he hasn't seen the light yet."

"He's seen this one, otherwise he wouldn't have stopped."

Only after he had walked halfway across the highway towards them did Jack acknowledge Cody's presence. "Howdy sheriff." He glanced at the flashing light. "If you ask me it's just a piece of aluminum foil or something like it that's made its way out there."

"You think so?"

"Sure. Look around you, sheriff. There's more trash on the side of the roads these days than you could shake a stick at. In case you haven't noticed, the wind's been blowin' pretty hard out here lately."

Cody wondered if perhaps he was right. The wind gusts did seem to be what the meteorologist forecasted back at the motel.

"We'll take that into consideration, Mr. Bauer." He cocked his head to one side then peered at the farmer's face over the rim of his sun glasses. He had already thought Jack's thin face looked like a slightly wilted strawberry with a crop of medium brown hair on top, but a new twist had been added since the last time he saw him. "It looks like you've fallen into a meat grinder face first, Mr. Bauer. Are you okay?"

Jack cleared his throat then ran his tongue across his upper lip as if he could wipe away the telltale sign of a recent altercation. "Oh, it's nuttin. It don't even hurt."

"Maybe not, Jack, but it sure hurts me just to look at you," Billy said. "What happened?"

"I...uh...I fell off the barn loft the other day, that's all. I'm okay."

Cody and Billy exchanged questioning glances then faced him again.

"We sure hope so," Billy said, grimacing.

"Anyways, like I said, I wouldn't waste my time over that."

"In case you don't know it, Mr. Bauer, we're here to serve and protect. And that includes responding to our citizens' concerns. We don't consider it a waste of time."

"Well then sheriff, knock yourself out." He pulled a heavily soiled, red bandana out of the pocket of his dirt-stiffened denim coveralls. "It's your time not mine." After lifting his cap and wiping his short-cropped, hair, he covered his bulbous nose, let out a loud honk, and then said, "See ya around."

"Mr. Bauer." Cody gestured towards the farmer's truck. "You'd better get that muffler taken care of before you get a citation with a little meat to it."

Jack didn't bother to look back after turning around to leave. As he neared his truck, he slowly lifted his arm, waved his hand and hollered, "Sure thing, sheriff. I'll take care of it as soon as I get home."

Cody waited until Jack got into his truck before turning back to Billy. "When was the last time we had him at headquarters?"

"Four months ago. He's currently on probation for DUI and assault."

"You buy that hayloft yarn?"

"Not really."

"Neither do I. Check with the city boys when you get back to the office. They may be able to tell us more on what happened to him."

"Don't worry, I will. I'm kind'a curious myself."

Cody took off his sunglasses and stuck them in his shirt pocket. While his eyes went back to Jack's vehicle as it took off, his mind drifted back to Clayton. The last time he had seen him, or his brother, Matt, was a little over two decades ago when their father shot and killed a man over in Midland.

He took a liking to Matt back then. And often wondered how the younger sibling, whose left shoulder occasionally jerked like an eye with a nervous twitch, turned out considering his brother's sadistic exploits and his parent's disdain for the law.

Since Cody didn't have a brother of his own, he had toyed with the idea of mentoring the nine year old boy, but the family moved away after the father was hit with a forty five year sentence for the offense. With time for good behavior, he could be out on the streets in a couple of years.

Matt didn't have much to say about his dad's predicament; perhaps because he was too young to understand the severity of the situation. Clayton, however, had plenty. In spite of the overwhelming evidence against the downtrodden farmer, he still believed his dad was just defending himself and should have been acquitted. He vowed to make the city and its justice system pay for what they had done. Most of the citizens in the area didn't take him serious. Cody did.

"Let's get back to this," he said, pressing his denim blue eyes against the binoculars' lenses until he was able to see the light. "Whatever's out there seems to be stuck inside a Creosote bush."

"That's what I thought."

"It's reflecting the Sun's rays."

"Maybe Jack's right." Billy lifted his hat with one hand and scratched his head. "This wind isn't exactly keeping that bush still. That could be why whatever it is looks like it's blinking."

With deep creases on his forehead, Cody lowered the binoculars for a brief moment then raised it again to confirm what he had seen. He handed them back to Billy and began kneading the back of his neck with his other hand. "If that's the case, why isn't the light swaying along with the bush?" he paused. "No. I don't think the wind has anything to do with this."

Suddenly he was back in Miss Applewhite's fourth grade classroom aiming the face of his Mickey Mouse watch towards the window on the east side of the building. Locking in on the rising sun's rays, he inadvertently bounced the beam towards her dead serious face instead of his friend, Jimmy. After seeing the look on her face, he dropped his arm and hid it under the desk. Unfortunately for him it was too late. The price paid for that one time antic quickly yanked him out of the classroom and back to the desert.

"Hey! It's gone," Billy said, excitedly.

"I know." He cradled his strong, square jaw between the thumb and index finger of his left hand for a moment then said, "Go ahead and call for backup while I go get my gear."

It wasn't unusual for the heat waves above the vast terrain to distort distant realities. However, he didn't think that or the wind had anything to do with what they were seeing.

Whatever it was appeared to have a controlled rhythmic motion, not unlike that of a signal light communicating from a navy ship, or someone trying to signal for help using a mirror or a piece of glass.

Back in the pickup, he took out his holstered weapon and attached it to his utility belt. As he closed the door, a white Chevy Blazer pulled up behind him.

Jeremy Sands, a baby-faced deputy with auburn hair, got out of it and immediately scanned the horizon with his narrowed, forest green eyes. "So what's out there?"

"We're not sure yet," Cody said, as he wrapped the belt around his thirty-six inch waist. He looked up at Billy. "See anything else out there besides the light?"

"No... did you?"

"I thought I saw something else moving behind the bush just before the light disappeared."

"You think maybe they're illegals or drug runners?" Billy asked.

"Could be."

Either way, he had to find out. Especially with the latest highway drug and drug currency interdiction methods learned at the Intelligence Center still fresh on his mind.

"You don't suppose they're trying to get help, do ya?" Billy asked.

"Now why in the world would they be drawing attention to themselves?" Jeremy asked, frowning. "That doesn't make sense."

"Not unless they're in a life and death situation. And if that's the case, we're obligated to assist them just as much as it is to round them up and turn them over to Immigration. Let's not take any chances, lieutenant. Get on the horn and see if you can get a hold of Kyle. Tell him what's going on out here and that we'll need to go through his property."

"You really believe someone's out there?" Jeremy asked Cody as Billy headed towards his vehicle.

"I reckon we'll soon find out."

Kyle's barbwire fence was located several feet off the highway and ran parallel about a mile and a half north and south. He figured if there was someone out there unbeknown to the rancher, he had to have broken through the fence somewhere along the line. And by the look on Billy's face when he returned from making the call, he was right.

"What'd he say?"

"Someone cut the fence further south from here. Whoever did it laid the wires neatly to the side of the poles as if opening a gate for a large vehicle."

"I thought so. Does he have any idea when it might've happened?"

"They discovered it four days ago. No tellin' how long it's been like that. Anyway, they replaced it that same day."

"Want me to check it out?" Jeremy asked.

"Go ahead. You should be able to spot the new wire easily. Look for tracks, prints, or anything else you can think of. While you're doing that, the lieutenant and I will go meet Kyle at the gate. I'm pretty sure it won't take him long to get over there. Join us as soon as you're finished."


When the restored WWII Army jeep reached the cattle gate, two of Kyle's ranch hands jumped out, dusted their chaps, and then sashayed over to the fence. Kyle put the emergency brakes on then got out and spent several seconds next to the jeep splattering a wad of brown juice on the ground. After the five feet, seven inch rancher swiped a forearm across his brown stained lips, he walked over to the cattle guard to join the deputies.

"Mornin', Kyle."

Kyle's prune like face sported a wooly worm mustache whose ends drooped about a half-inch down on each side of his lips. Above the mustache, a nose with a slightly swollen bridge leading to flared nostrils, and blue eyes that appeared to sink into their sockets whenever he blinked. With his thumb and index fingers touching the brim of his sweat-dark, cattlemen's style hat, the slim rancher in faded jeans and western denim shirt acknowledged Cody's greeting with a slight nod. "What's this all about, sheriff?"

"Don't really know yet, Kyle. Are any of your boys working near the base of the mountain?"

"No, why?"

"It looks like someone might be out there trying to get our attention." He leaned on the top rail of the galvanized steel gate and pointed towards the vicinity of the sighting. "Is there a trail from here that will get us close to that section of land?"

"The growth's pretty thick out that way but there are a couple of them that cut through most of it. They're kind'a rough, though. Big rocks, several deep ravines, and a couple of sink holes, as far as I can remember. Gotta watch out you don't run into them with this dust blowing around like it is. You might want to use a couple of my horses. I'd be more than happy to have my boys saddle them up for ya."

As Kyle unlocked and swung open the gate, Jeremy's vehicle pulled up and stopped on the south side of it. "Find anything?" Cody hollered, before Jeremy could even clear his opened door.

"Yes, sir. Tire tracks."

"You know anything about them, Kyle?"

"I checked them out myself, sheriff. Look to me like they might've been made by a pickup. Me and the boys followed them until they faded out. You know how this wind works around here."

"I'm afraid so."

Could there be a connection between the fence getting cut here and the great escape reported earlier by Billy's fingers?

"You wouldn't happen to be missing any from your stock, would ya?"

"As a matter of fact, I'm missing one of my mustangs. I've been meaning to report it for some time now but got hung up on my work. You know how that goes." He paused, looking out towards the horizon. "I reckon now's as good a time as any."

"The lieutenant here will take care of that. In the meantime, we'll just use our vehicle to get out there. If we need to, we'll get our department horses out here later."

"Then you can start by taking that trail over yonder." Kyle pointed. "It goes to the other side of my property. It may be a little out of the way, but it isn't as rough as the others. Beyond that you'll have to go through the back gate." He reached into his pants pocket. "Here's the key."

"Thanks." He stuck it into his jean pocket then turned to Jeremy. "You have your binoculars?"

"Yes, sir."

"Go back down the road. If you see anyone trying to make their way out of here, give us a holler."

He turned and faced the sixty four year old rancher who was reaching into his can of chewing tobacco. "You mind if one of your boys stays here for a while, just in case?"

"Not at all." He shoved a pinch into the left side of his jaw before saying, "As long as you drop him off at the barn when you get back. I can't afford to keep them idle too long."

"I understand. Deputy Sands will take care of that."

# 5

After unloading its cargo, Jack Bauer unhitched the trailer then parked the noisy pickup behind the barn. He got out, entered the barn through the back door, and then walked over to the grinder. He turned it on and began sharpening the only thing he had to keep the memory of his father alive; a hunting knife brought over from Germany by his grandfather, Erwin.

"Jack, breakfast's ready."

The loud, whirring sound of the grinding wheel kept him from hearing Nadine's first call. The second, however, came through loud and clear when he turned the machine off, slowing the wheel down to a low whir.

"Did you hear me? Breakfast's on the table."

Ignoring for the moment his mother's daily monotone, he slid the newly sharpened, eight and a quarter inch long blade across his left thumb, drawing blood as it sliced through the calloused skin. His eyes shifted from the bleeding finger down to the five by seven inch photo of a young female. He tightened his jaw, gritted his teeth, and then, in a wild eyed state, plunged the knife repeatedly at the photograph, each thrust accompanied by a deep grunt, each sending droplets of blood across the workbench.

It was the third photo he had taped to the workbench that week. It was also the third one left faceless, with nothing more to look at than the scenic background and the clothes she was wearing.

Exhausted by the relentless heat and his temporary frenzy, he put the knife down, then, while leaning over the photo, added insult to injury by raining down glistening drops of sweat on what was left. When his pulse rate stabilized, diminishing the redness of his face, he grabbed a rag and wiped the blood off the knife handle and his hands. He reached under the bench and pulled out the old cedar chest he had found a couple of days before Nadine's last visit to his aunt, Beverly.

"I want you to go up to the attic and find the purple and white patch quilt," she said, "I'm gonna give it to Beverly for her birthday. It isn't like the one she made but she won't know the difference anyway. I just can't believe she'll be sixty eight years old. My how time flies."

While searching for the quilt, he stumbled upon the chest hidden behind a pile of boots, clothing, purses, and furniture. It was a visual history of Nadine's life, and a section of the attic he was warned not to go near, let alone disturb. But her absence that day, coupled by his recent loss, lit a temporary spark of courage.

After blowing off what must have been decades of dust on the lid, he opened the chest, releasing a genie of musty odor into the speck filled attic air. He pulled back as if avoiding a left jab and waited for his lungs to get used to the antique odor. When they did, he sat on the back of his calves and, like some kid who had just opened his first Christmas present, rifled through its content. Within seconds he came across a bundle of photos and a two-inch thick stack of letters written during the 50's and early 60's. Some the photos were of Nadine and her sister Beverly. Others were those of a young man with facial features eerily similar to his. Could they have been of his dad, Carl? What really happened to him? Where was he now? Was this the only historical evidence of his existence?

Aunt Bev was the only person who was sure to have the answers. But they were lost forever in the Alzheimer's unit of the nursing home. As for Uncle Ron, he didn't' become a member of the family till after Carl took off. And if he did know anything, he never mentioned it.

There were so many photos to choose from in so little time. Several appeared to have been taken at Nadine's prom where she wore Starlet formal, glittering green high heels, and a purse to match. Others were of her sitting at the edge of the Comanche Springs pool in a one-piece yellow bathing suit sprinkled with lavender daisies.

27

But it was on his second forage through the treasure trove of the past that he came across what he considered the ultimate jackpot—a close-up photo that showed traces of Nadine's pursed lips, eyelashes covered thick with black mascara, and a black, bouffant styled wig adorning her head. He couldn't wait to take it to the whittling block.

"Come on, sweetheart, your breakfast's gonna get cold."

After putting the photo aside, he went to the door and, like some poor kid sneaking a peek at a minor league baseball game, pressed his right eye against the knothole. The sixty six year old, silver haired, Nadine, stood on the wooden front porch, and in the crosshairs of his mind. Her face was as weathered as the floorboards under her feet, and her gray eyes as tired as the old house she had lived in since the day she and Carl, who vanished after seven years of marriage, took their vows. And her head was adorned with a medieval bun, haphazardly held in place by a rubber band.

As the slender, sinewy, five foot seven inch tall woman waited for Jack to come out, the purring of Monique's body against her vein-streaked calf warmed her chilled heart. She bent down, picked the cat up, and then, with a mind that wandered off to an earlier time in her life, started stroking her.

"Have you seen him?" Nadine asked Beverly.

"Seen who? Ouch! Take it easy, will you. I'm not letting it grow long just so you could rip it off."

"That new boy from New Braunfels," she said, trying to avoid the knots in Beverly's blonde hair. "The one with the smile that could melt an iceberg," she continued, after a deep sigh. "I could just picture my fingers running through his hair. And those eyes. I've never seen such a light blue in my life. And did you see the way he walked? As if he's on top of the world and dares anyone to knock him off."

"Carl Bauer?"

"Of course."

"For God's sake, Nadine. Let him at least get his feet wet before you dry them off."

"Why should I," she said, with eyes peeking out through slits. "I'm not the only girl around with a towel, you know. Besides, you know dang well how slim the pickings are in this God forsaken town. He's going to be my future husband. I'm going to make sure of that."

"You're crazy. He's not going to give you a second look. What makes you so sure he'd want to spend the rest of his life with you? There are a lot of other girls here that could offer him more than you could ever dream of."

"Oh yeah. Well you just wait and see. He *will* spend the rest of his life with me. I'll make him so happy he'll never want to leave me. I'll make sure of that."

"You seem to forget momma said the same thing years ago, Nadine. Look where she is now."

"Yeah, well, momma just didn't know how to please a man. She didn't know what it takes to make him stick around."

"And you do? Give me a break, will you. When was the last time you looked in the mirror, huh?"

"Looks don't mean a thing, miss prissy. If you think those pearly whites and that pretty little smile of yours is all you need, you're in for a rude awakening."

Beverly huffed then rolled her eyes up. She saw no reason to pursue the matter any further—to argue as they always did. She gathered her schoolbooks, got up off the living room floor then strutted out the front door. As did Carl after he had mentioned the other woman at the dinner table several weeks before their eighth wedding anniversary.

On that memorable day, Beverly's childhood predictions came back to torment her, filling her mind as Carl sat across from her pouring his words out like gravy over meat that had just been tenderized with a sledge hammer.

With fire in her eyes, she watched him get up and traipse out the front door. As he was about to get into the family car, she ran out the door and on to the front porch where she stood, violently shaking and screaming, "You'd better get in here, or else."

Hearing the words that had accidently slipped out and brought her back, Jack mumbled, "or else what. Beat me to death with your broomstick."

Although he had seen her go out in space several times in the past, he had no idea what it was all about. And this time, why it ended with a threat.

She let go of the cat, placed her hands on her hips, and then waited with a look that would have sent a Pit Bull scurrying for cover. He, in turn, would have been content just to stay there and watch her stew, but the glare from the silver locket blinding his eye reminded him of the light the sheriff and his deputy were looking at earlier that day, and of the sheriff's warning. As luck would have it, out of the five beat up vehicles he had been refurbishing, that morning he chose to drive the one with the holes in the muffler. It was also the day he chose to tell Nadine about the chest and what he had found inside of it, but in light of what he had just witnessed, he decided to be put that off for yet another day. He walked back to the bench and grabbed Jim Beam by the throat. After capping it, he set the whiskey bottle on one of the rafters then slid the treasure chest back under the bench.

"I'm coming, mother," he yelled, loud enough for her to hear. Then he lowered the volume with the words, "Hold your horses."

Before leaving, he placed the tarp over the pickup he had been working on for the last several months. He walked over to the left side of the bench and put his tools into the mechanics toolbox. Then he turned off the light attached to the rafter by a thin chain.

Knowing all too well what was expected of him; he grabbed a dirty shop towel on the way out and wiped his forehead before shuffling towards the house. On the way there, he squinted at the sun then glared at her.

Each crack veined plank threatened to collapse as he made his way up to the porch. When he was one step shy from getting to her, she reached down and cupped his thin face between her slender, crepe paper skinned hands. "Honey, I thought you said you'd be hungry when you got back?"

Jim Beam took care of his hunger pangs most of the time, especially after their morning visit. But due to the task he had to complete that morning, their visit was cut short, making him vulnerable to the wrath that was sure to come.

"I... I'm sorry, mother. I thought I would be."

"Never mind, did you get the money?"

As he stepped up to the porch, he dug into his pocket and pulled out a wad the size of his tenuous wrist. "Every penny. Here."

She shuffled through the stack like a dealer at a blackjack table, then when she finished, she looked up and eyed him with a deep frown. "I don't know what's gotten into you. Ever since she took off you've been spending more time in that old barn playing with your toys than you spend with me."

"I ain't never gonna believe that, mother."

"Believe what?"

"That she took off without saying a word."

His words rumbled like thunder inside her head. She reared it back like a Cobra ready to strike, but instead she quickly chilled out and put on the charm. "Well you'd better cause that's exactly what she did. And you're much better off for it. Now let's stop this silly nonsense. That was a long time ago and I don't want to talk about it anymore."

"Why not. I was just gonna help her get a new start, that's all. I don't believe she'd a thrown that away. Why did ya have to stick your nose into our business, anyway?"

"What'd you say?"

"Nothing, mother, nothing," he replied, stuttering like some two year old kid learning to talk for the first time.

She took a deep breath, let it out, and then smiled, erasing the impact of the brief storm in her mind. "Good. For a minute there you had me worried."

"Can we go inside now?"

"Of course, sweetheart, but don't forget to wash your hands before going to the table."

He wondered if his father had heard those same words during their short time together, and whether he paid any attention to them. But that was all he could do—wonder.

It was as if someone had wiped off the memories of his father like dust from a piece of furniture. And as a result, he couldn't care less about the house, and it showed. The paint on the cracked walls gave up holding on a long time ago, and the roof was so bad even the roosters avoided it. The only thing he cared about was the barn. Perhaps because his father built it with his own hands, or because it was the one place she seldom set foot in. He had turned half of it into a workshop where he could spend time alone doing what he liked best—refurbishing junked vehicles and drinking his whiskey.

31

After pulling the tufted armchair away from the head of the table, he stood behind it like some waiter in a fancy restaurant.

She sat down as he pushed the chair closer to the table. Then she wrapped her hands around the end of the chair's armrest and surveyed the room like some Victorian queen about to address her subjects. The would-be waiter then took the embroidered cloth napkin off the table and gently placed it on her lap.

With the daily ritual completed, he walked over to the other end, sat down, then scooted up to the table.

"Really, Jack. Must you always come to the table looking like that?"

"We've been through this before, mother." He lowered his head to avoid her gaze and gave his bacon and two eggs the once over. "I don't have the time you have to put on the fancies. I thought you'd be use to it by now."

"I'll never get use to it. Why I let you get away with it, I'll never know."

With her elbows on the table, she cradled her chin on the back of her hands, and then gave him a Hawkeye stare as he cut his thick strip of bacon in half.

He brought the fork up, filled his mouth, and then, without lifting his head, rolled his eyes towards her. "I saw the sheriff today".

"You did?"

Thinking it was nothing more than a casual sighting; she picked up her fork and knife and began cutting her bacon into bite size pieces.

"Yeah," he said, egg tumbling around in his mouth like laundry inside an upright dryer. "He and that deputy of his were over by Mr. Wesley's property. They were looking at some sort of light out by the mountain."

"Light?"

"Yeah. I told them it was probably just a piece of _____"

"You what?" the fork bounced off the dish and on to the table with the bacon still hooked on it. "You stopped to talk to them?"

"I was just curious to_____"

"Are you crazy?" she shouted, leaning closer to the table. "Haven't you had enough run-ins with the law? When are you going to learn? The last thing we need is them sticking their noses into our business. What's wrong with you?"

The forty seven-year-old's sunken cheeks quivered. His eyes bulged. But then, like a flame suddenly doused with a bucket of water, he sat there fuming, his fingers running through his disheveled, dirty hair. "You shouldn't a sent me out so soon."

"Why you idiot," she growled. "You sound just like your ungrateful good for nothing father." She waved her crooked index finger in front of his face as if it was a flag of honor. "You should be thankful I'm even looking out for you. Why, there's no telling where you'd be today if it wasn't for me. And if____"

"Yes, mother, yes," he said, his hand squeezing the paper napkin as his eyes fell on the Winchester Model 94 rifle cradled on the wooden rack over the stone fireplace.

He could almost feel the butt plate held snugly against his shoulder, and the smoothness of the rifle's highly polished, Walnut wood stock on his hand. He could almost feel the slight kick, and hear the resounding blast as his long index finger squeezes off one 30-30 round, then another, then another, and another.

"Are you even listening to me?"

His battered thin lips curled as he pushed himself away from the table and stood up.

"Where are you going now? Wait, I didn't mean it. I'm sorry."

"I gotta get out of here." He snatched his hat off the deer antlers on the wall by the doorway and said, "I'll be back later."

"You're not going back to one of those devil's dens, are you? You know those places ain't for you. You know those wicked women just want to use you. Look what happened the last time," she yelled. "Sooner or later they're going to find out. Then what will I do."

"Mother, please, I'm just going for a spin. I'll be back before you know it."

"What about that Mexican?"

"What Mexican?"

"The one she was partying with."

"What about him?"

"It's been more than a week now and you still haven't told me who he is—or what he wanted."

"I didn't ask. I just wanted to get her out of there."

"So that's it. You tried to take her away from him, didn't you? That's why they're looking for you. Well, if you ask me, she and that brat of hers would've been better off south of the border than over here messing up your life."

"What's that suppose to mean?"

"It means your life's in danger. Those wetbacks don't fool around, you know. They're mean and vicious. They'd cut your throat just as soon as look at you, do you hear."

This time no amount of water or words could douse the reignited fire, or stop the severe turbulence. His lids narrowed. His cheeks quivered. His voice deepened with a slight rattle. His fists pounded the table. Dinnerware rattled. Table shook "You shouldn't have interfered. You should' a let me take care of It."

Suddenly the reason for his leaving changed. Without saying another word, he headed straight for the rifle. He lifted it off the rack.

"What are you doing?"

Under her scrutiny and in silence, he walked over to the china cabinet, opened the drawer and took out a box of ammunition.

"I asked you a question." The napkin slipped off her lap as she jumped up and slammed the table. "What are you up to?"

"I have some unfinished business to take care of."

"No you don't. Now put that thing back you hear."

After a brief moment with his head bowed down, he turned around and headed towards the front door with the rifle cradled in his left arm.

Her eye lids went up then slowly lowered like a window shade drawn down to minimize glare. "How dare you," she said, her emaciated body trembling as he walked out the door. After several seconds, she woke up from the perceived nightmare and hurried after him. Standing on the porch, she reared her head back and released the fury within. "You'll never leave me. Never. Never."

The deep, raspy tone stopped him at the bottom of the steps. He turned around and witnessed scraggly wrinkles deepening, teeth straining under pressure, eyes that were barely visible, and a quivering head. It was a look he had never seen before and hoped to never see again. After spending several seconds standing there trying to figure out what it was all about, he climbed behind the wheel of the cancer-riddled pickup and drove off.

For the second time in her life, all she could do was glare and shoot daggers at a family vehicle rumbling down the dirt road against her wishes.

# 6

Carlos Badillo was desperate. Time was running out, and so was his life expectancy. Throwing his usual caution to the wind, he recruited the services of a local street gang to expedite the completion of his mission.

Although it was risky, there was comfort in the fact that they had no knowledge of his real occupation, or his true motive for using them.

To finalize the deal, he chose to meet them at the Angels Dance Club. It wasn't the first time he had been there. And it wasn't exactly a place where his kind was welcomed with opened arms by the majority of its customers. Still, it was big, crowded, and noisy; the perfect place to discuss his predicament. The place where he had lost the best opportunity to retrieve the money and get back to Mexico before the authorities got wind of his whereabouts.

At the table, the raising of glass and bottles in a toast to their upcoming mission culminated in gulps, lips smacking, and then broad smiles.

"Now, listen to me carefully," he said, after running the back of his hand across his moist lips, "She has something that belongs to some very powerful people in Mexico. My job is to get it back no matter what."

The five foot six inch, skinny, twenty year old with the pimpled, peppered face sitting to his right was known around Fort Stockton as, "Flaco".

"I tink it must be money," he said. "Lots of money. Am I right?"

Carlos reached for the bottle of tequila. He held it lovingly with his beefy hand, capped it, and then leaned menacingly close to Flaco's face. "The only money you need to worry about is what I'm going to pay you. *Comprende.*"

"Yeah, man, I understand," he said, feeling the sudden heat coming over his body.

"Good."

Carlos wasn't about to let them know anything about the three quarter of a million dollars worth of cocaine stolen from a New York City affiliate of the Vasquez drug cartel. The proceeds from the sale, which was supposed to be delivered to Mexico, had been missing for over a year and a half now. As a result, Carlos was contracted to take care of the thieves and get the money back to them pronto. The first part of the contract was completed up in New York. The second was still pending.

The self-professed gang leader, tattooed with fear inducing slithering snakes, blood dripping daggers, and satanic symbols, sat across the table from Carlos. He tilted his shaved head slightly and said, "What? You expect us to do your dirty work for peanuts." With a smirk drawn across his face, he leaned back in his seat and waited for Carlos' response.

At that the shortest of the three, who could've easily passed for that puffy little white pastry chef people poke fingers at, let out a loud guffaw, breaking the awkward silence, and getting the full attention of everyone around him. "He must be stupid or sumting," he said, poking the leader sitting next to him in the ribs with his elbow. "We not migrant workers."

Carlos' dimpled cheeks quivered. His square jaw tightened. Then his dark brown eyes widened as he grabbed the bottle, unscrewed the cap and poured himself another shot. After sucking on the lime, he downed the Mexican mash without batting an eye, or spilling a drop. He slammed the glass down then reached into the pocket of his wrinkled, blue suit and pulled out a switch blade. He pushed the button on the side of the handle. Swoosh, click, thud.

The three boys nearly jumped out of their ground dragging pants when he plunged the knife into the table.

At the sight of it sticking straight up, twanging like a tuning fork, the leader's jaw dropped. His eyes strained to break out of their sockets. He had heard about the former welterweight's lightning speed, but thought time and circumstances had slowed him down. He was wrong. Other than an occasional twitching of his right eye and muscle tone that appeared to be heading south, Carlos Badillo, known throughout the boxing world as, "The Rock", showed no signs of slowing down.

After being demolished by a younger opponent, he satisfied his penchant for blood, gore, and glory as a hired assassin—a career which earned him even more money. One of the best the cartel had seen in years.

"So what you want us to do, huh?" asked the gang leader. "Go after him again? We almost got nailed the last time. I can't help it if the guy got lucky."

"Yes! And I don't care how you do it, when you do it, or what you do with him." In a deep, raspy voice, Carlos continued, "You just get me the information I need. I take care of the rest."

"You know, I think Flaco here is right. It is money. And it must be lots of it. That is why you don' want to talk about it." The leader's fat lips curled up at one corner and his eyes reflected dollar signs rather than the ominous figure in front of him. "What make you so sure we just don' keep it?" he said, tugging at the gold ring on his left earlobe gently, as if remembering the fate of the one torn out of his other ear by an admiring opponent.

Carlos' chin, darkened by a four o'clock shadow, quivered. His teeth clenched. He placed his right elbow on the table then held the index finger and thumb of his left hand together. "Because the three of you are just little *cucarachas* in a big man's world," he said. "You do and you will all join me in the grave."

After yanking the five-inch blade out of the table, he stuck it in his mouth, then waited a few seconds before taking it out and laying it down next to his glass. Then, with a broad smile, he exposed the desecrated tombstones and parts of the cockroach the three young men had failed to see crawling across the dimly lit table.

The leader, who didn't care much for being called a roach, released the earring he was fiddling with. He backed off as his smile took a dive. He would test Carlos no more. His nose wrinkled. His stomach churned.

Sensing impending danger, Flaco, by far the weakest link in

the ring, braced himself against the bench and slowly slithered away from Carlos. He wasn't about to get his spider like arms snapped and splintered.

"Can I get you another round of drinks, gentlemen?"

The waitress had on tight fitting jeans, its leggings tucked into cowgirl boots, and a white blouse meant to draw more attention to her than what was on her tray.

At the sound of her sexy voice, Carlos pressed his back against the rickety wooden bench. He eyed her small lean body as he ran a hand through his glistening, wavy black hair.

But the fleeting thought quickly vanished when he looked up at her face. Even in the near darkness, and through a potpourri of cigarette, pipe, and cigar smoke, he saw under the thick makeup someone who was considerably younger than she was made out to be. Someone who, for all he knew, was the same age as his daughter, Maria.

He smiled. "I think perhaps I quit for now, Chiquita," he said, and then swept his hand towards the others. "But maybe these fine gentlemen might care for more."

One right after the other turned down the offer after checking with their leader, who was more interested in getting started on the job. After all, he didn't come just to sit around some Honky Tonk canteen to engage in idle conversation. Nor did he come for a night of voyeurism.

Carlos waited till she left then reached into the inside pocket of his jacket. "Okay, I give you five hundred dollars each now and the rest after you bring me the information."

"Where?" the leader asked, tugging at the earring again.

Carlos leaned back and clasped his hands behind the back of his head. "I let you know where after you call me."

"Excuse me," she said, after returning. "Would you like your check now?"

He slid the knot of his yellow silk tie up to the unbuttoned collar of his white shirt. "Yes, please. Thank you." Then he waited till she left again before getting back to the business at hand. "Now, take the money and go. I take care of the bill here. Remember, you call me as soon as you find her, you hear."

The leader downed the rest of his beer, opened his mouth and expelled a blast of foul smelling air, then leered at Carlos. "What about her little girl?"

"Forget her."

"What you mean?"

"I mean you touch her and you answer to me. If she knows something, I'll take care of her myself. I don't want… wait."

He reached into his shirt pocket and took out the cell phone that was blaring Salsa music. He flipped it open. At the sight of the caller ID, tiny sweat beads began forming across his scarred, wrinkled forehead. He nodded towards the front door. "Go."

As the gang members slid out of their benches, they noticed the trembling index finger stretching his collar, the quivering cheeks, and the wide opened eyes.

The leader shrugged his shoulders at the others then motioned for them to follow him out

"*Si, Jeffe,*" Carlos said. He paused for a few seconds then continued. *"Todo estar bien."*

Carlos couldn't bring himself to tell his boss anything other than, "all is well." He wasn't ready to die just yet.

After hanging up, he looked down and studied the sharp blade on the table carefully. There were no qualms in using it but, in this case, he preferred to use less drastic measures if at all possible. Until he found what he came for, that is.

He picked it up, then, after forcing the blade back in against the spring until it locked in place, stuffed it back in his pocket.

# 7

As she stood in front of the dresser, the room filling aroma of his *English Leather* cologne brought back memories of the events that took place just before he left for work. Half asleep, and in the dim light of the bedroom lamp, he had accidently pinned his badge upside down to his tan uniform shirt. It was a mistake he didn't notice until he had put the shirt on and looked in the mirror.

"Give it here," she said, taking it from his fumbling hand, "I could see your mind's not on going to work this morning."

She was right. As it had been many times before, his mind was on his dream of becoming a rancher. That was one of the reasons for moving to Pecos County in the first place. But, to his dismay, it was a dream that had little chance of being fulfilled, especially after learning that less than one percent of the county was considered prime farmland. And, although oil and gas production had declined somewhat during the 80's, it was still one of the mainstays of the county, along with tourism and agriculture. All of which he had no desire to pursue.

This wasn't to say she didn't have her problems with the move to Texas either. For one thing, she had to learn all about their Independent School District system and dealing with their Independent School Boards. For another, she had to take a summer position at a local daycare center to keep her skills with children honed while she waited for the new school year to start.

"Look here, my lassie. Helping me with things like this is just one of the reasons I married you in the first place."

The twenty-six year-old never thought he'd be wearing another badge after he and Peggy moved to Fort Stockton from

Chicago. But then again, when he left the force, it wasn't without reservations by his colleagues concerning his dream.

They weren't aware of any third generation Irishmen making it big as ranchers in the plains of the West. And the words "city slicker", ran rampant throughout the department. Even so, he was determined to make it happen. After all, determination ran through his veins faster than beer ran through his father's.

Determination also ran through a mentor he had no idea would come into his life in Fort Stockton. Once Cody Johnson learned of his dream, he was more than willing to help him achieve it. Jeremy had spent many after duty hours at Cody's ranch watching and learning how to handle cattle and horses, and the business of buying and selling them. But after several months of trying, he wondered if perhaps his father was right. Was his dream a little too far fetched? Were his father's long ago predictions of a life filled with failures true? Or was he right in taking matters into his own hands.

"Oh yeah," she said, while pinning the badge, and looking deep into his eyes. "And just what other reasons did you have for marrying me?"

"Well, let's see now," he said, struggling desperately not to move his head while eyeing her up and down. "That tiny waist, those green, cat eyes under the long dark eyelashes, the full, deliciously tempting lips, those___"

"Okay, okay, that's enough." She laughed while playfully tapping his lean muscular shoulders.

"And let's not forget that perfectly round, smooth skinned face with the slight pug nose. On top of that, there's___"

"Alright already." She pressed hard against the badge with her palms. "I'm sorry I asked."

"Ouch! Well, I'm not."

The six foot two, lanky deputy, who gained most of his strength training for the Special Operations Unit of the Armed Forces, easily lifted the five foot one inch black haired girl from Michigan and kissed her gently on the lips.

"If you don't stop this nonsense," she said, "you're going to be late for work. Now put me down."

"Okay, be that way," he scoffed. After letting her down, he faced the dresser mirror and continued grooming. "Who are you going to take care of if I have a wreck chasing one of those roadrunners down the highway?"

Her laughter waned as she turned down the back of his collar. When she finished, she bowed her head and stared at the floor.

After seeing her reaction through the mirror, he rolled his eyes up to his forehead. "I'm sorry. I shouldn't have said that."

"That's okay. You can't help it. You don't understand."

"That's not fair, Peggy. I do understand. We've discussed this over and over again. You know the____"

"The choices? They're not mine, Jeremy. They're not going to make me complete in my eyes, or in anyone else's for that matter."

"Peggy, let's not go there right now, okay. I have to be able to give all my attention to what I'm doing out there. You know that."

"Yes, I know. It's just____"

"Come here." He turned around and faced her. Then he pulled her to him and gently placed her head against his chest. "It's okay," he said softly stroking the length of her hair. "We'll work it out, you'll see."

With tears welling, she looked straight into his eyes. Eyes that couldn't focus on the non-stoppable hands of the clock that ticked away the hours, days, and years of her life. Nor see the desire that was eating away at her inner being like some rapidly spreading cancer.

He wiped her teary eyes with his thumbs, then, holding her head in the palms of his hands, kissed her softly on the forehead "We're going to be alright," he said, "You'll see."

"I'm sorry," she said softly, grabbing a tissue from the box on top of the dresser. "I shouldn't hold you up like this." She glanced at the clock on the nightstand. It was already 5:30 am. "If you don't get with it you'll be late for work."

"Don't worry, I won't be," he said, walking over to his chest of drawers. He took out his utility belt and strapped it to his thirty-two inch waist. I'll be out there in plenty of time to protect the citizens of this fine county. Give me a kiss."

"By the way, how's the pickup running?"

"Much better now, thanks to Donnie.

"Good, now all you have to do is treat it as good as you do me." she laughed.

"That's a 10-4."

After their lips met, he bolted out, slamming the squeaky screen door behind him.

"Be careful," she hollered. "And say hello to Sheriff Johnson for me."

"I will," he yelled back as he got into the pickup.

The cold mist of *Emeraude spray* brought her back. She turned and looked at the clock on the nightstand. She had forty-five minutes to get to the center before working parents would start bringing their children in. She grabbed another tissue out of the box, got closer to the mirror and blotted the lipstick one more time. She straightened the collar of her blouse. Then she whispered, "be careful," one more time.

# 8

There were times when sand would blow across the territory like ocean waves in a raging storm. And then there were times it would barely drift across it. It was during the latter that Cody spotted a dark object in the distance. He reached for the binoculars and focused it in time to see a horse clear the rim of a ravine. Within seconds its thundering hooves kicked up enough dust to form a contrail that slithered like a sidewinder along one of the paths and through the maze of brush, cactus, and small mesquite trees.

It wasn't unusual to see a wild horse roaming the vast uninhabited parts of the southwest. Occasionally, one or two would even jump a weakened fence and trespass into someone's property. But, in this case, someone riding bareback with complete control of the horse was highly suspect, especially when he's trying desperately to put some distance between them.

Billy strained against his seat belt to get closer to the windshield, but couldn't see much through the dust that had settled on it. "What is it?"

"I got a feeling someone found Kyle's Mustang," Cody said, voice quivering from the jolting ride. "And he's out there burning the breeze with it."

"Where'd he come from?"

"Out of one of those ravines Kyle mentioned. The question I have, though, is who is he and why is he in such a hurry to leave the area? Keep him in sight. We might be able to cut him off somewhere up ...hold on a minute. Stop! Stop!" he said, his voice rising with each word.

A light brown mushroom of dust formed in front of the vehicle as it slid to a gravel grinding halt.

Billy took off his seat belt and got as close to the windshield as he could. He still couldn't see a thing. He turned to Cody, whose slanted eyes were desperately slicing through the dust, and asked, "You see something else out there?"

"I'm not sure."

Just before he ordered the unexpected stop, the air momentarily cleared between two large Creosotes. It could have been a calf that had wandered away from its mother, or a mule deer foraging for food, or it could have just been his imagination. But what it could have been and what his first impression was compelled him to check it out

"What about him?" Billy asked, nodding towards the rider who was quickly disappearing over the horizon."

"We'll worry about him later. Right now I want___"

He stopped in the middle of his sentence, narrowing his eyes once more towards several head high bushes.

Billy turned the vehicle and drove slowly in the direction of Cody's steady gaze, not having the slightest clue as to where they would wind up. Seconds later he lunged forward. His eyes widened as his nose almost touched the windshield.

"You see it too, don't you?" Cody said.

"That's got to be a mirage."

"I'm afraid not."

He guessed her to be around four or five years old, and somewhere between three to three and a half feet tall. The veritable Chameleon, dressed in what appeared to be tan khaki shorts, a polka dotted, white t-shirt, and a pair of pink and white tennis shoes, was walking away from them as if she was late for a very important date.

Once again, the vehicle came to a sudden stop. This time, both doors flew open. They got out, met at the front, and then looked at each other quizzically before giving her their full attention.

"What in the world is she doing out here?" Billy asked.

Through squinting eyes they could see she was getting further away.

"I don't know, but we'd better get to moving fast."

Gravel and coarse sand crunched rhythmically with each step

towards her. A stuffed teddy bear, limply hanging by her side, stared at them with big button eyes. It had a blue and white-checkered kerchief wrapped around its neck and a gray and blue stripped railroad engineer's cap on its head. And on its rotund body, more stitches than a major league baseball.

With each step they took, the smile on its face appeared to broaden in a, *catch me if you can,* fashion.

"One thing's for sure," Billy said, between breath catching gasps.

"What's that?"

"She's not Mexican."

"Hey, Darlin' wait," Cody called out, hoping to at least slow her down before she disappeared behind the scrub brushes or the next curtain of fine dust. "Hold on there. Wait a minute."

To his dismay, she kept walking away as if they didn't exist. In his mind, the thought that she had to have heard him in the tranquil realm of the desert where birds, wind, and flying insects ruled the airwaves? After several giant steps he got up alongside of her.

In spite of the suffocating stench of urine and feces, he reached down and took hold of the empty hand. It was clammy, warm, yet almost lifeless, unfeeling.

The last thing he wanted was to startle or frighten her by yanking her to a sudden stop. As difficult as it was for him to control his gait, he matched her stride for stride, oblivious to a nosey Jackrabbit several yards away.

Billy stopped, preferring to let the two of them go on as if they were taking a speedy stroll through a park. "We're in the desert, you know?" he hollered. "Things like this just don't happen out here."

"That's what I thought."

"How're you gonna stop her?"

"There's only one way I can think of."

He let go of her hand, then with his normal stride hurried out in front of her. After putting close to six feet between him and her, he quickly turned around and waited.

The occasional ebbing of the wind gust provided just enough visibility for Cody to see her clearer as she approached.

She stopped just inches away from him but didn't look up to

see the towering figure blocking her path. It was as if she had blindly sensed his presence.

Her golden brown eyes seemed vacant, as if he didn't exist in her world. Indeed, as if the world itself didn't exist. He dropped down on one knee and gazed into them. "Howdy." his voice was soft and gentle, his head slightly tilted. "What's your name darlin'?"

Billy came up alongside of him. As they waited for a response, their eyes wandered from her face down towards her shoes then towards each other. Billy spoke first. "Is that what I think it is?"

"I'm afraid so."

Each piece of her clothing appeared to have been splattered by a ceremonial flick of a brush dipped in a bowl of blood. Even the teddy bear, which was one-fourth her size, had dried blood on its mangy looking fur.

Billy searched his mind, bringing up recent incidents that could possibly explain her condition, but couldn't find one. "The last reported accident was over a week ago out on I-10," he said, "Everyone involved was accounted for and none of them were seriously injured."

"And as far as I know, there hasn't been any aircrafts or hikers reported missing either," Cody added. "We have a real mystery here."

"You don't suppose this was part of a satanic ritual, do you?" Billy asked, looking around as if expecting black robed fanatics to leap out of the bushes.

"That's hard to say. I understand some teenagers had gotten into that sort of thing up in Odessa, but I haven't heard of any down here. We'll have to keep that in mind, though."

The long, matted strands of her ponytail, the reddish tint to her fair skin, and the sand on her face were all understandable in light of the harsh environment. The rest wasn't.

Underneath it all, however, he saw a lovely little creature of innocence seemingly defiled by human insensitivity.

"Something doesn't add up here. Take a look." With his index finger under her chin, Cody gently lifted her head then took hold of her arms and did the same.

Billy carefully examined the cuts and bruises. Some of them

appeared to have been inflicted recently while others didn't. But that wasn't what got his attention.

"There's not a trace of blood anywhere on her bare skin. That doesn't make sense."

"Someone took the time to clean her up." Cody tilted his head towards the back of hers, "What kind of a ribbon is that?" He tucked his large hands under her chin and gently turned her head. Then he reached back and untied it.

"It's a piece off a vinyl table cloth," Billy said. "The kind mostly used on picnic tables."

"How do you know?"

"I have one at home just like it. If I'm not mistaken, it too is red and white checkered. It also has a flannel backing."

"Whoever did it has some experience tying bows." Although the material itself was ragged, wrinkled, and encrusted with dirt, he noticed that the ends of the bow appeared to have been meticulously looped then stretched out. It had to be a mother's touch. He gave it to Billy. "Go ahead and bag it." With his strong fingers, he stroked her scraggly, grime filled hair loose. "While you're at it, bring your camera back with you. After we get some photos of her and this area, we'll go over there where that danged fool took off. Those footprints coming from that direction look like they might be hers."

"So you think he dropped her off there?"

"Look at it this way. Kyle never mentioned a missing child. And the nearest house is miles away, which means if she came from there, she'd be burned a whole lot more than she is. He dropped her off alright." He set his large size hat on her head, smiled, and then tilted the hat back to expose her eyes. He rolled his from brush to brush looking for any signs of movement other than the flashing light seen earlier—which may or may not have been the work of the person on the Mustang. If it was, then he couldn't have had any other reason for his actions other than to get somebody's attention? He wanted her found.

Looking down he noticed her squeezing the teddy bear a wee bit tighter, yet the blank look and calmness didn't change. He passed his index finger in front of her face as if performing a sobriety check. Her eyes didn't follow. "Find anything?" he hollered over her right shoulder, taking his attention away from her, and away from conjuring up any more negative connotations concerning her state of mind.

"Not yet."

"Get on the radio and have them send an ambulance over to Kyle's ranch. Tell them we're bringing in a little girl who seems to be in shock. We'll meet them at the gate." He took her by the hand. "Let's see if we can get you something to drink, and then get the rest of this sand off your pretty little face, okay? I promise I won't hurt you." Then he led her to the vehicle. From the back of it, he took out the plastic bottle of water Billy routinely kept for emergencies. After rinsing Billy's paper coffee cup he filled it half way. Water dribbled down her chin as he placed it gently against her sun dried lips. Unable to part them, he brushed the sand off his hands then poured a little on his finger. He gently dabbed her lips then poured some onto his handkerchief. "Now what's this?" A gentle pull on a portion of the beaded necklace sticking out of her shirt exposed a quarter size silver crucifix.

"A rosary," Billy said, seeing it as he returned from searching for anything that would help identify her or the man on the horse. "I've never seen one around a child's neck before, or on an adult's for that matter."

"This might help us find out who she is and where she came from. Send a couple of deputies out to canvas the Catholic churches in the area as soon as we get a photo. Maybe we'll get lucky." He reached back behind her neck, unsnapped the latch, and then stuck the rosary in his shirt pocket.

He stood up and took in what was visible of the unforgiving landscape before him. There was no sign of the rider. He did, however see something else on the horizon: Vultures. They were a common sight in that part of the state, mostly ignored by the locals. But with the discovery of a child with blood stained clothes wandering in the desert, it had a whole new meaning. One he didn't particularly care for. He bent down to take the teddy bear before picking her up. She pulled away.

It was the first visible reaction encountered yet. She held on to it with a death like grip. Perhaps afraid to let go of the only security she's probably ever known.

"I guess it's gonna be the two of you or none." He picked them up then brought her head gently onto his shoulders the way he did Tammie's.

The doors left opened in their haste made it easier for him to back himself on to the edge of the driver's seat while still holding the newly acquired passengers. With the free hand, he reached over and adjusted the air conditioner so she wouldn't be immediately exposed to the cold air. Then he got out and closed both doors to hasten the comfort level of the interior.

Several minutes later, he opened the door and put her into the back seat. After removing his hat off of her, he ran his fingers through the stiff, tangled strands again. Then he playfully touched the tip of her little pug nose. "I'll be right back, darlin'."

With his hat secured back in place, he got out and watched Billy track and read the signs of life in the desert. Seeing nothing unusual himself, he wiped his forehead then hollered, "Anything yet?"

"I'm afraid not. Maybe we'll have better luck with more people out here."

"I think so too. Come on back."

While waiting for Billy to return, he took out one of those orange traffic cones from the back of the vehicle, went back to where they had found her and stuck it into the sand.

"Good idea," Billy said, glancing over Cody's shoulder towards the vehicle. "How is she?"

"Poor thing's exhausted."

"No telling what she's been through."

"Let's just get her out of here."

Billy's eyes narrowed as Cody opened the back door instead of going around to the front passenger side. "What are you doing?"

"I'm going to sit back here with her."

As Billy was opening the door to get in, his eyes were drawn to the mountain again. He stopped and stared at it with narrowed eyes for several minutes before getting in. Once inside, he leaned towards the windshield and said something in his native Comanche tongue.

When Billy leaned back onto the seat, Cody noticed the look on his eyes through the rear view mirror. After several seconds of death like silence, he asked, "What's wrong?"

"He's out there."

"Who's out there?"

"Hezekiah."

# 9

The outcome of mayhem and violence was nothing new to Jeremy. He had seen it all. But he could hardly believe what he heard over the radio; let alone what he saw coming out of the vehicle.

Cody, noticing the hypnotic stare, walked up beside him and put a hand on his shoulder. "Relax. Most of it isn't hers. She just has a few minor cuts and scratches."

After the brief moment of consolation, they both turned around at the sound of Kyle's jeep skidding close to the Expedition.

Kyle lifted his frazzled, straw hat and scratched his head when he saw the little girl in Billy's hand. "Well I'll be. What in Sam hill was she doing out there?"

"She wasn't the only one out there, Kyle," Billy said. "So was your Mustang."

"You found it?"

"No. Someone else did."

"Who?"

"We don't know," Cody said. "He lit out towards the mountain. You might as well get use to having us around for awhile, Kyle. We'll try not to interfere with your ranching."

"The last thing I need around here is a horse thief, sheriff. I'll be glad to help in any way I can."

"Good. Let's start with that break in the fence. Did you or any of the hands see or hear a vehicle around that area."

"I asked them back then and they said they ain't seen or heard nothin'. I'm pretty sure it happened during the night.

Besides, you can see the bunkhouse is quite a ways from here."

"I see."

"Those blood stains. You don't suppose there's been an accident out there, do you?" Jeremy asked Cody.

"There's a possibility someone bent on four wheeling could've cut that fence. But that's something we won't know for sure until we do a thorough search. In the meantime, let's make sure she's taken care of. Here come the medics."

Before the emergency medical personnel's feet could even hit the pavement, Cody motioned them over.

Like a worried father, he kept his eyes on them as they gently took her from Billy and put her and the bear on a stretcher. After strapping her down, they bombarded her with questions to check her responsiveness. They got none.

Cody grinned as they tried to separate her from her furry friend. Once they got her inside the ambulance, he continued to keep an eye on her as they checked her vitals and hooked her up to an IV saline solution.

Then a glimpse of the revolving, red light beacon on top of the ambulance got his full attention, eventually opening his mind's eye to the worst night of his life.

In it he saw Tammie, who had fallen asleep before she could finish counting the twinkling stars, or see the smiling moon playing peek-a-boo behind the dark clouds. Cradled on her frail arms; the blonde headed Ken, who had been separated from Barbie Doll ever since they had left San Antonio.

He saw Katelyn with her head resting on his shoulder. Perhaps dreaming of the wonderful time they had strolling through the Alamo city's River Walk after a full day at Six Flags Amusement park.

He saw himself drawing his head nearer to savor the herbal scent of the auburn, frizzled hair tucked under a baseball cap. He fought the urge to remove the cap, settling instead for a gentle kiss on the top so as not to wake her up.

Then he looked ahead and saw the vehicle whose driver had yet to dim his high beams as it approached from the south.

Cody brightened then dimmed his headlights several times to make the other driver, who was still a safe distance away, aware of his situation.

No response.

He ignored it at first, thinking sooner or later, as the gap between them got shorter, the driver would realize they were on and take appropriate action. He didn't.

As the increasing glare of the high beam engulfed the interior of the pickup, his worst nightmare unfolded before his squinting eyes. The vehicle was on the wrong side of the road and just seconds away from impact.

With a sinking feeling in his stomach, he turned the steering wheel hard right, presuming the other driver would realize the situation and instinctively do likewise in order to get back to his own lane.

The pickup, however, swerved violently one way then the other on its roller coaster ride to oblivion.

Katelyn jostled violently towards Tammie then back to Cody.

Tammie's head whiplashed from side to side.

Ken and Barbie disappeared somewhere under the dash.

He tried grabbing the steering wheel after Katelyn's shoulder knocked his hands off, but the wheel developed a mind of its own and took control of the situation.

The stars above spun in front of his eyes as if he were inside the cockpit of an F-16 fighter jet doing barrel rolls in the night sky.

Katelyn and Tammie's screams blended with the cacophony of metal scoring asphalt as the pickup slid several yards on its flattened roof.

The mangled truck eventually flew off the highway and into the desert. When it finally stopped, the only thing visible in the darkness was the dimmed beam of one headlight searching the stars on the horizon through a cloud of dust. In the end, three of the tires pointed skyward, spinning madly, breaking the eerie silence with their whirring death throes. The fourth wobbled down the highway like a drunkard attempting to make it home safely.

In a drunk like stupor, he unbuckled and freed himself from the cramped, neck breaking position. Through the narrow opening of what was once a window, he squeezed out. Every bone in his body felt like it had been shattered. Every muscle as if they had been run through a paper shredder.

The nightmare continued when he smelled the dreaded odor of gasoline. With bloodied fingers dug in the sand, he pushed himself up and crawled on all fours until he was several feet away from what was left of the vehicle. He tried calling out their names but the words were muffled by lungs that felt like they had been crushed. Then his arms and legs flailed wildly as he was catapulted through the air by the concussion.

He never got to see the huge fireball that lit the night sky, or feel the searing heat. Minutes later, the pungent, nauseating odor of burning rubber, leather, and flesh hit his nostrils like ammonia from a broken capsule.

The crescendo of sirens quickly filled his ears as emergency vehicles approached from each end of the highway.

His eyes fluttered until light began to penetrate the darkness. When they opened, his blood covered eyes revealed a blurred vision of lawmen, firemen, and medics silhouetted by the crackling tongues of flames.

After the firefighters doused the inferno all that was left was the smoldering, black heap of charred metal.

"Sheriff, please. Don't move."

He saw the familiar paramedic pushing down against his shoulders as he struggled in vain to sit up.

"Katelyn... Tammie. Where...where are they...? What happened?"

"There's been a bad accident. I'm afraid you might have some broken ribs and internal injuries. You need to lay still."

Through all the commotion, Cody couldn't see the tears shed by his side. He couldn't hear the Native American prayer offered to the good spirit in the sky. He tried again to sit up, but someone with a sledgehammer, he thought, pounded him back to the ground. Giving up on that, he reached up and grabbed a hold of Billy's collar. "Katelyn...Tammie"

Billy hid his teary eyes behind the brim of his hat then let the words trickle out, "They...they didn't make it, Cody. A passing motorist tried to get them out but was driven back by the heat."

Within seconds the floodgates opened. The thought of them suffering in such an inferno was too much to bear. A cold chill sent his body into feverish like tremors, and the lump in his throat threatened to block his airway.

Before they closed the back doors of the ambulance, he looked away from the red light in time to catch a glimpse of the oxygen mask being placed on the little girl's face. Even so, it didn't stop him from blurting out the words that had escaped the confines of his mind as the EMT approached. "What about the occupants of the other vehicle?"

Jeremy, hearing the strange question as he passed by him, turned around and asked, "What other vehicle?"

Although Cody had mentally rejoined them, the pallor of his skin and the confused look prompted Billy to rush over. He put a hand on his shoulder and stared into the glazed eyes.

The medic, who had stepped out of the ambulance to get some information on the little girl, also noticed. "What's the matter, sheriff? Are you sick?"

"No... No. I...I'm okay."

"Are you sure?" Billy asked.

He shook his head. "I'm okay."

"Good," the EMS said. "Is there a name I can put on my report?"

Although Jane Doe seemed to be the only name under the sun for the lost and unknown, it was the last one he wanted to use. As he scanned the horizon, a picture of a red, desert rose came to mind.

"Yes," he said. "Desert Rose."

He walked back to his pickup and placed his elbows on top of the hood. He leaned on it with his head hung low.

With a questioning look in his eyes, Jeremy shrugged his shoulders at Billy. "What's eating him?"

"The accident."

"That was a long time ago, wasn't it?"

"It has something to do with that other vehicle he believes caused it."

Before Jeremy could delve into the matter, the slamming of the ambulance doors grabbed his attention. He rushed over to the driver's side door just as they were about to leave. He knocked on the window. "Hey! Which hospital?"

The startled driver lowered the window. "County Memorial."

"Take it easy with her, will you. She's been through a lot."

"Don't worry. We'll take good care of her."

Billy, still concerned over Cody's behavior, walked up behind and tapped him on the shoulder. "Want to get a search team out there?"

"No," he said, lifting his head and straightening up. "Let's get back to this instinct of yours. What makes you think Hezekiah's out there?"

"About a month ago he was spotted on the other side of the mountain. He hasn't been seen anywhere else since."

"Get a hold of Deputies Seth and Earl. Have them bring their horses. The areas pretty thick with cactus and brush. Besides, if what you say turns out to be true, they'd stand a better chance of sneaking up, or even chasing him down. Have them bring yours also. I'll get DPS (Department of Public Safety) to send me a helicopter down here. I wanna make sure our desert rat doesn't leave this area without being spotted." He motioned for one of the deputies standing by. "Follow them back to the hospital then get her clothes over to the lab."

"I suppose you'll want a twenty-four hour watch set up," Billy said.

"You bet." He paused, bringing to the forefront the memo he had received from Child Protective Services several weeks earlier. The one he had glanced at then put aside for a later time. It concerned the arrival of their new supervisor, and her commitment to serve the community at large. "While you're at it, get a hold of a Miss Wheeler over in CPS and fill her in on the situation. We'll need her or someone from that department to advise us on the child's options if we can't find her parents."

Billy waited for the deputy to leave then came up beside him. In a voice that no one else could hear, he said, "The spirits of the past, huh?"

Cody whipped his head around. "What's *that* suppose to mean?"

"You're going to need help to make it go away, you know."

"Make what go away?"

"That far off look. Sort of like you're in a trance or something. I've seen it twice already. Three months ago at that accident over on 285. That Mexican family, remember? Mother and two little girls killed instantly. Look, it doesn't take a you know what to figure it out. You need help, my friend."

"You of all people should know what I've been through. What makes you think I need any more help?"

"Because of the fire that shows up in your eyes right after those episodes, or whatever you want to call them. I don't know if it's there to burn you or the person you believe was responsible for your loss. Either way, you're going to need help putting it out. If you don't, the demons will always return to remind you, to stoke your fire until it consumes you altogether."

"What about the Bulldog?"

"Bulldog?"

"Yes! The one that keeps throwing me to the ground before peeling back strips of flesh off my face. Is that the work of the demons also?"

"What are you talking about?"

"The nightmare. I've had it several times already. And each time its significance seems more important than the time before. There has to be some kind of connection between the bulldog and what happened that night."

"So that's it. How come you never mentioned this before?"

"I didn't want to bother you with it. Besides, I figured it would come to me sooner or later. I think it has something to do with that other vehicle."

"You were tired that night, Cody, wore out from that day's activities. Aponi and I even talked about it right after you left the house. You may have fallen asleep at the wheel and just can't remember it."

"I don't buy that, Billy."

"Okay then. Let's just suppose you're right and there was a second vehicle. Don't you think it's a little too late to get a vehicular manslaughter conviction based on a D.U.I. or negligence? You need to snuff it out, Cody."

"I know what you're getting at," he said. "No thanks. I've seen enough grief counselors to last me a lifetime."

"Okay, then, have you seen enough reporters?" He nodded towards the pack talking with the deputies. "They're getting a little restless."

"I know. As soon as those horses get here, try and track that varmint down. In the meantime, I'll go over there and give those vultures a short briefing before I put in the request for that helicopter."

# 10

Susan Wheeler's small apartment was a far cry from the one she had in lower Manhattan. That one boasted a living room big enough to accommodate forty members of the Women's City Club of New York, a bedroom fit for a queen, and a kitchen that would have made *Julia Child's* mouth salivate.

Not that she couldn't afford a similar one in Fort Stockton, if indeed there was one, but at the age of thirty-four, the apartment with contemporary styled, geometrically shaped furniture in bold colors gave her the comfort and satisfaction she needed. The only thing she missed about the one back east, besides Bill, was Freddy the doorman's friendly smile as she went in and out of her luxurious apartment building.

As for her mother and siblings, they understood, and were willing to accept the distance forced upon them by the events and her desire to start a new life.

She married Bill Wheeler, a Wall Street financier, when she was twenty-four, despite the misgivings voiced by friends and family concerning the ten years difference in age, and his desire to keep children out of the picture, at least until they reached his financial goal and ambition. But that didn't matter. Her work filled the passion to help abused and neglected children, a problem she knew all too well having lived in an environment dominated by an alcoholic stepfather who had physically and verbally abused her mother.

Thanks to him, she was determined to put off any thoughts of marriage, vying instead to put herself through college, eventually earning a degree in child psychology. With that she committed herself to a lifetime career with Child Protective Services.

You could say her transfer to Fort Stockton began on what was supposed to be a routine workday; one that had started with clear blue skies and a smaller workload than usual. She had also hoped it would turn out to be one that would give her an early start at the fitness center for her aerobics class. But all that changed when she saw the horror written across her friend Donna's face.

"You'd better get out here, quick." Donna said, as she stood at the threshold of the door nodding towards the break area. The small television next to the vending machines was tuned to the nationally broadcast *Today show*.

"Why? What's going on?"

The words had barely left her lips when she saw another co-worker pass by her door. His face was ashen, and he grabbed the cubicle walls outside her office for support.

She got up immediately, went to the entrance and followed him with her questioning eyes as he staggered to his work area. She never even noticed that Donna had run back to the break area, or the blaring sirens of the fire trucks passing by out on Maiden Lane.

Before long, screaming and crying could be heard throughout room 509 of the city's regional office.

"Can someone please tell me what's going on?" she yelled, as some of the employees ran by sobbing. There were others who seemed to have suddenly turned into walking zombies, with blank stares on ashen faces.

In front of the TV, several more employees sat stunned. By the time she walked close enough to see what was going on, the huge flames and smoke had engulfed the entire upper section of the North Tower.

"Oh, my God, what happened?"

"They're saying it was a plane," said one of her co-workers.

She refused to believe it at first, thinking it was a commercial for one of those cataclysmic movies of doom and gloom coming upon the earth. But then she heard the familiar voice of the show host say, "that was no accident," as a second plane sliced through the South Tower like a sharp knife through a stick of butter standing on its end.

The hairs on her neck stood up, and her heart felt like it had skipped several beats. Bill's punctuality surfaced when she looked up at the clock. 9:03 AM. He was sure to be at his desk. It was right by a large picture window. It was on the side struck head on by the plane. Did he see it coming? Did he stand a chance? "Bill." she gasped.

She ran back to the office. Maybe, just maybe, for the first time in years, he had left late for work. Maybe he's stuck in traffic. Maybe he stopped to get a newspaper. Maybe he's still on the elevator. The maybes kept coming until they ran out.

With hands that wouldn't keep still, she pulled the cell phone out of her purse and quickly punched the number to his thirtieth floor office at the South Tower. No answer. She punched in the number to his Cell phone.

The same.

She hung up then ran back to watch more of what was happening. Then she heard her desk phone ringing. She ran back and picked it up. "Bill."

"Susan, it's me. Have you heard?"

"My God, Betty, what's going on?"

"That's what I'd like to know. Have you heard from Bill?"

"No, I can't get through. What am I going to do?"

"Pray, Susan. Pray."

"I'm going down there."

"No, don't. You'll never get past all the emergency vehicles. Stay there until he calls. He may be on the way out of the building now."

Her sister-in-law was right. There had to be another way she could get in touch with him

"Listen, Betty, let me call you back."

"Okay, but see if there's anyone else up there you can call."

Before she could do anything else, a call came in from her mother. She had no more information to give her than what she had learned from the media.

"I'm sure he's okay, mom—he has to be. Let me call you right back."

With a fist to her mouth, she hung up, turned around and went to get her purse. Just as she was about to leave, screams, louder than those heard earlier, filled the air. She ran back and weaved her way through the small crowd that had now gathered in front of the television. At 9:59 am she watched in horror as her life crumbled along with the South Tower.

The shock wouldn't let her even scream at the sight or move a muscle. At the same time, anxious and bewildered co-workers ran to and fro not knowing what to expect or do next.

Those who knew Bill worked in the World Trade Center stopped long enough to glance at her with anxious looks, not knowing what to say.

Others passed by her as if she was a mere statue that had been recently placed in the middle of the room. And for all intent and purposes, she was.

In time, the grieving, the ceremonies, and the birth of the memorial, became part of history and memories of her past.

For a long time she had contemplated moving away from the tall buildings, the massive crowds, and the enticing target for more terrorist activities.

Money was no issue. She had enough now to go anywhere in the world she wanted. Her job however was. More than ever, she wanted to smother her life with the lives of those children in need.

She waited for an opening at a CPS agency somewhere out west, far away from the memories, and where her life had been dramatically changed. The waiting ended when she finally found one at the Texas Department of Family and Protective Services on 108 South Water, in Fort Stockton, Texas, a place she never even heard of, let alone knew anything about. After bidding Freddy and her family goodbye, she had the cab driver take her to the now infamous site for one last look. Then she headed straight for JFK international airport.

# 11

"That man was no tenderfoot, lieutenant. If it does turn out to be Hezekiah, where d'ya think he learned to ride like that?"

"That's a good question," Billy said. "The problem is we've never been able to find out anything about his past or where he's from, let alone what he's capable of."

"Well, with any luck we'll know before the day's over." he gestured towards the north end of the highway where two vehicle's towing horse trailers were fast approaching. "Here come our equalizers now."

After they pulled over to the side of the road, Jeremy watched with interest as the three deputies got out and unloaded their horses. When Cody walked by, Jeremy went up alongside of him asking "What about this Hezekiah? Who is he?"

"We really don't know who he is. The first time anybody around here's ever laid eyes on him was about two and a half years ago. He was rummaging through a McDonald's dumpster. When the manager came out and confronted him, he reportedly gave him a tightlipped, menacing stare. Afraid he was dealing with something he couldn't handle, the manager went back inside and called the city police, but by the time they got there, he was nowhere in sight."

"Is he homeless?"

"Well now that's hard to say since he's made himself home at an old abandoned farmhouse off highway 67." He gestured towards Billy. "Now he seems to think Hezekiah might be out there somewhere. I'm not really sure about that myself. As a matter of fact, we're not really sure if that's even his real name. The investigating officer got it from a drifter who claims to have spent some time with him up on the mountain. He was stuck with the name after the local papers ran a short piece on the incident." He glanced at his watch. "It's 9:40 now. Let's see if we can get a photo of her on the 12:00 O'clock news. Maybe someone will recognize her."

The strong, warm breath on the back of his neck brought a smile to his face. He turned around and patted the horse's nose. On the saddle, Deputy Earl Capps, a longtime veteran of the force, and an expert tracker, bent down closer to Cody. "The Lieutenant said Hezekiah's out there. Is that true?"

He put one hand on the horse's cheek and gave Billy the key to the back gate with the other. "Here. You're gonna need this. And if it turns out to be him then just remember what happened a while back."

Billy looked over at him with a knowing smile as he mounted his horse. He and his posse of two then rode through the gate and onto a swath cutting through the desert brush.

Jeremy, once again feeling left out, flipped his thumb back towards the posse as he and Cody turned around and started walking towards their vehicles. "What was that all about?"

"Six months ago three local bullies met Hezekiah hiking south on 67 and decided to have a little fun. Two of them grabbed a hold of him while the third one tried to improve on his kickboxing techniques."

"So what happened?"

"The Karate Kid didn't quite make it. After the smoke cleared, all three looked like they were tumbled in a commercial cloth dryer filled with rocks."

"You're kidding?"

"I'm afraid not. Our Mr. Hezekiah may be up in age, but that's about all. If you don't believe me, feel free to ask those poor fellas if and when you ever meet em." He looked up to the sky. "For now, though, we need to move fast on this. It won't be long before that sun takes its toll on us."

"Did you lock him up?"

"For what? There were enough witnesses driving by who testified *he* was the victim. By the time they called us it was all over."

"Self defense, huh."

"Yep. Which reminds me. I want you to go to the hospital and find out as much as you can about that defenseless child."

"I'd love to," he said, a broad smile flashing across his face.

"I know."

He couldn't think of a better person to send. Especially after seeing the way Jeremy's eyes also lingered on the child as she was taken to the ambulance. While passing on some of his knowledge of ranching, he had learned about the young couple's plight. He had an idea of what Peggy's reaction would be after learning a child had been found all alone out in that environment.

The whop, whop, sound of large blades beating the air caught his attention. He looked up and pointed towards the Glass Mountains. "I'll be up there if you need me."

# 12

As was his custom when seeing a child in one of the emergency room beds, Dr. Barnes looked around for at least one of the parents. With none seen by her side or in the immediate vicinity, he turned to the nurse who was familiar with his routine. "Where are they?"

"They're looking for them now. Here's her chart. Since they couldn't find anything to identify her, the sheriff suggested we put the name, Desert Rose, on it for the time being."

"From what I've heard and see here now, he made a pretty good choice." He took the report from her outstretched hand, gave it a quick glance, and then checked the bruises and cuts pointed out by the nurses.

He passed the beam of his pen light from one eye to the other. He checked for the presence of semen, knowing lack of penetration didn't necessarily mean she wasn't sexually abused in other ways.

"Take her to Radiology," he said, turning to the head nurse. "I want a CT scan of the brain. Let me know as soon as the films are available"

"Should we go ahead and admit her?"

"At least until we make sure there's no physical trauma to the brain. I'll sign the necessary papers later. Go ahead and dress those cuts then clean her up." After removing the latex gloves and discarding them, he turned to the deputy assigned to stay with her. "I understand there are reporters out in the lobby waiting for word on her condition, is that true?"

"Yes, sir."

"Well then, let's get this over with."

Out in the main lobby, a spokesman for the hospital introduced Dr. Barnes to a small contingent of reporters then motioned him to the microphone.

"Let me start by saying her vital signs appear to be normal and there are no indications of severe malnutrition or dehydration," he told them. "She does have a mild case of sunburn which the staff will be treating shortly. We will also be checking to make sure she has no fractures or any internal injuries. Those results won't be in until sometime later."

"How long will she be staying here?" asked one of the reporters.

"That I can't say, however, while under our care she will be monitored to make sure nothing's overlooked."

"Can you give us a description of the child?"

With that, a deputy stepped in and began handing out five by seven digital photos that were taken just before the ambulance took her away. As soon as a TV reporter got a hold of one, his camera man focused on it. The others reached for their cell phones as if it was a duel to see who would draw his weapon first.

"Anyone with information," the deputy said, "is asked to get in touch with either the Sheriff's Department or Child Protective Services as soon as possible. Your cooperation is crucial in helping us find out who she is. That's all for now. Thank you."

Doctor, Barnes started to go back to the emergency room when Jeremy approached him from behind. "Doctor, Barnes."

"Yes?"

"I'm deputy Sands. I've been assigned to keep tabs on her. Is she really going to be okay?"

"I'll tell you what. Why don't you just follow me over to Radiology and see for yourself. I'm sure they won't mind."

"Thanks."

Informed by the technician at the radiology department that the pictures, along with the patient, were already taken to room 33, they immediately turned around and went there. The deputy sitting by the door stood up and opened it for them. Once inside, Jeremy watched with interest as the doctor leaned over and gently lifted her eyelids. He pulled out his penlight and repeated the procedure over her eyes. As he checked them, another nurse entered with a large manila envelope in her hands.

"Here they are, Doctor."

Under the light over the headboard, he took more time to study the x-rays than Jeremy cared for.

"What's wrong, Doc?"

"I'd like to have a neurologist take a look at these, nurse. And while you're at it, get a hold of Doctor, Fieldson. I'm sure he'll want to see this." With his hands rubbing his chin, he turned back to Jeremy's question. "I need to talk to the sheriff as soon as possible."

# 13

Cody approached the slow moving blades of the DPS helicopter with one hand firmly on his hat and his head tucked between his shoulders like a turtle. After squeezing in and closing the door, he buckled up then grabbed the headset from the outstretched hand of the pilot.

"You're going to need those today," he said, loud enough to be heard over the increasing high-pitched whir of the turbine engine.

At first Cody thought he was talking about the headset, but then realized the pilot was nodding towards the dark aviator sunglasses sticking half way out of the door jacket. After adjusting the earpiece to minimize the noise in the cockpit, he took the sunglasses out and put them on. He gave the pilot the thumbs up sign.

As the *American Eurocopter* AS350B2 lifted, he looked down and noticed the reporters over by the staging area being held back by the deputies. The thought of one or more of them sneaking out to where she was found was interrupted by the voice coming through the earpiece. "So, where are we going?"

"Over to the east side of Panther Mesa."

"Okay, but I might as well warn you. We've got some pretty hefty wind gusts out there. We might not be able to get as close as you'd like."

"Do the best you can."

He was hoping to find something in that part of the mountain range before going further west and south where there were higher peaks and deeper canyons—an environment more difficult to search at best.

Through the chatter on the frequency, he learned that Billy and his posse had reached the location where Desert Rose had been found. He took the binoculars out of the seat pouch and scanned the horizon. He pointed. "There they are."

As the chopper got closer, a beam of light penetrated the windshield, forcing the pilot to shield his eyes even with the sunglasses on. "What was that?"

"I believe that's what started this whole business." Cody switched over to ground communication. "What is it?"

"A woman's compact mirror," Billy said. "It was stuck in the sand."

"Our runaway cowboy must've dropped it after seeing us coming, lieutenant. That's why we lost sight of it. Send it over to the lab then meet me at the base of the mountain."

Eyes closed and hands reached for hats as the helicopter, flying right above them, increased the velocity of grit and fine sand at ground level.

"Keep this thing low the rest of the way," he told the pilot. "I want to be able to get a good look at anything that doesn't belong out here."

Not far from the mountain, Cody scanned Kyle's property fence line until he came upon one particular section. "I thought so. Six zero two go over towards the area just below the highest peak. You won't need that key."

"Whatd'ya see?" the pilot asked.

"Barb wires kissing the ground. It wouldn't take much for a Chihuahua, let alone a Mustang, to clear what's left. When we get close enough to the base of the mountain, make a couple of passes around it. If we don't see anything there, take her to the top and level off."

After several minutes banking up and down the sides and scanning the summit, Cody lowered his binoculars.

"I don't see anything unusual up here. Let's take her over to the west side."

Deep down inside, he had doubts about Desert Rose's parents being anywhere near there. For one thing, what parent would subject a child to that environment even for one moment, let alone a day or more?

For another, how could she wander away from them without being noticed in the vast open countryside? Still, the question of

70

how she got there had to be answered.

"Six zero one."

"Go ahead."

"You were right. We found some signs indicating our mysterious rider was hiding in a deep gully when we came up on the child. He's probably somewhere near the base of the mountain."

"We're going to circle back around," Cody said. "Maybe we'll get lucky."

As they flew below the mountain top and skimmed the side, something caught his eye. He leaned forward, frowning. He put the binoculars to his eyes and focused on a narrow ledge not far from the base. "See how close you can get to that," he said, pointing."

"What is it?"

Cody zoomed in on the object, which appeared to be leaning up against a large rock. "It's a shovel." He lowered the binoculars for a brief moment to clear his vision then looked through it again. "I'm not sure, but it looks like the handle might be broken."

"What in the world would anyone do with a shovel up here?"

"I don't know but there's something else down there that's just as interesting." He lowered the binoculars again and turned to the pilot. "Take her down as close to the base of that mountain as possible."

"I'll see what I can do. Hang on."

Even though the engine was equipped with a sand filtration system, the pilot cut the engine as soon as he could to avoid any problems.

Cody wasted no time either. Before the blades had even slowed down, he unbuckled and opened the door. With the binoculars still in his hand, he got out and began looking at the mountainside through the dust.

When the three deputies on horseback arrived, Billy dismounted first and handed Seth the reins of his sweat soaked horse. "See anything interesting?" he hollered.

"A shovel."

"Where?"

"Half way up," Cody pointed. "Over by that ledge"

"I don't get it. As far as I know there's nothing up there worth digging for."

"And one shovel wouldn't exactly do for an official Paleontological or Archeological dig," Cody added. He brought the binoculars down and pointed to another ledge winding up the side of the mountain. "It looks like there might be enough room for our horses to make it up that far." As he spoke his eyes were drawn towards Seth's horse. "What's the matter with him?"

"I don't know. He's never acted like this before."

Cody grabbed the bit just as the horse started backing up. "Whoa, boy." He rubbed the horse's neck. "It looks to me like you don't want to go anywhere near that mountain. You know something we don't?" He took a quick glance towards the mountain. "Tell you what. Why don't we have Deputy Seth stay here just in case our friend decides to show himself while you and I go check out that big bad mountain, okay?"

Seth dismounted and handed him the reins to Apache, known to be the fastest and most dependable horse in their stable. But he had no intention of racing past any signs that could possibly lead him to the man who lit out of sight, or Desert Rose's parents. Nor did he have any inclination of racing the Mustang, who looked like he had the ability and speed to outrun any of the department's horses, including Apache. No. At this stage of the game, he'd settle for a mule, so long as he was able to find what he was looking for.

"I kind'a figured you'd be needing these," Billy said.

"Thanks."

After taking the pair of spurs from Billy's outstretched hand and putting them on, he checked the cinch around Apache to make sure it was still snug. Then with one hand wrapped around the saddle horn and one foot on the stirrup, he glided onto the saddle and patted the horse's neck to settle him down. With the rein in his left hand, he gently coaxed the horse towards the mountain.

Before mounting, Billy and Earl stood by their horses with their eyes on Cody as he sped off at a Gallup. The two deputies then glanced at each other and shrugged their shoulders.

"He must've seen something else besides the shovel," Earl said.

"I believe you're right. It's best we get going before we lose sight of him."

Near the base of the mountain, and close to where the shovel was spotted, Cody noticed two sets of footprints in the dirt. He pulled up on the reigns, stopping Apache before he could disturb them, then he motioned for Billy to come up beside him. When he did, he pointed to the set that appeared to be larger than the other. "It looks like someone wearing an old pair of cowboy boots was up here recently."

Billy grabbed the saddle horn then leaned down as close as he could to the set of smaller prints.

"Whatd'ya think?" Cody asked.

"Desert Rose."

"My thoughts exactly. Come on. Let's just see where they take us."

The trail raised then dipped like a miniature roller coaster hugging the side of the mountain. Along the way up, their ears filled with the sound of loose rocks and sand sliding down the mountainside, their hearts with apprehension.

While climbing, Cody kept an eye on Apache's ears, looking for any movement that would indicate something was amiss. If there was, the horse would more than likely detect it before he did.

Upon reaching a plateau, they're greeted by the rhythm of large, flapping wings beating against the wind. Apache stopped. His ears got taut, his flesh quivered, and his flared nostrils rattled. Cody sensed something other than the giant birds made the horse react like it did. And he didn't have to see what it was. He could smell it.

He laid a hand on Apache's neck to quiet him then bent down close to his pointing ear and whispered, "You picked it up too, didn't you, boy."

Even after being nudged, Apache gaited sideways as if seeking to avoid something up ahead. Only after considerable coaxing did he eventually lead Cody and the others to the source of the sickly, sweet odor of decaying flesh. And in that moment, in the solitude of the tranquil mountain, mingled the rattling of horse nostrils and the shallow breathing of three stunned deputies.

"Now we know what the shovel was for," Billy said, gazing at what appeared to be a body partially exposed in a shallow grave.

"It looks to me like someone took off before they could finish the job."

Maggots, along with the blowflies that had yet to lay their eggs, occupied the decomposing body. Her blue blouse and tan shorts were coated with a thick layer of dried blood, and they were both shredded by the neighborhood scavengers. Her mouth was wide opened as if frozen in one last desperate scream. One eye socket was empty, its contents pecked out by the black stealth squadron that had taken off just before Cody appeared. The other flattened, devoid of its fluid by the normal process of death.

"How long do you think she's been here?" Earl asked.

"I'm guessing three or four days," Cody replied, lifting his hat skyward towards the searing sun and then wiping his forehead with his sleeve. "Unfortunately, they've been some of the hottest ones yet." After dismounting, he walked over and stood by the remains making a mental sketch of its proximity to the trail that had led to her. "I reckon we'd better get the medical examiner up here."

"I'll notify him," Earl volunteered.

"Do you think that's her mother?" Billy asked.

"I have a feeling she is." He took a moment to take in the rough terrain and distance between where they were and the base of the mountain. "I sure would like to know how she made it up here barefooted."

"She was carried up here," Billy said. "As you can see, those boot prints leading up to this point are deep. Over there they're not. She was dropped off before the child was led over there."

"What about these other footprints?" Cody pointed. "I didn't see them on the trail."

"I saw traces of them earlier. They were made by hiking boots some time ago. These up here were made more recently. It looks like they're in desperate need of repairs also."

"So now all we need to know is who owns the cowboy boots and whether or not he was in cahoots with the hiker."

"Yep. But right now I'd like to know what made *you* come up here."

"That blouse." He pointed to the corpse. "Dark blue isn't exactly a color you'd find up here. It kind'a stood out like a sore thumb among all this rocky terrain."

"There's something else you wouldn't normally find up here either," Earl hollered as he stood at a good distance from them. "Come take a look."

When they met him, he turned around without saying a word and led them to a section of the plateau hidden by boulders taller than a city bus. There stood an altar composed of large rocks piled three feet high, two feet wide, and six feet across. It was strewn with burnt flesh, bones, and ashes from the kindling source.

"I noticed one of those vultures coming up from this area earlier," Earl said. "I figured there had to be a meal around here also."

That little girl may have witnessed something terrible here. Did they let her go thinking she was too young to know what had happened? Or did they know she couldn't or wouldn't talk?

"Come on, let's get back, lieutenant. I've seen enough. Did you get a hold of the Medical Examiner?" he asked Earl.

"The chopper's picking him and a couple of boys from forensics up right now. They should be here in about ten minutes or so."

"Did you bring the camera?"

"It's in my saddlebag. I'll go get it."

When Cody turned around, he noticed Billy glaring at the top of the mountain. "You still think he's up here, don't you?"

"Yes."

Although he was still skeptical, Cody joined him in looking up at the top. "Quite a ways from home, don't you think?"

"Not really. That old farmhouse is just on the other side of the Mesa north of here. It wouldn't bother him one bit or, for that matter, take him that long to hike out here."

"If he is up there, do you think he'll put up a fight?"

"That's hard to say." Billy pulled out his handkerchief and wiped the back of his neck. "If he decides to hunker down and put up a fight, he'll have the advantage. He probably has enough nooks and crannies mapped in his head to make our job that much harder."

"That's what I'm afraid of."

The side of the mountain was peppered here and there with crevices, holes, and cavities between large embedded boulders.

From where they stood there was no way to determine how deep they were, or if someone was hiding in them, waiting for a chance to pick them off. The whole scenario prompted him to postpone, at least for the time being, any attempts to bring Hezekiah, or whoever it may be, down until they could come back with reinforcements.

"I reckon we'd better get started," Billy said, walking back to his horse. He took a couple of latex gloves out of his saddlebag, snapped them on then tossed Cody a pair.

Cody waited for Earl to finish photographing the scene before carefully brushing some of the dirt off the remains. He searched the victim's pants pockets and found a book of matches. "Well, now, this is interesting."

"What?"

"Angels." he wiped his forehead with the sleeve of his shirt again then tossed the matchbook. "Here."

Billy snatched it in mid air then glanced at the cover. "The dance club over on East 20$^{th}$?"

"Yep."

When he opened it, he noticed only two matches were torn off. "She could've picked this up anywhere." He tossed it back.

"Maybe. But this and those tattoos on her right shoulder and left ankle is all we have that might help identify her. Make sure we get a couple of good close-up shots."

He didn't think the heart on the shoulder, which was somewhat faded and barely visible, would be of much use. The single rose just above the ankle, however, appeared to be fairly new, maybe even done in one of the city's tattoo parlors. At least that's what he was hoping for.

"Sheriff, you'd better have a look at this," Earl said, motioning to another area he had checked out while they were hovering over the body.

Leaving Billy at the gravesite to look around, he followed Earl to a site that looked more like the dirt floor of a rodeo arena than an undisturbed portion of a mountain. A multitude of footprints, sheltered from the strong winds by the higher terrain around them, covered the area.

"It looks like there must've been some kind of a brawl up

here." Cody got down on one knee and pointed. "These are from those same cowboy boots. The ones next to them look like they may be from the hiking shoes. From the way it looks, the cowboy walked away from the grave sight and joined the hiker here. The child stayed put where she was."

"Yeah." Billy said, as he joined them. "And if it was anywhere else but here, those impressions would either be a lot shallower or completely gone. I'd say the scuffle took place three, maybe four days ago." He did a slow three hundred and sixty degree turn, eyeing everything in sight. "To tell you the truth, they couldn't have picked a better place to dispose of her. Once you get past Kyle's property the traffic out this way is almost non-existent. I doubt if even Kyle or any of his hands venture out this far. In fact, if it wasn't for that little girl, this body may never have been found."

Hezekiah must've known that would be the case. Did he want them to find her? Or was their some other reason for getting them up there?

"We need to find out what brought this on and who got the upper hand. I want lots of pictures. After you're done, mark the perimeter. While you're taking care of that, the lieutenant and I will go back and have another look at the body."

Back at the gravesite, Cody squatted on one side while Billy the other. He stared at the body for a few seconds then looked up at Billy. "Whatd'ya you think?"

"We won't know for sure until we eliminate the damage done by the heat and the local varmints." He paused as he took a good look at the visible wounds. "But if I were a betting man, I'd say someone tried to slice and dice her from behind. She's got some pretty deep gashes on the back of her head, upper back, and neck. It had to be done by something fairly sharp and big."

"How about that shovel?"

"That's possible. We'll pick it up on the way back down."

"I saw hoof prints and tire tracks down below," Earl said. "And there's a piece of a wooden handle halfway down from here."

"Get pictures of the hoof prints and we'll compare them to the ones made by the Mustang. On your way down pick up that wooden handle. Lieutenant, you go get all the blood samples typed. Let's see if any of it matches those found on the child's clothing. What doesn't goes to CODIS (Combined DNA Index System).

"You do know it may take several weeks for the DNA results to get back to us," Billy reminded him.

"Have Martha put an expedite on it. In the meanwhile, let's hope what we've got so far will help solve this thing sooner than later."

"You're going to head this investigation yourself, aren't you?" Billy hollered as Cody walked away.

He hollered back, "Why not, lieutenant. I'm already involved. I might as well see it through. We'll get DPS to send a team up here to process the evidence. Our department will take care of the investigation."

"It's the child, isn't it?"

He stopped and turned around. "You might say that."

"I thought so. Don't forget, this is an impersonal career we've chosen. Try not to cross that fine line."

"Don't worry, I'll try not to."

"Good. So what's our next move?"

"While you're taking care of things up here, I'm going to have the pilot drop me off on the highway. You don't call for a medical examiner unless you found something. The last thing we need is a pack of reporters harassing Kyle for access through his property. Or worst yet, sneaking in and damaging evidence. I'll just give them a short briefing," He continued talking as he turned his back, "then head to the office. I have a gut feeling this is going to be the biggest thing that ever hit Pecos County."

# 14

Peggy's usual routine upon getting home after work was to take off her shoes then turn on the TV in the living room. Although seldom able to watch the early edition news, she was content to listen to it while preparing the evening meal.

With shoes in hand, she went to the bedroom, peeled off her work clothes then hung them up. As she reached for her housecoat, the biggest thing that ever hit the county had reached her ears. With a frowning look, she put on the housecoat then walked back into the living room in time to see Desert Rose's photo.

She lowered herself slowly onto the dark burgundy, reclining love seat behind her, eyes fixed on the child's face.

*"That's right, Gale. I'm here off of U.S. Highway 385,"* the reporter on the scene stated, *"About nineteen miles south of I-10. As you can see, Glass Mountains is right behind me. You won't be able to see them but a slew of deputies are at this moment out there, along with a DPS helicopter searching from above for any signs of her parents or guardian."*

*"Have they_____"*

*"Hold on a minute, Gale.. We've just received word that a body has been found in a shallow grave somewhere up on the mountain. No word yet on whether it is that of the little girl's mother or not. We will continue to monitor the situation from here and bring you the latest at our nine o'clock newscast. Back to you."*

After the initial shock, Jeremy came to mind. Cody's name being mentioned at the beginning of the broadcast gave her hope that Jeremy, in some way, was involved in the investigation. She couldn't wait for him to come home. She wanted to get as much information about the child as she could. And she knew he would have what the newscaster's wouldn't.

In a hypnotic like state, she continued to stare at the face on the screen. Before long, several tears appeared. She reached for the box of tissues used mainly for those tearjerker movies she loved to watch, and then hurried into the kitchen. She had to clear her mind before Jeremy came home.

# 15

The Big Apple, with its conglomerate of buildings packed together like headstones in a crowded Louisiana cemetery, was also experiencing some of the hottest days on record. And to Vincent Cassini, who was sitting on the sagging, tattered sofa, the stagnant air inside the two-bedroom apartment seemed to have gotten even hotter as he watched the 12 o'clock news on the old television.

He grabbed the lower part of his heavily soiled T-shirt and wiped the sweat off his bushy eyebrows.

He couldn't believe his eyes. He blinked several times, making sure that what he was seeing wasn't the result of the beers he had already consumed. But the photo of his niece, Olivia, didn't go away.

After confirming the sight in his mind, the five foot four inch man known as, *the Italian Buda*, by the neighborhood kids, and Vinnie by his friends, opened his fat lips, releasing the half smoked cigarette to the worn out, stained linoleum that had survived several tenants before him.

Realizing what he had done, he quickly stepped on the still smoldering cigarette with his bare feet then, oblivious to the burning sting, started hollering, "That's Livi. It's her. Get in here, quick. She's on TV."

With the dirty dishtowel draped on her shoulder, his wife Tina, disgusted with the interruption of her routine, waded through a minefield of empty beer bottles, shoes, crumpled cigarette packs, and toys to get to the living room. When she got there, her husband of five years was sitting straight up and pointing to the small television set.

"What are you hollering about?" she yelled, "Can't you see I'm busy?"

"Look!"

She followed the pointing, stubby finger.

"It's Livi."

Due to the age progression of the drawing, it took her a little more time than it did Vincent. But the minute she realized it was Olivia, her mouth flew open and her eyes got as big as the saucer she was wiping when rudely interrupted. In a zombie like state, she backed up to the sofa and dropped like a rock without saying a word.

The reporter stated once again that she was found wandering in the foothills of a mountain in Southwest Texas.

"Texas?" Vincent grabbed the bottle of beer on the end table and took a swig.

"Be quiet, you drunken fool."

*"Anyone with information about this child should contact the local authorities or call the number on the screen. In other news____"*

What'ya you doin'?" Vincent asked, after he vaguely saw her through foggy eyes jump up, rush over and turn off the TV.

"Get your ass in that kitchen and make some coffee."

The pot of gold, filled with the once in a lifetime opportunity to break out of the concrete jungle and smell the roses, had just showed up. This was her chance to look out of her window and see trees, hills, and more of the blue sky, instead of cave dwellers looking back out of theirs. This was her chance to visit places she had only dreamed of. Pitted nails and ingrown toenails were soon to be beautified, and a scaly, sweat prone torso kneaded.

All of it paid for by the upcoming financial reward for the child's life story in the form of a book, or even a movie.

She grabbed a piece of paper and jotted down the number still embellished in her feeble mind.

Knowing it would take a pot of coffee, and more time than she was willing to waste, she decided to call the TV station herself. Rather than give them too much information, she told them it was possible that the little girl in question was her husband's niece.

"It's been a while, about a year and a half now since we've seen her," She tells the station program manager on the other end, "but I believe it's Olivia."

The young manager, seeing an opportunity for a jump on a story that had just been put out by the Associated Press, couldn't resist. "Would you or your husband be willing to give us exclusive information about her and anything else you learn if we send you down there?"

"Why of course," she said. "My husband will be more than glad to help in any way possible."

"Great! After we verify your claim, we'll make all the arrangements to fly him out there."

"When?"

"Hopefully by sometime tomorrow."

"Tomorrow? Why so soon?"

"Look, Mrs. Cassini, we want first crack at an emotional reunion scene between uncle and niece. After that, an exclusive interview with the child. He'll be met at the airport by one of our affiliate reporters who'll take him over to the Sheriff Department. We'll call you right back and let you know what he'll need to take and the flight details."

"I guess that'll be okay."

After giving them their phone number, she hung up and smiled broadly. Mink coats, diamond bracelets, pearl necklaces, and lap bands danced around her head like stars in a planetarium ceiling.

Vinnie squeezed the bottle with all the strength he could muster as he sat in the living room listening to the conversation. It didn't break. He stopped gritting his teeth just long enough to say, "Why do I have to go down there?"

Tina opened the fridge door and took out a can of beer. "What about your sister?" she yelled, "Don't you wan'a know if she's alive? Ain't you forgettin' what they did to her old man? Besides, the least you can do is go down there and make sure your niece is all right."

He took another swig, grinned, and then, in a hushed voice, said, "Your not fooling me none. You don't care anything about her. You just think you're gonna get somethin' out of it."

"What'd you say?"

"I said, it doesn't look like I'm gonna get out of it."

She put the beer can down and straightened out the scraggly, dirt encrusted, brown hair.

"If you think I'm going to spend the rest of my life living in this shelled out dump you call home, you're crazy," she yelled.

"Oh, yeah, well where else can you find an apartment like this for what we're paying, huh? And, on top of that, where else can you find a manager willing to rent it to someone with three kids. You tell me."

"Don't forget, those two brats in the bedroom ain't mine," she said. "And if I hadn't opened my mouth, I would've been stuck with that niece too. I didn't know I was gonna be that little old lady in the shoe when I married you. Thanks a lot."

"Suppose I don't wanna go?"

"You're going whether you like it or not. Besides, it's no skin off your nose." She took a sip from the can of beer then, after a loud nauseating belch, continued, "They're paying for the trip down there. All you have to do is make sure they get whatever information the cops give you." She took another swallow. "Now just shut your trap, the other brat should be home from school any minute now."

"Shut my trap? What for?" he said. "You don't think they know what's going on already. Well I've got news for ya."

Olivia knew what was going on in her household. She had become part of it. That much was obvious to him after she refused to go near the water the last time he took her to the beach. If there was one thing she loved to do was sit in the sand and wait for the ripples to come and tickle her little toes.

"What's the matter Livi?" He asked, feeling her pull away before reaching the wet sand. "Don't you wanna swim with the other kids?"

She shook her head, ripped herself from his grip then turned around to go back to the blanket. On her way there, a breeze from the ocean side of the beach lifted her hair, exposing a dark bruise on her nape. "Hold on a minute, Livi," he said, grabbing her by the shoulder. "Where'd you get that bruise?"

He examined the rest of her body after noticing bruises under her arms also. Not finding any more he convinced himself they were caused by a fall. The less he knew the better off he'd be. Besides, there was nothing he could do about it anyway.

Several weeks before Tony disappeared, however, his denial switched over to acceptance of the truth.

"And I've got news for you too," Tina said, storming out of the kitchen, transporting him from the sandy beach back to the apartment. "They're going to notice a lump on your stupid head when they do come in. How d'ya like them apples?"

"Whatever you say, dear."

"You'd better believe it."

He staggered into the kitchen, grabbed a coffee can from the cabinet above the stained porcelain sink and made himself a fresh pot.

"You know, this could mean Francis is alive. Maybe she decided to drop the kid off thinking someone else would take better care of her."

He put a couple of scoops into the strainer then waited for her response before filling the maker with nine cups of water.

"Well, it's for sure we can't," Tina said. "We can barely take care of the three we got, let alone some other woman's brat." She crushed the empty beer can with her vise like hands and tossed it at the trashcan, snickering as it rolled off the heap and on to the floor. "Just make sure everyone down there knows you're her uncle. Sob a little if you have to. Play it up. I'm sure you can do that much."

Although he was back in the living room with the newspaper in his hands, what was in it was not on his mind. What if something happened to Francis? Would they be forced to take Olivia in? After all, there was no one else. He was the only relative left. He shuddered at the thought, realizing she wouldn't stand a chance there. Her life wouldn't be much different than what it was before.

"What time are they supposed to pick me up?"

"They're supposed to call and let us know so you'd better start packing."

"Don't forget, you'll have to make sure Emily gets to school and back while I'm gone."

"Don't worry. I know how to take care of miss-goody-two shoes. You just do what I tell ya."

"Livi's gonna tell, you know," he said. "She's a smart kid."

"Yeah, and she got it from her father, whoever that was."

# 16

"I had a feeling you'd be coming in before the day was over." Martha put down her low cal drink, got up, and then waddled over to the file cabinet behind her desk. "Especially after hearing what you found out there." She pulled out the night shift report, turned around, and, with a smirk on her plump face, held it out as if it was a gold ring waiting to be snatched by some child on a carousel. "Anyone else would have taken the whole day off as official travel time, you know."

Martha Cunningham was more than just his secretary. She was his unofficial mom, psychologist, and grief counselor. But during the last year and a half there was something else she had to deal with besides the normal grievance process.

Ever since the accident, he had stopped giving crime prevention talks in the area schools, opting instead to send one of the deputies. He stopped attending the Friday evening get together with his staff at the Comanche Truck Restaurant. And he didn't participate in the last Sheriff Department's annual picnic and rodeo.

These and other detours from the norm were becoming more and more frequent as time went by. That's why she had been trying to talk him into seeing a real counselor, or at the very least, taking an extended leave of absence.

"You know me too well, Martha, you and the lieutenant both." Without missing a step, he snatched the shift report out of her outstretched hands as he went by. "I'm gonna have to do something about that."

"Is that a threat or a promise?" she smiled at his one eye wink then remembered the phone on her desk. "While you're thinking about what to say, pick up on line three," she nodded. "It came in just before you walked through the door."

Inside his office, he dropped the report on top of the uncluttered mahogany desk then picked up the phone after pushing the blinking button.

"Sheriff Johnson here."

"Hello, sheriff." The voice was gravelly, low pitched, and definitely east coast. "My name is Taylor Hicks. I'm a homicide detective with the 42nd Precinct in the Bronx."

"Could you hold on for just a second?"

"Sure."

He switched the phone over to speaker mode, hung up the receiver, and then settled back in his high back, brown leather chair. "What can I do for you, detective?"

"That kid you found in the desert."

He raised his eyebrows then sat straight up. On the way in he had been told that her photo had made it to the local stations in time for the twelve o'clock news, but had no idea the story had spread that far and that fast. Or that it would bring such a quick response. "What about her?"

"A year and a half ago a mother and her daughter mysteriously disappeared from their home not far from the precinct. There's a slight resemblance between the photo shown on the one o'clock news and an age progressed drawing of that little girl. Our forensic artist is in the process of comparing them further as we speak. He should know something pretty soon. If he feels a trip down there is warranted, I'll fly down and fill you in on the case."

*Case? There must be more going on here than meets the eye.*

"I'll probably catch a commuter from the Midland Airport over to the Fort Stockton-Pecos County Airport. I'd appreciate it if someone from your department can pick me up."

"Sure. Just let my secretary know the time and flight number. She'll take care of the arrangements. What about a name Detective Hicks?"

"Olivia D'Angelo. She'll be six years old in a few days. I'll tell you more about her if and when I go there. In the meantime, I'd appreciate it if you would keep her name strictly confidential."

"I can do that."

"Thanks." Taylor hung up.

Before his train of thought could gather enough speed to figure out why the detective insisted on secrecy, the intercom buzzer brought it to a screeching halt.

"Yes, Martha."

"You have another call from New York on line four. This one's a Program Director from a Television station."

Back on the phone, he's told about an uncle named Vincent Cassini who would be flying out the next morning. And that they would like to set up an appointment to see him.

He grinned. "Is there anyone else up there interested in coming down?"

"What?"

"Never mind. Let me transfer you back to my secretary. She'll set the time up for you." He pushed the intercom button. "Martha, please take care of this gentlemen's needs."

"Yes, sir."

After hanging up, he walked out of the office with his head down reading the night shift report. Seconds later a sweet fragrance waffled through his nostrils, inadvertently derailing his train of thought. Before he could look up to find out what was mingling with his *Stetson* aftershave lotion, a pair of women's black, high heel dress shoes slipped into view. He stopped. His eyes locked on the shoes for a fraction of a second. On their way up to see who was wearing them, they passed by the dark blue pants outfit until they sighted the moist ruby lips. A lingering look, the kind you don't realize you're taking, the kind that results in a slow blush of embarrassment, crept up. But even that wasn't enough to stop him. He continued the visual journey up to the slim, slightly pointed nose and the inviting, almost transparent, blue eyes that were beautifully enhanced and complimented by crescent brows and long, dark eyelashes.

A fraction of a second later he zoomed in on the black, shimmering waterfall that parted on the left side of her head, cascaded down to her shoulders, and then curled inward.

The smile on the five foot ten inch stunner, standing just inches in front of him, sent butterflies scurrying throughout his body. It was a feeling he had not experienced in a long time, and for a few seconds, startled him.

His lips quivered slightly as she opened hers, emitting the voice of an angel. "Sheriff Johnson?"

The name rang a bell, but the fair skinned lady had managed to turn him, at least for that moment, into a fumbling mannequin. In an effort to regain control, he inflated his chest and tucked his chin in. His mouth, however, stayed shut, waiting for the confused mass inside his skull to reboot after the fatal crash. The feelings within were by no means intentional. His mouth struggled to bare the slightest resemblance of a grin.

Relief from his quirky reactions came with the look she shot at him. He sensed that she too was surprised. Either he wasn't exactly what she had expected, or she was in the wrong place. Immediately, the potbellied, tobacco chewing, mustached sheriff depicted on film came to mind.

After what seemed like an eternity, she asked again, "Sheriff?"

"You can answer her anytime you're ready," Martha said, making a smacking noise with her tongue as she shook her head.

"Huh. Oh. Yes." he cleared his throat. "Pardon me." A slight smile pursing his lips finally appeared. "That's me. I mean, yes Ma'am, I'm sheriff, Johnson. And who might you be?"

"This here's Miss Susan Wheeler, the new supervisor of CPS," Martha interjected, tilting her head back then rolling her eyes up in an *I don't believe this* fashion.

"Well, now, I had no idea. I mean," He paused, rolling his eyes to the brim of the hat he had forgotten to take off when he came in. In a split second it came down to his chest. "Pardon me."

"Is that the extent of your vocabulary?" she smiled again, revving his brain to an uncontrollable speed.

"Huh?" After realizing what she had meant, he grinned. "No. Not really. Believe it or not, I do have a few more words holstered up there."

"I see. Anyway, as you already know, I'm the new supervisor for the county's CPS office."

He racked his runaway brain, recalling some of the details in the letter of introduction sent by CPS over a month ago. Born in Brooklyn. Degree in Sociology. Ten years with the agency. He wished he had read it more carefully.

"This is quite a change, isn't it...? I mean from a Big Apple to a small Fort in Texas."

"A shocking one, believe me."

She's impressed that he took the time to learn a little bit about her. Big city cops rarely bothered.

"What can I do for you?" he asked, for the moment forgetting her role in the situation at hand.

"The child found in the desert."

"Yes. Of course." He put his hat back on. "I was on my way to see her myself. Perhaps I could give you a lift?"

She hesitated for a moment, then said, "Sure, why not."

He hesitated for a moment and said nothing.

"Well?"

*Did she say yes?* "Martha...uh... let me know if you hear from the medical examiner and the team out there."

"Yes, sir."

"This way, Ma'am."

"Sheriff."

"Yes, Martha."

"Welcome back."

# 17

"How is she?"

"She's resting comfortably right now," Jeremy said, surprised to see him walking in with a woman he had not seen before.

"Can she talk?"

"I'm afraid not."

"And there's a chance she might not for some time," Doctor Fieldson said, as he walked into the room. "I'm glad you're here, sheriff. I've been meaning to tell you this ever since my part of her examination was completed."

"What could have happened to her?"

"I'm not really sure at this time, Ms._____"

"Susan Wheeler. I'm with Child Protective Service."

"I see. Well, Ms. Wheeler, since there doesn't seem to be anything wrong with her vocal chords or motor skills, her inability to talk may have been caused either by acute bilateral damage _____"

"Damage?"

"Yes—to both cerebella hemispheres. It appears to have happened sometime in her past. Exactly when is anybody's guess. She also has signs of old fractures, sheriff. You might want to look into those. I'll send the X-rays over to your department right away."

"Or," Susan said, sensing there was more on his mind by the silence that followed.

"Or she could have either witnessed or been a part of a traumatic event which put her in a mental state comparable to shell shock, which, in some cases, have resulted in blindness, paralysis, and even loss of speech. From my understanding about the circumstances so far, this could very well be the cause of her muteness. Only time will tell."

"Is it going to be a permanent condition?"

"As far as I've been able to learn, muteness caused by a mental trauma usually lasts no more than three months. Maybe less with proper care." he paused for a moment as he approached the bed. "I believe she'll come out of it. When? Again it's anybody's guess." He sighed then turned to face Susan. "For now all we can do is get her into social anxiety therapy. That might help hasten her recovery."

"Until then, nobody's to know she can't talk," Cody said, firmly. "Especially anyone involved with the media."

"Secrecy is not a luxury around here with the number of employees we have, sheriff. All we can do is try our best."

"That'll be fine."

"Very well, I'll notify the hospital administrator. He'll put the word out to the staff."

"Thank you. I'll take care of my department personally." Cody shifted his eyes to the empty chair by the door. "So who's____?"

"Deputy Reed." As Jeremy cut him short, his eyes locked on to Susan's. "He's in the cafeteria getting a drink. I'm covering for him. He should be back any minute now."

"I'm on my way there myself. I'll tell him you're here," Dr. Fieldson said, before going out the door. "If there's any change in her status, I'll come back and check on her."

"Thanks doc. I appreciate that."

"My pleasure, sheriff." Before leaving he looked back over his shoulder. "I just wish I could've given you better news."

Cody realized as he noticed Jeremy's gaze that he had yet to introduce him to Susan. "Excuse me. Ms. Wheeler, this here's Deputy Jeremy Sands, one of our newest members. He comes from your neck of the woods."

"Nice meeting you, Jeremy."

"Likewise, Ms. Wheeler."

During the handshakes and pleasantries, Cody noticed the sly grin and the cocked brow on Jeremy's face. He took a deep breath and tried to loosen up a little not wanting to add to the deputy's keen perceptions. The last thing he needed was a firestorm of rumors consuming the department.

Susan, in the meanwhile, walked over to the side of the bed, placed both hands on the bedrail, and then leaned closer. What she saw was not what she had expected. Instead of a child suffering with severe sunburn and dehydration, there, sound asleep, was a child with naturally rosy cheeks and a body size commensurate with those of her age. A child whose little arm was wrapped snuggly around her teddy's neck.

"So this is the desert flower everyone's talking about?"

"That she is Ma'am," Jeremy said, as he and Cody joined her at the bedside.

"How can anyone abandon such a beautiful gift from God?"

"I don't know, Ms. Wheeler. I was hoping you could tell me."

"I wish I could, sheriff, but there is no right answer. Every time I see something like this, I ask in the hope that someone will give me one, or at least a clue that would satisfy my curiosity... Any idea who she is?"

"No. But there's someone claiming to be her uncle due to arrive here sometime tomorrow." After he had said it, he noticed the lines forming on Jeremy's forehead, the downward facing eyes, and the deflated chest. "He saw her picture on television."

"That's great news. What's her name?"

"I'm not at liberty to say, Ms. Wheeler. The caller insisted we keep her identity confidential until it can be confirmed."

He hated doing that, especially to the woman who had earlier scattered every piece of the jigsaw puzzle he had been putting together in his brain.

"Well then, can you at least give me the caller's name?"

Acting as if she wasn't there, or heard her words, he turned around to face Jeremy. "When did you say Deputy Reed would be back?"

"He's right behind you."

Cody looked back over his shoulder and saw the deputy walking through the door. "No one's to enter this room unless they've been authorized by the hospital or our department," he told him, "and even then, you make sure they show you some form of identification."

"Yes, sir."

He glanced at Jeremy and motioned. "Let's get back to headquarters." Then, with the customary tipping of his hat, turned to Susan and said, "Ms. Wheeler. You'll have to excuse us. We have some unfinished business to take care of."

Jeremy looked over in time to see her eye's opening wide and her jaw dropping. Not knowing what to say to cushion the blow, he shrugged his shoulders, put his hat back on then rushed to catch up to Cody who had already gone out the door.

Before they could get to the nurses station down the hall, Cody stopped abruptly, putting the breaks on Jeremy with an arm to his chest. "Wait here a minute, I forgot something."

"Yes, I know."

Cody went back and got Reed out into the hall. He got real close to his ear and said something to him in a low voice. Then he left Reed and rejoined Jeremy.

Out in the hospital parking lot, Jeremy, perplexed by Cody's actions, stopped just before they got to the vehicle and confronted him. "What was that all about?"

"I'll tell you later," he replied, as he continued walking towards his vehicle. "In the meantime..." Noticing Jeremy was no longer by his side, he turned around. "What are you looking at?"

"You. It's been a long time since I've seen a grown man smitten." He snickered like a schoolboy who had just discovered a big secret. "For a while back there, I thought you were going to drool all over her pretty outfit."

His words were like a steel tipped arrow that had penetrated his heart. Guilt and shame filled his mind, yet he couldn't ignore the tremors created by her very presence. Could he really allow himself to even think about her without the apparent outward signs?

"Never mind that," he said, opening the driver's side door. "Get in. we need to get back out there before the sun sets."

He released the emergency brake, put the vehicle in gear then got back on the highway. The chances of finding Hezekiah, still the most logical person of interest in mind, were now fading with the sun. All they could do on their return was deal with the small group of reporters awaiting them. And about the only thing he can tell them was that the victim had yet to be identified.

After whetting their appetite with that, and some information about the child's health status, he would post a couple of units in the area throughout the night.

Hezekiah, or anyone else that might be up there, won't be going anywhere soon.

"Will you look at that," he said, breaking his chain of thought and silence.

"What?" Jeremy's eyes darted to and fro.

Cody slid his sunglasses down lower on the bridge of his nose, looked over at him, and then nodded to the top part of his windshield. "That."

The one thing he avoided facing by leaving El Paso in the wee hours of the morning could not be avoided that evening as he drove west on Interstate 10.

# 18

Back behind her desk at the office, Susan, now knowing the man claiming to be the child's uncle was coming from the New York area, and that her picture had been broadcasted on TV, decided to do a little investigating of her own. She called the Statewide Central Register of Child Abuse and Maltreatment. If indeed a report had been made in the past that would substantiate Dr. Fieldson's findings, they would have it.

"How can we help you, Ms. Wheeler?" the caseworker asked, after Susan substantiated her credentials.

"Well, I'm not really sure you can, but has anyone there seen the news or heard about the little girl found in the desert down here in Pecos County, Texas? I understand it went national."

"Why, yes, as a matter of fact, some of us here were just talking about it."

"Great! Then perhaps you can help. One of your local TV networks called down here claiming they found the girl's uncle. I don't have a name but I'm sure someone at the network station, maybe even the person who called, might____ "

"Ms. Wheeler," she interrupted, "let me transfer you to my supervisor. Hold on, please."

The involvement of a supervisor was Susan's first clue that there may have been a file that was not fully investigated, or possibly mishandled. Though frustrated with the bureaucratic process, she held on for several seconds until the supervisor picked up on the other end. Susan then repeated all that she had said before and then some.

"Ms. Wheeler," the supervisor said. "No one here recognized the little girl, but we've had such a large turnover of case workers this year. It's possible one of those that left may have seen the news broadcast and recognized her. We'll get in touch with them. In the meantime, we'll also do a data base search of our files to see if there's a description that may be somewhat similar. We'll let you know as soon as we find out anything."

Though disappointed with their response, she brushed it off as an agency's precautionary measure. No doubt her employee identification and status will probably be corroborated even further before any discussion concerning a case would take place, especially over the phone.

"Thank you. I would appreciate that."

When she hung up, thoughts of finding a foster family, just in case she needed one, entered her mind. To her knowledge, it wasn't going to be such an easy task since the pickings in the area were considered slim. She shook her head and then got up and went to the file cabinet behind her.

After fifteen-minutes of going through her files, the phone at her desk rang again. Never in her wildest dream did she think it would concern the girl in question. Or that the information she received would set in motion a full-scale investigation that would lead to more than she had bargained for.

"Hello, this is Susan Wheeler, may I help you?"

"Hello, Ms. Wheeler, this is Dorothy Sloan from the Central Register's office."

Her heart skipped a beat. She got excited and apprehensive at the same time. She wanted to hear more about Desert Rose, but she was sure they couldn't have found something in such a short time. It had to be a no go.

"Yes?" she asked, biting her lower lip gently.

"We checked with the TV station and got the name of the man who's being sent down there. His name is Vincent Cassini. The child belongs to his sister, Francis D'Angelo. Her name is Olivia. An LDSS 2221A report was sent in by one of her teachers. We assigned a priority one status to it but never got the chance to complete our investigation. There's been some concern for her safety for quite some time."

"Why?"

"Her father was killed eighteen months ago."

97

"Killed?"

"Murdered to be exact. Anyway, mother and daughter disappeared not long after that happened. The authorities have been looking for them ever since."

After taking down all the information she needed, her eyes rolled up in search for anything in her past experience that would help her sort this one out.

"Can you send me a copy of the report?"

"Of course. The caseworker agreed to discuss the problem with you. I'll fax you her name and telephone number also. You may want to talk to her personally."

*Do I ever.*

Although the standard Child Abuse or Maltreatment report submitted has a lot of information on it, there were times when a caseworker was reluctant to add to it their own opinions or intuitive suspicions on the case. This would give her the opportunity to glean those and more on a one on one basis off the record private conversation.

"Thank you, I'd appreciate that."

After hanging up she raised her arms high and bellowed out a resounding, "Yes!"

At her file cabinet she pulled out a new folder, walked back to her desk, and then attached a label she had typed to it.

Olivia now occupied eighty percent of her mind. What remained was occupied by a tall sheriff who closely resembled the *Marlboro* man on the old    cigarette commercials, and who had impressed her with his manners and his casual attitude.

# 19

"You two know each other?" Cody asked, as he leaned against the door jam with his arms folded across his chest.

"Funny."

"You should feel honored, Billy. He's been ignoring me ever since I picked him up from the kennel. You would've thought I sent him to Siberia for the rest of his life."

"So what's this all about?"

"Either he's trying to get back at me, or he's trying to get back some of the attention he's lost since it happened."

"He misses them, doesn't he?"

"More than I realized." He patted Diablo in the back. "That's enough, boy. The last thing Billy needs is a slobbering tongue facial. Get down. Go get some water."

"Whew... Thanks." Billy brushed himself off while watching Diablo go to the dish on the other end of the ceramic tiled porch. "Mind if I come in?"

"As a matter of fact I wouldn't mind someone else besides him right about now." He stepped aside, holding the door open until Billy got in. "Can I get you something to drink?" he asked, closing the door behind him.

"If you had some, I'd ask for a beer, but for now, I'll take some of that." He pointed to the glass of lemonade on the round, cedar wood coffee table."

"Coming up. So, how'd it go after I left?"

"We gathered as much potential evidence as we could and sent them to the lab." As Billy passed in front of the fireplace, he noticed the gold framed photo that had stood on the oak mantle for years was now laying face down. It was the one of

Katelyn standing next to Patches in her cowgirl outfit. "So how'd yours go?"

"Not exactly what I'd expected, that's for sure. Here."

After taking the glass from Cody's outstretched hand, he slipped behind the coffee table, moved one of the four throw pillows aside, and then made himself at home on the brown leather sofa. "Thanks." He peered over the top of his glass. "In more ways than one, from what I hear."

After taking a sip and setting the glass down, he wiped his lips with his shirt sleeve and waited.

Moments passed in silence before Cody finally asked, "Okay. What's your mind?"

"I hear you ran into a little lady you haven't seen before."

"Deputy Sands, huh?"

"Not just him, my friend. There happened to be a few others who noticed."

"Noticed what?"

"Come on, Cody. We've known each other too long. Even I could detect a hint of that long lost glitter in your eyes."

Sitting on the matching leather chair in front of the sofa, Cody glanced back over his shoulder towards the mantle. "That's not going to make any difference, you know."

Billy got up and walked over to the chair. As he stood alongside it, facing the mantle behind the chair, he rested his left hand on Cody's left shoulder. "If that's the case," he turned away from the photo and looked down at Cody. "You might as well hook up with that hermit up on the mountain."

Cody looked up at him with deep furrowed brows.

"Don't you think it's time you tore down the wall," Billy said. "It's not meant for you to be alone, my friend. You have too much to offer and deserve a lot in return. Besides, you won't know what difference it *would* make unless you give it a chance."

The huge hole in his heart had yet to close. The emptiness within had yet to be filled. He tried all the different suggestions to cope with the feelings and despair that had overwhelmed him through the first six months but, like a spooked thoroughbred, he balked on entering the starting gate for the race that lay ahead. He looked down at the wooden floor and said, "Why does everyone think it's that easy?"

"No one ever said it was." Billy patted the shoulder. "No one's asking you to get serious, either. All I'm asking is for you to go with your feelings. It's the only way you'll be able to let the big spirit in the sky guide you to your destiny. Give him a chance to show you what he has in store."

Cody's chin touched his chest. "I don't know." he paused in deep thought. "So much has happened to me lately. I wouldn't know where to start. What to do."

"Start by getting to know this lady everyone's talking about. It looks like you're both gonna be working on this case anyway. Who knows what may come out of it."

"I guess it wouldn't hurt to be friends."

"It's either that or I take you to see that medicine man I told you about earlier."

"Say, how about some Chimichanga, rice, and refried beans. It won't take but a minute to heat them up."

"No thanks. I've got two frisky warriors waiting for me to take them to their little league games. Look, I just want to get that big galoot I used to have fun with back in my life, that's all."

"Tell you what. I'm not gonna make any promises. What I'll do is try to be more sociable, that's all."

"At least that's a start. Anyway, thanks for the drink and the ear. I guess I'll see you in the morning."

As Billy spoke, Cody's eyes wandered over to the large, rustic, wood framed painting over the sofa. It was oil on canvas. And it showed a chain of mountains with birds gliding above them, and different types of vegetation dotting the surrounding desert landscape.

The mountains were not unlike the Glass Mountains. Having paid little attention to it since Katelyn purchased it, he wondered if indeed it was. But even if it wasn't, it suddenly became a grim reminder.

"Before you go, I have a question." He leaned forward, hands clasped and elbows resting on his thighs.

"Okay."

"Do you think Hezekiah had something to do with that body?"

"I'm not really sure. But like I said before, we really don't know that much about him. For all we know he could be a

101

kidnapper, a sex offender, or even a serial killer. Or he could be one of the most respected law abiding citizens in the country. We just don't know. In any case, man wasn't made to spend his entire life alone. From what I've gathered, he's been living that way for quite some time now. Good or bad, there's no telling what affect that's had on him."

"I suppose you're right," he muttered. "But I just can't make myself believe anyone would leave a child out in that environment?"

"Once we find him, we'll ask him why. In the meantime, here's to you." He lifted his glass in a salute.

Cody reciprocated. "Thanks."

"No. Don't get up. I know my way out. You seem to forget, I've spent a lot of time in this once cheerful wigwam." He opened the door to leave but then stopped at the threshold and looked back. "By the way, I know Katelyn would want it this way. I knew her almost as well as you did, you know."

"I know."

"So what's our next move?"

"At first light take a couple of deputies and make one last pass. I want to make sure we didn't overlook anything. I'll be in the office at least for the first part of the day. Keep me posted."

"Okay. In the meantime, why don't you get something to eat then take it easy? Like you said, it's been a long day for you."

"Thanks, I think I will."

Before he could get a hold of the door knob, Billy looked down in thought for a fleeting second then turned around. "By the way. I checked with the city PD. Our Mr. Bauer was accosted by three young Mexicans not too long ago. The only thing that saved his rear end was the night club security guy. He managed to chase them away before the Police Department boys could get there."

"Mr. Bauer's a very lucky man."

"I'd say so."

Not long after Billy closed the door, Cody got up and went into the kitchen. The minute he opened the refrigerator, his thoughts drifted to the curvaceous cowgirl from the panhandle of Texas. After closing it without taking anything out, he walked into the formal dining room and turned on the light. The teardrop bulbs, attached under deer antlers, cast eerie shadows on the cedar wood table below and the three by six foot painting on the wall. It was a painting of wild horses grazing in a valley lit by the setting sun. It was the last one she had purchased. And it reminded him of their trip to Kerrville, a city in south Texas with many fine art galleries and studios.

A few steps down the hallway put him outside the room of a little girl whose dream of following in her mother's footsteps were shattered in a blink of an eye. He seldom entered it, leaving the occasional dusting to Juanita, the housekeeper who came once a week to clean house and do the laundry.

The opened door to the room across the hall revealed the bed with the green and tan checkered Percale bedding neatly spread over it. Against the headboard, sand colored throw pillows, stacked as if holding back the shore pounding waves depicted in the painting just above them. It was their room, their private little world. Could he share that world with someone else? Or must he abandon it for another.

For the most part—and for some time now—he considered the rest of the twenty five hundred square foot ranch house a giant, hollow museum, where the sound of footsteps accompanied by whispers echoed louder than the hum of the ceiling fans, and one that had been frozen in time by an unexpected chill. It was also one that housed a wedding ring as one of its valuable pieces.

"Perhaps you should consider getting away from the ranch for a while," the therapist suggested. "Take a vacation. Find a place where you could surround yourself with people instead of memories, horses, and cattle."

*Maybe I should have taken her advice.*

Back in the living room, he gave in to the paper. "Mystery child found wandering near Glass Mountains." He read it out loud. He had to hear something else besides the voices within.

She was a mystery all right, a veritable witness, who for some unknown reason, was allowed to live and perhaps, sometime in the near future, point a finger at a murderer. Worst yet, she was a witness whose life could be in danger.

Even though verification had yet to be established, he was almost positive the body found was that of the little girl's mother. Was the perpetrator that sure her daughter wouldn't talk? Or did she see anything at all?

And then there was Hezekiah. It didn't matter what he thought about the recluse. There was no way he could ignore the close proximity of the house, the altar, and the gravesite. If nothing else, Hezekiah had to have some inkling of what had happened up there.

With his eyelids feeling like window shades with cinder blocks tied to the draw strings, he walked over to the hat rack where Katelyn's Dallas Cowboy baseball cap hung just below his. He took it off the hook then, with misty eyes, put it on the top shelf of the hall closet.

With Susan on his mind, he stretched out, laying his head on the throw pillow. In the morning, he would pay a visit to two lovely people that had been thrust into his life, then afterwards, take some deputies over to that shack Hezekiah apparently uses as his home base.

# 20

"Hold it. Don't' move."

"What's the matter?"

"Look down."

When Earl did, he realized the tip of his boot was just inches away from it. He lifted his head and rolled his eyes from one bush to another. "Makes you wonder what else we'll find out here."

"Maybe we'd better not go any further." After removing his outstretched hand from Earl's chest, Seth reached for his shoulder-mounted two-way radio. "We have something over here you might want to take a look at, Lieutenant."

"I'll be right there."

Billy left the site where the tire tracks were found and hiked through the maze of brushes to their location. When he got there, Seth and Earl were standing over what was clearly a bleached white skeletal hand sticking straight up out of the ground. It looked as if a doomed human being, in a last ditch effort, had punched a hole through the surface of the earth in an attempt to escape death.

He lifted his hat and scratched his head as he gazed at the sight. "This is getting more interesting by the minute."

"This ain't all of it," Seth said, "take a look over there." He nodded towards what appeared to be an outdoor butcher shop surrounded by the discarded remains of rabbits, rats, coyotes, and a host of other unrecognizable creatures. Off to the side was a well prepared pyre ready to consume a hapless creature, or even a human being.

"I thought he only cooked up on the mountain," Earl said.

"Apparently not." Billy shook his head. "The sheriff's not going to like this."

"What about Kyle," Seth said. "This is right outside of his property. How d'ya think he's gonna react? I wonder if he even knows about it."

"Don't worry, pretty soon the whole county will. Go ahead and set up a perimeter while I notify the sheriff. Just watch where you're walking."

# 21

The minute Vincent crossed the threshold, Cody came out from behind the desk with his hand extended "Mr. Cassini," he said. "We've been expecting you. Welcome to Fort Stockton. Hope you had a pleasant flight?"

"It wasn't all that comfortable, I tell ya. Those seats are kind'a small."

"Believe me, I know what you mean." He gestured towards the chair in front of the desk. "Have a seat."

Vincent squeezed into the large armchair as Cody went around the desk and back into his. On the way, he nodded at the deputy who had brought Vincent in. "Bring me the box."

"Where's Livi?"

"I understand the media escorted you over here, Mr. Cassini, so first let's make sure you're related. I'm not about to expose her to you or anyone else until then. Did you bring a photo or some form of identification?"

"Yeah." He extricated himself from the chair, reached into his back pocket and pulled out his wallet. "I have a copy of her birth certificate."

"You mind taking it out?"

After flipping through the photo jackets, he leaned over and laid the certificate and a picture of Olivia on the desk. As Cody gathered them up, Vincent gazed at the glass enclosed case which contained the arm patches of all two hundred and fifty four County sheriff's departments in the state of Texas. From there his eyes wandered over to the metal file cabinet behind Cody's chair and then to the couch against the wall on his right.

When Cody finished checking the birth certificate, he took

the recent photo of Desert Rose out of his pocket and placed it alongside the one Vincent gave him. Even with the age difference, the similarities in features were enough to convince him she was indeed his niece.

"So where is she? Is she alright?"

Cody rose from the chair and walked around to the front of his desk. He leaned his buttock on the edge and folded his arms across his chest. "She's in one of our local hospitals. The doctors there seem to think she'll be okay," he told him. "For now, though, we need to get some information on her mother?"

"Where's Francis?"

After several knocks, the deputy entered with the box. Cody stood up and took it from him. "Thanks," he said. "Close the door on your way out." After turning back around, he set it on his desk and opened it. He took a pen out of his pocket and carefully fished out the rosary so that it wouldn't get tangled. "Have you ever seen this before, Mister Cassini?"

"No. Why?"

"Your niece was wearing it around her neck."

"No way. Francis would've never put something like that around Olivia's neck? My sister wasn't even a practicing Catholic."

"Then we'll need to find out who did."

Cody pulled out the checkered piece of cloth and held it in front of Vincent's face. "What about this?"

"What is it?"

"It was tied around her ponytail."

"Ponytail? Olivia never wore a ponytail either. Francis thought it was old fashioned— out of style."

"What about Francis? Were tattoos part of her fashion?"

"What'ya mean?"

"Did she have any tattoos on her body?"

"Yeah, sure. On her shoulder. Some kind'a flower, I think."

"Anywhere else?"

"Not that I know of, why?"

"Just a minute." He pushed the intercom button. "Martha, will you bring the tape recorder and your laptop in here please."

As he said it, he noticed the frown on Vincent's face. "You don't mind, do you?"

"Well, I…uh…I don't know. What's it for?"

Leaning back on the front of his desk again, he folded his hands across his chest before answering. "I'm sorry to have to tell you, Mr. Cassini, we found the remains of a woman yesterday up in the mountains. There's a chance it could be that of your sister, Francis. We want to make sure we have a record of you identifying this and some of the clothing we found on...excuse me." He got up, opened the door then took the recorder from Martha as soon as she entered. He walked back, set it on his desk in front of Vincent, and then assumed the same position he had before. "Martha here is going to be taking notes as well as witnessing the recording." The frown was still there. "Is there something wrong, Mr. Cassini?"

"I don't know." He shifted from one cheek to the other in his chair. "Maybe I should talk to my wife first."

Cody shot a low brow glance at Martha then faced Cassini.

"Is your wife an attorney?"

"Are you kidding?"

"Look, Mr. Cassini, all we're trying to do right now is to confirm whether or not the remains found up on the mountain are those of your sister, Francis... if you still wish to discuss this with your wife, fine. However, the sooner we get started, the better off we'll be."

Vincent lowered his head for several seconds before reluctantly nodding his consent.

"Good. Have a seat, Martha." He pointed to the couch. "Now where was I? Oh, yes." He looked down at the recorder then pushed the start button after flipping the voice activated recording switch. "The mother's name on the birth certificate is Francis Jean D'Angelo and, according to my calculations, she would've been twenty seven years old this year. Is that correct, Mr. Cassini?"

"Yeah," he said, momentarily lowering his head, "What happened to her?"

"We don't have the medical examiner's full report yet, but I'm sorry to say that it appears to be foul play."

Vincent's face fell.

Cody paused for a moment, noticing the shift in Vincent's eyes as he looked up, then said, "I can understand your anger and____"

"I knew they'd get her."

Cody's brows furrowed as he leaned closer to Vincent. "Who'd get her?"

"I don't know."

"Who would?"

"Tony."

Cody took another look at the birth certificate lying on his desk. "Her husband?"

"Yes! He was a gambler," Vincent continued. "He spent most of his measly paycheck betting on horses, dogs, cards, and boxing. None of it added a dime to his name. Before long he was dealing in drugs to pay off the debts. Even then, he would blow the money he collected—money that didn't belong to him."

"Who *did* it belong to?"

"The same ones who probably killed Francis."

"That's quite an accusation, Mr. Cassini. Where's your brother in law now?"

"He's dead... shot in the back of the head...they found his body on the railroad tracks under Hunts Point Avenue ."

Cody's eyes rolled up. Husband and wife murdered in two different parts of the country. Is there a connection here? Or is it just coincidence? "You wouldn't happen to know a Homicide Detective up in New York by the name of Taylor Hicks, would you?"

"Yeah, sure, he was the one in charge of the case. Why?"

"Nothing. Just curious."

"You know him?"

"No. But I have a funny feeling I will before all this is over. So tell me, when did this happen?"

"About a year and a half ago. Right before Francis and Livi disappeared. The cops think Francis might've had something to do with it."

"Why do you suppose they'd think that?"

Vincent gnashed his teeth. His hands squeezed the end of the armrests and his Lips curled inward. "He was a bum, that's why," he grumbled. "Treated her like trash."

"Is that so? What about Olivia?"

"What about her?"

"How'd he treat her?"

"Is she okay? How long will she be in the hospital?"

"I'm not a doctor, Mr. Cassini, but I suspect she might've witnessed something bad enough to have an impact on her mental well being."

"I'm surprised it didn't happen sooner."

"What makes you say that?"

His eyes glazed. His jaw tightened. "Tony was a wife beater, especially when he was drunk. He'd treat her like a queen in front of everyone, but I knew better. Francis wore black and blue bruises like they were the latest fashion. Half the times she looked like one of those—what d'ya call them—raccoon, that's it, a raccoon. She would always say she fell or walked into something. She didn't deserve this. She wasn't no saint either, but damn it, she didn't deserve this."

"Can you tell us a little bit about your sisters past, or anything that might give us a clue as to motive or a possible suspect?"

"I guess I could," He said in a low voice with his head bowed. "Who can it hurt now, right?"

"If anything, it might help."

"Hell, I don't even know where to start."

"How about starting with the worst case scenario?"

"The what?"

"The abuse, Mr. Cassini. Give me the worst case."

"Look, you gotta understand, I just happen to come in on the tail end of the bum's last attack. In fact," his eyes rolled up momentarily. "Most of what I know about them came from Francis. And she'd be having a fit if she was alive and knew I was talking to the cops?"

"I understand." Cody looked down at the recorder to make sure the volume controls were set to catch even the slightest whisper. "Let me know when you're ready."

Vincent sucked in a deep breath then nodded his acceptance Cody turned it on.

"It started at Clancy's_____"

"Who's Clancy?"

"He owns the Nighttime Bar over on Southern Boulevard."

"Go on."

"You'd think after spending most of his time drinking and gambling in the back room Clancy would float Tony a loan. But that wasn't about to happen that day. Even his buddies turned their backs on him. It was as if the word had gotten out not to give Tony a penny even if his life depended on it. He eventually ran out of money and became desperate. That night he went home drunk looking for cash."

Vincent's eyes showed little emotion as he recounted the details of Francis' last nightmare. Cody's had a disbelieving look about them—his mind unable to comprehend the viciousness in his story. "Where was Olivia during all this?" he asked him.

"In the closet. I guess she came out after it was all over."

He gazed at him with an incredulous look on his face. "I don't understand. Why wouldn't Olivia want it to stop?"

"She knew that if he did, she'd be next," Vincent said.

"Was she?"

"Not then. One of the tenants peeking out of his apartment door saw him stumbling down the stairs. I guess he decided to scram before the cops showed up. That's probably what saved her."

It was intense. More than Cody had expected. The more he thought about it, the greater the gnawing in the pit of his stomach. He had been involved with some of the most violent domestic disputes in the county, but none came even close to what Olivia and her mom had apparently gone through. He found it even more difficult to continue after noticing Martha's reddened eyes.

"Why don't we take a short break?" he said.

Martha needed that

He needed that.

He had to still his body, rein in his thoughts, and get back to the real issue—who murdered Olivia's mother.

As for Martha, she had to find composure so that her fingers could flow steadily across the laptop key pad.

"If it's alright with you, sheriff, I'd like to get this off my chest now."

Cody pushed himself away from the edge of the desk and walked back around to his chair. With his elbows on the desk, he cradled his temples, rubbed them, then looked over and sought Martha's approval to continue on.

She shook her head.

"Are you sure," Cody asked her.

"I'm okay."

"Then go ahead, Mr. Cassini."

"Thanks. Anyway, she kept begging him to let her arm go."

"Did he?"

"No!"

"What happened?"

Without saying a word, Vincent leaned forward in his chair, grabbed a pencil from Cody's desktop, and snapped it in half across his right knee.

"He broke her arm?"

For the second time since his return from El Paso, his boyhood friend, Clayton, came to mind, making it difficult to hold back feelings restricted by his indifference back then and by his authority and commitment to uphold the law without personal involvement now.

"At the elbow," Vincent said. "I guess he took off thinking he killed her. That's why Livi didn't hear anything after the scream. That's when she and Mr. Tibbs came out of the closet. Maybe she thought her mommy got away or something, I don't know."

"That's quite a story, Mister Cassini. Who's Mr. Tibbs?"

"Her teddy bear. I named him right after she got it." He paused, brought his hand up to his chin and began rubbing. "Hey. Where is he anyway? She wouldn't let him out of her sight for nuttin' in the world."

"She still won't, Mr. Cassini. As a matter of fact, he's with her right now."

"Good," he said, his chest inflated. "I gave it to her the day she was born."

"That I can believe." he smiled, recalling the bear's condition before he continued. "You say this happened in an apartment building. Did anyone call the police?"

"No!"

"No? Why not?"

"Does the name Kitty Genovese mean anything to you?" Vincent asked him.

He rolled his eyes up for a few seconds then said, "Can't say as it does."

"You might wanna ask Detective Hicks about her. Then maybe you'll know why."

"Thanks, I'll do that." He leaned back in his chair. "So how'd the authorities find out about it?"

"The cops saw her out on the ledge when they were driving down the block. They called the fire department. I didn't find out till a friend of hers living down the street called me. I got there as soon as I could. I really thought she was going to jump. I've never seen anything like it. The crowd got real big. Before long they had to bring in extra police and spotlights. It was like some Hollywood opening or something. Would you believe the blood thirsty mob cheered her on, screaming for her to jump?"

"Unfortunately I've seen things like that on news broadcasts. But what about Olivia, did she know her mother was out there?"

"Yeah, sure. The cops had to pull her away from the window. God knows how many times she tried to reach her mommy."

He wanted to stop the revelation right then and there, but after seeing Martha with a tissue to her eyes, he thought otherwise. If there was any positive aspect to Olivia's life after all that, he had to bring it out not just for Martha's sake, but for his also.

"Apparently they got her down and taken care of."

"They did," Vincent said. "They took em both to the hospital. That's when they saw all the bruises on Livi. For a while they had them see some kind of a shrink."

"What about Tony? Did they arrest him?"

"Yeah, but some big shot from a trucking company over in Jersey posted bond. About a week later they found Tony's body on the tracks. The cops figured Francis took care of him before he could finish her off."

"Francis? What about the person who posted bail? Did they bother to check him out?"

"I don't know. Why don't you ask Taylor?"

"Don't worry I will. In the meantime, let's get back to Francis. If they really believed she did it, why wasn't she indicted?"

"She disappeared before the grand jury could even get together."

"Do you have any idea why or how your sister wound up here? I mean in Texas."

"No I don't. Like I said, she disappeared. We didn't know anything until we seen Livi on the news." He paused with his head down. "Poor kid. Hell of a thing to lose your mother right before your birthday." .

114

"Yes, I know," said Cody, who had checked the date on the birth certificate after recalling what Detective Hicks had told him.

Martha stopped typing and looked up. She would normally stay out of any discussion between the sheriff and a visitor, but this time she couldn't hold back. "When is it?"

"Next month," Vincent said. "July 7."

After hearing what Olivia had gone through, Cody thought about giving her some sense of stability and continuity to her life. He would speak to Martha about that later. For now, though, the subject had to be changed. "Did Francis own a vehicle?"

"I heard she did. One of her friends told me she bought one several days after Tony's body was found. But I don't know if it's true or not. Where would she get that kind of money?"

From what he had learned so far, life insurance was highly unlikely, as was financing of any type. There was only one possibility left.

"What about her friend?"

"Are you kidding? She couldn't get a loan to buy a pastrami sandwich, let alone a car from her or anyone else."

"Did she say what kind of vehicle Francis bought?"

"An old Buick Regal, I believe."

"Year, color?"

"White. Don't know what year."

"What about detective Hicks? Did he know about this vehicle?"

"How the hell should I know?" he said, getting a little weary. "Are you through with me? I'd like to see Livi now."

"Not just yet. Would you happen to have a photo of Francis?"

After searching through his wallet again, he handed Cody an old photo of Francis holding a little girl who appeared to be around one year old.

"Your sister was a pretty lady, Mr. Cassini." He handed it over to Martha. "Make several copies. Save one for the lieutenant. I'm gonna have him check some of the motels and apartment managers in the area. She had to be staying somewhere. Send the rest out to the media. Someone else might have seen her around here besides the perpetrator."

"Hey." Vincent said. "What about the car. Did you find it?"

"No," he replied, with elbows back on his desk and his chin resting on the locked fingers of his hands. There was one other very important question on his mind, one that didn't have anything to do with the body. He was well aware that he may be crossing the line but he had to ask. "Mr. Cassini. How much did you know about your sister's personal life other than what you've already mentioned?"

"Whatd'ya mean?" his brow furrowed.

"I mean, was *she* abusive towards your niece also?"

He squirmed and swallowed while avoiding eye contact. When he didn't say a word, Cody decided not to press the issue, choosing instead to let CPS investigate the dead mother's past. Something he was more than willing to do now that he had met Susan.

"Okay, then. Why don't you and I just go over to the hospital and see Olivia." He looked past Vincent's left shoulder to Martha. "Go ahead and print several copies."

"I'll have them ready for you in a couple of minutes." She got up and walked out, closing the door behind her.

Even though he didn't care for warm coffee, he downed the rest before pushing away from his desk and walking over to the rack by the door. Just then a deputy, after knocking on the door, opened it and stuck his head in "Can I see you a minute."

Cody looked back over his shoulder. "Mr. Cassini, would you mind stepping outside for a moment. Grab a chair over by Martha's desk and make yourself at home. I have some unexpected business to take care of."

"Yeah, sure, whatever you say." He got up, turned around, and then walked out, passing by Cody and the deputy who had stepped aside at the doorway.

Cody then motioned for the deputy to come into the office. He closed the door behind them. "Whatd'ya have?"

"They came across some skeletal remains not far from the tire tracks down by the base of the mountain."

"What?"

Suddenly the words serial killer blinked in front of his eyes like a neon sign at a neighborhood bar.

"That's not all. They also found one of those stone altars nearby."

Cody opened the door and approached Vincent. "Mr. Cassini, this deputy here is going to take you over to the hospital. I'll be there later."

"Good," He said. "Maybe now that Tony's gone, I can get her to tell me what's been bothering her. I've been thinking about it ever since she and Francis took off."

He didn't tell Vincent she hadn't spoken since they had found her, or that she may not do so for a while yet. He opted instead to see if his presence would unlock the treasure chest.

After seeing them off, he walked back into the office and stood by the picture window thinking about serial killers like John Wayne Gasy Jr., who, after sodomizing thirty three young men, killed them and then buried them under his house, and Juan Corona, the machete murderer who had raped and killed twenty five migrant workers then buried them in the local orchards. He shook his head, mumbling, "I hope to God we don't have a killing field out there." He turned around and walked back out. As he passed by Martha's desk he told her to get a hold of Clinton, give him the location of the latest discovery, and that he would meet him out there. He looked back over his shoulder as he opened the outer door of the building. "While you're at it, get a hold of Ms. Wheeler over at the CPS office. Tell her the girl's uncle is on his way over to the hospital. She might want to be there."

"Anything else?"

"Yes. If you need to, call me on my cell phone. I don't want any of this on public scanners just yet."

# 22

After several hours worth of meticulous hand digging had exposed all of the skeletal remains, Clinton took a pen and notepad out of his white, short sleeve shirt, knelt down by the edge of the grave, and made note of every fracture, split, or deformity visible in each and every fragment of bone.

"Well?" asked Cody, after several minutes into the preliminary field examination.

"Female. I'd say around five foot five—slender frame."

"Any Idea what happened to her."

"The back of her skull is shattered. However, whether that caused her actual death or not won't be known until we do a full forensic examination. The biggest problem I could see right now is putting a face to it. For that we'll have to get a forensic anthropologist."

"A bone whisperer? Why?"

"Her jaw and upper teeth are missing. There's a possibility they may have been knocked out to hide her identity. I doubt if you'll ever find them. About the only things left that might give us a DNA profile are these few strands of hair. Other than that, there's not much more to work with. The anthropologist can garner more information from these bones than I can."

"Anyone in particular in mind?" Cody asked.

"There's a professor at the Texas State University in San Marcos who's been noted as one of the best. I'll have them sent down there."

Cody stood up. He began kneading the back of his neck as his eyes wandered and his mind wondered. Where in the world did she come from? Is there a link between the two?

"Any similarities to what may have happened to the one we found yesterday?" Billy asked, looking over Clinton's shoulder.

"That's what I'd like to know," Cody said. "How about it Clinton? Is there?"

Clinton stood up and reached into his back pocket. He pulled out his handkerchief and wiped the sweat off his balding head. "I just can't say right now. About the only thing I can tell you with any certainty is that she's been here a lot longer."

"What's your guess?"

"I'd say three or four years."

"That long?"

"I'm afraid so. I'll get in touch with the professor and let him know she's coming. In the meantime we need to get her back to my lab for safe keeping."

"The lieutenant here will make sure she gets there."

"There's something else," Clinton said.

"And what's that?"

"What's left of her panties is over by her shoulder blade. This could turn out to be a crime of passion. "

"That's going to be tough to prove with what we have to work with. I'm just going to turn this one over to a cold case unit until we know whether there's a link between the two."

Fearing the occasional wind gusts, he ordered the deputy by his side to photograph then quickly bag the hair and pieces of clothing. Then he turned around and looked past Billy's shoulder. "Did you tell Kyle about this latest find?"

"Yes I did, why?"

"Here he comes now."

On arrival, Kyle immediately jumped out of his jeep and approached. "What in tarnation's going on out here, sheriff?"

"You tell us, Kyle." He gestured over his shoulder towards Clinton, who was blocking their view as he supervised the removal of the bones. "Take a look over there."

He walked around Cody and got alongside Clinton. After looking down at the remains, he asked, "What is it?"

"What's left of another female, Kyle," Cody answered.

"Do you know if any of your boys been out this way lately?" Billy asked.

"Or up on the mountain?" Cody added.

Kyle rubbed his earlobe with the right thumb and index finger as his eyes narrowed. "Come to think about it, there was a drifter from Wyoming by the name of Josh Youngblood who went huntin' up there not too long ago. A part timer, you might say. He showed up the last few years for our roundup. He was great with horses—had to let him go, though."

"Why?" asked Cody.

"The last time he was here he got into a couple of scraps with the other hands."

"That's not unusual on a ranch this size."

"It is when you darn near send one of them to the hospital."

"Where's this cowboy now?"

"Last I heard he was somewhere up in Wyoming."

"I want all the information you have on him and every other hired hand who's worked for you during the last five years—by tomorrow if possible."

"Sure thing, sheriff. I'll get my secretary on it right away."

"Wait! Before you go, there's one more thing."

"What?"

"Have you or any one of your boys seen Hezekiah around here lately?"

"Not that I know of."

"For now I want everyone to notify me if they intend to travel out of the county. And that includes you too, Kyle"

"Don't worry, sheriff, there's enough work to keep me around here for as long as I live. I'll be at the ranch house if you need anything else."

While Cody was taking care of business with Kyle, Clinton and his assistant carefully removed all the small fragments of bone they could find and put them into boxes. The larger ones were put into plastic bags that were tagged with their anatomical names and then tied for transportation to the lab.

"I've done just about all I could out here," he said, as Cody was walking towards him. "I need to get back to the lab and get her ready for the trip."

"Thanks. Let the Lieutenant know what you learn as soon as you can. He's going to be handling this one until we turn it over to our cold case boys. In the meantime we'll pay a visit to Mr. Hezekiah's hangout."

# 23

The first phone call pertinent to the case came from the caseworker who handled the file on Olivia. From that, Susan learned more than she had expected. And since Cody felt compelled to keep what he knew from her, she was determined to reciprocate.

The second came from Martha, informing her that Vincent Cassini had just left to go to the hospital. He was the one person she definitely wanted to talk to, and it didn't take long for her to grab her purse and bolt out the door.

As she sat in the main lobby waiting, Vincent, escorted by a deputy, walked through the automatic doors. Eager to add a whole lot more of what she now knew about Olivia, she got up and blocked his path as he neared the information desk.

"Mr. Cassini?"

"Yeah."

"My name is Susan Wheeler. I'm with Child Protective Services."

It wasn't the name that reignited the fuse. It was the last three words.

"Look, lady, you people had your chance a long time ago and didn't do nuttin'," he spouted angrily. "Now you're down here like some guardian angel that's been hanging around just waiting for something like this to happen so you can jump right in and take over. Well, I've got nuttin' to say to you so buzz off. Go back where you came from." He brushed her off like a pesky gnat, stepped aside, and then went around her to continue his journey.

Stunned by the unexpected rudeness, she stood there for what seemed an eternity before turning around to face his back. The questions she had in mind were quickly replaced by a blunt warning. "Like it or not, you're going to have to talk to me sooner or later, Mr. Cassini," she blared. "Why not make it easy on yourself."

He stopped and faced the deputy by his side. "Do I have to talk to her?"

"Sooner or later, I reckon."

"I came here to see my niece. Can't you keep her off my back till then?"

The deputy looked back over his shoulder. "Mr. Cassini said he'll talk to you when he comes back out."

Although frustrated, she understood the deputy's dilemma. She reluctantly backed off. "That's alright, but I still have the right to visit the girl myself. So lead on."

The deputy sitting by the door to one of the rooms was Vincent's first clue to her whereabouts. He headed straight for the room with his escort by his side and Susan right behind.

"Can I go in?"

When Vincent's escort nodded the okay, the deputy stood up, opened the door then stepped to the side.

Vincent's eyes narrowed as he stood in the doorway of the dimly lit room. At the sight of Olivia, tears began to develop.

Susan squeezed past him and entered. Several feet in, she stopped, turned around, and then swept a hand towards the chair against the wall. "Would you like to sit down?"

He waved her off. "No. That's okay." Then he swiped the back of his right hand across his eyes.

Susan reached into her purse, pulled out a tissue and offered it to him. He took it as he passed by her on his way to Olivia. Leaning slightly towards Olivia's face, he whispered something then began stroking the hand that was sticking out of the blanket.

Susan got up beside him. "Is she your niece?"

He responded with a slight nod.

"I'm sorry, was that a yes?"

"Yeah... Is she going to be okay?"

"May I ask what's going on here?"

Susan recognized the nurse's voice and looked back over her shoulder. "It's okay. He's her uncle."

With the evil eye on Susan, the nurse walked over and checked the IV solution drip. "Please try to hold the noise down. The best thing for her right now is to get the sleep she needs."

"I promise, we'll be quiet," Susan said.

Not wanting to interfere with their time together, Susan sat down in the chair at the foot of the bed and watched. After a while, she noticed he stopped stroking Olivia's hand and had begun running his fingers through her hair. He leaned over and kissed her softly on the cheek, leaving a teardrop on her chin as he lifted his head. His chest heaved slightly. His lips quivered. He pinched the bridge of his nose and tightened his eyelids.

"I can't imagine how you feel right now, Mr. Cassini. And I'm here to do all I can to help you get through this. After your visit here, I would like to see you in my office."

"What for?"

"Well for one thing, we need to know a little more about her home life. And since both of her parents are deceased, we need to know how you can contribute to her future."

"Tony wasn't her real father," he blurted out.

"Yes, I know."

He frowned. "How'd you know?"

"We have our sources, Mr. Cassini. We also have documents on some of Olivia's problems at home—though, I'm afraid not enough to help us out. Is her biological father still around?"

"He took off long before Olivia was even born. Nobody knows where he is right now."

"It's not unusual for a child of a previous husband or boyfriend to be abused by the current husband, Mr. Cassini. We have numerous verified cases to that effect. Was Tony one of those? Or were they both guilty of doing that?"

"Look, you gotta understand, Francis was my baby sister," he said with gritted teeth. "You just don't turn your back on family. Where I come from you don't rat on your own flesh and blood."

With those words, Susan's tone changed dramatically. "What are you saying?" she let loose a low volume barrage, one that would penetrate his ears only. "What about her? Didn't she count as family? Didn't you turn your back on her? Right now she's going to need all the love and attention she can get—not to mention the professional help she'll probably have to have in the near future. " She paused for a moment, took a deep breath, then exhaled it in frustration, "How about___"

"Look lady, I don't need you to tell me what she needs."

"Are you willing to provide them, Mr. Cassini?"

"We can't… we can barely afford to take care of what we got now."

"Is there anyone else then? A grandparent? Or another aunt or uncle?"

He raised his head and said nothing for a few minutes then shook it. "No."

She took another deep breath, this time letting it out slowly before continuing. "Okay. Okay. Listen, this isn't getting us anywhere. Let's just start from the beginning." She slid her chair over to the wall, sat down, and then pointed to the one next to her. "Why don't you have a seat over here, Mr. Cassini? Maybe we can work something out right here. Perhaps___"

"Excuse me."

Susan, expecting to see another nurse, turned to see the shadow of a petite woman standing by the backlit-opened doorway. "Yes?"

"My name is Peggy Sands. Sheriff Johnson told my husband it was okay for me to visit her." She looked back over her shoulder. "The deputy out there said I could come in."

"So your husband must be the one I met yesterday," Susan said, as Peggy stepped further into the dim light of the room.

"Yes," Peggy, said, her face blushing red.

The smothering look in Peggy's eyes when they fell upon Olivia did not go unnoticed. Susan watched closely as she stepped aside and waved her towards the bed without saying a word.

Second thoughts crossed Peggy's mind. She hesitated at first, but then, like all the rest, melted as she got closer to the beauty of innocence. Her heart raced as a breath of air gently parted rose bud lips. She stepped back, afraid she might have gotten too close.

"It's okay," Susan assured her, "every once in awhile she'll do that. Unfortunately, that's all she does."

She let Peggy linger over the bed for a while before tapping her on the shoulder.

"I want you to meet her uncle." She nodded. "Mr. Vincent Cassini."

At this point, Peggy wasn't sure if she was glad to meet him or not. One side of her was hoping someone would come forth and claim the child. The other hoping that wouldn't happen. Reluctantly, she walked over to him.

"Hello, Mr. Cassini." She motioned back over her shoulder at Olivia. "You have a beautiful niece. I hope she's going to be alright."

"Yeah, sure." He stood up. "I hope so too." He turned to Susan. "How long is Livi going to be here? And who's going to pay for all this?"

According to what she had learned so far, there was no way the Cassini's could afford to raise and support Olivia financially. And now she even doubted they could support her emotionally. This case, she quickly realized, was going to be a long drawn out affair.

"To answer your first question," she said. "We don't know. We'll keep her here as long as it takes to get her back on her feet. As for the second, the state will take care of paying some of the bills. I can take care of the rest. However, having said that, the most important question that needs to be answered concerns her future. And that may have to be decided by the courts."

"Listen, I'm not getting involved in any court thing. I came here to see if she was Livi, that's all. I didn't even know her mother was dead."

"Are you sure that was your sister they found up there?"

"Yeah, I'm sure. So there's nothing I can do for them. I have to get back to my job—to my family."

The deputy, standing in the darkened corner of the room taking in all that was said, stepped forward and said, "I'm afraid, that's not going to be for a while yet. The sheriff has some more questions for you. And there's also the disposition of your sister. Someone has to make the necessary arrangements for burial."

"Not only that," Susan interjected, "When Olivia comes out of this, she's going to need someone familiar by her side, someone she knows, loves, and trusts."

# 24

As they approached the rustic cattle gate, a frown appeared when he glanced up at the large graying plank swinging gently between two twisted wooden stilts. Branded on it were the words, "High Roller Ranch", a verbal reminder of the prosperity among the cattle barons of the good old days.

The more his eyes took in, the more his own seventy five acre ranch came to mind. How long could he hang on to it? What would his future be like if he had to give it up? And where would he go?

With the house in view, he stopped the car, put the radio mike close to his lips, and then gave the instructions. "The lieutenant and I will take the front. The rest of you go around the back. Stay alert."

Both units acknowledged as they passed under the sign, which was located about a hundred yards from the main house.

Along the way, a loose gravel road threatened to announce their arrival with loud crunching noises. A windmill, with half its blades missing, joined in with an occasional squeak. Behind it, a decaying outbuilding, half hidden by overgrown vegetation, tuned in with a whistle. And not far away, empty stalls, that had lost their ability to hold in anything that could move, rattled.

In spite of the wind orchestrated noise, they got to within twelve feet from the left of the front porch without being detected. Billy brought his vehicle out from behind Cody's and stopped within ten feet to the left of it.

As Cody got out of his vehicle, he kept his eyes on the small tool shed and the ten by ten foot lean-to off to the right of the house. Perfect places from where one could easily ambush them the minute they exposed themselves. "Zero eight, are you in position?" His voice was low and apprehensive, closing the door of the cruiser quietly as he said it.

"We're ready."

"Okay, let's go. Keep a sharp eye on those other buildings. We don't want any surprises."

Jeremy got out and ran in a crouched position towards a dry well, located several yards from the back door. The other two deputies got out and hid behind a nearby empty water trough. Behind them a corral gate hung precariously by a single rusty hinge, poised to collapse at the slightest provocation.

The bone chilling squeal of the nearby windmill, a dirt devil obscuring their vision with fine grits, and the crack, pops, and squeaks accompanying every step taken on the warped floorboards of the front porch, joined to increase the tension.

As they got closer to the door, they straddled the butts of their forty-five caliber pistols with nervous hands.

Crouched along the wall to the right of the door, Cody inflated then deflated his lungs as he took one last look at Billy. He nodded, knocked, and then called in a loud voice, "Hezekiah, this is sheriff, Cody Johnson. Could you please step out here for a minute? I need to talk to you."

No answer.

He knocked again.

A sudden eerie silence magnified the thumping of hearts in their ears. Making matters even more nerve wracking was the pungent odor of rotting flesh that nearly gagged them.

As he pushed on the unlocked door, he kept his eye on the widening gap between the jam and the hinge, making sure no one was hiding behind it. When the door swung open, he grabbed his hat and ducked as a blizzard of dust and a flock of birds pelted his upper body. When the air stabilized, he dusted himself off, then, through a wide beam of light, saw the full scope of the trash littered front room. "All clear," he said, after carefully scanning the place. "Just watch where you're walking. I don't want anybody getting hurt."

What awaited them in the small kitchen was no different from what they had encountered passing thru the front room. On the wood burning stove, a frying pan caked with dried beans was host to a swarm of roaches and flies. Rotted meat hung like bats in a cave inside an opened pantry. And on the small table next to it, a tin military mess kit with bacon someone had forgotten to keep an eye on as it was cooking.

He ordered one of the deputies to open the window then took out his cell phone and called Martha. "Get me a probable cause search warrant for the High Roller ranch from Judge Baker. Don't know the address but I'm pretty sure there's a plat reference in the assayer's office. See if you can get it for him."

On overhearing his request, Jeremy's brows lowered. "On what basis?"

"Take a look over there," he said, pointing towards the far corner of the kitchen.

Jeremy walked over and noticed the red and white checkered cloth on the floor among the newspapers, trash, and clothing piled next to a badly scarred hutch. After picking it up, he turned it over and spread it out for all to see. "One of its corners is missing."

"If I'm not mistaken, I have the last piece of that jigsaw puzzle back in my office," Cody said. "Go ahead and bag it while I check this out."

He took a pen out of his shirt pocket, walked over to the fireplace mantle, and used it to lift the small, brown purse. Fairly clean, it stuck out like a sore thumb on the dust-covered mantle.

After examining it for signs of blood, he put it back in the exact position he found it. Looking down the other end of the mantle, he spotted the backside of a small photo. He carefully picked it up by the edges and turned it over.

"You're not gonna believe this." He showed it to Jeremy.

"That's Olivia."

"You bet it is."

He turned around to the deputies looking over his shoulder. "You two know what Hezekiah looks like, don't you?"

"Yes, sir."

"Stay here just in case he doubles back. If he does, don't let him touch a thing till we get that search warrant."

"6QN4 to six zero one."

"Go ahead," he said into his shoulder mounted radio.

It sounded like the chopper pilot's usual calm voice had taken a leave of absence. "I just spotted your man. He's at the foot of Panther Mesa. He's making a run up the east side. Some of the deputies are close by, but I'm afraid they're not going to get there in time."

"Try not to lose him. We'll be right there."

"I'll give it my best shot."

# 25

Hezekiah's ears perked at the sound of the blades beating the air below. He looked up just as the helicopter came over the rim of the narrow ledge. He tried desperately to reach a small crevice, but the eye in the sky forced him to hug the side of the mountain.

As the helicopter rose higher, sand and gravel swirled through the air like a miniature desert storm. He blinked several times before once again digging his raw, bloodied fingers between the embedded rocks. While lifting himself up as fast as he could, he looked back only to see lawmen fast approaching the mountain for the second time in as many days.

After reaching yet another ledge, he fell flat on his stomach and cradled his face with his forearms. His chest heaved like a bellows as it tried to stabilize itself to a manageable rhythm.

When it did, he summoned a burst of strength, rose, and continued climbing the mountain.

"It looks like he's trying to reach a plateau about a third of the way to the top," reported the pilot. "There appears to be deep crevices or caves nearby. You'd better hurry."

"Turn around and do another sweep," Cody ordered. "See if you can slow him down a bit."

"I'll give it try."

"Keep an eye on the chopper," Cody advised the others. "Lieutenant, have one of your men stay behind with the vehicles just in case he manages to sneak back down while we're up there. Take a couple of them over to the left side of the area where the chopper dips. I'll take the rest over to the right. With any luck we might be able to box him in."

He glanced over his shoulder and warned those behind him to spread out, use the boulders for cover, and keep their heads down as much as possible. With every step his chest pounded faster. With every step he scanned the mountain for a puff of smoke and the loud report that would quickly echo through the air soon after.

Before long, Jeremy, the youngest and the leanest, had managed to take the lead and be the first to spot Hezekiah.

"There he is," he hollered, pointing to the small figure climbing up about a hundred and ten yards above them.

"Don't let him get to those crevices," Cody hollered back. "And don't do anything foolish. Wait for the rest of us."

"He's heading towards what looks like an opening to a cave," the pilot said. "I'm going to buzz him and see if I could keep him down."

"Don't get too close," Cody warned, "we don't know if he's armed or not."

Out of all the possible hiding places available to Hezekiah, the ones that bothered Cody the most were the many caves sprinkled throughout the Trans-Pecos Mountains. Who knows how long it would take, or if they even could, to flush him out if he managed to reach any one of them? They had to stop him.

Billy and the others were just reaching the same level, a hundred feet apart and to the left of the main force.

"Go ahead and close in," Cody said over his portable radio. "He should be somewhere in between us. 6QN4 take her back to home base. We'll take over from here."

The last thing he wanted, if it came to it, was a stray bullet accidentally bringing down the helicopter, hurting, or possibly killing the pilot.

"Roger on that," the pilot said. "Good hunting."

As Hezekiah looked down at the approaching threat, the word, "pincer", crossed his mind, but he had no idea what it meant, or why it did. He knew, however, that the only chance to escape was to get to one of the cave entrances. But like a nursing home resident trying desperately to get up and run away, the mind willed, but the body couldn't. Sweat and saliva slobbered down his beard and on to his pain racked body. With his calf now looking and feeling like a balloon about to burst, the likelihood of him making it to safety was in jeopardy. The only options left were to surrender, or make his last and final stand right where he was.

After letting out a weird, prolonged scream that echoed throughout the mountainside, he squeezed into a narrow crevice whose opening was partially hidden with vegetation.

Birds scattered as if startled by a stalking cat. Jackrabbits stopped in their tracks, looked up and searched for the source of the hair-raising sound. So did the lawmen down below.

"What was that?"

"I'm afraid our friend up there isn't about to give up without a fight," Cody told the deputy next to him. "You might as well get ready for it."

Concerned for Jeremy, who he knew was closer to danger than the rest; he scanned the area ahead of him. But even with his sunglasses on, he was forced to wince constantly by the sun that had yet to crest the top of the mountain on its journey west.

In the meanwhile, Jeremy, whose adrenalin ran through his body like a freight train behind schedule, had no idea just how close he was to the man who had camouflaged his sweat covered body with sand. Nor did his mind register the rank body odor of someone who hadn't taken a bath in months. He even missed the roaming eyes that were following his every move as he passed by.

Unable to see the hunter who disappeared around the side of the mountain, Hezekiah leaned slightly forward, breaking through the natural cover and loosening gravel embedded in the walls of the crevice. The silence of the moment had been broken.

Jeremy turned around in time to catch a glimpse of Hezekiah as he pulled back into his hiding place. What he couldn't see were his hands. He drew his weapon and aimed. "Come out of there," he yelled. "Let me see your hands."

Hezekiah's fingers appeared first, assuring Jeremy he didn't have a weapon in his hand.

"Over here," Jeremy hollered. "Over here. I've got him. He's_____"

An ominous shadow, advancing in front of his feet like a growing pool of black oil, quickly silenced the rest of his thoughts and words. He took his eyes off Hezekiah and rolled them down towards the ground as the shadow grew larger.

Hezekiah quickly reached down and took the knife out of his boot.

Cody, catching a glimpse of what was about to happen as he came around the bend, took the forty five out of his holster, yelled, "freeze," and then fired just as Hezekiah sent the knife flying towards Jeremy.

Seconds later, a second shot echoed throughout the mountain.

Cody's hat flew off. His limp body melted to the ground.

With heart pounding and bullets kicking dirt all around him, Hezekiah hit the ground and crawled back to the crevice. He squeezed in and hugged the inside walls. Sand and rock shrapnel pelted him as a couple of more rounds slammed close to his body.

# 26

"She trusts me. You just ask her when she wakes up. She'll tell ya so. Won't ya Livi?"

"Olivia isn't talking, Mr. Cassini."

It took a while for Susan's words to sink in. When they did, he quickly straightened up from leaning over the bedrail and shot and eyeful towards her. "What d'ya mean she ain't talking? Why not? What's wrong?"

"Dr. Fieldson's not really sure yet if it's a condition known as Selective Mutism, or if it's the result of brain damage."

"Brain damage?"

"Yes. There were signs of a previous traumatic injury detected on the scan. He thinks that might have brought it on. In any case, if that wasn't it, then she's either too fearful or too anxious to talk."

"So that's it."

"What's it?" Susan asked.

"I noticed something was wrong the last time she came home from the hospital. At first I thought she was afraid to say anything in front of Tony, but even when he wasn't around, I couldn't get her to talk to me."

"Did she talk at all?"

"Yeah. Why?"

"Then it couldn't be the same thing. Nobody here has heard her say a word. There had to be another reason why she wouldn't talk to you back then. Can you think of any?"

"Maybe cause I tried to get Francis to take her back to the hospital? She was afraid of that."

Susan stood over the short man and peered into his eyes. "Why did you want her back in the hospital? Was she still hurting? Or were you hoping they'd catch on and do something about it?"

The answer to her questions didn't come in the form of words. His eyes glistened from a small amount of moisture that had accumulated at the bottom lids. His head lowered.

"Why didn't *you* report it? Why leave it to someone else?"

"You didn't know Tony, Ms. Wheeler. He would'a cut Francis' throat without batting an eye if I'd done that."

Reeling from what she had learned so far, Susan, exhausted and bewildered, slumped into the chair,

"You don't understand, Mr. Cassini." She looked over at Olivia. "Because of her condition, she can't be treated the same as other wards of the state. Finding a permanent home isn't going to be that easy. And then there's the nurturing factor, the physical and psychological care, and the special schooling she'll be needing." In her mind, everything she mentioned played out like future chapters in the life of Olivia D'Angelo. "That mountain she was walking towards is nothing compared to the one she faces now."

Peggy, with tears welling, strolled over to Olivia's bedside. "What's going to happen to her?"

"To be honest, I really don't know." Susan turned her attention back to Vincent. "Mr. Cassini."

"What?"

"I'm asking you once again. Are you going to help her get over that mountain?"

"I can't."

"You are all she has. No matter what, you have to be considered a prime candidate for her health and well being. Think about that."

He gritted his teeth. "No, you think about it. I already told you we ain't got the money to feed and clothe another mouth. Besides, my old lady would have a fit if I even thought about it. You do what you want. As soon as they're through with me here, I'm going back home." He turned around and went back to Olivia's bedside. "I ain't got nuttin more to say."

"That's exactly right, Mr. Cassini," the deputy said, stepping out of the shadowed corner of the room. "That is *all* you're going to say. The rest of you listen to me carefully. The sheriff doesn't want the public to know about her condition. She's a normal talkative little girl who's just been through a terrible ordeal, that's all. Is that clear?"

"Yes, but____"

"There's no but about it, Ms. Wheeler. Those are the sheriff's orders."

Peggy, Vincent, and Susan looked at each other in confusion before giving the deputy a questioning look.

With reddened eyes, Peggy glanced at Susan and then to Olivia. "My God, she doesn't stand a chance."

Susan put her hands on Peggy's shoulder.

"We'll have to put her into the system. She'll be a special case, of course. There's got to be someone in this area willing to take temporary custody until a permanent home could be found."

With piercing eyes toward Vincent, she said, "Of course you know, like it or not, this is going to wind up in the courts."

A whirlwind of thoughts filled Peggy's mind. Could she? Would she? How would Jeremy feel once he found out about Olivia's condition? Did he already know? Could they even afford to give it a try?

Her mouth opened, but the lips *would* not nor *could* not form words. Second thoughts kept crashing in like uninvited guests at a party.

Susan caught the expression. "Mrs. Sands? Did you want to say something?"

"Uh---no---no." She shook her head.

"I'm afraid you will have to leave now," the nurse in charge said as she entered. "We're going to give her another bath and try to see if she'll eat solid food." She walked over to the bed and lowered the side rails. "You could come back after we finish, if you'd like."

Peggy had seen and heard enough. She thought it best to leave, rather than stay and say something she might regret later. Or reach out for something she and Jeremy couldn't handle. "I guess I'd better go home now."

Encouragement was not on Susan's mind at this time. But neither was discouragement. A light at the end of the impending tunnel was about to leave the room, and she knew it.

"Mrs. Sands—may I call you Peggy?"

"Yes."

"Good. Perhaps we could get together later for lunch?"

"I suppose so." She said it reluctantly; afraid to get further involved "It will probably have to be on a weekend though. I'm going to be teaching at Apache Elementary this semester and I'll be tied up with preparations for that."

"That would be fine."

After exchanging home and cell phone numbers, Peggy left the room.

Susan turned her attention back to Vincent. "Mr. Cassini, I still want to see you in my office after the sheriff gets through with you. I'm sure he won't mind keeping you around for awhile, especially after I submit my report and the physician's diagnosis to the courts."

The struggle within was made obvious by the tormented look on his face. Still, her primary concern had to be focused on Olivia. She would have to wait until an investigation into his background and financial status could be verified and completed before passing final judgment.

"Can she do that?" he asked the deputy.

"Do what?"

"Keep me here."

"I'm afraid so. For now though, we're gonna have to get you back to headquarters. The sheriff's not exactly through with you."

# 27

You could almost hear a pin drop after Billy hollered several times for them to hold their fire. When the smoke cleared, two deputies had Hezekiah in their gun sights. The rest had theirs aimed high up on the mountain, scanning for the slightest spark, puff of smoke, or movement.

When looking down to see if any of the deputies had been hurt, Billy spotted Cody laying face up, his hat nearby speckled with blood from the swath that had been cut across the side of his head, inches above the right eye. He took off in a crouched position, zigzagging from one boulder to another. On the way to him, he got on the radio and hollered several times that the sheriff was down. After safely reaching him, he dropped to his knees, lifted Cody's head, and cradled it in his arms. He pulled out his handkerchief and placed it over the wound.

Cody reached up and grabbed a hold of his wrist. "Jeremy," he said. "Go check on Jeremy."

"I will after we get you taken care of." He spotted a deputy close by and yelled, "Get the chopper back here now."

"Lieutenant, over here," hollered another deputy. "You're not going to believe this."

Billy heard him but kept his hand on the handkerchief and his eyes on the deputies working their way up towards where they believed the shots might have come from. When he realized the deputies didn't draw fire to their counter offensive move, he turned his attention back to Cody who was pushing against the hand plastered to his temple.

"Help me up."

Although his head felt like it had been hit on the side with a small axe, he had to get up and make sure that what he had seen before the curtain closed in on him was not an illusion.

"It's best you don't move," Billy advised, "You'll only make it worse."

"I'll live. Besides, if you're talking about the headache, it couldn't get any worse." As he sat up, he noticed his weapon lying beside him. He picked it up. The hot barrel confirmed that he did indeed fire it, an action mentally lost when the apparent sniper took him momentarily out of the picture. "Did anybody see where it came from?"

"No. But I can tell you it was a high powered rifle—and it's not hunting season."

"It all depends on what you're trying to bag, doesn't it?" Cody said. "Did you call the chopper back?"

"Yes," he answered, spotting the chopper just above the horizon. "He should be here any minute now."

"Good. We'll need him to search that section up there." He pointed.

"Forget it. Whoever it was is either hunkered down in some hole by now or further south. It may take days to get him. We'll need the chopper to get you to the hospital."

Billy was right. The odds of finding him were slim. For the second time in the investigation, the possibility of an accomplice entered his mind. One who, for one reason or another, may have been trying his best to keep Hezekiah from falling into their hands. His thoughts quickly shifted back to the beginning of the ordeal and the welfare of his deputy. "What about Jeremy?"

"He's over here," hollered one of the deputies.

"Come on, give me a hand."

"Okay, just don't let go."

As he stood up, he winced and took short breaths in response to the drumbeats in his head. Feeling like a fish struggling against the gentle ripples of an incoming tide, he took Billy's advice and held on.

"Here's your hat," Billy said, his index finger sticking out through the newly made hole just above the brim.

"Keep it. I have a couple more back at the ranch."

Before all hell broke loose, Jeremy had failed to realize

Cody's demand to freeze was not directed at Hezekiah, but at him. And if he had listened, he may not have wound up flat on the ground with his lungs deflated by the sudden and unexpected impact.

How am I gonna write this one up? Cody thought. Better yet, who's going to believe it?

Visibly shaken by his ordeal and the sight in front of him, he proceeded cautiously. As did Billy and the others, who had no idea what had happened to Jeremy prior to the shootout. As they stood there in a veritable state of shock, the puddle of blood under Jeremy's neck grew from the size of a silver dollar to that of a dinner plate. Billy wasn't sure if it was Jeremy's life fluid emptying on the ground, or that of the male mountain lion straddled on Jeremy's back. He motioned for one of the deputies to hold on to Cody then took a chance and bent down to check.

"How is he?" Cody asked, his weapon, along with that of the deputy standing alongside of him, pointed squarely between the black-tipped ears of the lion's small head.

"He's dead."

"What about Deputy Sands?"

"He'll be okay."

contorted by the weight of the animal's head on top of his.

"That's not your blood."

Jeremy felt the warm, thick saliva on the back of his neck as it dribbled out of the lion's opened mouth. He inched his head to one side and found himself eyeball to eyeball with the one hundred and thirty pound, five-foot long carnivore.

The pounding in Jeremy's compressed chest grew louder in his ears as he realized what had happened. "Are you sure he's dead?"

"Believe me," Cody said, "if he wasn't, we wouldn't be standing this close to you."

Hezekiah didn't hesitate. Nor did he consider the consequences. He hurled the knife just as the mountain lion that had been stalking him for the last several weeks leaped from the giant boulder behind Jeremy. And now the predator was spread out like a fireplace rug on top of Jeremy with the knife stuck in its outstretched neck.

Although still a little disoriented, Cody managed to squat down next to the stunned deputy. "Hey, are you sure you're okay?"

"I will be." he grunted. "After you get him off, that is."

Cody motioned to the deputies. When they removed the carcass, he noticed the gaping hole just under the lion's left front leg. The bullet that had creased his skull made him miss what he was aiming for—the lion's chest.

After he was helped to his feet, Jeremy ran his trembling fingers through his dirt encrusted hair then looked down at the source of his newly acquired aches. He backed off and shuddered.

"Where'd he come from?"

"I can only tell you where he was going. And if it wasn't for him." Cody nodded painfully towards Hezekiah. "The chances of you being among the living would've been slim to none."

Hezekiah, whittled by exhaustion and the bullet that had grazed his shoulder, leaned against the side of the mountain behind him. His squared chin, hidden by the dirt-encrusted, sun bleached hair, dropped till it touched his chest. Spittle hung off his lips, and blood dripped like a leaking faucet off his fingertips. His eyes rolled up at the sound of the helicopter passing overhead.

The orders to get his hands up came through loud and clear, but darkness was about to supersede them. The deputies grabbed him before he could hit the ground. They pinned him back against the side of the mound and handcuffed him.

"I don't get it."

"I don't either," Cody said. "He could've let the big cat take you right out of the picture. Instead he chose to take care of the cat."

It didn't make sense to anyone but Hezekiah. The long awaited confrontation with the lion had finally taken place. For weeks they had been playing cat and mouse with each other. But once again, Hezekiah had become the victor, the survivor, and the controller of his own destiny.

"Things like this don't happen in Chicago you know," Jeremy said, picking up his hat and, like some cowboy that had just been thrown off a wild bronco, dusted off his pants.

"Here lately, lots of things seem to be happening where you'd least expect, or for that matter, make any sense." Billy said.

Cody wasn't sure if Hezekiah was really concerned for the deputy's life, or if he was just playing the part of the, "Good Samaritan", to soften the blow that might be in his future. He approached him. With hands that were still trembling, he parted the front of Hezekiah's hair. He gazed into the windows of the soul partly hidden under Neanderthal like eyebrows. "Look at me," he said.

The gleam in his eyes and the wry smile on his face was not what Cody had expected. He wondered if the suspected killer was taunting him. "Who's your friend up there?" He asked, nodding towards the spot where the sniper was apparently hiding.

When a long period of silence followed, Billy shook his head. "I'm afraid he's not going to tell you a thing."

"All right then, you listen to me carefully," he said. "Yesterday we found a little girl not far…" He paused at the sight of Hezekiah's eyes rolling downward along with the corners of his chapped lips. "You know who I'm talking about, don't you?"

Without saying a word, Hezekiah lowered his head and closed the curtain of hair.

"Why'd you leave her out there?" Although he didn't really expect answers, he was determined to plant the questions in his mind, to make him ponder them no matter where this took him. "What about those two bodies?" he continued. "Do you know anything about *them*?"

The head shot back up. He shook it several times, exposing questioning eyes, as if he had no idea what Cody was talking about. Even so, Cody felt he knew enough to put him behind bars where they can keep an eye on him until they could sort things out. He turned and gave the order to take him away.

As Cody walked by him, Jeremy turned and followed, "What's going to happen to him?"

"Right now, all we can do is hold him on suspicion of murder. Those items found in that shack should be enough to do that."

142

"The helicopter's down below waiting," Billy said. "He's going to take both of you to the hospital."

"Go ahead and take care of him. I'll be okay."

Billy shook his head, looked up and spoke several words in his native tongue.

"Wait," Jeremy hollered. "I need to know."

That need was all too familiar to Cody. And the last thing he wanted was to deny Jeremy the opportunity to at least try. "Go ahead. Ask him."

"While he's doing that, how about letting me wrap that head of yours," Billy said.

Billy had an inkling Cody would stall his departure. He sent a deputy down to get a first aid kit long before the helicopter even landed.

Cody winced as Billy wrapped the gauze bandage several times around his head then taped it. He felt relief when the warm water, poured onto a gauze pad, washed the dried blood off his cheek and chin

Jeremy, in the meanwhile, walked over and took his turn at Hezekiah. With his index finger under Hezekiah's bearded chin, he lifted it up. Unlike Cody, he didn't bother to try and part the hair. "Why?" he asked.

No response.

Jeremy took his finger away. Hezekiah's head dropped as if he had just died.

"I figured it'd be like this," Cody said, his hands on Jeremy's shoulder. "We have a possible witness who can't talk, and a possible serial killer who won't. I reckon we have our work cut out for us."

"Now that we have reasonable cause to legally print him, we should be able to find out who he really is," Billy said. "I'll have Martha send them to the FBI."

"Let me know right away what they come up with," He motioned to the deputies. "Make sure you read him his rights before you take him away. Watch him carefully, though, you're no faster than that big cat was. I'll be there as soon as we finish up here."

"I'd like to go with them," Jeremy said.

"Hold on a minute," Cody hollered, noticing the way Hezekiah was limping as they led him away. He walked over to where they had stopped, tipped his head to one side and took a good look at it. "What's wrong with your left leg?"

Again, he didn't say a word. Instead, he stared at him, confused by the concerned tone in Cody's voice.

"Okay," Cody said. "We'll see to it the doctor checks that also." He nodded again and they escorted him down the mountain to the waiting helicopter.

Cody's cell phone rang. Before he took it out of its holder, he turned to Jeremy. "Yes, you can go with them. And while you're there, have his clothing sent to the lab. I have a feeling some of those blood stains are not from those animals he's been butchering."

"Yes, sir."

"Sheriff, a Mr. Alex Ramirez wants you to give him a call," Martha said. "He claims to have some information concerning the remains you found."

"Which one?"

"He didn't say."

"I see... How about that search warrant?"

"Judge Baker signed it. I have it right here on my desk."

"Good. Tell Mr. Ramirez I'll be in to see him sometime this afternoon." He hung up. "I was hoping he'd call."

"Who?"

"Gordo."

"Isn't that a Hispanic word for fat?" Jeremy asked.

"Yep." He reached into his pocket and took out the matchbook. "It's also his middle name and the one he goes by. Apparently he was a big baby. Anyway, he's a bartender at the Angels Dance Club. He must've seen the photo of Francis on television." He motioned Billy over. "Martha has that search warrant. After you pick it up go back out to that house. Have the lab boys hit it with a fine tooth comb while I go visit Mr. Ramirez."

"You're lucky he didn't aim more to the right," Billy said. "Have any idea what that was all about?"

"Either Hezekiah's got a friend we don't know about, or I've got an enemy *I* don't know about."

"Then again maybe he's got an enemy *he* doesn't know about," Billy added.

"What makes you say that?"

"There are several bullet holes over by where he was hiding. I'd be willing to bet we didn't make them."

"We'll know for sure after we dig them out, won't we."

"Why don't we worry about that later?" Billy said. "Right now you need to take care of that head of yours before it gets infected."

"I'll stop at The Family Health Care Center on my way to the dance club."

# 28

"May I help you?"

"She's awake," the nurse in the room said. "Notify the doctor on duty."

After hearing her talking to the nurse's station then looking up and seeing the light above the door blinking, Deputy Reed rose from his chair and entered the room. "Is everything okay?"

"We'll know soon enough. Right now, I'm going to check her pulse and temperature."

"I'll be out here if you need me then."

The word had spread throughout the hospital like a blazing wildfire, prompting the few reporters holding vigil in the lobby to scurry like rats for the upcoming morsel.

When he was notified, the hospital spokesperson left his office and headed straight for the girls room hoping to get as much information as he could before facing the media. On the way there he met the doctor who had just gotten the word, and who was also anticipating an immediate barrage of questions.

"Hello sweetheart. My name is Doctor, Stevens. What's your name?" After several seconds of no response, he turned to the nurse. "She's awake but I'm afraid her condition remains the same." He took out his penlight and checked her pupils. I'm afraid Dr. Fieldson's right. She is going to need physiological therapy."

Susan and Peggy walked past the small contingent gathered by the door and entered. "Has she said anything yet?"

"No, Ms. Wheeler."

Peggy, in the background with her hands covering her mouth, took them down and stepped forward. "I thought Dr. Fieldson said this would just be temporary?"

"Unfortunately no one really knows how the brain works when pushed to its limit, Mrs. Sands. Amnesia, shock, insanity—these are but a few of the escape routes it takes when confronted with something it can't deal with. All we can do is hope she comes out of it with no long-term consequences. We've done just about all we could here. We'll set her up for speech therapy to see if that will help also."

"We've already taken care of that, Doctor," the nurse said. "She has an appointment with a child psychologist also. It will have to be as an outpatient, though. Admissions have no idea how long we can justify an inpatient status without insurance coverage."

Susan looked back over her shoulder. "You do whatever has to be done. The state will take care of it. Right now, it doesn't look like she has anyone who could help with that except her aunt and uncle. Unfortunately, they don't seem to have the means or the desire."

The doctor rubbed his chin. "As far as I'm concerned, she'd be better off in a home environment." With hands outstretched, he continued, "familiar surroundings would probably help her more than being confined in a hospital."

"That's the problem," Susan said. "We don't have a place for her to stay, let alone one that would be familiar to her."

"Well then, I hope everything works out for her. She's a lovely child. And she needs to be in a better environment than what she's apparently been in." He got up to leave the room.

"Wait," Susan said.

He stopped just as his hand touched the doorknob and turned around.

"Can she be taken out of here tomorrow?" she thought for a moment. "What I mean is will she be able to leave soon?"

"I would prefer to release her sooner than later. One more good checkup and an assurance of follow-up opportunities are all we need to do that."

After hearing that, the next thing Susan Wheeler wanted was to talk to the Sands couple alone. She had already gone through the department's list of possible long term foster parents and determined them unsuitable to take care of someone in Olivia's situation.

Jeremy's undeniable concern and attitude towards Olivia seemed to be embellished in her mind. He and Peggy were the right age and, according to what she had learned, had no children of their own. She made up her mind. It may take some time to get them checked out and cleared but she thought it would be the best thing to do.

"Why don't you and I go to the cafeteria where we can get better acquainted?" She asked Peggy. "I'll buy the coffee."

"Yes, of course."

Susan waved a hand towards the door. "After you."

Having heard the doctor's advice, Reed waited till everyone left the room then took out his cell phone and dialed Cody's number.

# 29

The last thing he needed after having his wound cleaned and stitched was exposure to the cacophony of billiards mingling with explosive Honky Tonk music. Information has its price, though, and under the circumstances, he was more than willing to pay for it.

He stood at the opened door waiting for his pupils to adjust to the near darkness before venturing on to its two thousand square foot dance floor. When they did, he strolled into the smoke filled, cavernous interior under the scrutiny of a few hard-core early bird celebrants bellied up to the small bar

Through the eye stinging haze, he met their gazes. He grinned as several heavily tattooed bruisers, dressed in undershirts and jeans, downed their drinks then, like proud peacocks looking to score, strutted past him on their way out.

Before he could get to the larger of the two bars, a young, black haired waitress, in an attempt to get the sudden chill out of the air, approached quickly with tray in hand "What can I get you, sheriff?"

He cupped the back of his ear like some old man whose level of hearing decreased as his age increased. "What?"

"Drink," she shouted into his ear. "What can I get you to drink?"

He bent down, getting as close to the five feet, five inch, slender girl as he could without intruding into her space. "Where's Alex?"

"Out back." she flipped her head towards the door behind the left side of the smaller bar. "He should be... there he is now."

Alex's apron, which looked like it had just finished a wine tasting contest, strained to stay above his belly as he struggled through the door. The cautious two hundred and ninety pound bartender's jowls, adorning the dark-skinned round face, jiggled with every step he took. He looked up just as she pointed her long nailed finger towards him.

Spotting Cody, he put down the case of beer, wiped his beefy, calloused hands on the apron, and then approached. "I take care of thees." He nodded for her to leave as his big brown eyes locked onto the peepers of a couple of nosey Hispanic nationals.

On turning his attention back to Cody, he noticed a piece of the four-inch gauze bandage sticking out and the hole in the hat. "Wha' hoppen to you?"

"I had a little mishap earlier." He rolled his eyes up. "Nothing serious."

"How about drink?" He motioned towards the stool at the far end of the large bar. "Might help you forget pain."

"No thanks. That's the only thing I can handle right about now. I understand you have some information for me."

As Alex made his way behind the bar, Cody made his to the front of it and sat. He gave a courtesy nod to the tipsy patron two stools away.

Alex leaned over the bar, getting as close to Cody's face as he could. "Look, Amigo, just to make look like social visit, let me pour you coke or sumting, okay?"

Cody looked into the mirror behind the bar and saw why Alex was concerned. He was drawing quite a bit of attention from the few Mexican construction workers who were perhaps worried about not having their green cards or proof of citizenship.

"Okay, if it makes you feel better," Cody said. "How about a Sprite?"

"That gude enough."

Alex didn't hesitate to go all the way with the charade. With hands hidden behind the bar, he popped open a can, poured its content into one of those fancy, wide-mouthed glasses, and then topped it off with a green olive.

"Now how's that gonna look. You know I don't drink. And even if I did, I'm on duty."

"Thees will give them sumting to talk about, eh. Besides, their wurd don't really mean a thing outside thees place."

After setting the drink in front of Cody, he took out a pre-smoked stogie and stuck it between his fat lips. Having dealt with Cody in the past, he refrained from lighting it.

Cody grinned as he eyed the olive then raised the glass and finished a third of it off before setting it back down. "Okay, let's have it. What's on your mind?"

"A couple weeks ago, on Saturday night," he said. Noticing the attention still on them, he took the towel off his shoulder and began wiping the counter as he continued. "That lady on the news, she cum een here."

"What time?"

"I say around seex, maybe a leettle afta. Anyway, around thee time thee evening crowd start comeeng in. She sat over in that booth." He nodded towards the corner on the other side of the large dance floor.

Cody looked back over his right shoulder, squinted at the barely visible booth, and then turned his head back around.

"Go on."

"Well, thee first thing I notice was her waitress comeeng up here with twenties and fifties. Crisp, unwrinkled, almost like they just come out of meent plant over in Fort Worth."

"You mean the U.S Currency plant, don't you?"

"Yeah, that right. Anyway, she just didn't look like thee type that would have that kind of doe."

"What'ya mean?"

"I mean she no look like what you call, debutante." He grabbed a glass and started wiping it off. "Her hair look like it no sees brush for weeks. No makeup. Bolsa's."

"What?"

"You know—bags." He touched below his eye. "Black. She no that bad lookin'. I theenk if she take care, she be, uh—how you say—nuckout"

"You mean a knockout."

"Si…si. Anyway, her clothes look like she sleep in them for weeks."

"How long did she stay?"

"She go around 1:00 am." He spit a wad of tobacco into the trashcan behind him then continued. "The guy, he left after."

"What guy?"

Cody took his hat off and fanned the air around him.

"Actually, two of them. The first one, he here for a while before he go to her around nine. Maybe hour later, thees other guy he come and go right to their table."

"Did they know her?"

"I don know."

*If she looked as bad as he said then what could've attracted them?*

Alex leaned over the counter. "She was flashing lots of money before the Mexican walked to their table, though."

*Money? Was that it?*

"Have you seen them in here before?" he asked.

"I don pay dat much attention to them unless they regulars. Besides, you can see," he nodded towards the corner of the room again "It pretty dark over theere."

"I see," he agreed. "What about the waitress. Did she know them? Has she seen them in here before?"

"Why don you ask her yourself?"

Alex motioned her over just as she finished serving drinks at one of the tables.

She set her tray down at the server's counter then walked over to where Cody was sitting. After giving him a quick glance, she leaned against the bar and waited.

"Norma, thees here Sheriff Johnson. He got some questions for you."

"Oh, yeah. What kind of questions?" she took the wad of chewing gum out of her mouth then stuck it on the side of Cody's glass

Before answering, he glanced at the glass, grinned, and then looked back at her. "Do you remember that lady whose picture was on the news earlier this afternoon?"

"I sure do. She dropped fifty dollars on the table just before her old man left."

"You saw her do that?"

"Yeah! And he wasn't too happy about it either. He tried to get her to go home, but when he saw he wasn't getting anywhere he got up and left. Boy was he fuming."

"That mad, huh?"

"Yeah! Said he had a good notion to knock her lights out."

"Can you describe him?"

He was hoping the size of the tip had induced a photographic image that may help the investigation.

"He was tall and skinny. I'd say somewhere between thirty-five and forty." She wrinkled her nose. "Kind of scrubby looking. Dirty."

"Hair, eyes, those sorts of things?"

"Can't tell you much about his eyes... his hair was kind'a short. From what I could see it was sort of brown, or was it blonde? I'm not sure."

"How about a light brown?"

"That's it. He also had a slight hook to his nose. Sorta like an Eagle's."

"What was he wearing?"

"Denim coveralls. They were faded and dirty, even had a funny smell to them."

"Like what?"

"Cow or sheep dung, I suppose. I don't know."

"Anything else you can think of."

"Yeah," She said. "He was disgusting."

"Why do you say that?"

"He took this big, red bandana out of his pocket and blew his nose while people were eating at the next table. I thought for sure they'd get up and walk out."

She didn't have to go any further. He found himself back on highway 385 with Billy, a flashing light, and the occupant of an old Chevy pickup. Besides her description, the red flag, or in this case, bandana, was too coincidental to ignore.

"What about the other guy?"

"The wetback?"

"You mean Mexican, don't you?"

"Whaaat everrr."

"What did he look like?"

"He had an olive complexion and slick, black hair that was sort of wavy. He looked like he might've been a good-looking hunk at one time. That's about all I can remember ... Oh yeah, his nose. It was crooked. Like maybe it was broken at one time."

For the first time in his life, he was glad a female paid more attention to the nose than the eyes. Her description of the farmer drew a familiar picture in his mind. Now all he needed was enough information to draw another.

"It sounds like you remember him better than you do her old man."

"He was better looking, remember."

"How'd he get along with him?"

"I thought sure he would get up and belt him when they started arguing but he didn't. He just sat there and watched. I guess he was afraid to start something in here."

"Did he leave with her?"

"He left for a while then came back."

"Thee suit was blue," Alex said. "I no get to see hees face but I got gude look at suit when he go to the Bano."

"The bathroom?"

"Si."

"How long was he in there?"

"About five meenutes or so. Long enough for lady to vamoose out front door."

"Oh yeah, I forgot." Norma looked over her shoulder as she went to the end of the bar to pick up her tray. "His English wasn't all that bad," she said, glancing at Alex, "even with the accent."

"Hey! You forgot something else." Cody nodded to his glass.

She turned around and walked back. "Sorry."

Before she could peel the hard wad of gum off the glass and stick it back in her mouth, Cody asked, "Did any of them mention anything about a little girl?"

Norma thought for a moment then said, "Yeah, not long after her old man came in, he asked about the kid. She told him the girl was asleep out in the car."

"Did you happen to get a look at the car?"

"Are you kidding? This joint was jumping. We had a full house. I didn't even have time to go to the bathroom."

"Thanks, Norma. You've been a mighty big help."

"Sure."

"What about me? Don't you want my help?"

The velvety voice coming from behind him was familiar even in the din of the club. Turning around brought his eyes first to the top of the light auburn hair that flowed down to her shoulders, then down to her tanned, oval shaped face where they lingered on the dark, green inviting eyes.

"Ms. Miller?" he said, brows furrowed.

Her thin arched eyebrows lifted as her moist lips spewed the words, "Ms. Miller?"

The stunning lady, filling every inch of her slim cut western jeans, penetrated his comfort zone before she continued, "What ever happened to plain ole Bonnie? Has it been that long?" She looked up at the wound on his head "Or is that more serious than it looks."

Cody rolled his eyes up for the second time since he had walked in. "No, not really." He took off his hat. "What are you doing here? The last I heard you were over in Sweetwater."

"I thought a change of pace would do me good," she said, imbedding him in visions of the past. "You know what they say about living your life in the same ole rut. I'm not getting any younger, you know."

"Come on, Bonnie. You don't look like you've aged a bit since the last time I saw you. What? five—six years?"

"How about seven." She smiled. "You always were the complimentary type. Thanks."

"My pleasure." He downed the rest of his sprite. "So, what's the change?"

"She no longer serves drink, dat what." Alex bit another piece off the stogie then spit it on the floor. "She own thees place."

"Alex's only half right. Bud Watkins and I are partners now. He takes care of the business end while I take care of the entertainment and the drinks."

Cody's brows lifted. "Congratulations."

"Why, thank you again, Cody Johnson."

"It sound to me like you two already know each other. Sure you don want real drink?"

"No thanks." Cody put his hand up when Alex slapped a bottle of whiskey on the counter.

"What about you?" Alex said, turning to Bonnie.

"I'll have the usual. That's if the sheriff here doesn't mind, of course."

"Of course not." he grinned. "Go right ahead."

"I heard about what happened, Cody," she said, after sipping on her Rum and Coke. "I can't even imagine what it's like to lose your family. I'm truly sorry."

"Thanks, Bonnie. I appreciate that."

"Sure you don't want to have a drink with me?"

"Maybe some other time, okay?"

"Is that a promise?" Her long eyelashes fluttered.

"Listen, Bonnie, I really can't make any promises. Right now I'm tied up on a big case. I'm just here trying to get some information."

"Now, aren't you going to ask me what kind of help I was talking about?"

"Sure. What is it?"

"That man with the crooked nose." She touched the tip of his. "I've seen him before."

"You have?"

"Yes." She pointed at a table. "He was sitting there last Friday with three young Mexicans. It looked like they were having a serious pow- wow."

First the Mexican sitting at the same table with Francis on the twelfth, and then a week later he meets with these boys. He was almost certain now that she met her fate sometime around the 20$^{th}$.

"Are you sure it was the same man?"

"Hey, if you'd seen this guy, you'd never forget him."

He glanced at Norma who was serving drinks at the table in question. "So I've heard. What else can you tell me about him?"

"He's staying at the Comanche Motel over on East Dickinson."

"How do you know that?"

"A couple of days ago I was in the motel office looking for an old friend of mine when he walked in complaining about his bed not being made right. It kicked up a little Latin temper, that's for sure. I thought the old man at the desk was gonna have a heart attack."

"Can you give me a more detailed description than Norma did? Height, weight, those sorts of things."

"I'd say about five ten, a hundred and sixty, or sixty five pounds. He had dark, mean looking eyes under thin black eyebrows, sunken cheeks, and a hard looking square chin. He's probably in his early forties."

The corner of his mouth went up slightly. "Why don't you just show me a picture?"

Her lips came close to his as she practically stood on her toes, stretching apart the blue, western shirt with the top two buttons undone. "I just did."

He swallowed hard again as he tipped the brim of his hat. "Thanks Bonnie, I best be going now."

"She must really be something."

"Who?"

"The one holding the rein, that's who."

For a fleeting moment her eyes reflected the face that had been embedded in his mind ever since he bumped into her at the office. He shook his head. "I'm sorry, what'd you say?"

"Boy, you do have it bad."

"Those three men you mentioned. Did you see what they looked like?"

"To be honest with you, I couldn't____"

"I could," said Norma, hearing part of the conversation as she neared them.

"Apparently she has better eyesight then I do," Bonnie said.

"It's not that. I saw the one with the gold ear ring in the *Stop and Go* gas station several days before they came in here."

"He wore earrings?" Cody asked.

"Just one," she said, grinning. "That's all he *could* wear."

"Why?"

"Someone took a big chunk of his left ear lobe off, that's why."

"Ouch! That'll teach him to mess around with Chiquita," Bonnie said, then smiled.

"Anything else?"

"Yeah. The guy looked like a walking commercial for tattoo parlors."

"I'm going to need you to come down to headquarters and look at some photos, Norma. Does tomorrow morning sound okay?"

"Yeah, sure."

"Bonnie, nice seeing you again," he said, tipping his brim.

"See you around, cowboy." She winked.

He had a pretty good idea who the, so called, old man was. It was the other fellow and his entourage that had him wondering. Where do they fit in? And what was their connection to Francis?

He was about to get into his vehicle when Norma rushed out the front door of the bar frantically waving her arms. "Wait! Wait a minute. There was another man."

"Another one?"

Closing the door, he walked over and met her in front of the vehicle.

"Yeah. He seemed to be very interested in her. He asked me if I knew where she lived, and if she spent a lot of time in here."

He could have been just another Romeo testing the waters. Nevertheless, Cody figured he'd better get some information about him just in case.

"Okay, so what can you tell me about him?"

"Not much. He kept his head back in the dark corner most of the night. All I could see was his eyes."

"And?" he asked, noticing the sudden deep frown.

"Dark. Hungry. As if he was craving a forbidden fruit he couldn't have. You know what I mean?"

"No, I don't. Why don't you tell me?"

"Like when someone sees a chick he likes but she won't give him the right time of day. I see their type in here all the time. Most of them are just looking to have a good time, but…"

"But what?"

"There was something different about this one. His eyes. They gave me the creeps."

Reaching into his wallet, he pulled out a card. "Give me a call if you happen to think of anything else that might be important. That's my number at the top."

"Sure."

He was beginning to think this whole investigation was deliberately brought about and edged on by the sun as its glare caught his attention. Reaching into his shirt pocket, he took out his sunglasses. When he put them on and glanced into the rearview mirror, his brows lifted. He looked back over his shoulder. Across the street, parked in alley way, was a white Buick Regal. It was a 1991 model. And it had a New York State license tag.

He quickly turned back around, stuck his head out the window and hollered, "Norma, wait."

Hearing him just as she opened the front door of the establishment, she turned around and walked back. "What?"

"That car parked between those two buildings," he nodded. "Do you know who it belongs to?"

"No."

"Do you have any idea how long it's been there?"

"I'm not sure. Maybe a week or so. Why?"

"It looks similar to one we're interested in."

"Can I go now? Alex wouldn't appreciate me being out here too long."

"Sure. Thanks for your help."

He watched her go back in then got on the radio. After giving dispatcher the tag numbers, make and model, he got out and walked across the street to check it out.

Peering inside, he saw on the back seat a pile of clothes, including some belonging to a little girl. Fast food wrappers, empty whiskey bottles, and crushed beer cans were scattered on the front passenger side floorboard. The mobile trashcan testified to both an unplanned outing and Alex's perception of Francis' lifestyle.

Now almost certain it was her car, he called Martha and told her to secure another search warrant.

While waiting, his thoughts locked in on Francis. The kind of life she had, and the impact it might have on her daughter's future. He was about to turn his attention to the evidence he had stored in his mind when one of the department's vehicles approached.

After filling the deputy in on his suspicions, a locksmith was summoned to standby.

Several minutes later the word came back from dispatch. The vehicle was indeed registered to Francis D'Angelo. Right after that, Martha called him on his cell phone. The judge had signed the search warrant.

He and the others stood back as evidence processors, arriving shortly after the locksmith obtained access to the inside of the vehicle, swarmed over it like bees on a hive.

After photographing the interior from every angle possible, they carefully vacuumed it and the inside of the trunk.

The minute one of the technicians came within five feet of him, Cody nodded towards the vehicle. "Find anything?"

"We found a good set of prints."

"How about bloodstains?"

"Not that we can see. We're going to have to take it to the garage and hit it with luminal. In the meantime, here are all the documents out of the glove compartment."

"She paid cash," Cody said, looking over the bill of sales and registration papers. "Go ahead and put it with the other evidence."

Another technician approached him with a couple of plastic bags in his hand. "It doesn't matter whose car it is. We found what looks like pieces of brown thread in the back seat and several strands of blonde hair in the front. We just have to compare the former with Mr. Tibb's and the latter with the deceased. If they match, it will be one made in heaven. There's only one thing that doesn't match." The deputy nodded towards the tires.

"So what you're saying is the car wasn't near the mountain."

"That's right."

"There's the tow truck now," Cody said. "Tell him to hold off. I need to make a call."

"Okay."

He took out his cell phone and dialed the office. "Martha it's me. Is Mr. Cassini still at the hospital?"

"No, he's gone to make arrangements for his sister's burial."

"Get a hold of him and tell him to be in my office tomorrow morning at nine."

"Okay, but before you hang up, I have a message for you. I just received a call from the Drug Enforcement Agency. An agent by the name of Robert Albrecht wants you to give him a call. I have his number right here."

"Did he say what he wanted?"

"No, he didn't."

He thought perhaps the call might just be a follow up to the drug intervention program he had recently attended. But that quickly faded when he wrote the first three numbers down. 214. Dallas area code.

He hung up then dialed the number.

"Agent Albrecht here."

"This is Sheriff Johnson from the Pecos County Sheriff's Department returning your call."

"Hey, I hear you found the remains of a Mrs. Francis D'Angelo down there."

From the way he talked, Cody pegged him as yet another Easterner. "Tell me something, agent Albrecht. How'd you find out so soon? We haven't made an official announcement concerning her identification."

"Mr. Cassini called his wife last night."

"And she notified you?"

"She didn't have to."

Cody's eyes rolled up. *Wiretap? Now why would the DEA listen in on them this late in the game* "So, what can we do for you, agent Albrecht?"

The agent hesitated for a few seconds then said, "Sheriff, let me just fill you in on what's going on. Francis' husband, Tony, was an undercover informant feeding us information on a Mexican cartel that's been smuggling drugs to most of the major cities up and down the east coast.

"An informant? How'd you manage that?"

"It was a case of one thing leading to another, sheriff. He mounted a debt he couldn't pay off. And in order to get the loan sharks off his back, he started dealing drugs. When he was busted, we offered him pleas bargain in return for critical information on the whole network."

"It didn't work out, though, did it?"

"No. The fool decided to get rich quick and disappear. He and a friend busted into one of the cartel's drug distribution centers up in the Bronx. They stole quite a bit of money and drugs."

"Now that's something I didn't know. How much money are we talking about?"

"I'd rather not say just yet."

"I see. Well, I know what happened to Tony, but __"

"Yeah, I know too."

It wasn't the interruption that caught Cody by surprise. It was the noticeable anger in Robert's tone as the words spilled out. Cody thought it strange. He filed it in the back of his mind.

"What about his accomplice?" Cody continued, "Is he still on the loose?"

"I'm afraid not. He wound up in the East river with a bullet in the back of the head."

"Same fate as Tony, huh?"

"You could say that."

"So with both of them gone and no sign of the stolen items, you're thinking maybe his wife took off with them."

"Chances are she did. We were just hoping they wouldn't get to her before we had a chance to find out for sure."

"So you think *they* killed her?"

"I don't know. You tell me."

"Well, I haven't got the medical examiner's full report yet, but it appears she was beaten to death with a sharp object. Does that sound like their M.O. to you?"

"It all depends on the circumstances. No matter what method they use, though, they wouldn't have finished her off unless they got the money and the drugs, or at the very least learned where they can get their hands on it."

Cody couldn't think of a better time to jerk the line and reel him in. "Let me ask *you* a question."

"Go right ahead."

"Did Francis or her husband have anything to do with a Mexican with light brown hair and a slightly crooked nose?"

"Brown?"

From the sudden change in tone and the hesitation that followed, the color he mentioned didn't seem to go along with the rest of the description. Either Robert knew the Mexican, or knew enough about him to know his natural hair wasn't brown.

Although he was curious to find out what was really going on, he decided to wait and see what other information came with the rest of the conversation.

"Never mind. So tell me, why would the government care if an illegal drug operation gets ripped off?"

"The drugs, sheriff. It could be anywhere between a half to a million dollars worth. It's our job to find it before it hits the streets. Right now the only person left alive who can help us do that is in your hands."

For a brief moment, Cody's priority switched from finding a killer to protecting a potential witness.

"That's right. And since she's the only ace in our hand, I have every intention of making sure she's okay before anyone, including myself, can question her—and I'm not about to make her prey for a pack of wolves looking to save their hides, or keep from facing embarrassing questions either."

"Tell you what. I understand she's in the hospital right now recuperating from her ordeal. I'll give you a couple of days before I send one of my colleagues down there. In the meantime, you're obligated by law to fill me in on what you have?"

"I have no problem with that. Right now I have the remains of two females."

"Two?"

"Yes. We found those of a younger victim not far from where Mrs. D'Angelo was found."

"There's no connection, is there? I mean…is that possible?"

"It sounds like you know more about this case than we do. You tell me."

"I wish I could. All I can do is send my colleague down with what we have on Tony D'Angelo. You might find it useful."

"I'd be much obliged."

"No problem. Always glad to assist the local lawman. He'll also confirm what you've found so far and get copies of all the documents for us. Together we might be able to get you your answers."

"In that case let me ask *you* a question."

"Go right ahead."

"How long have you been working at the Dallas field office?"

"A couple of weeks now, why?"

"Nothing. Just curious, that's all."

As he got back into his vehicle a call came in from Jeremy. "I think you'd better come over to our subjects place," he said. "There's something you need to see."

"I'll be right there."

Then Reed's call came in on his cell phone.

"Yes."

"The doctor said she could be released soon, sheriff."

"Does Ms. Wheeler know that?"

"Yes, sir."

"You know what to do. I'm on my way to Hezekiah's place. Let me know if you run into any problems."

# 30

"The good news is that the bullet passed through without doing damage to the bones," the emergency room physician said, looking at the X-rays. "The bad news is that you have a sprained MCL (Medial Collateral Ligament). With a little bit of rest and therapy the knee should be as good as new. As for the shoulder wound, we'll clean it up to make sure it doesn't get infected and give you some antibiotic and pain medication."

Hezekiah wasn't paying any attention to what the doctor was telling him. His mind was on the news being aired on the wall-mounted television in the corner of the room. With wide-opened eyes, he watched as a picture of Olivia appeared on the screen.

He listened carefully and then grunted as the reporter announced her condition. But that response turned out to be nothing compared to what happened when the reporter stated Olivia was in that same hospital. His back arched, his biceps tightened, and his chest expanded. More ominous than that, he became oblivious to the pain in his leg and shoulder.

It didn't take long for the nurse tending him to interpret the threatening look in his eyes. She had seen that kind of look before at the hospital's mental illness ward. And she had a pretty good idea of what could be coming next.

"Doctor," she said, her eyes shifting from him to Hezekiah and then back.

Having been made aware of Hezekiah's past history of violence, It didn't take *him* long to get the message either. "Better get the deputy in here."

Before she could open the curtain, Hezekiah, whose legs they had failed to shackle, managed to slither a hand out of the cuff, ripping some of the skin off in the process. He flipped off the bed and then braced one foot against it. A metal snapping crack followed as he ripped off the side rail he was handcuffed to.

The deputy outside of the emergency room, hearing the commotion, ran into a situation he couldn't handle. Hezekiah, with a large metal tube now firmly in his hands, met him immediately. The deputy never saw what hit him. Another one rushed in only to come face to face with a solid hard fist.

Grunts, howls, and spit poured out of Hezekiah's grimacing mouth as he attacked with the fury of a cornered animal. He unleashed a barrage of powerful kicks and punches at humans and med trays alike, launching sutures, knives, and scissors through the air like miniature missiles.

Doctors and nurses cowered in the corner of the room, watching in horror as both deputies slammed against the walls and slithered down. Neither one had a chance to reach for their mace, let alone their weapons.

He yanked the key chain off the prone deputy's belt. Then after fumbling for a second, found the key that gave him freedom.

With resistance out of the way, he picked up a wooden chair by the partition that had been knocked down and slammed it against the wall until it splintered. With one of its legs in hand, he sped from the emergency room and through the doors leading to the main lobby, bowling over med carts and staff nurses on the way.

Several elderly female hospital volunteers, who had come out of the gift shop to see what was going on, screamed at the menacing eyes and animal like grunts getting closer and closer to them.

In the hallway, visitors and waiting patients scattered as the half naked, wild looking madman ran amuck.

He ran down the long corridor past the lab until he reached the Nurses' station. At the sight of him approaching from one of the three halls that projected from the outer wall of the semi-circular room like bicycle spokes, nurses and their aides ran to the back room for cover.

A security officer sprung to action as the code green announcement blared on speakers.

In the gift shop, Reed, who had just put the loose change from the soda machine into his pocket, looked up after hearing the volunteers screaming as they ran back inside.

Hezekiah, whom he knew was brought in for treatment, immediately came to mind. He dropped the cup and ran to room 27. He grabbed the doorknob. But before he could turn it, an ominous shadow caught his attention. He turned around only to see the growling, slobbering mouth of the man he inadvertently led right to where he wanted to go.

Caught by surprise, all he could do was reach for his mace. But like the others, his reaction was no match. The cringing thud of flesh and wood reverberated all the way to the nurse's station. Reed never knew what hit him. His head hit the door like a battering ram. The rest of his body blasted through it.

Hezekiah looked down and then stepped over the fallen deputy lying unconscious in the doorway. He now had complete access to his prey. As he approached her, his eyes squinted and his growling ceased.

Since she was tucked up to her neck in blankets, all he could see was the back of her head. Lying on top of the blanket was the wide-eyed teddy bear looking up to the ceiling.

He tipped his head from side to side as he stared at her before making his way around towards the other side of the bed to get a closer look at her face.

Hearing the code and the subsequent commotion, Susan put down her cup of coffee.

"I'd better go check on Olivia."

"Want me to go with you?"

"Right now you have other children to worry about, Peggy. Besides, this might not have anything to do with Olivia."

"You're right. I do need to get back to work."

"I'll get in touch with you later, if that's okay."

"Sure."

Susan saw her off then turned around and headed down the hall. Seeing the result of his rage when she passed by the emergency room entrance, she quickened her pace to Olivia's room.

At the sight of the deputy's feet sticking out into the hallway, she cupped her mouth and gasped. After the initial shock, she garnered up enough courage to walk over him and approach Hezekiah.

"Please don't hurt her," she begged, standing at the doorway.

He stopped, turned around and eyed Susan menacingly. He stiffened.

With trembling hands outstretched, she continued walking towards him. "Please don't hurt her."

Within a matter of seconds, the hospital's unarmed security personnel, completely out of breath, showed up at the entrance to the room. He grabbed the fallen deputy's ankles and slid him out into the hallway. Once he got him out of harm's way, he started to go in but thought better after he noticed the chair leg in Hezekiah's hand.

"Ma'am, step back and away," he said. "Don't do anything foolish. Don't go near him."

"She's a very sick little girl," she said, hoping to divert Hezekiah's attention.

Instead, he turned back around to Olivia. Hovering over the still sleeping child, he said what sounded to Susan like an apology for something he did.

"She can't hurt you," She said. "She doesn't even know you're here."

"Ma'am, please get back. Let me handle this."

"You're Hezekiah, aren't you?" she waved the security man away.

Hezekiah grunted again.

"Look, I don't know much about you but I would like to learn. Why don't you step outside so we can talk and get acquainted? I'm sure we can work something out."

She had no idea where the nerve suddenly came from, or for that matter, what to do with it. All she knew was that she had to do something, anything, before things got out of hand. She had already seen enough heartbreak and tragedies to last her a lifetime. She wanted no more.

# 31

"What d'ya have?"

"Come take a look." Jeremy turned around and led Cody thru the house until they reached the opened back door. There he stepped aside and pointed to the field out back.

"What is it?"

"I guess you could say a private landfill. We didn't pay much attention to it when we first got here. Too busy concentrating on finding Hezekiah,- I suppose. Anyway, take a look." He pointed to a large, black plastic trash bag. One of about thirty scattered on top of a mountain of trash. Its importance, however, was noticeable by the presence of two deputies hovering over it.

Squishing, cracking, and snapping filled the putrid smelling air as they trudged through fifteen yards of discarded waste to reach the top. Once there, he bent down and looked inside the bag held open by the deputies.

"Is this the way you found it?"

"Yes, sir," Jeremy said. "We didn't want to disturb it until you had a chance to see it."

Shoes, a ladies purse, and several pieces of wrinkled clothing were stuffed inside the bag.

Cody straightened up, stepped to the side, and then gave the deputy with the camera the okay to start taking pictures. After that was done, he snapped on the pair of latex gloves Jeremy gave him then reached in and carefully fished out the purse. "I want all of you to witness this."

"How about this here board?" One of the deputies said.

With everyone looking over his shoulder, and the camera flashing, he set the purse down on the four by eight, heavily damaged particle board and carefully opened it.

"It looks like dried blood on the outside, doesn't it?" Jeremy said, as he bent down next to him

"I'm afraid so."

"If you ask me, he intended to burn it along with the rest of the trash. He just didn't get around to it."

"By the looks of it, I think you're right." he looked back over his shoulder at the farmhouse. "Do you have that search warrant with you?"

"Yes, sir, I have it right here."

"Good! Let's just see what we have in here first."

Opening the purse was easy. Retrieving its content wasn't. Besides being jammed tight into the photo jackets, a sticky brown substance added to the difficulty of pulling out the driver's license, pictures, and cards.

Cody took the picture Vincent gave him out of his pocket and compared it to one he eventually managed to retrieve.

"Well, that and the clothing should prove he had something to do with Francis," Jeremy said.

"It looks that way." He went back into the purse and pulled out several crisp new twenty-dollar bills. "Go ahead and bag these then let's you and I go inside and check the contents of that other purse. The rest of you check some of those other bags."

Back inside, cups, cans, pots, and pans took flight with one swipe of Jeremy's arm across the rickety table. Cody retrieved the purse and turned it upside down over the table, spilling several photos, an old makeup applicator, a black tube of dried lipstick, and a plastic compact case, which he opened right away. He looked up with a grin on his face then showed the case to Jeremy. "Notice what's missing?"

"The mirror."

"You think maybe the one we found out there will fit?"

"It just might."

Cody closed the compact then put it back on the table. He picked up the expired driver's license and read it out loud. "Louisiana. Holly Nelson. Born, Oct 3, 1967."

"Pretty girl," Jeremy said, looking at one of the photos. "You think she's the one Earl almost stepped on?"

"Let's make sure she's not out there driving around with a new license before we jump to any conclusions. It says here she lived in New Orleans. Take down the number and check with their Office of Motor vehicles."

"Yes, sir." Jeremy's eye's wandered to one of the other photos spread out on the table. "Here she is leaning against a 97 Cougar."

"I'm more interested in the gentlemen by her side. Get it blown up then send a copy to the Louisiana authorities. Let's see if we can put a name to the face and a number to that license plate."

As he started out the front door, one of the deputies came in through the back door with a knife held gingerly by the point of the blade. "More blood."

Cody stopped and turned around. "That makes two of them. You know what to do with it. The rest of you keep looking around."

"We've already been through here with a fine tooth comb," Jeremy said. "What else are we suppose to be looking for?"

"What might be left of a half to a million dollars. Twenties, fifties, and hundreds, I believe."

Whistles filled the hot air as they eyed each other with confused looks.

"What were they, bank robbers?" a deputy asked.

"Francis may have been better off if she was."

"You're serious, aren't you?" Jeremy said, following him out the door and onto the porch.

"I'm afraid so."

"So tell me, what makes you think Hezekiah didn't bury it somewhere out there? Surely he would've known if she had that kind of money on her."

"Maybe he was smart enough to figure out it wasn't hers."

"Huh?"

"I'll explain later. Right now we need to focus on the lab results from the shovel and Hezekiah's clothing. If the blood from them and what we found here match, I'll turn the case over to the District Attorney's Office."

"What about this Holly Nelson? How does she fit in?"

He got to the bottom of the front porch then looked back and said, "She doesn't."

"Control to six zero one."

He reached into the truck and grabbed the mike. "Zero one here."

"You'd better get over to the hospital quick. Our number one person of interest is on the loose."

"I'm on my way." He looked up at Jeremy. "You come with me." Then he shouted to the others inside. "After you finish cataloging the evidence I want this place locked and sealed as a crime scene. One of you stays here till you're relieved. Make sure no one goes in without my permission."

# 32

His heart went to his stomach. His hands went immediately to the butt of his weapon.

"Ms. Wheeler. Please step aside. Move away slowly."

Recognizing Cody's voice, she glanced back over her shoulder and noticed the bandage under the brim of his hat. She had heard about what happened to him up on the mountain, but the situation in front of her kept her from thinking about it any further. She quickly turned back around to face the immediate threat.

Out in the hallway, Jeremy went down on one knee and checked Reed's condition. He motioned to one of the nurses cowering nearby. "Get him some help, will you?"

In the meanwhile, Susan waved Cody off. "She's okay. He's not going to hurt her. Isn't that right Mr. Hezekiah? You just came to visit her. You know who she is, don't you?"

Cody swallowed hard and his eyes widened at the sight of the chair leg in Hezekiah's right hand. He unsnapped the butt strap, took out his weapon and pointed it at Hezekiah's upper torso—praying he wouldn't have to use it.

"It's best you put that thing down, mister," he warned. "Put it down now. Ms. Wheeler, step away from him."

On his way there he called for backup, but that was before he even knew Susan was still there, let alone in harm's way. There was no time to wait. All he could do now, in spite of the emotions he had not felt in quite some time, was hope and pray they'd be able to subdue Hezekiah before the situation worsened.

When Jeremy entered with his weapon drawn, Cody nodded at him and said in a low voice, "I'll take this side. You take the other. If he makes the slightest move towards her with that chair leg, take him."

With his back against the wall, Jeremy slithered to a spot where he could get a clear view of Hezekiah.

Cody, in the meanwhile, worked his way to the other side of the room where he had to contend with Susan, who seemed to be purposely blocking his view of Hezekiah.

"Ms. Wheeler, please," he said again, "Let us take care of this. Just step to the side and back up."

"Hezekiah," Susan said, ignoring Cody's plea. "We're taking good care of her. I'm sure she'll want to see you when she gets well. Wouldn't you like that?"

*What is she thinking? Olivia's the only witness who could testify against him. If only she knew.* He had to get enough separation between her and Hezekiah.

"Listen to her," he said. "Don't do anything you might regret later. Besides, there's no way you're going to get out of here. Look," he flipped his head towards the window to the right of the headboard hoping for a chance to make a move on him. "The place is completely surrounded by now. Why don't you and I step outside and talk things over. I'm sure we can work something out."

The ruse didn't work. Instead, Hezekiah's eyes widened menacingly. His muscles tightened. And then he let out a loud, hoarse, menacing growl as he swung the wooden leg at Jeremy.

Jeremy ducked, distracting him long enough for Cody to lunge at Susan, sending both of them against the bed.

She crumbled to the floor under the weight of his body.

Hezekiah stepped back, spun around, and lunged.

Jeremy stepped aside and, using Hezekiah's own forward momentum, slammed him against the wall.

Cody got up, ran over, and grabbed Hezekiah's right arm. He slammed it against the wall several times until he released the chair leg.

Bodies got tangled as other deputies ran in and jumped into the fray. Once they got him down to the floor, they pinned him with a knee then forced his arms behind him.

"You okay?" Cody asked Jeremy, who was bent over trying to catch his breath.

"Yeah, I'm okay, but you'd better go check on her."

He rushed over to Susan who was lying on her stomach moaning.

"Can you sit up?" he asked, gently turning her over.

"I'm not so...sure I want to... I...I feel like I've been run over by a truck... Did you have to do that?"

"I'm sorry. He didn't leave me much choice. Take a couple of deep breaths."

"Why don't you take her down to the emergency room and let them check her?" a nurse suggested.

"No, that's okay. I...I'll be fine." She gazed into his eyes. "Just help me up."

Her eyes didn't leave his as he slipped one arm under her knees and the other under her back. Before long, a feather floated through her mind as he lifted her up then gently lowered her into the chair. During the whole time aloft she was speechless.

"Are you sure you're alright?"

"Huh? Yes...I...I'm sure," she said, with a shallow breath. "You'd better go take care of him." She pointed to Hezekiah who was now handcuffed and shackled.

"Maybe I'd better," he said. "I'll be right back."

He walked over and, after picking up his hat, came face to face with the man held firmly by two deputies. "Are you ready to settle down now?"

Hezekiah nodded without saying a word.

"Good." He turned to Jeremy. "Take him back to the ER and have them re-bandage that shoulder. When they're through, book him on attempted escape, resisting arrest, and assault with a deadly weapon."

"Maybe now we can print him and find out who he really is," Jeremy said.

"You bet."

"What about Ms. Wheeler?"

"On your way out see if you can get one of those nurses to come in and check on her. I've got some unfinished business to take care of."

174

Once he knew the situation was under control, his thoughts turned to someone else of interest. He hurried out to his vehicle and called Billy.

"I want you to go over to the Comanche Motel and check on a Mexican who occupied a room there about a week or so ago," he said. "He has dark hair, a square chin, and a crooked nose. I understand he had some kind of a problem with his room. Also find out if he's had any visitors, or if they can tell us anything about his movements. Get back with me as soon as you can."

"Ten four."

Back in Olivia's room, Susan was pondering what she had just experienced when she noticed something strange. She looked curiously at the nurses and interns crowding the hallway.

Even after everything had settled down, not one of them bothered to go in and check on Olivia. Stranger yet, how could she have slept through such a knockout, drag out fight, which included the violent jarring of her bed.

In spite of the aches wracking every bone in her body, she got up out of the chair and hobbled over to Olivia. Near the bed, she noticed a slight difference in the color of Olivia's hair. She pulled the blanket down. She gasped. "Oh my God."

Cody walked back into the room just as her hands went up to her mouth.

# 33

The Comanche Motel and Hostel on East Dickinson was noted more for the southern décor painted on its exterior walls than its modest interior accommodations. Still, it was a place where someone could spend the night at a decent price. And with a few of its twenty five rooms furnished with several bunk beds, the place could house a family of ten, if not more, for as long as they'd like.

"Let's see," the manager said, putting on his glasses. "Here it is. Mr. Julio Calderon, room 18. He's the only one I recall staying here recently who fits that description."

"Including the crooked nose?"

"Yes, sir. He probably got it in the ring."

"Ring?"

"Boxing ring. He must've been a boxer at one time."

"What makes you say that?"

"Well, besides the nose there's the fists. He bragged about them, saying they were used in his business back when he was a little younger."

"How long did he stay?" Billy asked, stretching his neck over the counter to get a glimpse of the old computer screen.

"A couple of weeks. He came in on a Monday and checked out early this morning."

"Do you still have the make and tag number of his vehicle?"

"Sure." His trembling fingers danced carefully across the keyboard. "Here it is, a black Toyota—an Avis rental."

"Number?"

"6Y8M3K."

176

"Did he have any visitors that you know of while he was here?"

"Only one time that I—hey, wait a minute. Someone else came in here asking the same questions."

Billy's eyes narrowed as they shifted from his note pad to the clerk. "When?"

"Yesterday afternoon."

"Male or female?"

"Male."

"Can you describe him?"

He rolled his eyes up then said, "He was a tall fella...around six two or three… shoulder length blonde hair...a slightly tanned face. He had an official air about him?"

"Whatd'ya mean?"

"You know. Black suit, black tie, dark sunglasses. He looked like one of them government type. As a matter of fact, he came out of a black van with dark windows." He gestured over his shoulder at the wall-mounted television in the lobby. "Like the kind you see in them spy movies. That's right. Like that."

Billy had to think about that for a moment before asking, "I'd like to take a look at Mr. Calderon's room if I can."

"Sure," he said, going back to the computer. "Providing there's no one in there right now. Let's see. Nope. This must be your lucky day. The room's empty. Let me just go to the back and get the desk clerk out here. It'll only take a minute."

After he came back out with the clerk, he grabbed the key to the room.

Billy followed close behind as they left the office and headed towards it. At the door to the room, he stood behind the stooped over senior, whose trembling hand guided the key into the lock after several failed attempts.

"Here we go." He glanced over his shoulder then stepped aside. "Sorry about that. They say it's part of the Golden Years."

Inside were a couple of single beds. One looked like it had not been slept in, the others unmade.

"Which one was his?"

"The one over by the corner."

Billy scanned the room then went into the small bathroom. Unable to find anything there that might've been left behind, he came out and walked over to the bed.

"That his nightstand?"

"Yep!"

He sat on the edge of the bed and opened the drawers of the homebuilt nightstand. The top one was empty. The bottom one contained the usual Gideon Bible. Immediately, his thoughts went to Hezekiah. He picked it up and, for a fleeting moment, thought about opening it.

"They take the towels, soap, and pencil, but leave that behind. I'll never figure that one out," the manager said.

"I know what you mean." As he started getting up, something on the floor, wedged between the leg of the nightstand and the wall, caught his eye. He took out his handkerchief, bent down and picked it up. After laying it on top of the nightstand, he looked up at the manager. "Do you put these in every room also?" He pointed to the familiar looking matchbook.

"No. A lot of our guests go there and bring back more than just those matches."

"I'm going to have this room dusted for prints. I want you to lock it up until we get the lab boys down here to go over it."

"For how long?"

"It shouldn't take them too long—an hour and a half at the most. In the meantime give us a call if Mr. Calderon decides to come back for another visit."

"Yes, sir. I sure will."

The manager walked out the door. Billy, not far behind, got on the radio and requested what he needed.

# 34

Cody hurried over and put his hands on Susan's shoulder. "It's okay," he said. "We had to do that. Believe me. She's okay."

"What's going on here?" After ripping herself away from his grip, she reached over the bedrail and picked up the Styrofoam female head with the wig pinned on it. "What's the meaning of this?"

"We borrowed it from the cancer resource center. You see___"

"See what, mister. That I put my life on the line and she wasn't even here. Have you any idea what you've put me through? Are you crazy? What's wrong with you?" She glanced up at his bandaged head. "Did that bullet knock the senses out of that brain of yours?"

He didn't see the fumes.

He didn't have to.

He felt the searing heat.

"Look, I'm sorry. I sort of figured the news broadcast on her whereabouts might just attract her mother's killer. I didn't want to take any chances."

"What are you talking about?" her body stiffened as she got louder. "You already had him."

"To be honest with you, Hezekiah was the last person I'd expected would come here. And I sure as heck didn't expect *you* to be here."

"Well, Mr. big man, he came. I came. Is there anyone else you're not expecting so I can prepare myself?"

"I really am sorry." He took his hat off and held it against his chest as if that would protect him from the wrath. "I don't know what else to say."

With glaring eyes and hands on hip, she asked, "Where is she? What have you done with her?"

"She's okay. I had her moved to another room."

"Where?—if you don't mind my asking."

"She's over on the next hall. Room 39."

"Get out of my way."

Although he instinctively dropped his hat to the floor at the sight of the Styrofoam head being thrust towards his chest, he didn't budge. He felt the strength of a woman in charge, one who knew what she wanted and how to get it. With the Styrofoam head in his hands and his head tilted, he eyed her as she walked around him and raced towards the door.

Seeing the fire in her eyes the minute she opened the door, Jeremy quickly sidestepped out of her path, and watched her storm out. "Wow! What was that?"

"That, Deputy Sands, was a true Texas tornado." With a sly grin, he rolled his eyes up. "Just don't get in her way."

"Thanks for the warning." he bent down and picked up Cody's hat. "I almost did. Here. What the_____?"

"Now don't you go off on me," he said, following Jeremy's gaze towards the Styrofoam head he was cradling. "She's over in the next hall. I gave Deputy Reed orders to have her moved to another room just in case something like this would happen."

"And here I thought you were going back to apologize to the lady."

"I thought getting this done was more important at the time."

"I see. Olivia's okay then?"

"Sure," he said. "You're welcome to go check on her. Just don't stir things up anymore than they already are."

"Here. You'd better put this back on before you wind with more collateral damage."

"Thanks." Cody stuffed the Styrofoam head under his armpit and grabbed the hat. "I'm not sure it can take any more."

The sight of the Styrofoam head under the armpit stopped Billy cold just as *he* crossed the threshold. He gazed at it for a second then tucked his chin in as his eyes met Cody's. "I'm not even gonna ask."

"Then don't," Cody said. "What d'ya you have?"

"Well, for starters, Ms. Holly Nelson was a disturbed young lady."

"Disturbed?"

"Yes. She served time for possession of cocaine, shop lifting, and prostitution. The address on the driver's license belongs to her mother who was divorced at the time she lived there. According to her, Holly came home late one night talking about going out to California with her boyfriend who, by the way, was a well known drug dealer. The next morning Holly got up and took off with him. She had several hundred dollars in cash on her."

"That's interesting."

"I'll tell you what was even more interesting. That was her Cougar in the photo."

"Something else to look for," Cody said."

"That's right. Anyway, the last time she was heard from was about three years ago. She called a couple of times from somewhere in Fort Stockton. On her first call, she mentioned something about the boyfriend dumping her and taking off with some woman he'd met at a bar over in Midland."

"Did she say anything about going back home?"

"No, sir. On the second one, she said something about finding someone here who wanted to take care of her."

"Or her money. There wasn't any cash in her purse. Did her mother ever make out a missing person report?"

"Yes. After the phone calls stopped. Holly never gave her mother a number or a way to get in touch with her so she called the police. Detectives there notified the city force down here in order to appease her mother. With the background she had they probably assumed she just wanted to get away from the area."

"Have you talked to the city boys?"

"I just got off the phone. They're going to check their files."

"There are still some things that don't make sense, though," Cody said

"Like what?"

"The way I see it, if Hezekiah was responsible for her death, he wouldn't have left her purse on the mantle, especially with all that information inside. I've been thinking all along there's more to this man than meets the eye."

"Maybe so but those purses didn't just get up and walk into his place," Earl said as he entered the room. "Someone had to put them there. And then there's the shovel. The blood on it came from Olivia's mother."

"Do we know that for a fact?"

"We do now." He handed Cody the lab report.

"Any prints?"

"Yes, sir. Probably Hezekiah's."

"I don't know about that. Why wouldn't he bother to use gloves? Or at least wipe the thing clean. He may be acting irrational, but I have a gut feeling he's not that careless or stupid."

"If you ask me," Billy said. "None of it adds up."

"They don't. Right now, though, I'd better get down to that room and make sure Ms. Wheeler's alright."

"Don't you think it would be safer to wait awhile," Jeremy suggested. "Like maybe two or three days."

"No!"

"How about some backup, then?" Billy asked.

"Funny. Just make sure whoever's guarding this room doesn't let anyone else in besides her, Mr. Cassini, or Mrs. Sands."


Down the hall, Cody took a deep breath, let it out, and then opened the door. Inside, Susan, leaning over the bedrail, was brushing Olivia's hair with her long delicate fingers as she whispered into her ear.

The same scene played out in his mind but with different characters, and in a different place and time. Katelyn wrapping strands of Tammie's hair around her fingers while whispering good night and I love you into her ears. And just as he stood by the door back then, he savored the opportunity to stand there and do the same again.

"Can I come in?"

Not that he was wearing one, but the gaze shot his way wasn't searing enough to burn a hole through a bulletproof vest.

He saw it as an opportunity to further calm the woman he'd just recently met and managed to set off. He put on his best, lowering his head, and fumbling with the brim of his hat as he held it down by his chest for the second time that day. He waited for her response before making another move.

"Sure, why not. You seem to have the run of the place anyway."

"Now that's not fair. I couldn't tell you she was out of harm's way without compromising the plan. Besides, like I said before, we weren't expecting her to have any concerned visitors this afternoon. If I'd of known you were coming, I would've offered to take you out to dinner, or done whatever I could to keep you away from here."

"Tell me something? What made you think he wouldn't be the one to come here after her?"

"Well, for one thing, he was already in custody. For another, he's probably the only one who knew, besides us, that she couldn't talk. Why would he take a chance at even coming close to her?"

"Wrong," said the nurse standing in the doorway.

"What?" He looked back over his shoulder.

"There's someone else who knows she can't talk."

"Who?"

"The man who just called the nurse's station."

"What'd he say?"

"He wanted information on little Mudo's condition and room number."

Susan's brow furrowed. "Mudo?"

"That means mute in Spanish," he said. "I'm afraid she's right. Whoever it is knows she can't tell us anything. Now you have to wonder how he found out about her condition and why he's interested in her whereabouts."

"It's not easy keeping secrets these days," Susan said. "Especially with the number of people involved with her case."

"How true." He turned back to the nurse. "He didn't give a name, did he?"

"No, sir."

"I didn't think so."

"But I can tell you where he called from."

"Where?"

"An airport. The nurse who took the call said she could hear someone announcing flight information and people talking in the background. She even heard the whining of jet engines."

"Crooked nose," he said. *Probably has a one-way ticket to Mexico.*

"Who?" Susan asked.

"A person of interest. Will you excuse me a minute? I need to make a phone call."

"Of course," she said, reaching into her purse. "While you're doing that, I'll go to the ladies room and repair some of the damage you caused."

He dialed the Midland Odessa Airport Security office number on his contact list. After giving them a description, they assured him if it wasn't too late, they would stop him from boarding an aircraft.

Susan came out of the restroom just as he hung up. His knees weakened and his heart fluttered as his eyes fell on her long, well formed legs. He decided to take Billy's advice now that the situation had stabilized and the adrenalin had not worn off completely. "There's not much we can do here right now," he said. "She's sound asleep and Hezekiah's on his way to the jailhouse. Things should be a lot quieter."

"Are you sure?"

"Trust me." He assured her with a smile then glanced at his watch. "Look, I know of a Mexican restaurant in town that has the best meals this side of Dallas. How about letting me make this up to you? "

It was the first time since they had met that she noticed the telltale sign on his ring finger. Even so, there was still a slight hesitation. "I...I don't know."

"I'm sorry," he apologized. "Maybe I'm getting a little too hasty and _____ "

"Oh, no. It's not that. It's just that so much has happened in such a short time. I need a little time to settle down. As you know, I have a lot to take care of now."

"I understand," he said. "Why don't you just give me a call when you're ready? I promise I won't tackle you."

She smiled.

"Can I take that as a yes?"

"You may."

A sigh of relief was almost followed by an outburst of joy. Almost being the key word at the time. He turned his attention quickly to the deputy at the door. "Keep your eyes open."

"So," she said, nearing the main entrance to the hospital. "If they've taken him away, what does he have to keep his eyes open for? I thought you said things would be quieter now?"

"A little precaution, that's all."

"That's his trademark, ma'am," the officer added as he came through the automatic doors.

"Well, now. What brings you here?"

"First things first, Cody," he said, turning his attention to Susan.

"Oh, yes, sorry. Ms. Wheeler, this here's Sergeant, Stephen Boyd of the Fort Stockton Police Department."

"Ms. Wheeler," Stephen said, taking off his hat. "Pleasure meeting you."

"She's with CPS."

"She is? So how is it we haven't met yet, Ms. Wheeler? Has this ole boy been hiding you somewhere?"

"You should have received a letter of introduction by now, Sergeant, Boyd. I sent them to all the law enforcement agencies in the area over a week ago."

"I probably have," he said. "I'm just sorry I haven't gotten around to opening it yet."

"You still haven't answered my question, Stephen."

"Didn't I," he said, his eyes unable to move away from Susan. "So, how long are you going to be with us, Ms. Wheeler?"

"I'm not sure just yet," she said, glaring at Cody. "It all depends on how much more excitement I can handle."

"Which reminds me," Cody interrupted, glancing at his watch. "You'll have to excuse us, Stephen. She has to get home as soon as possible."

"I'm sure she does. Anyway, to answer your question, I'm here visiting an old friend of yours."

"Who?"

"A Mr. Jack Bauer."

"He's not exactly who I'd call an old friend. What's he doing in here?"

185

"He's in room 21." He nodded towards the corridor closest to the nurse's station "You just passed by there. Last night one of our units happened to drive behind a local bar just as three young Mexicans were using him as a Piñata."

"What? Again?"

Susan gasped. "Is he going to be alright?"

"He might've been better off if they were blindfolded, Ma'am. As it is, he'll just be nursing some bumps, broken ribs, and a concussion for a while, that's all."

"Did you catch any of the party goers?" Cody asked.

"Yeah, we got one. A young fellow by the name of Flaco. He's downtown right now. Won't talk, though. Claims he 'no speaky de English,' if you can believe that. I've got one of our bilinguals working on him right now."

"I don't get it," Cody said, rubbing the back of his neck. "All of a sudden our farmer's taking a shine to mixing it up with Mexicans."

"Well, as funny as it might sound, it appeared these guys were trying to rob Mr. Bauer."

"You're kidding." Cody frowned. "Does he look like someone with lots of money to you?"

"Not exactly. I'm going to have him taken to the station for interrogation after the doctors give him a clean bill of health. A different environment might just loosen up the tongue a little."

"You wouldn't happen to have anything on one that's about five foot ten inches with a unique crooked nose, would you?"

"Not to my knowledge, why?"

"He, Mr. Bauer, and the deceased we found up on the mountain were seen together at the Angels Dance Club. I'd sure like to know what their little get together was all about, or at least, what they had in common. What about the other two? Have they been identified?"

"All we know is that they're members of a local street gang. We have the gang unit on the hunt right now."

"Let us know as soon as you get a description. I may have someone who might help verify what you have."

"Be glad to. Anything to get them off the streets."

"Mind if I pay Mr. Bauer a visit?" Cody asked, recalling Jack's visit out on the highway, and the description given to him by Norma.

"Not at all. I'll let the officer in his room know you're coming. Good seeing you again, Cody."

"Likewise." Cody grinned then fired the parting salvo. "Give my regards to the wife and kids."

"Thanks, I will." After putting his hat back on, he tipped it forward. "Like I said, ma'am, pleasure."

"Is that visit going to be business or personal," Susan asked as they watched the sergeant walk down the hallway towards the rooms.

"Business. He may have been one of the last persons to see Francis alive."

"Really?"

"Yes Ma'am."

Hearing the conversation as he caught up to them, Billy asked, "What about Ms. Nelson? What's her connection to Francis?"

"At first I thought there wasn't any. Now I'm thinking it might just be the same perpetrator?"

"That last one doesn't fit. Francis was apparently hacked with the shovel. According to Clinton, Holly may have been bludgeoned with a blunt instrument." Billy thought for a minute. "Reckon who ever killed the Nelson girl changed his M.O.?"

"The Anthropologist's report will shed some light on that. In the meantime, we'll let the cold case unit coordinate their investigation with the New Orleans detectives. We just have to make sure they get everything we found so far."

# 35

"Subject just entered the terminal." Robert's voice was low, subdued. His countenance made devilish by the red dome light inside the customized surveillance van.

He adjusted his headset, and then turned up the volume on the communication control panel, making sure he could clearly hear the DEA agents inside the busy terminal.

Having arrived at the airport, Carlos proceeded to the Avis rental desk, turned in the Toyota, and then took the shuttle over to the main terminal—all the while unaware he was followed from the minute he left the motel.

After being dropped off in front of the terminal, agent, Frank Peterson, one of several who had been assigned to Robert's unit, followed Carlos through the main entrance. "I have him in sight," he said into his lapel microphone "Get someone else over here in case I have to pass him on."

"Dean's on his way," Robert said.

The back door to the van flew open and Agent Dean McDaniel stepped out. He donned his dark sunglasses and then proceeded to the main entrance. Unlike his partner, who was dressed in a gray suit, white shirt, and blue tie, McDaniel wore a red polo shirt, jeans, and a Texas Ranger baseball cap. To enhance the casual look even further, he carried a small gym bag.

Once inside the terminal, he spotted the subject walking past Frank. "Got em. He's on his cell phone." He pulled the visor of the baseball cap down over his eyes then blended in with the waiting passengers after grabbing a newspaper from an empty seat and sitting down.

"Subject's at the Airline counter now," Frank said, stopping in front of a glass enclosed, advertising kiosk. He straightened his tie while keeping a close eye on the reflection of the subject behind him. "Should we make a move?"

"Hold on a minute," Robert said. He reached into his shirt pocket and took out his cell phone. "We have him at the airport getting ready to go thru security. Should we pick him up?" A frown came over his face, as he listened carefully then glanced at the agent sitting next to him. "Are you sure? Okay...if that's what they want." *Damn it.* He closed the phone and then readjusted the headset. "No, do not apprehend. I repeat, under no circumstances apprehend."

Thinking he was hearing wrong, Dean inconspicuously adjusted his earpiece. "Say again."

"I said, do not apprehend."   Robert took off his headset and gave the radio operator a blank stare.

"What's going on?" the operator asked.

"They're expecting him at JFK international," Robert said. "There's another unit waiting to pick him up there."

"How'd that happen?"

*Somehow he must've cut some kind of a deal.* "We're to make sure he got on the plane before we break it off. That's all I know."

Dean, with his eyes just above the edge of the newspaper, glared at Frank and then shrugged.

Frank returned the gesture as he passed by just a few feet away.

"Here's your boarding pass, Mr. Calderon," the airline agent said, handing over the packet that was awaiting his arrival. "Your plane leaves in forty five minutes. Enjoy your flight."

"Thank you."

It wasn't so much the discovery of Francis' body that sealed Carlos' fate. It was that Olivia was in the hands of the authorities. A jury of his own peers rendered the death sentence. Worst yet, in a court where the judge and the executioner are one and the same, and where plea-bargaining, bail, and mercy were non-existent. Neither was escape.

Carlos, though, had been a fighter from the time he was old enough to run around the streets of Presidio. He wasn't about to be the target of a hungry assassin. His only chance was to turn states evidence, hide in the core of the big apple, and pray that none of its eight million plus cave dwellers would take the notion to spit him out to the wolf who would soon take his place in the organization.

His eyes darted to and fro as he stood in line at the checkpoint. Before long, tiny drops of apprehension appeared on his forehead. Standing still was almost impossible. He glanced at his *Rolex*. Whatever years remained of his natural life were just a few feet away. Any delay, he knew, would probably result in a premature journey into the abyss. He gave a big sigh of relief as he placed his overnight bag on the conveyor. Then a member of the Transportation Security Agency walked up and tapped him on the shoulder.

"Sir, would you come with us, please," the security officer said as he stood face to face with him.

Another security officer picked up the small suitcase and grabbed Carlos' arm.

"What's the matter?" he asked, trying to pull his arms out of the grips of the officer.

"We just want to ask a few questions, that's all. There seems to be some discrepancy with the information on your ticket and we need to straighten it out. Just relax."

"Okay, okay," Carlos said. "Take it easy, man. I'm an American citizen you know. I have rights, you know."

"Hey! Something's wrong," Dean said, sliding his baseball cap back.

"What? What's going on?" Robert pressed the headphones tighter against his ears. "Somebody talk to me. What's going on out there?"

"They're taking him away."

"Who's taking him away?" Robert snapped his finger at the agent in the van, motioning for him to pickup a headset.

Frank pulled on the collar of his white shirt. "Two airport security officers just hauled our subject off." He glanced at Dean, and then turned around to face the kiosk.

"Sit tight while I find out what's going on here," Robert ordered, removing his headset. He grabbed the cell phone again and called DEA headquarters.

"They just took him inside the airport security office," Frank said, watching them through the glass of the Kiosk."

Robert, having passed the information on to Arlington,

closed the cell phone. "Stay with him until we find out what's going on. The Eagle is checking it out right now."

"The Eagle better flap his wings a little faster," Dean suggested, pulling his visor back down. "It looks like we're not the only ones interested in this guy."

"What are you talking about now?" Robert said, shaking the van as he bolted out of his chair.

"Two sheriff's deputies just went inside the airport security office."

"Okay...okay." Robert ran fingers through his hair. "Headquarters doesn't know yet what's going on. There getting in touch with the law down here. We're to stay with the subject all the way."

"They're coming out now." Frank pulled out a handkerchief from the lapel pocket of his suit and covered his nose as if he was blowing it.

"Okay, here we go," Dean said, pushing his cap down further. "It looks like our deputies are taking him in. I see a couple of black and whites out in front of the terminal."

"What the hell's going on," the agent said, removing his headset and setting it in front of the radio

Robert's jaw tightened. "It's that sheriff, Johnson," he said. With one hand on his hip and the other cradling his forehead, he paced back and forth a couple of times in the back of the van.

"Johnson?" the agent asked. "What does *he* know about Carlos?"

"I don't know," Robert replied, thinking back to the phone conversation earlier. "He mentioned something about a Mexican with a crooked nose. I told him I didn't know anyone fitting that description. Apparently he did."

"You don't suppose____."

"No," Robert said. "It has something to do with Francis D'Angelo. What that is, I don't know. I don't think he has a clue on what's really going down, though. Get those guys back in here. Let's see where they take him."

# 36

Two days went by since his bid for a dinner date. Part of the days was spent reviewing the evidence gathered, visiting Olivia, who was still in the hospital receiving therapy, and checking out several tips that had been phoned in to headquarters. None of which amounted to anything. What was left was spent trying to catch up on the paper work that had backed up during his stay in El Paso.

At home he spent time rearranging some of the furniture in his bedroom, and putting the photos of Katelyn, that were displayed on his fireplace, into their family album.

In the meantime, Susan spent the same two days putting together a new portfolio for Olivia, combining what she had learned from the main office in New York and what had happened the past few days. In between, she and her staff searched the local files for and visited several suitable candidates for the temporary care of Olivia. She also submitted the necessary vouchers to take care of Olivia's expenses.

As busy as they were, however, their minds eye occasionally played reruns of their recent encounters and emotions, each wondering what the future had in store.

Susan couldn't quite understand why Cody, a good looking man with manners, consideration, and kindness, was not wearing a wedding ring. The last thing she wanted, though, was to find out through others. She would do it in her own way, and at the right time.

As for Cody, the right time came with the one call he was anxiously waiting for.

After sprucing up in a tan dress slack and a western style, brown shirt, he picked Susan up at her apartment and drove her to the restaurant he had mentioned. The ride there was spent mostly in silence and in thought. But once they had entered, thoughts turned to words. The first few were about the murals, the colorful Mexican sombreros on the walls, the Piñatas hanging from the ceiling, and the Spanish serenades occupying the airwaves.

"*Senor, Johnson, Mucho tiempo no se ver. Como esta?*"

"I know," Cody said. "It has been a long time, Consuela, but I'm doing well, thank you."

"*y como esta la Senora?*"

"I believe she's doing well also" He gave Susan raised eyebrows. "At least I hope she is."

"*Hablar Espano?*"

"She's asking if you speak Spanish."

"Yes. I know." Susan smiled as she looked up at her. "I picked up a little bit working with the Puerto Ricans up in New York. Not enough to carry on a long conversation, I'm afraid."

"I'm sorry, Miss?" Consuela said.

"Susan Wheeler. And there's no need to apologize."

"You are dining weeth a very gude man, Ms. Wheeler. Welcome to our restaurant. I go now and make sure every thing okay in kitchen. Hope you enjoyed."

"Thank you. I did."

"Did you really?" Cody asked.

"Yes. It was surprisingly good. But then again, I've always heard you can get some of the best foods in little places like this."

The *Mi Casita Mexican* restaurant just happened to be one of those places. Though small in size, it was big on serving the best meals around. He was just glad he recommended the sample platter after learning she didn't care that much for greasy sauce.

The *Chile Relleno* or *Asado Puerco* he ordered for himself might have sent her back east on the first available flight. Needless to say, the last thing he wanted was to lose her over stuffed Chile or roasted pork, especially after seeing the way she was dressed when he picked her up.

193

She wore a blouse cut low enough to expose part of what had perfectly filled her workplace attire, and a summer skirt just high enough to reveal the strength of her smooth thighs.

"Is everything okay, Senora?" asked the waitress, the spout of her pitcher aimed perfectly at Susan's empty glass. "Would you like more tea?"

"Yes, please."

"And you, Senor?"

"No, thanks," he said. "I reckon this'll hold me for a while."

With her eyes locked on his, Susan thanked the petite waitress, wrapped her long fingers around the tall glass, and then seized on the one opportunity to satisfy a nagging curiosity.

"By the way Consuela acted, you and your family must come here quite often."

He lapsed into a momentary silence before the words trickled out. "They're no longer with me. My wife and daughter died in an automobile accident."

It was not what she had expected. The smile on her face took a turn downward. Her eyes rolled upwards as she took a deep breath then let it out. "I'm sorry. That wasn't very nice of me. Please forgive me."

"No, that's okay. You had no way of knowing. Besides, it happened a long time ago. They're both resting in peace now."

For the second time since they met, she reached over and put a hand over his. "Are you?"

"I think so. My job and my friends have helped me some."

If he were, would he fight the overwhelming urge to turn his hand over, to feel the warmth on his palm, and to lock fingers? Would he still refuse to let go of the past and live his life in the present? His slightly tanned face flushed as he lifted the glass with his free hand and took a sip. "What about you?" he asked, staring at her left hand.

She pulled it back slowly. "I lost him on 911."

A slight flutter filled his chest as his mind suddenly raced. There in front of him sat the one person he could reach out to, someone who has more than likely experienced the same emotions and the same emptiness. The encounter sessions recommended by the department's grief counselor was not his cup of tea. Could this be? Could this also be the time Billy was talking about? "Now it's my turn to apologize," he blurted out, avoiding eye contact once again.

"That's okay," she assured him. "I've been given the best gift of all by my friends back east."

"And what was that?"

"The gift of healing."

He rubbed the back of his neck. As he stared into her eyes, he saw the wrapping, the ribbon, and the bow. *His* gift was sitting just a few feet across from him, and all he had to do was reach out and unwrap it. His eyes rolled up as he asked for strength to continue without falling apart. "Tell me something, Ms. Wheeler___"

"I would think after that uplifting experience at the hospital you would know me well enough to call me by my first name now."

"Okay," he said, clearing his throat. "Susan. What's going to happen to Olivia? I mean, where does she go from here?"

"I'm afraid since we can't find any one in her extended family willing to step up to the plate, she'll be placed under the unable to complete category. There won't be any reason to initiate an investigation into the possibility of past abuses either since both her parents are deceased."

"And?"

"And as far as where she'll go, I've managed to find a couple here in Fort Stockton who's had some experience dealing with handicapped children for the department. They've agreed to take her in temporarily until we can process her into a permanent home."

"I've heard that in a case like this, finding one could take a long time." He wiped his lips with his napkin.

"The system does have its drawbacks, and I'm afraid this case is going to be entangled in one of them. All we can do is give it our full attention and hope for the best."

Not wanting to spoil the rest of the evening, he thought it best to change to a different subject, one he knew little about, but thought to be crucial to the case.

"How much do you know about this Mutism business?"

"What little I do know comes from what I've read, why?"

"I hate to sound ignorant, but I really don't know a thing about it. I'm willing to learn whatever I can, though."

With the stroke of a key, he could have easily found all the information he wanted on the Internet, but, he'd rather listen to the mellow voice, than goggle a static computer monitor in his bleak home office.

"For one thing," she said, "Selective Mutism, means just that, selective. He or she is different from someone who is mute because of physical or psychological reasons. Selectivity may have been caused by a traumatic experience. For example, I read somewhere about a child who became mute after witnessing his father murder his mother."

"So there's a possibility we have a similar situation here."

"The doctor seems to think so. Even if he didn't, we couldn't rule it out. In any case, we really need to place her in a stable environment, one that may bring her out of it."

He wondered if perhaps he should mention Peggy's candidacy. Although the couple were fairly new to the area, he made it a point to learn as much about their past as he could. And from that he developed a picture of honesty, integrity, and security. As far as he was concerned, they had all the qualifications needed and then some. The opening was now there. He had to at least plant the idea into her mind.

"That deputy I introduced you to at the hospital, he and his wife___"

"Peggy?"

"You know her?"

"Not really, I___"

"Would you care for some *Sopapilla* now?" the waitress asked.

Cody smiled. "I don't think I can handle honey on pastry after what we had. How about you?"

"No thanks, I won't be able to sleep if I take another bite."

"Can I take these away?"

"Sure." Cody said, taking out his billfold. "Go ahead and bring the bill."

"*Si Senor.* I be right back."

"Now, you were saying."

"I met Peggy at the hospital when she stopped by to see Olivia. She seems like a very nice person."

"So whatd'ya you think? Is it possible?"

With all that's been going on, she hadn't really given much thought to the permanent solution. That usually came after a quick temporary one could be put in place. His sincere concern, now added to hers, however, just stamped an ASAP on the situation.

"Well, that all depends," she said. "As you know, a full background check has to be made, a certain level of income has to be met, and parenting skills checked out. Then there's the legal aspect to consider. It's not as easy as you might think."

"Here you are, *Senor.*"

"Thanks." He opened the leather binder, glanced at the bill, and then pulled out a couple of twenties and a ten. He slid them in the binder. "It's just a suggestion, Susan."

This time the name spilled out easily, as if he had known her all his life. His heart fluttered ever so slightly, afraid perhaps anything stronger might be detected. "I just thought maybe since they were young and don't have children of their own, they might be good candidates."

"If it makes you feel better, their concern for the child didn't go unnoticed. Peggy comes across as a very caring person, one with a deluge of love waiting to drown a child." She smiled. "It's very noble of you to think about them."

"Thanks. I just think Olivia needs all the love and attention she can get right now."

Suddenly, she too felt a flush as she looked at the innocent but stern looking face. "Okay, now, what else were we talking about?"

"May I take this now?"

As much as he hated to, he took his eyes off Susan. "Sure, and keep the change."

"Thank you."

"Listen, Susan, I have_____"

"Don't you think you'd better answer that?" she said, pointing to the lapel pocket that appeared to be vibrating.

It wasn't his heart after all.

"I'm sorry," he said. "Pardon me?"

"That's okay. I need to freshen up a bit anyway."

She stood up.

He stood up.

As she walked towards the ladies room, he sat back down, took the cell phone out and flipped it open. It was Martha.

"What d'ya have?"

"The results from blood analysis came in," she said. "There's no trace of human blood on Hezekiah's knife. What was found came from several different species of animals."

"What about the blood stains on the photographs?"

"Those on the photo of Olivia came from her mother. The ones on the items found on the mantle came from Holly Nelson."

"I was afraid of that."

"I got a hold of Holly's mother and told her about the discovery. It didn't sound like she believed it was her daughter but she agreed to send us samples for further DNA testing anyway. Also your package has arrived."

"Must be good news," Susan said, noticing the smile on his face when she returned.

He pulled the phone away from his ear as she sat down. "It is. We've got him."

"Crooked nose?"

He shook his head. "Martha, does he have a name?"

"He was using the name Julio Calderon, but when the FBI ran those prints found at the motel, the name Carlos B. Badillo came up."

"Carlos B. Badillo," he repeated, "Carlos...Badillo. Where've I heard that name before?"

Susan's eyes lit up. "He wouldn't happen to be that Mexican boxer who lost the championship bout some years back, would he?"

"Martha, did they say anything about his occupation?"

"As a matter of fact, they did. He's a former boxer." After several seconds of dead silence, Martha had to make sure he was still on the line. "Sheriff?"

"What?"

"Do you want him processed?"

"Yes. Then check with the Feds and see what you can get from them." He closed the phone.

"You should see the look on your face." Susan laughed.

"How'd you____?"

"Know?" She smiled. "My husband used to be a big fan of boxing. He could name just about every boxer from the Golden Gloves to the pros. He used to go to Madison Square Garden quite a lot when he was young."

"Your husband must've been quite a man."

"Bill was," she said, head bowed. Wishing to avoid bringing up more memories, she glanced at her watch awkwardly and said, "I...I really should be getting home. Morning comes around fast these days."

"Okay, but before I take you home, I have a request."

"And what might that be?"

"The doctors say Olivia will be able to leave the hospital tomorrow. Is there any chance she could stay with you for a while?"

"What?"

"Just for a day or two. I could bring over a galley of photos for her to look at. Maybe if she sees someone familiar, it____ "

"You don't know what you're asking. I...I don't know that it's ever been done. I mean, we're not supposed to get personally involved with any of our cases, let alone take them home with us."

"I understand that. But maybe CPS can make an exception. After all, this is a pretty unusual situation. Here we have a child who can't talk, who may have witnessed the murder of her mother, and who seems to have drawn the interest of some unsavory characters."

"I don't know," She said, her right elbow on the table, her forehead between thumb and index finger. "I'd have to check with the home office. I mean there's the legal aspect to consider—not to mention agency policies."

His request was important to him. Still, he could just about picture the flood of information speeding through her mind like a virus program scanning a hard drive before she bothered to ask, "why me?"

Did he dare tell her? Would she think badly of him? After careful consideration, he decided to wait.

"You know more about her than anyone else around here, Susan, including the fact that she can't talk. The others who know have been advised not to tell anyone, especially members of the press. If she wound up going anywhere else, it may get out."

"Let's suppose I *can* do this. Then what?"

"Maybe if she recognizes one of the men in the photo lineup she'll show some kind of emotion or reaction. That would be a big help in our investigation. Who knows, it might even bring her out of whatever she has sooner than expected."

"Can you do that? I mean, is it legal?"

"I'll talk it over with the DA's office and see what they say. Even if she does point someone out, I doubt it could be used in a court of law. Still, it's worth a try. In the meantime, you could check with your department."

"What if something goes wrong, Cody? Aren't you afraid of an adverse affect on her mental state if you go through with this?"

"I've already discussed this with the doctors at the hospital___"

"And?"

"Doctor Barnes seems to think it might help also. Anyway, he left it up to me. She's our only hope of breaking this thing wide open, Susan. The only witness we have."

"I just hope you know what you're doing."

"So do I."

"Now," She said. "What is the other reason?"

She knew. And he should have. She was just as much an investigator as he was. She was reading his eyes like a professional interrogator.

"Okay," he said. "You've got me. I do have an ulterior motive."

"I know," she said with a smile. "So what is it?"

"Vincent Cassini mentioned something about taking Olivia to Coney Island occasionally. I thought perhaps you, me, and the Sands couple could take her to the Fourth of July celebration at Rooney Park. If the photos don't do the trick, then maybe a day in a similar environment might. If nothing else, it will give her a chance to be with the young couple and around kids her own age."

Her mind drifted back to the sandy beach, the long, wide, wooden boardwalk, the various amusement parks, and her experiences as a child among the screams, clangs, whistles, and bangs around what was once one of New York City's most famous neighborhoods.

"I don't know." She paused. "It might be a little too soon for that."

"When is the right time, Susan?" he leaned over the table. "That's something even grownups have trouble with."

"How well I know," she said, remembering her friend Donna's constant prodding for her to go out and meet people, perhaps even join a singles club. She shook the thought off and diverted her mind's eye with a question of her own. "Now what else do you have in mind?"

"Olivia's gonna be six years old the day after tomorrow. If I make all the arrangements, would you help me throw a party for her? Nothing fancy mind you, just you me and the Sands again. I'll take care of all the expenses."

All that he requested was out in the open, the real reason wasn't. As much as he wanted to he couldn't bring himself to disclose that. Not yet.

"That's quite a load you're willing to carry, Mr. Johnson. I just hope you can pull it off."

"I've seen bigger loads through its completion in the past, Susan." He hesitated for a moment as her eyes rolled up in thought then asked, "Well? What d'ya think?"

"I think a party would be very nice. And I'd be glad to do what ever I can to help. But for now I should be going home. I've had a busy day." She gazed into his eyes. "Thank you for the wonderful meal."

"You're welcome." He smiled. "Perhaps we can do this again."

"Maybe." She smiled.

That was all he needed. After escorting her to her vehicle, he went to his pickup with one more person in mind—the other patient he needed to visit in the morning.

# 37

Jack Bauer was worst off than Cody had been led to believe. Even so, from what he had gathered from the hospital staff, Jack still had it in him to be belligerent, refusing needed medication, and insisting on leaving the premises immediately. What was missing, he had learned real fast, was his willingness to talk.

As soon as he lifted his head off the pillow and saw Cody, he mumbled something unintelligible, winced as he dropped his bandaged head back down, and then turned on his side to face the window.

"I know darn well the traffic out there isn't that interesting."

"Whatd'ya want?"

"First of all, how are you feeling?"

"Why should you care how I feel?"

"Oh, I don't know. Maybe I just might want to compare it to how I felt after that bullet grazed my head."

"I've already said all I'm going to say. How'd you get in here anyway?"

Without answering, Cody walked back to the officer who stood up after Jack began stirring. "How about leaving us alone for a few minutes? I'll take full responsibility."

"I'll be right outside if you need me."

"Thanks."

Cody waited till the officer closed the door behind him then went back to take care of business

"Okay, Mr. Bauer, it's just you and me now." He grabbed a chair, slid it over to the side of the bed then straddled it. He rested his forearms on top of the chair's back. "You wouldn't mind if I ask you a few questions, would you?"

"Oh, yeah. Like what?"

"Like how much do you know about Carlos Badillo?"

Jack turned his head around and gave him a quizzical look. "Who?"

"Let's not play games, Mr. Bauer. I've been told you, Mr. Badillo, and a certain lady were seen together in the Angels Dance Club. Not that long ago as a matter of fact. How about it?"

"So what? There ain't no law against talking to strangers." He turned back around and faced the window again.

"Is that what you consider them?"

"Like I said. I don't know nuttin'. Go away."

*This isn't gonna work. Might be a good time to shift gears.* "Okay, then let's talk about your admirers."

"Who?"

"The ones who trampled all over your face, that's who. What were they looking for? Booze? Drugs? Or a portion of at least a half million dollars?"

This time, pain took a back seat. Jack whipped back around and sat up on his elbows. An even greater quizzical look appeared on his bruised face. "Are you crazy? Do I look like I have that kind of money?"

"That's funny. I asked that same thing about you not too long ago. What about Francis D'Angelo?"

"What about Fra...?" His mouth clamped shut. He got about as twitchy as a cat on his way to a hot bath.

That alone was enough to keep him from showing Jack the photo of Francis.

"You knew her, didn't you?"

With threatening eyes and bared teeth, Jack growled, "I don't know who you're talking about."

"You should. She was that certain lady I mentioned earlier. Did *she* look like she had that kind of money?"

"I ain't saying nuttin'."

"Let's go back in time then, Mr. Bauer." This time he took out the other photo and held it close to Jack's face. "What about her?"

For a brief moment after the long gaze, Cody thought he saw the beginning of a tear developing just before Jack dropped his head. A nerve, unlike the kind he had expected, had been touched, connecting a link to the chain of events.

"Her name is Holly Nelson," Cody continued. "And I get the impression you know her also. Am I right?"

"I...I never saw her before in my life. Now leave me alone."

Almost certain Jack had at least some knowledge of both women, he decided to file the information in the back of his mind and force himself to pace the interrogation in order to squeeze what ever else he could out of him. "Not before I'm through," he said, as he put the photo back into his pocket. "Have you ever been inside that old farmhouse where Hezekiah hangs out?"

"No."

"But you do know him."

"Who doesn't? He's that loco who hangs out around the mountain." Fire developed in his eyes as his jaw tightened. "How many times do I have to tell you I don't know nuttin' about nuttin, huh? Why don't you just get out of here?"

"Okay then. Let's just try this again later. Perhaps you'll be in a better mood. In the meantime, do what the doctor's tell you. It's for your own good, you know."

After getting up, he put the chair back where he got it then walked to the door

"Close the door on your way out."

Cody wasn't finished just yet. There was one more name to drop. He opened the door halfway then stopped and turned around. "By the way, Olivia said hi, and that she hopes to see you soon."

His eyes almost came out of their sockets.

"Did I say something wrong, Mr. Bauer?"

Without answering, Jack turned around to face the window for the third time.

Cody opened the door the rest of the way. He looked at the officer then nodded back towards Jack. "Take good care of him, will ya."

"I'll do my best."     .

Down the hallway, several feet away from the room, he called headquarters to have someone go over to the dance club, pick up Norma, and then bring her to Olivia's room where he would be waiting.

# 38

"How is she?"

"Okay, I guess," the deputy said. "All she does is lay there staring at the ceiling with her arms around that teddy bear."

"How about leaving us alone for a couple of minutes."

"Yea, sure. I'll be in the cafeteria if you need me. "

It was the first opportunity he's had to be alone with her since the time he had found her. He tiptoed quietly just in case she was asleep.

She wasn't.

He grabbed a chair, carried it over to the side of the bed and sat. "Olivia, sweetheart, do you remember me?" After several seconds of silence, he leaned closer and took hold of her hand in the chance that maybe she would acknowledge his touch with her eyes. She didn't. He sighed. "I can't even begin to imagine what you've been through," he said in a low voice. "And I don't particularly care to bring any of it up. But right now you may have the key to solving this case before it grows cold." How ironic, he thought. Of all those involved with the case, the one who couldn't talk was just several rooms down the hall from the one who wouldn't.

Teddy bear's beady eyes drew his attention, bringing a smile and a slight head shake. If only you could talk. "I bet he loves you very much, doesn't he?" he asked, turning his attention back to Olivia. "What's his name?"

After a long period of silence, futility sank in. with a sigh of resignation, he leaned back in the chair, cupped his face between the palms of his hands then pondered what and when his next move would be. Would a place with people who would shower her with love and attention bring her around? Or would he really need to have her relive the recent events of her life. He had read something about a little girl, in almost the same situation, who was shocked back to reality when taken to the scene of the crime. Would he dare take her up on the mountain?

Time flew by as he sat there staring at her. Soon his thoughts were interrupted by a knock on the door.

"Come in."

"Sheriff, there's a Ms. Paterson here to see you," the deputy said.

"Send her in."

Cody could tell Norma had no idea what was going on by her hesitation at the door. "Its okay, Norma." He got up off the chair and motioned for her to come in.

"Oh my God. Is that her?" She said, her eyes getting wider as she approached the bed.

"Yes it is. Her name is Olivia."

"What happened to her?"

"We really don't know. We're hoping she could tell us when she gets over this." The tears welling in Norma's eyes were exactly what he was hoping for. He turned around, reached into the box of tissues on the nightstand and gave her one. "You have a chance to help find her mother's killer, Norma."

After wiping her eyes, she gave him a startled look. "Me? How?"

"To begin with, we need to check every person who's had recent contact with her mother while she was still alive. There's a good chance you may have been one of them."

Norma's eyes widened and she began to fidget. Cody had a pretty good idea she knew what was coming next.

"What can *I* do?"

"There's someone down the hall I'd like you to take a look at." He put his hand on her shoulder. "Why don't you and I take a walk?"

They both turned around and headed towards the door. Norma, however, looked back over her shoulder several times before they cleared the doorway.

They were just about to reach the door to Jack's room when the police officer on duty got up from his chair and told them Jack had a visitor.

"Who?" Cody asked.

"His mother. She got in touch with the chief and demanded to see her son. She showed up right after you left."

"It may not be a good time for this," Cody said, looking down at Norma. "Let's just come back later."

"I can't afford to keep taking off work like this. Why can't we do it now?"

He was beginning to take a liking to her grit and courage. Of all those involved in the case so far, she, he thought, would be the one to take the heat of cross-examination without breaking a drop of sweat, or missing a beat of her gum chewing jaw.

"Okay, if that's the way you want it. Let's go."

The officer acknowledged Cody's nod by opening the door. Nadine was standing at the side of the bed wiping Jack's forehead with a damp wash cloth. The minute their presence was felt, she stopped what she was doing and looked up.

"Mrs. Bauer?"

"Yes."

"I'm Sheriff, Cody Johnson," he said, with the customary tipping of his hat. "And this here's Norma Paterson, a friend of your son."

She straightened up, walked over to where they stood, and got within inches of Norma's face. "My son doesn't have any friends. Who are you and what do you want?"

Cody didn't much care for her attitude but thought it wise to keep their meeting cordial for Norma's sake. Not that she would scare easy. He just wanted to make it more pleasant for her to cooperate.

"Now, Mrs. Bauer, we just want to ask your son a few questions that's all, we'll be out of your way as soon as we're done."

"She still hasn't answered my question."

While they were talking, Norma walked away from them and got closer to the bed. "That's him," she said.

At that, Nadine turned around and gave Norma an evil glare "That's who?"

"That's the guy who was sitting in the booth with her and that Mexican, sheriff. I'm sure of it."

"What's she talking about?"

"It seems your son was seen talking to a Mrs. Francis D'Angelo more than a week ago over at the Angels Dance Club."

He noticed a sudden shift in her eyes and then the rise and fall of her Adams apple. It couldn't have been the dance club. Almost everyone in the city has heard of it. It had to be the name, Francis. Mother and son's reactions were too much of a coincidence, and more importantly, almost identical.

"You know who I'm talking about also, don't you, Mrs. Bauer?"

"No, I don't. And neither does my son. So why don't you two get out of here and leave us alone." She waved her arms as if shooing a couple of hound dogs out of her house. "Can't you see he needs rest?"

"Now wait just a minute, Mrs. Bauer," Cody said. "Why don't you let him speak for____?"

"You heard mother," he shouted. "I already told you I don't know who you're talking about, so get out of here."

"He's lying, sheriff," Norma said, getting even closer to the bed. "You're a liar, Mr. I seen you there with my own eyes."

"Who the hell are you?" he shouted.

Cody walked over to Norma and put his hands on her shoulders. He gently pulled her back away from the bed and said, "Its okay. You can go on back to work. I'll take it from here."

As he escorted Norma out the door, he motioned to the officer sitting outside the room. "See if you can get Mrs. Bauer out of there for awhile. I want to talk to him alone."

"Yes, sir."

"I'm going to need you to come down to headquarters, Norma, so don't plan any long trips away from home, Okay."

"Don't worry," she said, walking down the hallway. "I can't afford to go anywhere. Besides, I don't cotton to nobody making me out to be a liar."

While Cody watched her leave, the officer came out with a grumbling Mrs. Bauer, fussing about her rights to see her son, and his rights to be left alone, unbothered.

Cody re-entered without saying a word to her as they passed by each other. He pulled up a chair. "Okay, Mr. Bauer, are you ready to talk?"

Dead silence.

"Well, I'll tell you what. I believe there's enough evidence to take you in for further questioning. You won't be going home anytime soon. If you change your mind before the city boys get through with you, give me a call. If I'm not in my office, just leave a message. Have a good day, Mr. Bauer."

He got up and walked out the door. He confronted the officer guarding the room and said, "Let someone from my department know if he has any other visitors, or any new developments.

"Yes, sir."

# 39

"There's someone over there waiting to see you."

Cody stopped in front of her desk and glanced down the short corridor. On the bench outside and to the right of his office door sat a man dressed in a tan sports jacket, brown pants, and an open collar white shirt. "Who is he?"

"Agent, Robert Albrecht, from DEA."

"Albrecht?"

She shrugged without taking her eyes off her work, and then gave him a sense of impending trouble ahead when, in a low voice, she said, "He's not exactly a happy camper. You might want to take one of the deputies in there with you."

Cody grinned. "I don't think that'll be necessary, thank you. Anything else?"

"Yes. Detective Hicks called early this morning from the airport. I sent a deputy out to get him. He should be here shortly."

"Let me know when he comes in."

Robert stood up the minute he spotted Cody coming towards him. "Sheriff Johnson?"

"Yes."

"I'm agent, Albrecht." He reached into his pocket and pulled out his government ID.

"So, you decided to come down yourself."

"There are times when face to face discussions become necessary."

"If that's the case then we'd better step into my office." Cody motioned him in after opening the door then walked around to his chair, sat down and leaned back "Have a seat." He wondered how much more the armrests could take after watching Robert squeeze in. "Now," he said, looking deep into the angry looking eyes. "What can I do for you?"

"For starters, I want you to release the man your deputies picked up at the airport earlier this morning," he said forcefully, with authority, leaning forward in the chair. "Let him go."

"I don't know exactly how you found out about this, and I don't particularly care, but, as you already know, I'm in the middle of investigating what appears to be a double homicide, agent Albrecht. And the way things look right now, your man, Mr. Badillo, is a person of interest to me. I'm afraid you'll have to wait until I'm through with him—if, of course, he has nothing to do with either one of them."

Robert's big nose flared as he stood up. With both hands resting on Cody's desk for support, he got within a foot away from his face. "I'm afraid that's impossible, sheriff. You tell Mr. Badillo it's all been a terrible mistake and that you'll be glad to have him taken back to the airport as soon as possible. Is that clear?"

Cody bolted up with gritted teeth. "Now you listen to me, Mr. Agent. I'm not releasing anyone until I'm through with what I have to do here. And even then, it depends on what the medical examiner, the Anthropologist, and the lab technicians have to say. What's clear is that it doesn't make me any difference where you came from or who you work for, you can leave anytime and come back later after we're through with him, or you can stay and enjoy our hospitality. You might even want to visit the Annie Riggs Memorial, or the Wheels and Frills Museum while you're here. Both places tend to have a calming effect on visitors."

"Look, Sheriff, I don't have the time or the patience to be playing ____"

"Sheriff, the lieutenant's here to see you?"

"Will you excuse me a minute?" He could almost see the steam coming out of Albrecht's ears, which seemed to lay flat against his face. He fought to stifle the smirk, as he spoke into the intercom. "Send him in."

Billy could feel the tension the minute he opened the door and saw the face to face confrontation. The air in the room was thick enough to cut with a scalping knife. He hesitated.

"It's okay. Come on in." Cody waved a hand as he sat back down. "I'd like you to meet Agent, Robert Albrecht from the DEA."

"DEA?" Billy was certain now that something big was going down and, by the serious look on his face, Cody wasn't exactly happy about it. "Glad to meet you."

He turned around and met Billy's extended hand.

"What brings you to these parts," Billy asked.

"I'm here to pick up a package the sheriff here has been kind enough to keep for me." He glared over his shoulder at Cody. "Isn't that right, sheriff?"

"Of course." He shot Billy a grin he was sure to catch. "We don't have probable cause to arrest our well known guest, but we could ask for his autograph. From what I hear, he'd be more than willing to do that."

Robert whipped his head around, leaned on Cody's desk again, and got even closer to his face than he did minutes earlier. "You do that and you'll sabotage three years of hard work, not to mention___"

A knock on the door put a damper on the conflagration that was about to flare up.

"Come in."

Martha, feeling the same tension Billy did, walked gingerly over to Cody, handed him a piece of paper without saying a word, then quickly turned around and headed back out.

After reading it, he glared at Robert then gave Billy a defeated look. One that was accompanied by a sigh and a slight head turn to the left. "After you get done with Mr. Badillo, let him go."

"What?"

Glaring at Robert, he handed Billy the fax, which came directly from DEA headquarters in Virginia, and which the director of the agency himself signed.

"It looks like we have no choice," Billy said, handing it back.

Cody didn't care for the smirk on Albrecht's face as he sat back down. He knew there was no way he could use the information in a court of law, but he requested it anyway. "See if he'll take a picture with you and have him autograph it, lieutenant. Tell him it's for your kids."

"You're bound and determined, aren't you?" Robert said, running the fingers of one hand from the front to the back of his curly, chestnut brown hair.

"You better believe it." Cody stood up. "Is there anything else I can do for you?"

Robert looked at Billy as if the deputy could help him persuade his boss to cooperate, but was met instead with a bewildered look. He turned back to Cody in frustration. "You haven't heard the last of this. I just hope you know what you're doing."

Cody smiled. "That's funny. Someone else said the same thing to me not too long ago. She was a lot prettier though… Agent Albrecht… Have a great day."

The chair nearly came up with him as he shot up, turned around and, without saying a word, stormed towards the door, bumping Billy's shoulder on the way. Once out he slammed the door behind him.

"Whew!" Billy said, running the back of his thumb across his forehead as if wiping sweat. "What was that all about?"

"That's what I'd like to know. You have something for me?"

"Yes! We found the Mustang a couple of miles from the crime scene. He's on his way over to our stables right now. Kyle's on his way there also. He wants to make sure it's his."

"Was there anything else around the vicinity?"

"Just pieces of an old faded, credit card receipt from a Motel. We found it near one of his campsites."

Chances were it had nothing to do with the case. Still it had gotten to the point where anything having to do with that area was now more interesting to him than ever before.

"What's on it?" he asked.

"Most of the writing's faded so we sent it over to the lab for analysis. The only word they were able to really make out was, Buffalo."

"Buffalo, New York?"

"Could be. We're not really sure. There's at least a half dozen or more other cities named Buffalo in the country."

"Sheriff, your other visitor is here?"

"Have him wait a few minutes, Martha." He knew Billy wasn't finished yet by the look on his face. "Okay, what else?"

"That man next to Holly in the photo. His name is Harold Jacobs. He has a rap sheet a mile long. Time served for running a prostitution ring, burglary, bad checks, and—get this—domestic violence."

"Now that's interesting. Let's see if we can get a hold of this young man. Have any idea where he is now?"

"Yes." He tilted his head and gave him a sideways look down. "He's in a cemetery."

"What?"

"He died from Aids complication. Not long after he and Holly split up, from what I've been told."

"Just what we needed," Cody said, rubbing his chin. "Have any more good news?"

Billy started getting up. "Nope. You want me to leave now?"

"No, stick around. Let's hear what New York City's finest has to say. Who knows, they may even have the key to this whole mess. After we're through, see if you could narrow that Buffalo down to one state."

Martha opened the door and then stepped aside.

"Detective Hicks, come on in."

Taylor Hicks stood five foot, nine inches tall, had puffy cheeks, deep set, dark turquoise eyes, and a head with a rim of black hair resembling that of a Monastery monk. His light blue suit looked like it had been slept in during the entire flight there.

"How was your trip?"

"It was fine, thank you. I'm not interrupting anything, am I?" he asked, glancing first at Billy then Cody.

"Detective Hicks, this here is Lieutenant, Billy Parker. He was just filling me in on some of the latest information relevant to our current case."

"Pleased to meet you," Billy said, shooting a sly grin at Cody.

"Grab that chair over there and join us," Cody said. Back down in his chair, he set both elbows on his desk, clasped his hands and watched with interest as the detective unbuttoned his jacket to relieve the strain on it before sitting. "Now, where were we, lieutenant?"

"Unfortunately there's not enough on that motel receipt to work with," he said, as he grabbed the other chair and slid it next to Taylor. "Even the Feds need a little more than the few letters they can pull out to come up with the person's name."

"Let's just hope he has nothing to do with this case. File it just in case something does come up. Make sure you let me know of any other developments."

"Yes, sir." Getting up and turning around almost got him on a collision course with Martha, who was coming in. "Excuse me, Martha." He tipped his hat then winked at her. "He's all yours."

"Thanks a lot."

"What d'ya have, Martha?"

She walked over to his desk and handed him a fax sheet.

"So our Mr. Badillo is suspected of several drug related executions."

"The latest ten months ago over in Mexico," Martha added.

Informant or not, he could only think of one good reason the DEA would want him to release an apparent assassin. He's bait. They're hoping Carlos will lead them to a bigger fish. At the moment, though, it didn't really matter. Come hell or high water, he was going to do whatever it took to find out if Carlos had anything to do with either of the victims.

"See if you can get a hold of someone over at the Dallas field office who can tell us when and why Agent Albrecht was sent down here."

"Good luck," Taylor interjected. "I've never had any in my dealings with them."

He must not be aware of Tony's involvement with DEA, Cody thought, Maybe we'd better not mention it just yet. "Well, we'll see what kind of luck we have." Cody glanced at the envelope still in Taylor's beefy hand. "So, whatd'ya have there?"

"Oh, yes. This here's all the info on Tony's murder investigation." Reaching across the desk, he handed it over. "Of course, it's all condensed to the most important details."

"I don't get it. From what I've heard, Francis was your prime suspect. If that's true then it's over. Case closed." He sat up on his chair and gave Taylor a quizzical look. "Or do you have someone else in mind?"

"That all depends. Now that she's gone, we could close the case. But whoever killed her might have something to do with Tony's past. If that turns out to be the case, then we'll have to look into it."

"I see. Well, we won't know for a while yet if we have the right man or not. In the meantime, is there anything else you need to know?"

"Well, for starters, I'd like to know how the little girl's doing."

"Olivia?" She's fine. If you'd like, I can have one of my deputies take you over to see her."

Cody would've never pegged him for a big teddy bear. He leaned back in his chair, pleased that someone familiar with her is concerned enough to ask, someone who probably knows just as much about her background as CPS.

"I'd like that, sheriff. As you know, I've had to deal with her mother just before she disappeared. I have an idea of what life must've been like for her with someone like Tony."

"Then why didn't somebody do something about it?"

"The system, sheriff. It's not as perfect as we would like it to be. They're under funded and under manned. We were lucky to get them involved at all. And when we did, the family refused to cooperate."

"Meaning Mr. Vincent Cassini."

"Meaning his wife."

"Is that so?"

"Sheriff?"

"Excuse me a minute. Yes Martha?"

"Hezekiah's court appointed attorney is on his way to the interrogation room."

"Thank you." When he looked up he noticed the frown on Taylor's face. "Would you care to join me? At the moment, he's our prime suspect in the murder of Francis D'Angelo. He may also be responsible for the death of a young lady by the name of Holly Nelson."

"If you don't mind."

"Not at all."

Cody led him down the hall and into a ten by ten room furnished with a table and three chairs. Waiting there was Deputy, Dave Hammer, a tall, burly, former army intelligence officer experienced in interrogation techniques. There also was George Lacey, Hezekiah's court appointed attorney; a mild mannered, five foot, eleven inch with fifteen years experience defending career criminals in the Texas judicial system.

After formal introductions, Dave and George sat while Cody and Taylor chose to stand against the wall behind them.

Dave picked up the phone on the table. "Bring the prisoner in, please."

In handcuffs and leg shackles, Hezekiah shuffled through the door escorted by two guards. He was seated across the table. His long hair, at times concealing eyes which appeared more subdued then menacing, touched the table as he slumped over it at a forty five degree angle.

Before they could even begin, Taylor tipped his head to one side, leaned forward, and said, "Wait a minute."

As Taylor walked over to Hezekiah, Cody took note of his narrowed, piercing eyes. "What's the matter?" He asked.

Taylor spotted a small portion of a tattoo visible just below the hem of Hezekiah's short sleeve shirt. "Do me a favor will you, sheriff? Have him roll that sleeve up to his shoulder," he asked, pointing to Hezekiah's left arm. "I'd like to see something."

"This is highly unusual and uncalled for, sheriff," George said "My client's here to be questioned, not to be subjected to stripping by someone who has no jurisdiction here nor any part in the official investigation."

Curious to see how Cody would handle Taylor's request, Dave turned around and waited.

Cody noticed Hezekiah's peering eyes aimed at him. He decided to let Taylor have his way for the moment. "I'll take that into consideration, counselor."

Once Dave saw the agreeing nod from Cody, he turned back around to Hezekiah. "Do as he said."

Hezekiah, with his head still lowered, hesitated for a moment, then, without bothering to look up started rolling up his sleeve.

Taylor's eyes followed every move, opening wider as more of the tattoo was exposed. When the sleeve had reached the top of Hezekiah's shoulder, Taylor leaned closer to his bicep. After studying it for several seconds, he said, "I've seen that before."

The compass, about two inches in diameter, had its needle pointing up to the capital letter N, and in the hub of the needle, the letters PAM.

Cody had seen it before also. He even checked to see if any criminal profile database, including the FBI's, had anything tying

Hezekiah's description, prints, and tattoo with any past criminal offenses. He's still waiting to hear from them. In the meantime, he let the situation play itself out to see where Taylor was going with it. "There could be hundreds, even thousands of tattoos like that out there," he told him. "What's your point?"

Taylor backed off then made another unusual request. "Have him stand up and roll up his right pants leg."

"This is getting out of hand," George protested again as he bolted out of his chair. "I'm putting you under advice. If this continues, I'll be forced to take the matter to the DA's office."

"I understand," Cody said, not thinking much of it either. "Taylor, don't you think this is going____?"

"Please, sheriff, indulge me. If I'm wrong I'll gladly take the heat off your back."

Aware of the thin line, Cody took in a deep breath then faced the attorney. "For the record, let's just see what the detective has in mind, George, okay. I won't let it go too far. I promise. What d'ya say?"

"I'm going to hold you to it, sheriff." George warned, and then sat back down.

Hezekiah's facial expression gave Cody the impression that he didn't have a clue to what this was all about. But he could tell by the tightening of his jaw and the pulsation of the veins on his temple that he didn't exactly care for the way he was being treated.

"Let's not make it any more difficult than it already is," Cody warned. "Roll up your pants leg."

Under the watchful eyes of all in the room, Hezekiah stood up and shuffled away from the table where everyone could see him. He bent down and slowly rolled the pants leg up above his knees.

"Like you said, sheriff, there may be many tattoos like the one on his bicep out there but how many have that?" He pointed to the ugly scar just below Hezekiah's kneecap. "And a wife named Pam to go with it." He looked back over his shoulder. "Tell me something, sheriff. That receipt the lieutenant mentioned earlier. Were they able to make out where the motel was located?"

"The city but not the state. Buffalo. Why?"

At the mention of Buffalo, Hezekiah looked up and gazed at

the bright ceiling light. Within seconds colorful strobe lights invaded his mind, blinding him, forcing him to blink repeatedly. Music beat upon his ear drums. The tinkling of glass upon glass, the sweet odor of liquor, and laughter consumed the smoke filled air. Fuzzy figures gyrated as they spun around him like a runaway carousel.

"I have to admit I wasn't sure at first because of the long hair and beard." He nodded towards Hezekiah, "but I'd like you to meet Mr. Benjamin Ephraim. The man whose receipt you found out there in the desert."

# 40

Carlos stood between two of the Pecos County Court House's six huge pillars cracking his knuckles and taking in the fresh air. Confident now that his interrupted trip to the promise land would be completed, he thought about going across the street and killing time in the Annie Riggs Museum before heading to the airport. But that idea quickly vanished at the sight of the black van in the small parking lot to the right of the courthouse.

He peeked over his dark sunglasses as he came down the six steps and flashed a defiant grin for the surveillance cameras he knew were focused on him. Then he strutted right past them and headed towards South Main Street.

In spite of the fact he felt humiliated by the treatment during his brief captivity; Carlos Badillo still thought he had beaten the system. Won the fight, you might say. After all, DEA kept the local authorities from obtaining anything else other than his autograph on a picture taken for some deputy's kids. Which he gave willingly, with an inflated chest, a stiff upper lip, and a chin held high, without realizing what he had done, or what the consequences could be.

He considered the switchblade that was confiscated a prized gift to the department from the greatest boxer that ever lived. He even went so far as to autograph that, thinking it would increase in value and perhaps put him back into the limelight of the sports world.

After leaving Cody's office, Robert gathered his agents and parked the van by the courthouse in preparation for Carlos' release. He didn't much care for the location, but with a big assault trial in session, the invasion of summer tourists, and the Comanche Springs Pool faithful milling around town, parking on South Main and West Callaghan was at a premium.

While Carlos was relishing his imagined rebirth on the courthouse steps, Agent Jim Fox, sitting in the driver's seat of the van, caught a glimpse of him. Peeking over his dark sunglasses, he lowered the Styrofoam cup of coffee from his lips and then looked back over his right shoulder. "Here he is now."

"Good, maybe now we can finish what we started," Robert said.

Once Carlos was spotted, agent Frank, who had entered through the back doors of the courthouse and positioned himself inside the Health and Sanitation office, received word to return to the van immediately.

Robert, not wanting a repeat of what happened at the airport, was determined to cover all the bases. He got the cameras rolling then told Dean to stay on the east side of Main in case Carlos crosses over.

After getting them in position, Robert worked his way to the front of the van and sat on the passenger's side in order to keep an eye on Carlos himself.

"Where is he?"

Jim pressed his upper body into the back of the seat, giving Robert a clear shot across the street as cars passed by. "He just crossed Callaghan."

"He's heading your way, Dean," Robert said. "Do you see him?"

The street in front of the Happy Daze place brimmed with the jostling of tourists dumped out of several busses: men in shorts, sports shirts, and visor caps, and women in shorts, peddle pushers, and sleeveless blouses—all of them AARP qualified.

"Are you kidding? I can't even see the sidewalk."

Jim, getting glimpses of the target now and then suddenly lost him also. "I don't see him. He must've slipped into that crowd."

Robert shot a glance himself. "I don't see him either. Frank, did you hear that?" he said, in a high and furious voice. "We lost contact."

"Of all the times to release him, they pick lunch time," Jim said.

The thought of Cody doing this on purpose crossed Robert's mind. His jaw got tight enough to crack.

"I heard," Frank acknowledged, eyeballing the large crowd milling around the area where Carlos was last seen. "I've got news for you. He's not in there."

"What?"

"He's not there. He may have gone into one of the shops."

"Dean," Robert's voice rose a little higher yet. "Do *you* have an eye on him?"

"No, sir."

Robert came out of the passenger side door like he had been shot out of a cannon. He started across the street, prompting a volley of blaring horns from swerving vehicles. Halfway there he noticed a black Chevy Suburban peeling out of its parking space about a block north from where he stood. With a deafening squeal and smoking tires, the vehicle weaved wildly in and out of the line of traffic at a high speed, prompting his heart to quicken. A lump lodged in his throat.

At the sound of the tires, Frank and Dean shot a quick look at the vehicle then at each other. They didn't have to hear Robert's subsequent order to get back into the van. They had already turned around and were on their way there. The pair jumped through the opened back doors of the van while Robert jumped in the passenger's side.

"Where are they?" Robert buckled up as the van peeled out of the parking lot. It took longer than he cared for to jump into the heavy traffic on Main.

"Up ahead—about twelve vehicles between us. They're picking up speed."

"Can't you get closer?" Robert asked.

"Not in this pea soup. Keep your fingers crossed we don't hit a red light or a bottle neck up ahead, otherwise, you can forget about it."

White-knuckle hands hung on tight as the van threaded its way between vehicles coming and going.

"If we lose this guy, my head's going to roll."

"He must've jumped into that Suburban as we were getting into position," Frank said.

"They're turning left on Ninth," Jim said. "Hang on."

"Did you get a hold of the department yet?" Robert asked.

"Yes," replied the communications man. "They don't know anything about this. It could be those young hoods he was spotted with, or worse yet, a delegation from Mexico."

"Great! That's all I need." He wiped his forehead with his handkerchief then looked over at Jim. "Whatever you do, don't lose him."

"I got him. It looks like he's heading towards____"

"Look out!"

Jim caught a glimpse of the truck just as Robert yelled his warning. He jammed the breaks, stopping the vehicle just inches away from the driver's side of the trash truck that had run through the stop sign of a narrow street and stopped in the middle of the intersection.

Inside the van, Frank and Dean tumbled towards the back of the front seats. The only one not joining them was the buckled in communications agent who struggled to hang on to the loose materials on his desk.

"You guys okay," Robert asked, after composing himself.

Frank got up off the van floor and shot a look out the windshield. "What the hell happened?"

Robert shook his head and stuck it out the window. "Get out of the way. Move it!"

"*Si Senor. Un minuto, por favor,*" the beefy, mustached Mexican driver said, with his head sticking out the window, smiling.

"Hey! He's got us blocked," Dean hollered. "There's no way to get around him."

"The traffic's backed up and we've got parked cars on both sides of the street," Frank added.

"I don't have a minute," Robert yelled, on the verge of exploding with rage. "I don't have a second. Get that piece of junk out of the way now, you hear me. Now!"

"*Si, Si, un minuto,*" the driver said again, as the engine sputtered, trying to restart.

Robert realized it was too late to get a copter up in the air. "We have to stop him before he gets on the ramp. As soon as that idiot gets the truck out of the way, pour it on."

Several seconds went by before the loud blast. Smoke blew out of the truck's tail pipe. After forcing some of the oncoming traffic off to one side, the truck chugalugged past them with the driver still smiling broadly and waving goodbye.

The van, after weaving its way through slow moving traffic, swerved and bounced as it hit speeds of 60 to 70 miles per hour.

Dean pointed "There he is up ahead. He's getting on the West I-10 ramp."

"See if you can get the tag number and run a check on it before we lose him," Robert yelled.

Frank grabbed the binoculars. Seconds later he yelled back, "Got it."

Several feet from the rear of the Suburban, Jim steered the vehicle to the left and picked up speed he didn't know it had, but knew he couldn't maintain.

With the standard pit maneuver on his mind, he eventually got the front of the van even with the rear fender of the Suburban then bumped it, making it swerve violently. Without warning, the Suburban began to stabilize and slow down. Jim let up on the accelerator, backed off, and positioned himself behind it.

"He's going to stop," Robert said. "Talk to me, Dean."

"It's hot. It was reported stolen a couple of days ago. It seems a Mexican national rented it for a day and never returned it."

He took out his nine millimeter. "I'm not surprised. Get ready to move just in case they try to bail out and make a run for it."

"Okay, he stopped," Jim said.

Robert looked back over his shoulder. "Let's take them down. Watch your backs. Don't shoot unless you have to."

As the dust enveloped both vehicles, the agents spilled out like fire ants from a disturbed mound.

"Come out with your hands up," Robert yelled. "Come out now."

The darkened window on the driver's side lowered, revealing a hand meekly coming out and waving.

In the meanwhile, Frank and Dean crouched behind the rear of the vehicle, guns pointed towards the front, yelling for anyone else in the vehicle to come out.

Fingers tensed as the driver's side door opened. The driver exited with his hands in the air.

"Turn around and back away from the vehicle."

"Get on the ground," Frank yelled, his weapon aimed at the driver. "Get down. Get down."

Robert went around to the passenger side and yanked that door open. The only thing on the seat was a cell phone.

As soon as the driver got close enough to them, they forced his arms behind his back and plastered him to the ground.

The young man was in his early twenties. He was tall and lanky. And not at all what they had expected.

After they handcuffed him, Robert yanked open the back door on his side and took a quick peek. There was no sign of Carlos. He slammed the door shut then bolted around the vehicle to the driver's side where the young man lay on his stomach. He bent down.

"What's going on here? Where is he?" he asked.

"Where's who?"

"Don't play stupid with me." He grabbed a handful of blonde hair and lifted the young man's head up off the graveled shoulder of the road. "Where's Carlos."

"Carlos?" he asked, spitting sand and gravel. "I don't know any Carlos. What's this all about?"

"Get him up," Robert said, releasing his grip on the hair.

After lifting and padding him down, they did a thorough search. From his back pocket they took out his wallet and handed it to Robert.

"Okay, Mr. Woodley," he said, looking at the young man's license. "Who are you working for?"

"The super 8," he screamed. "I'm the night shift clerk. What's this all about?"

"Where'd you get the Suburban?"

"It was in the motel parking lot. He gave me the keys yesterday."

"Who gave you the keys?"

"The man in the lobby. He told me to wait for his call and he'd tell me what to do."

"What did he look like?"

"A Mexican."

"Come on, come on. What else?"

"He was big. His hair and mustache were black."

"What was he wearing?"

"A white shirt and dark blue pants."

"We've been had. There are two of these vehicles—both identical," Frank said.

Frank was right, and Robert didn't like it one bit. The other Suburban with Carlos in it cut back to Ninth when the trash truck blocked their way. This innocent lackey was sent on his way to lead them on a wild goose chase. The whole thing was planned and timed perfectly. And it worked.

"So what did this mysterious guy tell you to do?" Robert asked him.

"I was to pick up his friend at the gas station just west of the city and take him to the airport. He gave me a hundred dollars and said he'd give me another hundred when I got back."

"What was the big hurry?" Dean asked. "You were doing 75 in a 55 mile zone."

"He said his friend was already at the gas station waiting and would miss his flight if I didn't hurry up and get there."

Fury raged within him. Once again, the allusive Carlos slipped right through his fingers. What will he tell his superior? More importantly, what will his future look like now? He decided to wait and see if Carlos would be spotted again, perhaps even picked up by the local authorities.

"What do we do now?" Frank asked.

"Let him go," Robert grumbled. "I'm willing to bet his other hundred dollars the other vehicle's half way to Mexico by now. Put out an APB and see if we can stop him at the border crossing. If that doesn't work, we'll just have to wait and see if we get word through our sources over there."

"What about that sheriff?" Dean asked.

"What about him?"

"He's not going to like the fact we lost his man," Frank said.

"I don't care what he likes or dislikes. He should've thought about that before he had him picked up at the airport. Right now I've got more important things to worry about."

# 41

By the look on Hezekiah's face, the word, "Buffalo", cracked open a window in time that had been closed long ago—one Cody was willing to open all the way if needed. But before he could do that, he had to be sure the detective knew what he was talking about. There had to be records, documents, something tangible that could be used to verify Taylor's revelation, and maybe even help the investigation. And if what Taylor claimed was true, something readily available.

"We've been trying to figure out if Hezekiah was his real name or not for some time now. Are you sure he's who you say he is?" Cody asked.

"That's what I would like to know," George said. "If this is true, we'll have to start from square one. Every piece of document on file here and in the court will have to be changed and resubmitted."

"You might as well start then because I'd stake my reputation on it," Taylor said, glaring at the skepticism written all over Cody's face.

He nodded towards Hezekiah. "If you don't believe me just ask him?"

On that advice, Cody got within inches of Hezekiah. "Look at me." He waited several seconds as Hezekiah slowly lifted his head. "Is he telling the truth? Is that your name?"

"Most of those he dealt with knew him as Ben, sheriff. Try using that. You just might get him to talk."

"Well Mr. What's it gonna be? Hezekiah? Or Ben?"

Once again he refused to make eye contact, let alone utter a sound. He hung his head, closing the long curtain of hair as he opened his mind's eye. He swayed dizzily as numerous black letters swirled around in his head, trapped in a whirlpool of green, slimy liquid, spinning faster and faster towards the abyss where they united, forming the words Ben and Pam until they disappeared. Hezekiah stopped the slight swaying and lifted his head, this time making contact with Cody's questioning eyes.

"You'd better sit down before you fall," Cody said, nodding for the guards to help him. He was about to recommend getting medical help but then noticed the defiant look in Hezekiah's eyes. Weakness was not in his vocabulary.

Frustrated by that and the turn of events, Cody took another deep breath then let it out as he looked up at the ceiling, realizing even Miranda might have taken a hit with this new revelation. "Okay, then," he said, lowering his head to eye level with Hezekiah's. "Whoever you are, let me read you your rights again. You have the right to remain silent ____"

"That's not necessary, sheriff," Taylor interrupted. "He knows Miranda better than you and most of the criminals out there."

"And why's that?"

With a knowing grin and a face that bore the gleam of someone tickled by the irony of it all, Taylor said, "Mr. Ephraim happens to be a well known attorney from New York."

Hezekiah whipped his head up and shot a questioning look at Taylor.

Cody's jaw dropped. "You're kidding, right?"

"I'm afraid not," Taylor answered with a grin on his face. "Right now he doesn't fit the profile. If I told you he was a former hippie from the 60's, you wouldn't think twice about it. But I couldn't be more serious if my life depended on it."

Cody flipped his head to one side, motioning for Taylor to follow him. He led him closer to the door of the room where Hezekiah would have a harder time hearing.

"Now run that by me again," Cody asked in a low voice.

"Like I said, he's an attorney. A pretty wealthy one at that, I might add. He and his wife own a couple of apartment buildings on Madison Avenue, a six thousand square foot mansion in Florida, and a race horse that's won them several big purses at the track."

"That answers one of my questions."

"Whatd'ya mean?"

"I've been wondering where he'd learned to handle a horse."

"I've got news for you. Ben Ephraim was raised around horses. Grandpa owned a horse breeding ranch somewhere in Fredericksburg, Virginia. Quarter horses from what I've heard. He put the kid on one of them before he even learned to walk.

And if that wasn't enough to jump start his fortune, Gramps also left him enough money to last him for a very long time."

Cody's interest in the life of Hezekiah had suddenly taken a giant leap forward. The man apparently had enough money to hire an entire law firm and post the maximum bond available to date. That was something he knew would make the DA's office and the courts more than happy to learn.

Now more than ever he was determined to find out all he could about the man who showed up out of nowhere and has managed to turn the department upside down. He shot a thumb towards the door at the deputy. "Let's play it safe. Read him his rights again then take him back to his cell." He turned around to Lacey and said, "It looks like he won't need your free services after all."

"And you won't need me for a while, either," Dave said. He picked up his note pad and followed Lacey and Hezekiah out the door.

Cody waited until they were gone before turning back to Taylor. "Let's you and I go back to my office. I have a funny feeling you know a lot more about Mr. Ephraim than you've already spit out."

It wasn't the sudden identification, which he had expected would come sooner or later, it was the amount of information and its source that caught him by surprise. Anxious to learn more, Cody motioned towards one of the chairs by the wall as he walked into the office. Once Taylor dragged it to the front of the desk and seated himself, Cody sat, planted his elbows on the desk, and then met his eyes head on. "So he's an attorney. What else should l know about him?"

"First of all, I wasn't really sure it was him until I remembered the description in the APB put out by the Buffalo

Police Department, and that he was registered in a motel up there just before he disappeared.

"And when exactly did *that* happen?"

"Three years ago," Taylor said. "His wife notified the authorities when he was overdue back from a routine business trip. Three days later they found his locked *Mercedes* in a nightclub parking lot. His cell phone and remote key were found under the car, his wallet two miles south of there. His driver's license was in it but the seven hundred in cash plus his credit cards weren't. At first they suspected a possible kidnapping for ransom__"

"Ransom?"

"We're talking real money here, sheriff. Between the stable, stock holdings, real estate investments, and his law firm, your suspect was able to push Gramps seed money into the millions."

"Did the FBI get involved?"

"They did, but after a month without a trace, or a call demanding money, they turned it over to the local authorities. In the end, they concluded he was either a victim of a local mugging, foul play, or he staged the whole thing to run off with another woman."

"Leaving all that money behind?"

"Go figure." he shrugged his shoulders. "All we know is that he hasn't been seen since—until now that is."

"How in the world did he wind up down here?"

"Only he knows the answer to that."

"His prints must be on file then."

"I would think so."

"Excuse me a minute. Yes, Martha?"

"I put the folder with the autopsy and forensic reports in your inbox?"

"Thanks," he said, after spotting it. "Anything yet on Hezekiah's prints?"

"Not yet. It seems they're having problems with their database. It should be up and running shortly."

"Let me know as soon as you hear something."

"I will, but before I forget, Mr. Albrecht called. He sounded like he needs to vent some more. He wants you to give him a call right away."

"I'll call him as soon as I get through here." He turned away from the intercom to continue his discussion with Taylor. "Now, where were we?"

"Mind filling me in on what you have there?"

Cody reached for the folder and opened it. Under the watchful eyes of Taylor, he scanned through the documents.

"According to the ME's examination the first victim was hacked to death with a shovel."

"Francis?"

"I'm afraid so. The other one died of blunt force trauma to the head."

"Hence the worried look," Taylor said. "There's a possibility the two cases aren't related."

"Let me put it this way, it makes things a little more complicated than I like. The only sure things I have at the moment are those items found at that house he uses. They could tie him to Francis' murder. If so it should be enough to take it to a grand jury."

"There seems to be something else bothering you, though." Taylor said, seeing Cody reach for the back of his neck.

"As a matter of fact there is. A while ago I got the impression Ben had no idea what or whom you were talking about."

"If it makes you feel better, sheriff, I got that same impression."

"I'll mention it to the DA and see what he says."

"Before you go too far with this," Taylor said. "You might want to have your DA look into Ben's war record. It's quite impressive. It may even influence the outcome of any legal proceedings."

"Thanks, I'll let him know."

"In the meantime, do you mind if I ask you a question?"

"Go right ahead."

"What's the DEA's interest in all this?"

"Good question. I'll let you know once I get in touch with agent Albrecht. What about Ben? What's NYPD gonna do now that you found him?"

"I can't say for sure that he's well, but he's definitely alive. Once you get through with him, we'll get all the details on what exactly happened to him and take it from there. In the meantime, we'll go ahead and let his wife know where he is. I'm sure you'll be hearing from her right after that."

"While you're at it, you might as well tell her he'll be our guest for a while."

"Don't worry, by the time I get through you'll be hearing from his associates at the law firm as well." He extended a hand. "Thanks for your hospitality. If it's alright with you, I'll stop by the hospital to see Olivia after I get a room for the night. I'll be leaving sometime tomorrow afternoon."

"You bet," Cody said. "Another familiar face might just help bring her back to us."

Taylor rose and headed towards the door.

Cody waited till he was gone before picking up the phone and dialing Robert's cell phone. And when he did, the news wasn't exactly what he wanted to hear. "Whatd'ya you mean you lost him?"

"You heard me," Robert howled. "And if it wasn't for you, this wouldn't have happened."

"What's that supposed to mean?"

"I'll tell you loud and clear," he said, "It means if you hadn't picked him up at the airport, we'd still have a bead on him."

"Where? In Mexico? Don't forget, you're the ones who gave him that free pass out of Jail. It looks now like we're the ones having to take it away. Just hang your hat somewhere for awhile and let us handle the situation. I'll put out a statewide BOLO (Be on the Lookout) right away."

"You do that," Robert yelled."

Cody hung up then called Martha back in.

"Here, get this out on the airwaves," he handed her the paper with Carlos' description and the photo taken during his brief stay in the holding pen. "He should be easy to spot."

"Yes, sir," she said, looking at Cody's drooping eyelids. "In the meantime, why don't you go home and get some rest? Mr. Ephraim is in custody and there's not much more you can do here until the rest of the reports come in."

He rubbed his eyes with palms of his hands as he rested his elbows on the desk. "I suppose you're right. I'm still back in El Paso."

"You've been through a lot these last few days, and tomorrow's the funeral service. How about letting the

233

lieutenant have it for awhile. I'll give you a call if anything important develops."

Tired or not, he dreaded going home to an empty house. For a brief moment he toyed with the idea of inviting Susan over for some porch time. But like a child playing with the same toy for so long, he pushed it aside.

"Let me clear my desk then I'll head on out of here."

"Good. Enjoy what's left of the weekend," she said. "I'll see you Monday morning."

# 42

Olivia was in a veritable world of fantasy, yet there wasn't a trace of anticipation, excitement, or a gleam in her eyes.

Rooney Park was packed with hundreds anxiously waiting for the Fourth of July fireworks to light up the night sky. Many of them gathered in clusters enjoying picnics, games, and the food offered by the numerous vendors there. Music, blaring out of radios, CD players, and the live band, competed for air space.

Children bounced, slid, or tumbled inside giant, inflatable rooms, while others spent time riding around in carts, waving little American flags and laughing as they passed by their caretakers.

Cody's heart revved up a notch and had not slowed down from the minute he picked Susan up at her apartment. Even as he sat opposite her on the blanket, he couldn't keep his eyes off what had filled the clothing he had seen her in previously.

Each date, or what he would like to think of as dates, revealed more of her inner and outer beauty. She had on a light blue, short sleeve halter-top and one of those black shorts with the big pockets. Both of which made her look like a young teen on her first date.

He wondered what she thought about him being out of his realm with his snug fitting *Wrangler* and tan, open collar sports shirt. It had been a long time since he had relaxed enough to even contemplate dressing down, let alone picnic in the park with a woman he had just recently met, even if it was with another couple

"Is she going to be alright?" he asked.

"I don't know," Susan said. "She gave me quite a scare this morning. She wasn't in bed when I woke up."

"Was she in a closet?"

"Why yes. She was sitting there rocking back and forth. How did you know?"

"It's a long story, Susan. I'm hoping the time will come when we can all talk about it."

"What about you?" Peggy asked Cody. "Are you going to be alright?"

Although busy making sure Jeremy and they were fed, she found time to notice the subtle attraction developing between Cody and Susan.

"I'm just fine, thanks."

Just before leaving the ranch, he had promised himself to stay in control—that he wouldn't embarrass himself. But it was apparent he had left the promise back at the ranch.

"How do you like Olivia's new outfit?" Jeremy asked, with a proud fatherly tone in his voice. "Peggy got it for her yesterday after calculating her size."

"It's a good thing she did," Susan said. "I had no idea what to get her. I'm thrilled you brought them over last night." She gave Cody a smile. "And I'm even more thrilled that you brought us out here today."

"Right now, Mr. Tibbs seems to be showing more enthusiasm for what's going on than she is, though," Cody said, pointing to the only object that had Olivia's undivided attention. "I thought maybe this would bring the child within her back into our world. I guess I was wrong."

"No, Cody. Don't say that. This was a wonderful idea," Susan said, loud enough to be heard over the din, yet aimed directly towards him. It had been quite some time since the child within *her* made its presence known. There was glitter in her eyes and an ear-to-ear smile on her face. Her hair flung freely as she turned her head to and fro soaking up all the joy that surrounded them. "It's too early to tell what may come out of this. Let's just wait and see."

It had been a long time for the child within him also.

The whole atmosphere was a far cry from the solemn one inside St. Agnes Catholic Church the day before during Francis' funeral service.

236

Not only was it attended by all those personally involved with Olivia's plight, but also by hundreds of citizens whose heart was touched by it, who had kept daily vigils on her through the various media outlets, and who had even donated money to a fund set up for her education.

In the crowded church, Olivia and Tibbs sat between him and Susan, an arrangement approved by Vinnie who, with remorse and in tears, sat directly behind his niece. And as the service progressed, Cody threatened to join him as memories of the last funeral service he had attended briefly surfaced.

After radio station KFST offered to pay, Vinnie decided to have Francis' remains cremated right after the service was over, then, having done all he could for the investigation, take her back home.

"I don't think she'll hold on to it," Susan said, noticing Cody eyeing the masses of colored balloons tethered above an approaching hawker's head.

"We won't know for sure unless we try, won't we?" With a wave of his arm, he flagged the hawker down and then pointed. "I'll take that yellow one." After paying and taking hold of the string, he turned to Peggy. "Here, why don't *you* give it to her?"

With a look of apprehension, she sought encouragement and strength from Jeremy. The smile on his face and the nod was all she needed. She took it from Cody's outstretched hand then bent down and offered it to her.

As far as Olivia was concerned, though, the balloon was non-existent. There was no eye contact with it. Nor did she attempt to latch on to the string. If anything, Mr. Tibbs found himself in an even tighter squeeze than earlier.

"I was afraid of that," Susan said. "Perhaps it's just too early."

"Tie it to the bear's paw," Jeremy suggested, not wanting to lose the moment. "I'm sure he won't mind holding it for her."

"That's a good idea," agreed Susan, her lips curling up slightly. "A soft teddy bear may have a bigger part in bringing a wall down than one realizes."

She was looking at Jeremy, yet her words bounced around Cody's head like a pinball ricocheting down the board towards the pocket.

"Maybe we should take her on that," Peggy said, gesturing towards one of the inflated game rooms.

Cody, seeing an opportunity to give her and Susan some time alone, readily agreed, suggesting he and Jeremy get some sodas at one of the vendor's booth before checking to see if tickets were needed for the game rooms. He gave Susan a smile and a gesture towards Peggy as a clue to what was on his mind.

As it was, Susan had already thought about gauging Peggy's reaction to what she had to say. What puzzled her was the way she was able to read Cody's. As if they'd known each other forever. As if she knew his next move without him having to say a word. She never knew what Bill was going to do or say next until it happened.

Her thoughts went back to the young couple's financial qualifications and past history. They were acceptable and viable—perfect candidates. All she needed now was to make them the offer. One she hoped would be accepted.

Peggy's eyes gleamed as she watched Jeremy walk away and meld into the crowd.

To Susan it spoke volumes. "He's a good husband, isn't he," she said. "You must be very happy." Susan waited for an answer. When she noticed the hesitation, she quickly said, "Look, I'm sorry. It's really none of my____"

"That's okay... he really is."

"There is a problem, though, isn't there?"

"I'm the problem," she admitted, looking at Olivia. "I can't seem to accept ____"

"The fact that you cannot carry a child."

"How did you____"

"I took the liberty to do some checking. I'm truly sorry Peggy. I hope you don't mind."

"I don't...but why? What for?"

She reached out and took hold of Peggy's hand. "For the three foot tall angel you can't seem to take your eyes off."

Peggy pulled her hands away from Susan's gentle grip. She shook her head. "No, please. I know what you're thinking. Buying her clothes is one thing, but something like that is another. I...I just can't bring myself to even think about it."

"I know it's not easy, Peggy. Even I would have trouble considering it. But in this case, time is of the essence. A decision based upon the facts available has to be made as soon as possible. All I'm asking is that you keep an open mind."

"I know all that, Susan. It's just_____"

"It's just a chance to do what I believe would be right. Not only for yourself, but for someone who's in desperate need of what you have to offer. I would hate to see it go to waste. And I would certainly hate to see someone, who I feel would be just as great a father as he is a husband, lose the opportunity to be one."

"What do you mean?"

"What I mean is this. There's no hope for a decent happy life without love. Olivia needs that now, before she's grown up and molded by a world without it. You have to realize the urge to love and share yours with a child may fade with time, Peggy, and time is something that won't stop for you or anyone else on this planet. Think about that."

"I just don't know if I could cope with it."

"You don't have to cope with anything alone. There's plenty of help available out there. Besides, according to the doctors, her condition isn't known to be one of permanence. In fact, in her case, its length of duration seems to be highly unusual. Sooner or later, she's going to come out of this. We just haven't found the right key."

"Well, maybe_____"

The blast and its subsequent shockwave cut her short as the sparkling ball in the sky expanded into a huge globe, engulfing the park in an eerie reddish glow. Engrossed in their conversation, they had failed to notice it had gotten dark enough for the fireworks display to begin.

Noticing in the light Olivia's frightened eyes; Susan reached out and took hold of her. She pressed her face against her breasts, and began to rock her.

"Is she okay?" Peggy asked."

"She's fine. Startled that's all."

She began to question her agreement to Cody's judgment. Perhaps it was too early to expose her to the heart pounding shockwaves or the ear piercing screams that follow.

Peggy, after making sure Olivia was taken care of, stood up for a better look over the heads of those standing in front of the blanket. Seconds later, the impact jarred her head back as if she had been accidentally rear ended by an automobile.

It was no accident. Nor was it the concussion from the last big bang. Someone had deliberately bumped into her. Pain sped down her spine as she fell forward. Her face hit the corner of the metal ice chest.

Susan gasped at the sight of Peggy bouncing off then rolling to the ground in agony.

The perpetrator took off running, knocking people aside like bowling pins as he cut a swath through the crowd.

In the red light provided by the last display, Susan scanned the devilish looking faces of onlookers but was unable to pick out the perpetrator. As the next round of sparkles rained down, she turned and caught a glimpse of blood flowing from the gash on Peggy's forehead. She reached into the picnic basket and pulled out a handful of clean napkins. She lifted Peggy's head and, with a slight pressure, placed them against the wound. "We need to get you to the first aid station."

"No. I'll be okay, I think. Just help me up."

"Okay, but you really should have it looked at."

Peggy took over and held the napkins. "If it doesn't stop I'll have Jeremy take me there, I promise." Soon after she had said it, her face changed from one flushed from embarrassment to one drained of its natural color altogether. "Susan?"

"What?"

"Olivia."

"She's right...where is she? Oh my God!"

In her haste to help Peggy, she let go of Olivia. Within seconds, the darkness and the crowd that had gathered swallowed the child.

Susan's knees began to buckle. She gasped. She called in a loud frightening tone, "Olivia!" Chills ran up the back of her neck as her eyes darted through the darkness, keying on anything that even came close to resembling Olivia, or as she realized quickly, someone carrying a child.

Hysterically, she went from one person to another asking if they had seen her. Some shook their heads while others simply said, "No."

Then, out of the corner of her eye, as the park was showered in blue, she saw a little boy looking up at her and pointing towards the games. "Her daddy picked her up and took her over there."

"I'd better get Cody, Peggy. Stay here just in case."

As one rocket after another blasted off, she scanned the lines formed around the vendor's booths. Only one straw cowboy hat stood high above the rest. It had to be Cody. But as far away as he was, there was no way she could get to him in time. Instead, she picked up her purse and took out her cell phone."

"What are you doing?"

"It's the only way, Peggy. He'll never hear me in all this."

She opened her contact list and called his number.

The vibration and ring tone penetrated the oohs and ahs between the explosions. He took the cell phone out of his pocket, opened it and saw that it was Susan.

"Hi."

"Cody, someone took Olivia. He knocked Peggy down and_____"

"What?...What? Susan slow down, I can't make out what you're saying."

"Olivia's gone," she screamed.

In the light, Jeremy saw Cody's head whip around to look back over his shoulder, his eyes gazing towards the area where they had left the girls. "What's the matter?"

"Something's wrong."

Finding it difficult to differentiate between the cacophony surrounding them and the rest of Susan's words, he said, "Stay where you are, we'll be right there." He hung up. "We need to go back."

He took off at a fast pace, sidestepping those he could, and shoving the others gently out of his way. Jeremy was right behind him like a running back following his blocker.

Jeremy rushed over to Peggy when he noticed her pressing the blood soaked napkins against her temple. "What happened?"

Susan's words came out fast and furious. "Olivia's gone. She's gone."

"Whatd'ya mean gone?" Cody asked. "How?"

"Someone in the crowd knocked Peggy down. Olivia's gone. She's gone. I just left her for a second. I...I___"

"Take it easy," Cody yelled, gently but firmly shaking her shoulders. "Don't worry, we'll find her. Did you see which way she went?"

"I don't know... I didn't see. Some boy said he saw her with a man going towards those game rooms."

"He couldn't have gotten far in this crowd. Stay here and make sure Peggy's okay."

If ever he needed Diablo, this would be the time. Between the mob and the darkness, it was almost impossible to see whoever took her. Then he remembered the one thing she would never let go of. He turned around. "Susan, where's Mr. Tibbs?"

"I don't know. He must still be with her."

*I thought so.* He craned his neck and canvassed the area full circle as the fireworks intermittently lit up the park. There were quite a few balloons, but only one caught his undivided attention. It was lagging close behind someone who appeared to be weaving through the maze of picnic tables, blankets, and people. It was also higher than the others, and heading towards a parking lot that was as long and wide as a football field. If the perpetrator was able to reach it, the hide and seek game would involve more players than just him and Jeremy.

Women screamed, children cried, and old folks struggled to stay on their timeworn legs as he bowled his way through them. None knew what was going on, only that a man claiming to be a sheriff was bound and determined to leave the park in a big hurry.

Several feet from the street in front of the park, he spotted Olivia in the arms of a young man who had just passed through the two-foot opening between police barricades. The yellow and black wooden horses were lined up like a train at the curb to keep vehicles from blocking the entrance. Fortunately, for Cody, they also forced the would-be kidnapper to slow down as pedestrians on their way in filed between them. This gave him the opportunity to get closer.

"Freeze! Stop where you are," he yelled, his adrenalin higher than the showers of light above. "Stop right there."

As he ran towards the suspect, a black Nissan, which had skidded to a stop across the street from the park, caught his attention. The driver reached back and pushed open the rear door on his side. But when he looked up and saw Cody running right behind his expected passengers, he turned back around and floored the accelerator, engulfing all of them in the smoke from burning rubber.

The sudden jerk forward swung the back door shut just as Olivia was about to be tossed inside. Within seconds, the vehicle weaved in and out between stalled vehicles until it disappeared from sight, leaving its would-be passengers stranded in the middle of the traffic-laden street.

The acrid smoke slowed Cody down, giving the panicked kidnapper time to make a mad dash towards the parking lot.

Jeremy came up alongside of Cody who was pointing. "They're in there. We're going to need backup."

"Don't look now, but the Calvary's right behind us."

One of the Fort Stockton police officers, unsure of what was going on, yelled, "Stop where you are," several times as he approached. Another one yelled, "Get on the ground, now."

Even with the prevailing cacophony of screams, music, and fireworks, their orders were loud and clear. Cody could tell they meant business, even though he had identified himself loud enough for others nearby to hear. His words to them, however, were drowned by the fact he and Jeremy were in off duty attire. Being in the dark didn't help matters either.

He could tell by the crack in his voice that the youngest, and perhaps the newest of the three officers running behind them, was getting a little impatient and nervous.

Anxious as he was to pursue the suspected kidnapper, he wasn't about to take any chances. He reluctantly motioned for Jeremy to do as they say. "We're wasting time. Hurry, get down."

"I hope this doesn't get back to the guys in Chicago," Jeremy said under his breath as he went down on his knees. "I'll never live this down."

For the first time in his life, Cody felt the pressure and pain of law enforcement officer's knees on his back. The urge to resist their attempt to pull his arms behind his back to be handcuffed was overwhelming. "It's me, Sheriff Johnson," he hollered, spitting grass and dirt as he lay face down. "And he's Deputy Sands. Make it fast. Someone just kidnapped a little girl and the culprit's in there." He motioned towards the parking lot.

"Hey! This one's got a badge, sarge," one of the officers said, the beam from his flashlight focused on Jeremy's black leather, badge holder. "He's a deputy."

"The sergeant shined the light on Cody's face. "Cody? What in the world's going on?"

"I'll fill you in later," Cody said. "Now help me up."

Cody was able to get up on one knee with the sergeant's help then go the rest of the way on his own. "Thanks. Now let's just hope he's still over there. How about the three of you taking the north end of the lot while Deputy Sand's and I take the south. I'm not sure if he's armed or not, but he's got the child. That means no weapons if at all possible."

He and Jeremy then ran through the maze of vehicles that had slowed down to gawk at the fireworks. After reaching the perimeter of the lot, he sent Jeremy off to the left and then, in a crouched position, went from one row of parked vehicles to another, peering inside each one with the flashlight given to him by the sergeant. Occasionally he would get down on one knee and look underneath. Halfway into the search, he heard Jeremy shouting from the fourth row in. He took off running after catching a glimpse of Jeremy waving frantically. So did the others.

Apparently abandoned by the kidnapper, Olivia was sitting on the ground with her back against the right front tire of a Ford pickup. Jeremy picked her up just as Cody arrived. The first things he checked with the flashlight were her arms and legs. "She looks to be okay."

"Yeah," Jeremy said, smiling at teddy. "I guess the guy felt the two of them were too much to handle."

"The hat wasn't," he said, his flashlight aimed at a dark blue baseball cap lying on the ground next to the tire. "I think he's still in here somewhere. Take her back to the ladies. I'm sure they're worried to death by now."

"What are you going to do?"

"I'll stay here and help the others with the search."

"Watch yourself."

As Jeremy took off, Cody knelt down to check under a vehicle. When he stood back up, he heard one of the officers yelling for the others. A white, sparkling mushroom in the sky lit the area in time for him to see the officer pointing to the figure running from behind a vehicle. To Cody's surprise, the suspect was running back towards the park.

He knew the chances of finding him there were slim to none. So did the kidnapper. All he had to do was blend in until the fireworks ended then walk out among the thousand or so homeward bound.

Given no other choice but the one that had entered his mind earlier, he put his pinkies to his mouth and gave a loud, shrill whistle. Several rows away, Diablo heard. He jumped out of the truck bed and within seconds was by Cody's side. The two of them then zigzagged between vehicles and hurried back to the park. The games, engulfed in a sea of grownups and children, drew his attention. He squatted and put the baseball cap to Diablo's snout. "Go find him, boy."

Not far from the entrance to one of the inflated tumbling rooms, Diablo froze, growled, and then bolted. So did the suspect, knocking down people as he shot out of the crowd and headed towards a street filled with those trying to beat the last minute rush out of the park.

Suddenly, a loud horrible thud stiffened the hairs on Cody's neck. The shrill yelp that followed weakened his knees.

A white Lincoln Navigator, whose driver was paying more attention to the fireworks than what was in front of her, hit first the suspect, then Diablo. Confused and disoriented, the elderly driver continued going until those in the crowd screamed for her to stop. But by then it was too late. The kidnapper tumbled like a rag doll under the vehicle. Traffic came to a complete standstill. What followed next was a chaotic scene as concerned pedestrians gathered around the vehicle.

Did he just lose the last member of his family? Did fate deal him yet another blow? The drumbeat within quickened as the thought filled his head. He swallowed hard. He knew Diablo was close to the suspect. Maybe even on top of him. With swim like strokes he pushed and pulled his way through the mob that encircled the vehicle.

When he broke through, his eyes fell on Diablo's limp body as it lay several feet behind the vehicle. With flashlight still in hand, he rushed over, knelt down, and shined the light on Diablo's head. The rolled up eyes sent a cold chill throughout his body. He lifted Diablo's head and felt the warmth of the blood pouring out of his snout and on to his hand. Looking further, he noticed the left leg was grotesquely shaped like a boomerang.

Jeremy, after spotting Cody, broke away from the officers checking the suspect's condition and walked over to him. "How is he?" he asked, putting a hand on Cody's shoulder.

"Not good. We need to get him to the animal hospital right away."

As the words left his mouth, Susan and Peggy managed to work their way to the front of the mob surrounding the victims. Susan sucked in a deep breath as her cupped hands went up to the mouth. Peggy pressed Olivia's face against her bosom.

"Get her out of here, Peggy," Jeremy hollered over his shoulder. Then he turned to Cody. "I'll take him to the vet."

"Here. Take the truck."

After Jeremy got the keys, he ran to the parking lot, jumped into the truck cab and then, with the help of an officer at the scene, weaved his way through the stalled traffic. When he got close enough, he jumped out and helped Cody lift Diablo into the bed. Another officer grabbed a blanket out of his squad car and covered him up.

"You drive carefully, you hear?"

"Don't worry," Jeremy assured him. "I've hauled precious cargo before. I'll get in touch as soon as I hear anything."

"God, Cody, I hope he'll be okay," Susan said, as Jeremy, with a light flashing, siren blaring escort leading the way, headed for the nearest veterinarian hospital.

"I hope so, too."

"I think maybe you should go over and check on that young man." She took hold of his hand in an attempt to comfort him. "I'll wait for you over here."

"Yes, sure," he said, with misty eyes focused on his pickup as it left the area.

The accident scene was quickly secured by officers pushing onlookers back, setting flares, and chalking the position of the body. They were just about to cover him when Cody came up to them. "Hold on a minute. I want to have a look."

"Sure thing, sheriff," said one the officers, "Let us know when you're finished."

He winced at the thought of losing his chance to question the suspect.

Sergeant Boyd, who had been dispatched to investigate the accident, came up behind him. He gazed over Cody's shoulder at the mangled body. "Poor bastard didn't have a chance?"

"I'm afraid not. I just wish we could've spent more time together."

Boyd's brow arched at the sincerity in Cody's voice. "You knew him?"

"Let's just say I knew of him."

With his blood splattered, shaved head laying right side up on the street, the earlobe stood out like a rabbit chewed cauliflower. Standing out also was a kaleidoscope of colorful spiders, roses, daggers, and skulls on his muscular arms and thick neck.

To confirm his suspicion, he motioned for one of the officer's who already had his latex gloves on to turn the victim's head. Struggling against the onset of rigor mortis, he lifted it and twisted until the gold earring on the left ear glittered in the beam of his flashlight.

"Who is he?" Boyd asked, curious about Cody's intense look.

"I don't know. I'm hoping your gang unit does. And if they do, I want a list of all his known associates."

Now more than ever he wanted to get Carlos back. The former Mexican boxer's link to this victim and Francis was enough to hold him for questioning. Regardless of what the DEA had to say.

"I hate to tear you two apart," Boyd said. "But we have to get this investigation and traffic going."

"Do me a big favor, will you?" Cody motioned over his shoulder. "How about getting me one of those photos they took a few minutes ago. I have a young lady who just might give us a definite link between this guy and our case."

"You bet. I'll have one ready for you by tomorrow morning."

"Thanks."

"Cody?" Susan asked, "Are you okay?"

"Yes," he assured her as he kneaded the back of his neck. "How's Olivia?"

"I don't think it phased her one bit, Cody. I don't like that."

"Where is she now?"

"Peggy took her to the pavilion." She walked up to him and got within inches of his chest. "Cody."

"Yes?"

"I'm sorry for the way I acted at the hospital. You were right all along. Her life *was* in danger."

"That's okay, Susan. I wasn't really sure I was doing the right thing myself. I just had a hunch something like this might happen and I ran with it. Let's just forget it, okay?"

She looked up with questioning eyes. "That young man at the park. What could he have possibly wanted with Olivia?"

"That's what I've been trying to figure out. Remember Carlos Badillo?"

"What about him?"

"Carlos was seen with him and some of his friends in the Angels Dance Club a couple of weeks ago. Not only that, about a week later Carlos was seen there with Francis and Jack Bauer."

"The man in the hospital?"

"Yes. The only one who hasn't made an attempt to get to Olivia. The others, including Ben, either tried to or inquired as to her whereabouts."

Susan shook her head. "But why? She can't hurt anyone. Right now she can't even talk."

"Either they're trying to make sure her condition never changes or she has something they want." He put his hand on her shoulders. "I'm going to have Peggy drop me off at the vets before taking you and Olivia back to your place. I want you to stay there until I sort things out. I'll have a deputy posted nearby. Whatever you do don't open the door for anyone. Do you understand?"

"Yes, but_____"

"Susan, please. I really believe her life is still in danger."

"Yes, of course. I'll go back and get them now." She took hold of his hand. "I'm sorry about Diablo?"

"So am I. He and I have been through a lot together. I'd hate to see it end like this."

# 43

After a quick breakfast at the Comanche Springs Restaurant, he stopped by the clinic to check on Diablo before heading to work. With his canine partner's wellbeing weighing heavily on his mind, he entered without even noticing who was sitting on the bench in the waiting room.

"Cody."

He turned around and stared in disbelief. "Susan? What are you doing here?"

"I had to see for myself. You don't mind do you?"

"Are you kidding? Of course not." Her words were all he needed to hear, and her face was all he needed to see. Now more than ever, Billy's words echoed in his ear and inadvertently spilled out. "Who knows what may come of it."

"What?"

Ignoring her question, he nodded at two other animal lovers sitting in the room then shot a questioning glance at Susan. "Where's Olivia?"

"She's with that couple I mentioned earlier. I took her there this morning."

He was about to say something when his cell phone rang. It was Martha. "Agent Albrecht called. He wants to see you right away," she said, with a noticeable hint of impending trouble in her tone.

"Did he say what for?"

"They found Mr. Badillo."

"Great. Maybe now we can get some answers. Where is he?"

"At the Sanitation Department's landfill."

The corners of his lips went south as he slowly lowered the phone. He shook his head in disgust. Martha needn't go any further. The local landfill wasn't exactly a place either Carlos or Robert would visit willingly. He developed a knot in his stomach at the feeling he had just lost another person of interest? Suddenly, Agatha Christie's, *Ten Little Indians*, crossed his mind. Was *he* on the verge of ending with none? "Just what I needed to hear."

"What's wrong?" Susan asked, noting the deep creases on his forehead.

Since Ben was safe in jail, Jack Bauer suddenly went to the top of his most wanted list. Now all he had to do was get to him before anyone else interested in his well-being could.

"I'm afraid Mr. Badillo met the same fate as that young man did last night."

"Sheriff?" Martha said, after several seconds of silence.

Plunged deep in thought, he had forgotten she was still on the line. He got back on the phone.

"Yes, Martha. I'm still here."

"I was just going to say, our Mr. Robert sounded a little upset."

"He's not alone...are any of our units over there?"

"Yes, the lieutenant and several deputies are out there right now."

"Tell them I'm on my way."

As he was hanging up, the veterinarian came out and spoke to both of them.

"There's no sign of internal injury, and as far as the leg is concerned, the flexible cast, which will allow some movement of the joint, should help it heal a little sooner."

"What about the snout?"

"The blood came from a deep gash in the left nostril. It required a number of stitches. I'd like to keep him here where he could be monitored for at least the rest of the day before I send him home."

"That's okay with me, doc," he said, turning his attention to Susan. "I want to thank you for stopping by. That was mighty kind of you."

"You're more than welcome. If you need me for anything, you have my number."

The soothing warmth of her hand gave him a sense of peace and assurance. He didn't want to let go but knew he had to get to work.

And so did she.


It wasn't the number of vehicles with US Government license plates that bothered him. Nor was it the putrid odor that gagged him even inside the air-conditioned cab of his pickup. It was the sight of vultures sprinkled like pepper among the white cowbirds above, and the look on Billy's face below. He got out of the truck just as Billy started giving him the news.

"You're not going to like this."

"That bad, huh."

"I'm afraid so."

Cody removed his sunglasses and squinted as the sun's rays reflected off every conceivable, manmade shining object there.

Billy nodded over his shoulder. "The reception committee's waiting for you."

"Another mountain of trash," he said. "That's just what we need. Come on, let's not keep them waiting."

At the crunching of plastic, glass, and cans, several of his deputies, along with a half dozen agents wearing their ominous dark sunglass, turned to face him. Robert, who was bent over an object half buried under the pile of trash, was in their midst, hidden from his view. As the agents parted, Robert straightened up and approached.

"Well, look who's here." Robert said. He nodded towards the trash heap. "Take a good look…I hope you're satisfied."

Cody wasn't exactly sure which was worst, the garlic blast or the contorted face just inches away from his. "Mr., I don't even let the meanest bull in the rodeo get that close to my face. I strongly suggest you back off a might."

"What? Was that a threat? Is that what I'm hearing?" He took the advice and backed off, but then loosened his tie, and started removing his suit jacket. But before he could take it off, the agents and sheriff's deputies alike rushed over to the foreseeable confrontation, prepared, if necessary, to intercede before it developed into another desert storm battle.

"Come on, you two," Frank said. "We're supposed to be on the same side, remember."

"If that's the case, then ask him why he interfered with our investigation. As far as I'm concerned, it's his fault this happened."

Cody's face reddened. The hairs on the back of his neck stood up even higher than the last time. A knot formed in his stomach.

"Now look here, partner," he said, trying desperately to hold back. "You seem to forget who took him out of our hands. Maybe—just maybe—he'd be alive today if you hadn't pulled strings like some hot shot, egotistical puppeteer."

The last thing Cody wanted was a full-blown confrontation, but when he turned around and started to walk away, Robert grabbed his bicep and yanked him back around.

Billy and several agents immediately formed a wedge between them.

"Take it easy," Billy said his palms up against Cody's chest. "It's not worth it, okay?"

"Come on, Robert," Dean said. "Grow up. It's bad enough the chief's not going to like what's happened here already. We don't need to make it any worst."

With his hands now up on Cody's shoulder, Billy pleaded, "Let it go. We don't need this either."

"I will as long as he stays out of my face."

"Okay, okay," Robert, said, under the restraining arms of several agents. After being released, he shook his shoulders, glared at Cody, and then straightened his jacket and tie.

"That's better," Billy said. "How about we all take a short break, okay?"

"You haven't heard the last of this, mister." Robert hollered.

"That's fine with me," Cody said. "But as you can see, Mr. Badillo won't be helping you anymore. And as far as that missing money is concerned, it's probably made it across the border by now. I don't see any reason for you to stick around."

"I'm afraid there is, sheriff," Frank said. "There are still some materials that haven't been accounted for."

Robert got closer, testing the ground one more time. "That's right. And we're not leaving till they are."

"Suit yourself," Cody shot back. "Just don't interfere with my investigation."

"Does that go for me too?" Taylor asked.

Cody didn't even notice him watching the brief episode from a safe distance. He waited for the detective to weave his way through the small gathering before confronting him. "So what do you have to say about all this?"

"Whoa. Take it easy, will ya." He held his arms out as if to ward off a charging bull. "I just happened to hear about this and decided to see who it was they found, that's all."

Cody waited until the agents took Robert over to one of their vehicles to cool off before turning his attention to Taylor. "What'ya doing here, anyway?" Cody asked him. "I thought you were flying out today."

"You can blame it on DEA's involvement. I just had to satisfy my curiosity."

"I see," he said, glaring at Robert. "So what'd you find out?"

"From what I gather, Mr. Badillo there was given a new eye socket in the back of the head then dumped here sometime during the night. Early this morning the sanitation worker on the front-end loader dropped half of his load before spotting him."

"It must've happened right after they snatched him then," Cody said. "

"It looks that way. And if you ask me, Robert's ticked off at himself more than anyone else. He's just trying to palm the guilt off on you."

"That's not gonna work."

"Well, as far as I'm concerned, this will probably close the book on Tony's murder. I'll be out of your hair by tomorrow morning."

"What d'ya mean?"

"What goes around comes around, sheriff. We've known about Badillo and his occupation for some time now. We also knew he was last seen with Tony in a nightclub over on Southern Boulevard, which, by the way, was just a couple of blocks from where his body was found."

"I had a feeling you knew him when I mentioned his name back in the office. Why didn't you tell me all this back then?"

"Like the song says, 'You gotta know when to hold them', remember. You never know when you might need them later. Besides, I wasn't really sure he was the same Carlos we had on our suspect list."

"Are you sure that's him now?"

"Let's put it this way," he said, looking over his shoulder towards the mound, "If I'm not sure now, I will be after I get this back home." He held out the photo given to him earlier by Cody's own department. "About a month after Francis disappeared, a witness, who saw him and Tony out in the alley behind the club, came forth. He claims Carlos forced Tony into a car at gun point. That was the last time Tony was seen alive. Which reminds me, you might as well consider closing the book on Francis. The way I see it, Carlos tracked her down here and got what he was looking for."

Cody didn't much buy his last statement. Francis had been dead for some time now. Why would Carlos hang around if he found the money everyone's looking for? For that matter, why would Robert hang around? Could it be Ben had the money? Does Olivia know where it is?

Taylor took out his handkerchief, looked up at the sun, and then wiped his forehead. "I could sure use a cold one right about now."

"You could always get one here," Billy said, holding in his right hand a matchbook that had been found in Carlos' lapel pocket.

"Let me guess. Angels Dance Club, right?" Taylor asked.

"Yep."

"Is that supposed to be a good place?"

"I don't know," Cody said. "Out of the three persons of interest seen huddled together at the club that night, Jack Bauer's the only one still alive."

Carlos' fate had all the earmarks of a professional job. Francis' didn't. Jack's life, he figured, wouldn't be in jeopardy unless he knew something about her past, or the money. Both of which he must now take into consideration.

"Whether it's a good place or bad one depends on how you act around the clientele, detective," Billy said. He turned to face Cody. "Martha wants you to give her a call."

He excused himself from the pack and walked away to make the call. And when he did, the one person he was hoping to hear from was ready to talk. He told Martha to get a hold of Ben's attorney and make all the necessary arrangements to record the meeting.

After hanging up he joined Billy and Taylor who were still huddled outside the circle of activity and said, "I want you to get just as much information from here as they do, lieutenant." He nodded towards the agents. "Then get back with me at headquarters."

"Before you go," Billy said. "I have some good news for you."

"Diablo?"

"Yes. It just came over the airwaves. He's waiting for you to take him home."

"Now that is good news."

# 44

The air was thick with anticipation even before Cody had entered the interrogation room. Ben Ephraim, handcuffed and shackled, sat slumped like a whipped puppy at the six-foot long table. Sitting next to him, Lacy, his thick bifocals resting at the tip of his pointed nose, his long slim fingers rustling through some documents stashed in his black attaché.

Behind him stood two prison guards with their backs to the wall, both fully aware of what had happened at the hospital, and mentally prepared for a possible repeat.

After greeting everyone in the room upon entering, Cody pulled up a chair and sat right across from Ben. The tape recorder had already been set up and waiting to be turned on. The video camera, hidden inside an air vent high up on the wall behind him, was already turned on and rolling.

Watching the video monitor in another room were the state's district attorney, Brian Keith and prison psychologist, Dr. Louis Weaver, who was there to determine, if at all possible, whether Ben had a problem they should know about and evaluated further, or if he was putting on an academy award winning performance.

Looking at Ben, Cody saw for the first time a man who appeared lost and weakened—a man who had surrendered without a fight to the misfortunes of life. It was a complete contradiction to what he had seen up on the mountain.

After putting down the large manila envelope, Cody nodded his readiness to proceed. He set his elbows on the table. In a low, calm voice, he said, "Ben. I'm sure you know that anything you say here can and will be used against you in a court of law. Are you sure you want to do this?"

Ben mumbled something which no one could really understand. Cody leaned closer. "I didn't catch that. You'll have to talk a little louder."

"Yes."

In the beginning, the words sounded forced, as if coming from a one year old just learning to speak for the first time, but, as the interrogation proceeded, his voice took on a slight hint of bravado and confidence. Nevertheless, Cody knew the recorder had picked it up when, out of the corner of his eyes, he spotted the red, voice activation light blinking.

"For the record, we're going to use the name Ben? Is that okay with you?"

"Ben," he said it more to himself than anyone else, with his head bowed low, and his beard, once again, touching the table.

The name had been pounding his head like rolling thunder ever since the whirlpool vision. After a while he raised his head and made eye to eye contact with Cody. "Who's Ben?"

"According to detective Taylor, your name is Benjamin Ephraim," Cody said, wondering if the man really knew or not. He leaned back in the chair and stared at him for a few seconds before continuing. "I'm going to be the only one asking questions, Ben. If I don't make myself clear, let me know and I'll repeat them. Also, the court has elected to keep Mr. Lacey here as your attorney until such time it can confirm your financial status. Do you have any objections to this?"

Ben hesitated for a brief moment before shifting his eyes slowly towards Lacey. Then, after dropping his head said, "No."

"Good. Now, before we begin, could we get you something to drink?"

To that, the lengthy hair, its blonde hue made lighter by a long overdue shampoo job, swayed from side to side as if lazily swabbing a ship's deck.

"Okay. I want you to take your time. Speak loud enough so we can hear you. Let's start with Olivia. What do you know about her?"

"Nothing."

"What about her mother? Did you know her? Did you have anything to do with her death?"

Lacey jumped in before Ben could open his mouth. "Don't answer that." He turned to Cody. "If you have evidence I'm not aware of then you must present it to me prior to the court proceedings. I have the right to examine____"

"No... I didn't," Ben answered, glaring at Cody with menacing eyes. "He did."

Cody and Lacy turned away from each other and sat straight up. The two deputies behind Ben left the wall they were leaning against and looked at each other. Those in the other room got as close to the black and white monitor as they could.

Cody decided to change tactics and let Ben, who appeared willing to talk his head off, take the lead.

"You're right, Ben. There was another man up there. And from what we've gathered so far, he had on cowboy boots and drove a vehicle to the foot of the mountain. So why don't you just start from the beginning? Maybe then we can get a clearer picture of what happened and who this other man is."

"Be advised I have the right to stop him at any point I deem necessary."

"I'm well aware of that, counselor," Cody said. "Let's just hope you don't have to. The more we learn, the sooner we could put this thing behind us."

Ben drew a deep breath then exhaled as if the weight of the world was about to be lifted off his shoulders. "It's okay. You probably won't believe me anyway." He lowered his head and gazed down at the table. "I was half asleep under a low hanging crag when I heard this rumbling noise. It quit just as I opened my eyes so I wrote it off as a dream and went back to sleep. Sometime later a man's voice woke me up. It sounded like he was talking to someone." He paused for a brief moment, trying to recall what he had seen before continuing. "I saw him come out of the shadows. He...he was holding something rolled up over his shoulder with his left hand and...and a shovel with his right. He dropped them both then bent down and rolled out a large object. At first I thought it was a storefront mannequin, but after a while I got to thinking____"

"You're trailing off, Ben," Cody said. "Speak a little louder. Now, what were you thinking?"

"Who in the world would go up there at night to bury a

dummy? It had to be a body. When I focused my attention on it I realized it...it was a woman."

"What about Olivia?"

"I didn't see her until she came out of the shadows. That's when I saw her eyes. They had this look about them." He paused, shook his head for a brief moment, and then covered his eyes with the palms of his handcuffed hands."

"Ben?"

He dropped his hands and met Cody's questioning eyes. "They mirrored fear...I...I've seen that before," he said, in a low voice. "I just can't figure out where or when. I just knew I had to do something... anything."

"Is that when all hell broke loose?"

"I guess you could say that. He just gasped and froze when I came out to confront him, but then he picked up the shovel and swung it at my leg when I got close. Talk about hell. We rolled, grunted, kicked, threw punches, you name it we did it. I finally got him into a position where I was able to land one on his nose. I knew I got him good when I felt his warm blood splatter on my face. Right after that we both went down from exhaustion. I guess the heat that night got into the fray."

"When did all this happen?"

"If you mean what day or time, forget it." Ben lowered his head again. "Those things don't mean a thing to me. Maybe...Just maybe...if they did, I'd be able to figure out what the hell's going on."

"I can't make any promises, Ben," Cody said. "But we just might be able to help you with that after all this is over. That is, if you're willing to accept it."

"I understand."

"Good. Now, what happened after that?"

"I don't really know. Everything after that was fuzzy. It was like I had passed out or something. The next thing I remember was waking up to the child standing over me. I thought I was dead until I felt the pain in my calf."

"Now we know for sure why he never got to finish digging the grave," Cody commented.

"I tried to finish it myself. I figured if she were found up there, I'd be the one getting the fatal injection. Then everything inside of me boiled over. I had to stop. I just couldn't handle it anymore. I slammed the shovel against a boulder until the handle split in half. I could hear it ricochet down the mountain like a pinball. I couldn't see where it wound up, though."

"We have it."

He gazed into Cody's eyes for several seconds. "I had a feeling you did."

"I don't understand. You say you couldn't finish burying the body? What about your tour of duty in Vietnam? I'm sure you've seen____"

"I don't know what you're talking about." Ben said, frowning. "I've never been to Vietnam."

Heads turned. Shoulders shrugged. Those outside the room watching turned away from the monitor and looked at the psychologist, who leaned closer to it.

Taylor was right. After several inquiries, Cody learned quite a bit about Ben Ephraim's military exploits. He was, indeed, a highly decorated Vietnam veteran. A Green Beret with several face to face kills. Towards the end of the war, he had escaped from the Vietcong, not once but twice, eluding the last massive search in the jungle with his survival skills and ingenuity. There's no logical reason to deny that part of his life, Cody thought, as he shot a puzzled look at the camera.

Lacey glanced at Ben over his bifocals. "Perhaps we should postpone this for a later time."

Ben's eyes rolled up as his mind's eye opened up once again. Under the light of a distant street lamp, a glistening, silver Mercedes, the only vehicle on the outskirts of the parking lot, meets his foggy sight. Music pounded his eardrums. Colored lights penetrated his pupils. Laughter, giggling, and loud conversations engulfed him. In the semi-darkness his outstretched shaking hand pointed a remote door opener at the vehicle. Then a shadow appeared at his side. He struggled to turn around without losing control, but the heavens spin. He drops like a rock. Then darkness overtakes him.

"Ben?"

The voice penetrated the privacy of his inner world, bringing him back to reality. In silence, his eyes slowly rolled down.

"Let the records show the interrogation as being held against the will of the attorney and the defendant," Lacy said, interrupting the silent standoff between Cody and Ben.

"Who has yet to complain or request we stop," Cody added, with a stern look at Lacy. "Now, let's talk about the most important subject." He turned his attention back to Ben. "I'm going to ask you one more time. Why did you leave her out there alone?"

"What?"

"Why didn't you bring her in to the authorities? If you're telling us the truth then you had nothing to worry about."

The confused look appeared first, then the swallow, the tightening of the jaw, and the eye of the storm.

With the incident at the hospital still fresh on his mind, Cody nodded at the two guards. The last thing he wanted was another tornado.

"I didn't," Ben yelled, table shaking under the pounding of handcuffed fists.

When he started to get up, the guards made a move towards him but stopped at the sight of Cody's outstretched hand. So did Ben. "That's okay," he told them. "Mr. Ephraim's just trying to get his point across. Isn't that right, Ben?"

Without saying a word, Ben floated back into his chair like a bird feather tossed into the breeze.

"Now," Cody said, his voice calmed. "What were you about to say?"

"I knew she wouldn't be alone long. I didn't leave until I was sure you were coming."

"Why'd you leave at all?"

"Like I said, who's going to believe I didn't kill that lady?"

He had a point. Even though his story might have been true, it wasn't that easy to swallow or prove. The lack of blood on the sand around Francis' head, however, did point to her being killed somewhere else and then taken to the mountain for disposal. But who's to say that someone wasn't Ben? There were no witnesses other than Olivia. And as far as that goes, he might've known about her condition and felt safe in letting her live

Cody opened the envelope, brought out the photos of Francis and Holly, and then dropped them on the table in front of Ben. "We found their purses, Ben—one inside the farmhouse, the other out back. What d'ya you know about them?"

Ben leaned over and gazed at the photos. "I found the young girl's purse near the base of the mountain several months ago. I thought she might have been a hiker or a naturalist and lost it. The only thing in it was a driver's license that had expired over two years ago. I took out the compact mirror then put the purse on the mantle. I meant to throw it away. I guess I forgot."

"What about the other one?"

"I don't know anything about it."

"Why not? It was found up there in your trash heap."

Before Cody and the prison guards could react, he shot out of the chair again, slobbering as he shouted, "I don't care where you found it. I'm telling you I never saw it."

The stunned guards grabbed his arms and pinned him back to the chair. They held him down until he fizzled out.

For a fleeting moment, the possibility someone else might have dumped the bag there entered Cody's mind. But that, again, was something he would keep to himself for the time being. "Let's get back to Olivia," he said, returning the items to the envelope. "How long was she up there?"

"Long enough to meet him."

"Who?"

"That mountain lion. He showed up right after I put her in my sleeping bag. I thought sure we were going to be his meal for the week. "

"What stopped him?"

"I don't know. Maybe something else got his attention... either that or he was just toying with us, waiting for a better time."

"Or maybe he realized he was outnumbered."

"What do you mean?"

"Your friend," Cody said. "The one who put this crease on my temple? For all we know, he was up there with you."

"I don't know what you're talking about. I have no friends."

He sat back, gazed at Cody for a few seconds, and then slowly rose from his chair.

"It appears my client has nothing more to say."

"I have one more item to take care of, consular." He leaned closer to Ben. "Have you ever owned a *Mercedes*?"

Ben's eyes went up for several seconds recalling the vision again before he said, "No."

"What about the horse you were riding out there?"

"I found him wandering out near the mountain a couple of months ago. He followed me to my campsite and wouldn't go away. I never tethered him in case his owner showed up. No one ever did."

Cody was eager to learn if Taylor knew what he was talking about. He had to ask. "Where'd you learn to handle a horse—to ride one bareback at that?"

Ben's eyes rolled up in search for an answer.

After several seconds without a response, Cody stood up. "Let's try this again some other time." He nodded at the guards. "Go ahead and take him back to his cell."

Lacy gathered his documents and stuffed them back into his case. He got up and confronted Cody. "Unless you have irrefutable evidence, I'd be careful with the questions."

"Thanks. I'll take that into consideration also." He turned off the recorder, took out the tape and stuffed it into his pocket. Left alone in the room, he contemplated for a few seconds on what was said then got up and walked out.

Billy had arrived at the viewing room in time to catch most of the interrogation. But Cody wasn't interested in talking to him just then. He walked right past him and confronted Dr. Weaver. "Well, what d'ya you think?"

"It's what *he* thinks that's important here, sheriff. I detect sincerity in his voice and expressions. In fact, he seems to believe every word he's said." He paused, rubbed his chin, and then turned to Brian. "To your knowledge, has he had a physical examination recently?"

"I doubt it, why?"

"You might want to consider having him undergo a brain scan. At the very least, an examination for a possible history of trauma."

"I'd rather know what I'm up against sooner than later," Brian said. "I'll see to it he gets whatever you recommend."

"What about you, lieutenant?" Cody asked. "What do you think?"

"First of all, his name really is Ben Ephraim. We just got word from AFIS. As far as what you're asking, I don't know. Some of what he said in there could be true. After all, it did look like the grave wasn't really completed. Besides the difference in the footprints, there are those slugs we took out of the crevice wall. They didn't come from our weapons. The way I see it, they were meant for him."

He thought for a moment then said, "There's only one way I know of to find out once and for all if he's really telling the truth. In the meantime, I want you to get a hold of a lunar calendar and check which day of the last two weeks had a full moon on it. After you take care of that, send a couple of deputies back up the mountain. There's got to be shells, footprints, or something up there that can help us find that shooter."

"That's easier said than done," Billy said. "You're talking about the summit. That's a long ways up from where we were. And it's made up of rocks, hard clay, crevices, and caves. It'll be like looking for a needle in a haystack."

"Then use a magnet," he grinned. "Let me know right away if they do find something."

# 45

The minute you step onto the black and white checkered floor you knew the Happy Daze on North Main was not your typical diner. Along one wall, hanging between large black musical notes, were poster size photos of Marilyn, Dean, Lucy, and Desi. Opposite that wall, a soda fountain counter with red vinyl covered stools where patrons could still spin themselves dizzy while waiting for their malts, sundaes, or root beer floats.

It was a place where they could picture themselves on the set of the movie, *Grease,* and dance to all the 50's music the old Jukebox had stored in its carousel. It was one of Cody and Katelyn's favorite haunts.

The manager went to great lengths in providing everything Cody had requested. Balloons of all sizes and colors, tied to the backs of each chair with long strings, bobbed precariously several feet above their heads. Colorful streamers hung like spider webs from the Styrofoam paneled ceiling. And a large white banner above the entrance greeted everyone that came in with the words, "*Happy Birthday, Olivia*", in dark pink letters.

In the end, it turned out to be one of the most unforgettable parties he had ever attended. What he didn't provide were the smiles on the faces of all those who recognized the name on the banner and her face from the media coverage of the last several days.

Surprised as they were upon entering the 50's style diner and soda Shoppe, Susan, Jeremy, and Peggy were unaware Cody, with a little help from Martha, had made the arrangement for the affair a couple of days before, insisting the manager, whom he knew well, not tell anyone about it, not even the employees, until the last minute. The last thing he wanted was publicity of any kind to mar the happy occasion, or spoil the surprise he had in store.

Cards and wrapped gifts, mostly provided by the Sheriffs Department personnel, who were also sworn to secrecy, were neatly stacked at one end of the long, red vinyl upholstered bench outside of the kitchen wall.

The foursome that had bonded the last few days also had their places at the table prearranged. Cody and Susan sat on one side while Jeremy and Peggy occupied the other.

At one end, facing the entrance to the restaurant, sat the birthday girl in her new pink, cotton dress and white, patent leather shoes. At the other, the ever-present Mr. Tibbs was propped up in a child's highchair, looking like a bear that had already filled himself to capacity in anticipation of the hibernating season.

Susan was decked out in a snug fitting purple, tiered v-neck dress, coincidently befitting the surroundings.

He wore his light tan, *Cambridge Classic* pants and an *Arrow*, dark brown shirt that toned down his olive complexion.

As they chatted, he glanced at his watch and then at the manager who was informed not to begin the festivities until given a prearranged signal.

"So," he said, pointing to Mr. Tibbs, "are you going to tell us how you managed that?"

"Believe me it wasn't easy," She said. "I told her he had to run an errand, and that he would be back in time for breakfast. I thought separating them would open the way for others to take his place and make a positive impact on her life. I'm hoping she'll feel a little more comfortable with us as time goes by."

"She bought that?" Jeremy asked.

"Not exactly. It took me thirty minutes of holding her in my arms before she released him."

Their eyes shifted to the young waitress approaching with the menus. For Olivia, Susan ordered from the child's menu the chicken strips with fries. She opted for the grilled chicken salad. Peggy ordered the same thing. As for the men, they settled for the famous Happy Daze Panther burger and fries.

"Do you think she'll eat the chicken?" Peggy asked.

"I haven't heard of a kid yet who wouldn't," Cody said, rubbing together the palms of his hands.

"I see," she said, noting the sparkle in his eyes and the ear-to-ear grin.

"And that includes me," Jeremy added.

Peggy gave him an agreeing smile then reached over and parted the glistening bangs adorning Olivia's forehead. A ponytail, bow tied with a red ribbon, flowed down the back of her neck. In the light filtering through the transparent balloons, her eyes appeared to have a slight glow, and her lips fuller.

"Well, the fourth of July celebration didn't go off exactly the way I wanted it to," Cody said. "Maybe this will make up for some of it."

"You're really getting frustrated aren't you?" Susan asked

"You bet. We just can't seem to unlock that fear or whatever it is that has this hold on her. And if we can't do that, there's no way we could bring out the happiness she's been cheated out of, let alone determine who killed her mother. I'd hate to see that last one turn into a cold case file with little chance of solving."

"I have to agree," Peggy said, with a downcast look on her face. "It doesn't seem like anything is working."

Jeremy wrapped his arms around Peggy's shoulder and drew her near. "Sooner or later something's going to click."

"We'll just have to be patient," Peggy said. "For now, though, let's just concentrate on our meal."

Not long after they had finished eating and the table was cleared, a drone like chorus replaced the lowered volume of the piped in music. Everyone's attention was drawn towards the back of the diner as several waitresses, came out clapping and singing.

Another waitress was lagging behind carrying a birthday cake with six lit candles. Before long all the patrons joined in the festivity.

"This is much more than I had expected," Susan said over the loud chorus.

"It's what I wanted," Cody said. "If nothing else, she might remember this later on."

Once again, they focused on Olivia, searching for some kind of reaction to what was unfolding in front of her. But the only thing visible was a hypnotic like stare at the burning candles.

The waitress set the cake down gently in front of Olivia. But when the birthday girl was prodded to blow them out after the singing had stopped, she wouldn't.

"Why don't we just cut the cake and see what happens," Peggy suggested.

Jeremy agreed. He reached for the knife and handed it to her. "Why don't you help her?"

Peggy rose from the chair. Standing over and slightly behind Olivia, she placed the knife in her right hand, and then closed her eyes as the sweet scent of baby shampoo entered her lungs. With lips curled up and eyes now gleaming, Peggy guided the knife down slowly, savoring every second the warmness of Olivia's smooth skinned hand.

"Cody?" Susan said. "Is anything wrong?"

"No, why?"

"That's the third time you've looked at your watch. Do you need to be somewhere else?"

"No. Not really. It's just____"

He stopped short after noticing Olivia fidgeting, growing increasingly anxious.

Susan followed his stare in time to see her start getting down from her chair.

"Where are you going, sweetheart?" she asked, reaching across the corner of the table to grab her.

"No. Let her go."

"What?" While pulling back in shock, something even more unusual than Cody's stern tone got her attention.

Peggy noticed Susan's jaw drop and her eyes widen. She elbowed Jeremy. He, in turn, shrugged his shoulder, not knowing what to think or tell her.

Once they had all followed Susan's gaze to the entrance of the diner, they understood. There, half encircled by Billy and three other deputies, stood Ben Ephraim with his head hung low. His hands, cuffed in front, were hidden under a sports jacket that had been draped over his arms like a wet garment on a clothesline. Even his leg chains were hidden by the long, baggy Khakis borrowed from a slightly taller deputy. Over his barrel chest, he wore a dark blue sports shirt, which brought out the sheen on his hair and beard. For all intent and purpose, and if it wasn't for the armed escort, he would have been considered just another patron waiting to be seated by the hostess.

On spotting him, Jeremy pushed his chair back and started getting up. "Hey! What's going on here?"

"Sit down," Cody said, forcefully. "Stay right where you are. That goes for the rest of you."

Peggy gasped at the sight of Ben.

Susan's eyes darted from Cody to Olivia, looking for some kind of action that would stop the child from leaving the table.

Olivia got down. For a few seconds, she stood by her chair motionless, her eyes glued to Ben's face. Before long she took one step, and then two.

Shock and awe was written in everyone's eyes as Olivia shuffled straight towards Ben.

Peggy's hands went to her mouth as if to keep her heart from coming out of her throat. She wanted to scream but couldn't.

Jeremy tensed with the urge to jump up and stop her no matter what Cody said.

Susan's nails dug deep into the palms of her trembling hands as she gave Cody a questioning look. She couldn't understand his calmness at the unfolding situation.

Inches away from Ben, Olivia's eyes rolled up to meet his.

"Cody how could you?" Susan whispered with a slight hint of fire in her eyes.

"It's okay. They're watching him closely."

After a few seconds of staring at each other, Olivia opened her arms wide. She wrapped them around Ben's legs then pressed the side of her face against them.

The jacket fell to the floor as Ben lifted his arms above her head then lowered them behind her back. He bent down, drew her head under his chin, and held it there for what seemed to Susan an eternity.

It was a picture perfect moment of love that had captivated all those watching in amazement.

Jeremy's jaw, like the rest of them still sitting at the table, dropped. "You have got to be kidding."

Peggy wanted desperately to say something, but nothing would come out of her mouth, even though it was still agape.

Billy and the deputies, not knowing what to expect, took steps towards Ben, but as soon as they saw Cody's outstretched hand, they quickly backed off.

After the unexpected emotional reunion, smiles and tears appeared on the faces of just about everyone there. Even a teardrop or two managed to fill the lower lids of Susan and Peggy's eyes.

Jeremy just shook his head in disbelief.

"I guess I've seen enough," Cody said.

At his nod, Billy placed a hand on Ben's shoulder and said, "It's time to go back now."

Before turning around, Ben kissed Olivia on top of the head. Then, after lifting his arms back over, cupped her chin in his hand and gazed into her eyes.

Billy picked the jacket up off the floor and hung it over Ben's arms once again.

"You can go get her now, Susan," Cody said.

She stood up, went to Olivia and placed a hand on her shoulder. Meeting Ben's eyes, she nodded, and said, "Thank you." Then she turned Olivia, who had taken a step to follow Ben out the door, around to take her back to their table.

As they were taking Ben away, he looked back over his shoulder and caught Olivia's action out of the corner of misty eyes.

After helping Olivia back on the chair, Susan turned around and gave Cody a knowing smile. She too had her doubts about Ben. His behavior in Olivia's room left her with many questions. She had thought about discussing them with Cody then, but interfering with his investigation was the last thing she had wanted to do, especially since she considered herself to be the new kid on the block. But now she couldn't hold back any longer. She had to know if he also had doubts back then. "You knew, didn't you?"

"Let's just say, I had my suspicions. And this was the only way I knew how to confirm them."

"I guess in some ways the unconventional can teach us a lot."

"It taught me love can blossom in just a few days," he said, knowing how long Olivia had been with Ben, and how long he himself had known Susan.

"What about that incident at the hospital?" Jeremy asked. "He was trying to get to her then."

"Maybe," Cody said, shooting a sly look at Susan, as if the two had shared a secret. "But then again, maybe not. If he's telling the truth, then the real killer is out there waiting to get his hands on Olivia. Ben knew this. I believe he went to her room to protect her. I guess he thought he could do a better job than we could."

"So what happens now?" Jeremy asked.

"Unless we could come up with a witness or some solid evidence that would stand up in court, we'll have to release him or change the charges. Let's face it. He leaves the purse of a women who may have been killed a long time ago out in the open where we could find it, but stuffs a recent victims items into a trash bag, without setting fire to it right away, mind you. Does any of that make any sense to you?"

"Now that I think about it, no."

"Right now, as far as I'm concerned, whoever took those shots at us has reached the top of my person of interest list."

"Anyone particular in mind?"

"I think we need to pay Mr. Bauer another friendly visit."

# 46

Susan gave him a sideways glance just before they arrived at the Bauer farm. "Tell me this isn't going to be another one of your surprises."

He gave her a sly grin and a headshake at a question he had suspected might come his way. "Could be," he said. "Remember what I said awhile back about him being the last person to see Francis alive?"

"Yes."

"He claims he never saw or heard of her, yet, according to a witness, he was with her at the Angels Dance club a couple of weeks ago. The witness claims Jack was pretty upset over Francis leaving Olivia in the vehicle parked outside. If that's true, if he was that concerned, then why hasn't he made an attempt to visit her? Why does he deny knowing her? Surely he knows she's alive. Just about everyone in the country knows that. Let's just see how he reacts to seeing her now."

"You got lucky with Ben. What makes you think Mr. Bauer won't try to harm her?"

"Don't worry. There's no way I'd put you, Olivia, or Diablo in any kind of danger."

She looked at Olivia, who was sound asleep with Mr. Tibbs on her lap. The last several days had finally taken its toll and forced the heavy eyelids to shut down completely five minutes into the ride.

As they passed highway 385 heading west on I-10, his eyes instinctively rolled towards the vast area to the south. "There's where we found her." he nodded. "Between that mountain out there and the highway we just passed."

"My God." she squeezed Olivia a little closer to her. "It's a miracle she was found at all."

"I guess in a way we can thank Ben for that."

After turning off the highway, they drove through the opened gate and on to a long dirt road with a weathered beaten wooden fence running along both sides. A small herd of cattle, some mowing the tall grass while others nibbled on haystacks, was scattered around the field on the other side of both fences.

The jarring ride over bumps, dips, and rocks, afforded little opportunity for any intelligible conversation. But as they neared the building, Susan couldn't hold back any longer. "Are you sure they live here?" she asked, her voice chattering as if she were on a roller coaster.

From her perspective, the house, with its chip peppered clapboard, sagging roof, and skewed shingles, couldn't possibly be inhabitable.

"Don't let its appearance fool you. See those trucks over by the barn? He fixes them up between tending to the cattle—hang on

Olivia, shaken by the deep rutted road, began to stir long before they reached the front of the house.

"If she's not awake by now, she will be in a minute," Susan said.

"That's okay. I want to see his reaction when he sees her. It shouldn't take that long."

For Olivia's sake, after getting out, he closed the door quietly as the blare of nearby cattle reached his ears. At the back of the truck, he ordered Diablo to stay, and then climbed the creaking steps to the front door.

He knocked. No answer. "Mr. Bauer." he said it loud enough to counteract the squeak of a window shutter swinging at the command of the gusting wind. He knocked again. "Anybody home? Sheriff Johnson here."

After several moments of silence from within, he looked back over his shoulder at Susan and shrugged.

At the front window of the house, he cupped his hand over his eyes to block the glare then peered through a laced curtain that had been yellowed by the brush of father time.

The front room was empty. He walked over to the corner of the house where the hot breeze from the south rustled his hair as he stuck his head around. No one was there. On his way back to the front door he noticed Susan's lips moving. But between the closed windows of the pickup and the clattering diesel engine, he couldn't hear what she was saying.

Before he could ask, a loud clanging noise came from inside the barn. He took one step away from the front door, turned his head to the right and gazed at the barn that was roughly thirty feet away.

Olivia stirred once again, this time opening her eyes wider. She lifted her head off Susan's side, then turned and looked out the window. She began to fidget, not the type a child does from weariness, but from anxiety. Noticing it, Susan lowered the window half way and hollered. "Cody, something's wrong. She's getting restless."

"Maybe she's just tired of sitting," he shouted. "Why don't you bring her out for a while and let her stretch her legs."

Olivia's back arched. A wide-eyed look and a grimace appeared on her face. She struggled with the buckle on her seat belt.

In an attempt to calm her down, Susan put her hands over hers, but the little fingers continued to fight for supremacy.

Susan was completely caught off guard by the strong will to escape from the grip of the seatbelt. It was by far the most purposeful movement she had seen yet. "Wait a minute," she said. "Wait. I'll let you out."

When finally freed, Olivia flung herself over Susan's lap and with outstretched arms continued her mission, this time with the door handle. Susan wrapped her arms around Olivia's waist in an attempt to hold her back.

Cody looked back in time to see Olivia clawing at the window like a wildcat trying to break out of a cage.

"What's the matter?" He yelled.

"I don't know." Looking past Cody's shoulder she noticed something different about the double doors of the barn. "Cody!"

"What?" He looked back over his shoulder as she pointed towards the barn.

"That door was halfway open when we got here. Now it's closed. There may be someone in there."

The breeze had picked up somewhat since they had arrived, but not enough to move a door of that size and weight.

When Susan finally opened the passenger door, Olivia squirmed off her lap then slid out of the truck. Susan reached out to grab her but missed. Olivia ran around to the back of the truck then veered off the road and headed towards an open field as fast as her little legs could take her.

Cody debated whether to go after her or check the barn. Fearing whoever was inside might get away; he cupped his hands over his mouth and gave Diablo the command to go get Olivia.

Completely ignoring the restriction and consequences, Diablo jumped from the bed of the pickup and hobbled after her. He passed Susan, who was almost out of breath, and quickly reached Olivia. As gentle as a German Sheppard could, he locked his fangs on the hem of her Khaki shorts and held her in place until Susan caught up.

In the meanwhile, Cody, not knowing who or why the person inside wouldn't come out and greet them, cautiously edged his way to the barn. Rather than opening the door right away, he stood off to the side and put his ear to the wall. Hearing nothing, he hollered, "Anyone in there, this is Sheriff Johnson."

He stepped to the side of the door, grabbed the handle, and cracked the door open just enough to peek inside. The cavernous interior was flooded with slivers of light coming through the numerous cracks on the walls. Countless particles of dust and flying insects danced through the slivers as if they were performing aerial stunts under spotlights.

His nose turned up at the stronger than normal stench of animal manure mixed with wet straw—a sure sign of neglect.

A mare tied in a stall flipped his tail at the flies then rattled his moist nostrils with a blast of air. A large rat, off in the corner, feasting on a rotting apple, ran for cover.

He took a chance and opened the door wide enough to enter. As he surveyed the interior he noticed the manual chain hoist and trolley bolted to one of the beams above his head. He walked under the steel hook hanging on the end of its chain. On the walls were several block and tackles with ropes looped around their pulleys. Thick ropes, like jungle vines, also hung from several rafters.

It was apparent part of the forty by sixty-foot wide pole barn had been converted into a well-equipped auto repair shop. The other part still had remnants of stalls with hitches, tacks, and other riding accessories hanging on the walls.

Recalling Jack's purported fall, he rolled his eyes up to the loft. Stacked by the edge were several small bales of hay. Looking down he noticed an empty stall. Inside it, a metal bucket lay on its side. He trudged through the soaked, straw covered floor and picked it up. Thinking nothing of it, he set it down and continued his search.

On top of an eight-foot long workbench stood the tabletop drill press, grinder, and an ammo shell loader. There were other things on it, though, which were more interesting: the photo, the box of used 30-30 rifle shells, and signs of dried blood splatter.

He blew the wood shavings off the photo and gazed at it. Making out the face was virtually impossible. It was almost completely gone. His eyes narrowed in confusion.

Panning to his left, he spotted the tarp-covered pickup. Looking at the exposed lower part, he noticed the rusty hubcaps and bumpers.

Curious, he walked over to the front of it, grabbed the bottom hem of the tarp, and then rolled it off the hood. A blinding sliver of light, bouncing off the hood ornament, took him back in time. In it he saw the vehicle fast approaching on his side of the road. Katelyn lifting her head just before he jerked the steering wheel and then hearing the words, "look out."

But this time the voice was rough, crude, and definitely masculine.

It was Jack Bauer's.

# 47

"What's going to happen to her now?" Ben asked.

"Don't worry," Billy said. "She'll be well taken care of. Right now the only person you have to worry about is yourself. What happened at the restaurant doesn't exactly exonerate you. We're still searching for more clues and tying together what we already have. In the meantime, you'll be taken back to your cell by these two fine gentlemen." He gave the two deputies the nod.

"Do you still think he's responsible for those killings?" Martha asked, watching them take Ben away as she walked back to her desk.

"That's up to the courts to decide."

"If it turns out he's really an attorney, he could probably shoot holes in what we have so far," Martha said. "Especially if Olivia regains her ability to talk and verifies his story."

"The problem is he doesn't know he's an attorney, or so he says. Till then, we'll keep a good eye on him. Especially since it seems someone's trying to silence him also."

Just then, deputy Earl walked through the door waving two small brown bags in front of him.

"Whatd'ya have there?" Billy asked.

"We've finally located the exact spot where the shots came from. Take a look."

Billy grabbed the first bag from Earl's outstretched hand and set it on Martha's desk. He opened it.

"Spent shells. 30-30. this'll come in handy. What's in the other one?"

"We followed several footprints down from there and found this about a hundred yards south of the base. It was snagged on a Creosote bush." Earl set the second bag on the desk.

When Billy opened it and looked inside, his eyes opened wide. He looked at Earl then at Martha.

"Where's the sheriff?" he asked her.

"He said something about going over to the Bauer place, why?"

"Get dispatch to send all available units over there right now," he told her, and then turned to Earl. "We don't have much time. Let's go."

"What's going on," she asked.

"We'll tell you when we get back. Get on the horn now."

# 48

Nadine's ear-piercing scream as she charged at him with the pitchfork sent shivers down his spine. But before Cody could turn around to see it coming, Jack Bauer ran in and shielded him from the fast approaching Nadine with his body.

At the sight of her son suddenly standing between her and the intended target of her wrath, Nadine tried to stop her momentum but couldn't. Nor could she stop from literally skewing Jack as if he were a piece of meat on a hot barbecue grill.

Cody could not believe his eyes as portions of the bloodstained tines ripped out of Jack's lower back.

In shock, and with the wind completely knocked out of him, Jack wrapped his trembling hands around the handle of the imbedded pitchfork and attempted to pull it out. He couldn't. With eyes opened wide in disbelief, he gazed at Nadine then dropped to his knees like a wilting weed, his insides burning with fire, his mind filling with fear of death.

For the first time since the frightening scream, Cody was able to see jack's eyes straining to escape from their sockets. Nadine, who was standing in front of her son with her hands cupped over her mouth, was also in a state of disbelief and shock.

The scream brought Susan and Olivia running. Entering right behind them, Diablo, who, upon sensing the threat, headed straight for Nadine. His speed and weight sent her flying back towards the stall where she had started her banzai charge towards Cody.

He drew his weapon and aimed it at her. Once he realized

she was under Diablo's control, he quickly put it back into his holster.

Susan gasped at the sight of Jack writhing in pain on the foul smelling dirt floor.

Olivia emitted for the first time a muffled noise that could have been a feeble attempt to scream.

Cody, reacting to Olivia's wide eyed look, and the onset of tremors, waved his arm frantically, yelling, "Get her out of here." At the same time, thankful he did not get a chance to go through with the idea of exposing her to any part of what had happened to her mother in the hope of bringing her out of her condition.

Susan picked her up, shielded her eyes with the palm of her right hand, and then ran back out.

"Good job, boy. Good work. I'll take it from here."

Still growling, Diablo reluctantly backed away, allowing Cody to get close enough to roll her over and place her in handcuffs.

"Is he dead?" she asked, "Is he dead?" she repeated, tears welling.

"Let's hope for your sake he isn't, Mr.'s Bauer."

He turned his attention to Jack, who was lying on his side with the impaled pitchfork. He knelt down and checked his pulse. It was as weak as his breathing, and his face was as white as a ghost. For the time being, the bleeding had been minimized by the flesh closing around the tines. The real threat now was the likelihood of internal injuries and infection. "Don't move," Cody said. "I'll get help out here right away."

He got up and ran out to the pickup, passing Susan who was consoling the sobbing Olivia. On the radio, he called for assistance and an ambulance. From behind the seat, he pulled out the first aid kit. On his way back he stopped by Susan long enough to make sure Olivia was okay.

"I think so," Susan said, as she held Olivia close to her bosom. "She's just frightened."

"She wasn't the only one. I wasn't exactly expecting anyone to come out of hiding like that. Apparently, she was the one who closed the barn door when we got here."

"Cody, look."

The sirens got louder as she pointed down the dirt road towards several department vehicles fast approaching."

"Stay here and point them to the barn," he said. "I have to go take care of Mr. Bauer."

Back inside, and on his knees again, Cody noticed Nadine had managed to change the initial course of her charge enough to only impale Jack with three out of the pitchfork's five tines.

He got back up and hurried over to the workbench where earlier he had spotted a box cutter. With it, he cut and ripped most of Jack's shirt off. Fearing contamination from animal fecal matter, he wiped as much blood as he could from the flesh and tips of the tines with the shirt. Looking around, he spotted a horse blanket slung over a stalls gate. As he got up to get it, Diablo's growl made him look back at Nadine who was attempting to get on her feet. "Don't move, Mrs. Bauer. He'll tear you apart, believe me."

He grabbed the blanket and gently covered Jack then walked over and helped her up.

With tears now flowing, she gazed at Jack, and then lowered her head. "I didn't mean it. Why did you get in the way? Why?" she asked. "Now they'll take you away from me."

"I wouldn't exactly say that, Mr.'s Bauer. "It looks like it's gonna be the other way around."

# 49

After they had cut a major portion of the pitchfork's handle, Jack was flown by Care Fight to the Odessa Regional Medical Center where he underwent two-hours of surgery to remove the tines, stop the internal bleeding, and clean the wounds. X-rays and Cat scans revealed the tines had missed all of his internal vital organs.

Inside Cody's pickup, Olivia pointed at the tearful, twisted face plastered against the window of the Sheriffs Department vehicle parked next to them and said, "bad lady," just before Nadine was whisked away to the county jail for attempted murder. Even though Susan hated its connotation, she was overjoyed by the rebirth of Olivia's soft, squeaky voice. She lifted Olivia's chin and looked straight into her gleaming eyes. "Did that bad lady hurt you?"

She nodded.

"Well she won't be hurting you anymore," Susan assured her.

"How is she?" Billy asked after seeing the exchange of embraces inside the pickup.

Susan lowered the window. "I think she'll be alright now," she said, stroking Olivia's hair. Susan looked at Cody, who was at the front of the barn appearing hesitant at the prospect of reentering. "Right now, I'm worried about him."

"That makes two of us. I'll go check on him."

Through all that had transpired Cody had yet to fully see what that one sliver of light reflected off—what sent him momentarily back to that dreadful night.

Billy came up behind him and laid his hand on his shoulder. "You okay?"

"I think so. But tell me something. How'd you manage to get out here so soon? I just got a hold of control a couple of minutes ago."

"We found Jack's red bandana near the mountain."

"You did?"

"Yep. I recognized it the minute I saw it. He must've dropped it after he took off. I thought maybe you might run into a little bit of trouble with him."

"So you think he was the shooter."

"I believe so."

"Before we go, there's something in there *I* recognized." He nodded towards the barn.

"Okay, why don't you and I go in and find out what it is?"

The moving sun no longer brightened the same spots inside the barn. A whole different picture unfolded before his eyes. As they passed by the workbench, Billy noticed the mutilated photo. He stopped and, with deep creases on his forehead, hovered over it. "What's this?"

Cody turned around and joined him at the bench. "I'm not really sure. By the looks of it, somebody's been doing a pretty good job of whittling away at it. If you look closely at the bench top you'll see more gouges. And they all seem to be inside the tape marks."

"I wonder what it means."

"I guess we'll have to wait and see what the Bauer family has to say. They probably have the answers to a lot of questions."

"Like why she tried to kill you?"

"That's just one of them."

Billy noticed the box of spent shells. He picked it up and took one out. "I have a funny feeling these hammer marks are gonna match those on the ones we have back at headquarters."

"You're probably right." He left the bench and continued his journey over to the truck. "Well whatd'ya know," he said, standing in front of the hood. "We finally meet."

Billy's eyes narrowed as he looked around to see who Cody was talking to. He soon realized the words were directed at the chrome steel, hood ornament; a miniature Bull dog posed to leap.

It was the nightmare monster picked up by Cody's headlights as both vehicles passed each other that fateful night, the monster that hid in his subconscious mind, occasionally appearing in his nightmare.

"Billy. I would like you to meet the other vehicle."

"Are you sure?"

"I'm willing to bet my life on it."

"Life on what?" Susan asked as she entered.

Turning around, Cody noticed something about Olivia apparently missed by the others. "Where's Mr. Tibbs?"

The words had barely come out when Diablo entered the barn with part of Mr. Tibbs' belly in the clutch of his razor sharp fangs.

"Bring it here."

To Cody's surprise, Diablo dropped it, put one paw on it, and started gnawing at it with a vengeance.

"What are you doing?" Cody asked in disbelief. "Stop that. Back off."

Diablo's apparent fury against the bear was relentless. He continued to tear into his prey in spite of Cody's harsh sounding words.

"Cody, do something," Susan yelled. "He's destroying it."

With his fangs dug into the hapless bear's throat, he picked it up and swung it violently from side to side, backing up as he did so to get away from Cody's advance towards him.

Cody was completely at a loss. What was going through Diablo's head? Had he gone mad?

"Careful," Billy said, sneaking over to one side of Diablo. "He's not about to let that go."

The attack on Mr. Tibbs proved fatal. The ripping sound was followed by small balls of cotton flying everywhere. Along with them, more than a dozen little white packets, each with a rubber band around it. Mr. Tibbs had spilled his guts in more ways than one.

Cody's eye's narrowed.

Billy's head went back.

Susan gasped.

"Is that what I think it is?" Billy asked.

Cody stooped down. He picked up one of the packets and carefully un-wrapped it. He stuck his finger into the white substance then put it to his tongue. "Well I'll be… Cocaine."

"You're kidding," Susan said.

"No wonder he had such a big smile," Billy said.

Cody looked up at him in agreement. "Now we know what this was all about—what Carlos was looking for. And why his young friends tried to snatch Olivia."

"What about Francis. Do you think she knew about this?"

"That stuff didn't get in there by itself, Susan." Billy said. "Someone had to do it."

"I'm afraid we'll never know now that Francis is gone." Diablo kept his head still long enough for Cody to gaze into his eyes. "You did your job, partner, now put the poor thing down. Go back to the truck and stay there."

"I guess we'd better perform a little more surgery on him," Billy said. "There's no telling how much more our furry friend has swallowed."

"I'll take care of that, if you don't mind."

The voice came from someone hiding in the shadow filled corner behind the old pickup.

Billy turned around to see who it was before Cody could get back on his feet.

Susan tightened her grip on Olivia's hand.

Seen first was the white of the mysterious person's eyes. Seconds later, their eyes focused on the nine-millimeter pistol held firmly in his hands.

"Take them out and throw them over here," he said, nodding towards their holstered weapons. "Don't make any stupid moves."

The words, "never give up your weapons," ran through Cody's mind like a stampede of horses. He was sure it was going through Billy's also. But, with Olivia and Susan standing nearby, he had to make sure Billy would comply. "Do as he says, Billy."

Billy gave Cody a questioning look.

"That's right, lieutenant," the man said, as he bent down in the darkness and picked up the two pistols. "The sheriff knows best." He tossed them behind the same hay stack where Nadine had started her rampage.

Diablo. Would he dare risk whistling for him?

In the hope of shielding Olivia from harm, Susan stepped in front of her. A chill ran through her slender body, her quivering lips parted. "Who are you? What do you want?"

"Why don't you come out and introduce yourself to the lady," Cody said. "Then tell her why you're here."

"Since it sounds to me like you already know," he said, before coming out, "why don't you tell her?"

"Susan, I'd like you to meet Agent, Robert Albrecht, from the Drug Enforcement Agency. He's supposed to be on the side of law and order in these here United States. Unfortunately, greed seems to have put him on the other side."

He came out. "Is that what you believe, sheriff?"

"It's the way I see it, Robert. Apparently you're involved in some way with this here cocaine. You probably had some kind of business ties with Tony D'Angelo. Am I right so far?"

"Not bad." Robert grinned. "Let's hear the rest."

"The stuff disappears. Tony gets killed. The treasure hunt begins. I've been wondering why you were so upset about Carlos' demise. You were hoping he'd lead you to the drugs. Maybe even the money Tony stole from the agency." He paused for a moment in thought then continued, "Or was that last one something you took care of?"

"Not bad again, sheriff. You're right. Carlos would've led me to it eventually, but since he was taken out of the picture I figured you'd do just as well. That's why I've been keeping tabs on you. A while ago the whole county knew you were up here. What they don't know now is that you and your friends stayed after everyone else left. I did."

"He must've snuck up while we were all in here," Billy murmured. "I must be losing my senses."

"Don't torture yourself, Cochise. Thanks to the confusion and the number of people milling around here, I was able to park behind the shed unnoticed. Once all the others left, I snuck up here and came through the back door while you were admiring my property. It was as easy as that."

While he was rambling, Olivia pushed on Susan's wrist and wiggled out of her grip. She took off running out the front door.

"Wait! Olivia, come back." Susan turned to go after her.

"Stay where you are," Robert said. "Let her go. She can't get far."

"You lay a hand on her and I'll____"

"Do what, sheriff? Hang me from the nearest tree? Those days are long gone, remember."

"What're you going to do, Mr.?" Billy asked. "Shoot us all. They'll hunt you down like an animal. You'll never get away with it."

"That's a pretty big desert out there, deputy. It could be days, weeks, even months before they'd find you. And by that time I'll be sitting pretty in South America."

"They'll trace that gun to you in a heartbeat." Billy nodded towards it.

"Come now, you don't really think I'd use my own service revolver do you? As a matter of fact, I got this at one of your local gun shows a couple of days ago. They make it so easy."

Robert thought of everything. And now he was gloating over it—showing off his intelligence as if he was being interviewed for his next promotion.

Cody shot a sinister smile at him. *That's okay, you just keep talking.*

"Now, why don't we all take a ride in the desert?" Robert said. "I hear the scenery's absolutely fascinating this time of the year."

He herded them outside at gunpoint. Halfway to the vehicles, Olivia's sobbing could be heard in the serine atmosphere of the southwest desert. It was coming from behind an empty wooden barrel where she had put herself back inside her closet, wishing it would stop once and for all, and hoping no one would see her.

"Get her out of there."

"Listen, Robert, there's no way she could hurt you," Cody said. "Just leave her here. Someone's bound to come and find her."

"Please," Susan said, ready to get on her knees if she had to. "She's just a baby. Her whole life is still ahead of her. Give her a chance."

"You heard me. Now move," he screamed.

Susan reached down and took her by the hand. "Come on, baby. Everything's going to be alright. Nobody's going to hurt you, I promise."

Cody's ears were tuned to all that was said, but his mind was in third gear trying to steer a safe course for the road ahead. Their only chance was Diablo. It had been almost five years since his retirement from the K-9 unit. Whether Diablo would instinctively attack or have to be prompted weighed heavily on his mind. So did Diablo's hind leg. Would he even be able to do the job? Would it damage it further? He had no choice. He had to make the decision.

"Move it," Robert yelled again. "You and the kid first, lady. Now let's go."

Cody and Billy followed several feet behind Susan. With their hands on the back of their heads they continued towards their inevitable fate. Timing was everything.

From a distance Cody noticed Diablo anxiously pacing back and forth in the bed of the truck, stopping occasionally to stand with his front paws on the top edge.

Unnoticed by Robert, Cody worked his way closer to Billy's side and whispered, "Pick up the pace."

"What?"

"The pace."

He had to get separation between them so Diablo could see the gun in Robert's hand as they neared the pickup.

When the gap between life and death widened, Diablo stopped whining and started growling. Before Robert could react, Diablo jumped from the truck and hobbled quickly towards him. He leaped then locked his jaw on Roberts' wrist. He shook it from side to side as if it were a mere rag doll.

In pain and fear, Robert dropped the gun and started kicking Diablo's belly.

Seizing the opportunity, Billy turned around and threw a body block on the busy Robert who went down with Diablo still hanging on.

As the scuffle intensified, Susan picked up Olivia and ran back into the barn.

Cody picked up the gun. "Let him go, boy. Good boy. It's Okay. Billy's got him."

Diablo reluctantly let go and backed away, giving Billy enough room to wrap his arm around Robert's neck.

After Cody holstered the gun, he took hold of Diablo's collar. "Give it up or I'll let him go," he hollered, straining to keep the barking dog from dragging him closer to Robert.

Realizing the futility of fighting against man and beast, Robert succumbed, whittling down to a beaten man. After Billy rolled him over on his stomach, he forced his arms behind his back and ratcheted the cuffs on.

As Diablo settled down to a growl, Cody kneeled next to him and checked the hind leg. Finding everything okay, he lovingly wrapped his arm around him. "You didn't forget after all, did you boy? You've earned your keep today, that's for sure. It's okay now. Go on back to the truck. I'll be right there."

"Is he okay?" Billy asked.

"I think so. I'll have the vet check him when this is all over just to make sure."

"How'd you know he'd do that?"

"I didn't. We were just lucky I didn't take away too much of his past, or that his hurt leg wouldn't keep him from attacking." He turned his attention back to Robert who was still lying on the ground. "Get him up."

"It's a good thing I stuck around," Billy said. He grabbed Robert's arms and pulled him up. "I don't think we'd all fit in that vehicle of yours."

"Take him in. We'll be right behind you."

He was about to take Robert away when he looked past Cody's shoulder and saw a trail of dust off at a distance. "We've got company."

Following his gaze, Cody turned around. A dark colored vehicle was fast approaching on the dirt road leading to the barn. "Now who can that be?"

"I don't know but he's in a mighty big hurry."

"Cody, what's going on," Susan asked, noticing the vehicle as she and Olivia came out of the barn.

"We'll soon find out. Take Olivia and get in the truck."

The vehicle skidded to a stop several yards in front of them. The passenger got out first then the driver. Both men, one in a gray, pinstriped suit, white shirt and tie, the other in a black suit and a white shirt with its collar opened, approached with their outstretched hands displaying FBI credentials.

"Agent Snyder and, let's see…agent Philip," Cody said, holding a hand in front of his eyes to shield the glare of the sun behind the agents. "Well now, what can we do for you boys?"

"We have an arrest warrant for DEA agent, Robert Albrecht, sheriff. If it's alright with you, we'll take him off your hands."

Cody stepped in front of them as they approached Robert and Billy. "Now you just hold on, boys. I'm not turning anyone over till I get to the bottom of all this. Right now I have both a criminal case to take care of and the jurisdiction to do it. If you want to pursue this, just stop by my office and we'll discuss the matter in an orderly fashion. In the meantime, my deputy here will take Mr. Albrecht and lock him up for safe keeping. I'm not about to lose another prisoner just yet."

After putting their credentials back into their pockets, they glanced at each other then faced Cody. "Okay then, if you don't mind, we'd like to obtain a search warrant for this property."

"What do you expect to find around here?"

"We're checking every place agent Albrecht has set foot on, sheriff."

"It's the money, isn't it?"

"We'll explain it all tomorrow morning. In the meantime, we'll get some of our people down here to do a thorough search once we get that warrant."

"By the way, how'd you know he was here?"

"We've been keeping an eye on him ever since he arrived in Dallas." Having said that, they turned around, walked back to their vehicle, and then they sped away, engulfing Cody, Billy, and Robert in a cloud of throat choking dust.

When the air cleared, Cody put Robert in the back of Billy's vehicle then went back to his truck where, after letting the tailgate down, he helped Diablo up into the bed. Once sure that his canine friend was okay, he got into the driver's seat and for a while, sat there staring at the northern tip of the Glass Mountains.

"Cody? Is everything Okay?" Susan asked.

"It is now. Let's get out of here before anyone else crawls out of the dirt."

# 50

Contrary to the reception given them back at Nadine's place, Cody greeted them with a smile and an extended hand across his desk. "Come on in, gentlemen." He pointed to the two chairs preset in front of his desk. "Have a seat."

After shaking Cody's hand and introducing himself, Ted Snyder, the apparent senior agent, stuffed his stocky, five foot six inch frame in the armchair. He immediately unbuttoned his gray suit jacket then straightened his silver colored tie.

His younger partner, Gene Philip, who looked like a professional surfer with his six foot two inch, slender frame, long blonde hair, and a light tan, quickly followed suit. He was dressed in a tan sports jacket, dark brown pants, white shirt, and red tie.

"Everything you need to release him is right here," Ted said, as he leaned closer to Cody's desk. "All we need now is your signature."

"Good." Cody took the documents from his outstretched hand, put them aside on his desk then, in his usual congenial manner, offered them both freshly brewed coffee. Gene turned it down while Ted was more than happy to accept. After placing their orders with Martha, Cody turned his attention back to them. "Now, where were we? Oh, yes." He reached down, picked up the documents and, as he leaned back in his chair, read each page carefully. "Well, they seem to be in order."

"So, when could we have him?"

"Not so fast, Mr. Philips. Remember what I said back at the farm." He sat straight up, laid the papers down again then folded his arms across his chest. "Now, do you mind telling me what's going on here? I've had more people from the east coast visiting me lately than I've had in my entire life. I'd like to know how a local murder case like this has managed to attract all this attention. If you don't mind my asking, what's the connection?"

At that, both agents turned their heads and looked at each other as if contemplating whether to answer him or not. After a brief standoff, Ted nodded his approval then turned to face Cody.

"It appears you've gotten yourself between a Mexican cartel's stateside operation and a DEA agent working both sides of the fence, sheriff."

"Cartel? In the states?"

"I'm afraid so."

"You see," Gene said, taking over. "Not only have their tentacles reached parts of our country, they've also managed to recruit some of our own citizens to do their dirty work. We're talking growing, packaging, distribution, the whole ball of wax."

Gene shifted his eyes towards Ted and nodded for him to continue.

"Agent Albrecht was freelancing for himself, sheriff. As you already know, Tony was a DEA informant. One whom they trusted enough to dish out twenty grand for a drug buy that would've gotten him noticed by the cartel. The problem was that the money they gave him, along with what he stole from the drug operation, disappeared. Once Robert learned that Tony reneged on the plea bargain deal and ripped both the DEA and the cartel off, he saw dollar signs. He figured he could turn the tables on Tony and do likewise."

"Did he really think he could get away with that?"

"Why not," Gene said. "What were the chances of Tony reporting the theft to the authorities or, worst yet, exposing his whereabouts to the cartel? It may not sound like a big sum of money considering the latter's total intake, but there's a big difference between losing that much to the feds and losing it to a two bit loser like Tony. A severe lesson had to be taught here, sheriff. That's why he wound up on their most wanted list."

"How was he able to steal drugs from their distribution center? They must've had some type of security system."

"I'll let Ted answer that."

"Simple. First he managed to find out where the safe was. Then he got hungry after finding out they only had one guard watching the place at night.

"One guard?"

"The cartel must've figured too many would draw unwanted attention. Besides, nobody in their right mind would have the guts to go near there, let alone steal from them."

"Except someone like Tony, that is," Cody said.

"And a career thief named Joey Blanco," Gene added. "Together they overpowered the guard, torched their way in, and then hauled off cash plus seven hundred and fifty thousand dollars worth of pure cocaine. They would've probably gotten away with it if Joey had kept his mouth shut. When the word hit the streets about Joey's new found riches, Carlos got wind of it. He eventually caught up with the guy and persuaded him to talk."

"Of course, that was before Joey wound up in the East River," Ted added.

"So I heard," Cody said.

"Anyway," Gene continued. "Before Joey became a floater, he fingered Tony. After that, it didn't take Carlos long to find him. Under severe duress, he told him his wife, Francis, had the stuff. That meant Carlos didn't need him anymore so he whacked him, which, by the way, was his biggest mistake."

"Why's that?"

"As soon as Tony's wife got the word that her husband was dead, she bought a car then took the kid and split. Carlos couldn't find her so he went back to Mexico. Somehow he persuaded his boss to give him an extension on the contract. I guess it was his celebrity status and his reputation for getting the job done eventually that bought him a reprieve."

"What put Robert on to Carlos?"

"Robert had a good idea Carlos wouldn't have killed Tony unless he was able to squeeze information on the stolen goods whereabouts. Knowing that, Robert started hunting for Carlos, or should I say, looking for our minnow. He wasn't about to let him or the cartel get away with his new found fortune. He figured Carlos would come back sooner or later to get it.

"In other words, it was a race to see who would get to the stolen items first."

293

"That's right," Ted said.

Martha came in with the tray. She put two coasters on Cody's desk then set the cups on them. "Can I get you anything else?"

"No. This'll do for now, thanks." He waited for her to leave before giving them the okay to continue.

"Right now we're here to deal with Robert's extracurricular activities," Ted said, taking a sip then wiping his graying mustache with the napkin Martha had provided.

"Meaning?"

"His job was to find out who their stateside boss was through Tony. If nothing else, get information on their operation____"

"But then Tony was killed before he was able to do either, so the FBI and DEA switched their focus to Carlos and he became the bait, right?"

"Right," Gene said.

"I had a feeling there was a big fish in the picture, but if you think Robert's gonna open up and point to it, you might be in for a big surprise."

"We're used to surprises, Sheriff," Ted said. "Thanks for the warning."

"Before you leave, there's one more thing."

"And what's that?" Gene asked.

"Who ordered the hit on Carlos?"

"Our sources tell us it was the cartel in Mexico," he answered. "I guess they finally got tired of waiting."

"Which reminds me, sheriff," Ted said. "Our search of Mrs. Bauer's property didn't yield what we were looking for. You have just a portion of the cocaine. The seed money he stole from DEA, or what was made from the sale of the rest, is still missing. Do you have any idea where that might be?"

"No I don't. We tore Francis' car apart and came up empty handed. We got the same results at that old farmhouse Ben stayed at. It's my guess either Tony hid it somewhere up north and lied to Carlos, or Francis hid it down here and took its whereabouts to the grave with her. We'll probably never find it."

"I'm afraid you're right, sheriff," Gene said. "If it's alright with you we'd like to get the prisoner. There's a flight leaving here a couple of hours from now. We'd like to make that."

Cody signed the extradition papers then returned them. "They'll have him ready for you by the time you get down there. I hope you get whatever it is out of him."

At the threshold of the door, he turned his attention to the one person sitting on the bench outside his office who was inadvertently involved in the case, and who he had dreaded facing the most.

"Sorry to keep you waiting," he said. "Please come in."

Her eyes, dabbed occasionally with the wadded up tissue in her trembling hand, were reddened. Her face slightly paled by the long awaited news. Of all those who had occupied the seat in front of his desk the past few days, she was the only one he carefully helped get into it. Once seated, he walked back to his chair and sat down with his forearms crossed on top of his desk.

"First of all, Mrs. Nelson, please accept my sincere condolences on the death of your daughter, Holly. As you already know, DNA has confirmed our suspicions and we do have the perpetrator in custody."

"Thank you, you're very kind." She dabbed her eyes again before continuing. "I'm just glad to finally have closure. That means so much to me."

"Believe me, I understand." He dropped his eyes momentarily before continuing. "If it's alright with you, I'll have my secretary make all the arrangements to have Holly's remains sent back home. Just let her know where and when. We'll make sure she gets there."

"Thank you. I appreciate that."

"In the meantime, if there's anything you need, or that we can do for you, just let us know. We'd be more than happy to help you in any way we can. Thank you for your cooperation, Mrs. Nelson, and most of all your patience."

After helping her up, he escorted her out to Martha's desk and said his farewell.

# 51

Inside the Department's vehicle, Jack leaned back, closed his eyes, and let his mind's eye take him back to that fatal night, where every word spoken and every action taken  inside the barn would haunt him for the rest of his life.

When he entered it, he gave Nadine a look that would've stopped a charging bull dead in its track. "What happened?"

"We got into an argument at the house…she wouldn't listen to reason. She lit out and came in here. I followed right behind. That's when she started laughing at me, calling me a psycho, a lunatic." Nadine paused with a sigh. "So I took care of her. You have to understand, Jack. You and I belong together, sweetheart. Without each other, we'd be lost. I need you. You're the only good thing your father's ever given me. I couldn't stand to lose you too."

"Whatd'ya think is gonna happen now, mother, huh? Do you think they're going to let us stay together as if nothing ever happened?"

"If you just do what I say, no one will ever know."

As he was bent down over Francis' body, he could feel the knobby fingers kneading his tough skinned back and neck as her words continued to spew out. "Remember how it used to be before she showed up. I always took care of you, sweetheart. You've never needed anything other than my love." She paused to let her manipulation take affect, and then said, "I want you to take her up the mountain and____"

"The mountain?"

"Yes! They'll never think of looking for her there. Besides, if they do find her, who do you think they'll go looking for?"

"That crazy old hermit?"

"That's right. Just about everyone knows he's hanging around up there. All you have to do is bury her anywhere close to it." She stopped kneading and walked over to one of the stalls. With a shop towel in her hand, she picked up the bloodied shovel and set it down next to him. "Here. Put on one of your work gloves and take this with you. I already wiped it clean. After you finish, leave it somewhere close by."

As she spoke, one more detail that had to be taken care of entered her mind. She walked over to the bench and picked up a hammer.

"What're gonna do with that," he asked.

"We have to knock out her teeth."

"Are you crazy," he hollered. "What the hell for?"

"So they won't be able to identify her." She paused at the sight of his shocked look. "Come now. Do what momma says. Everything's going to be alright. I promise."

He stood up, snatched the hammer out of her hands and flung it into one of the stalls. "Over my dead body," he snarled. "You leave her alone. I'll take care of her."

There was just one little thing she had failed to mention. He looked past her shoulder. "What about her?"

Nadine spun around and spotted Olivia standing just several feet away with her clothes and face splattered with blood, her eyes wide open, and gasping for air.

"Look at her. She was here, wasn't she? She saw you do this."

"I didn't see her," Nadine said. "I had no idea she was in here."

"Now what? Are you going to take care of her too?"

"No. Of course not. She can't hurt us. Who's going to believe anything she says? She's just a baby." She lowered her head and squeezed it between her hands as if scrambling a bunch of ideas to pick at random. "Take her with you."

"And do what?"

"Just leave her up there. Nature will take care of her. No one will ever find her."

He filled his lungs, let out a rush of air, and then walked over to the workbench. He reached up over the rafter and for the first time exposed his friend Jim for the entire world to see.

"So that's where you've been hiding it." He didn't say a word. His Adams apple was too busy rising and falling with each swallow until not a drop was left of the once half filled bottle. He tossed the bottle into a stack of hay then faced Nadine. "I'd better take her back to the house."

"You go ahead and do that then come back and help me."

He lifted the silent Olivia and whispered into her ear. "Mommy's okay. She's okay. She just had a little accident. We're going to take her to the hospital soon."

Before he reached the door, he turned and confronted Nadine with one more question in mind. "What about her car? Her belongings? We can't keep them here."

"Take the car and park it somewhere near that club. I'm sure she was seen there with that Mexican. Then take her purse and clothing over to that old abandoned shack near the mountain."

"Hezekiah's place?"

She smiled. "Of course, dear. Can you think of a better place?"

"You thought of everything, didn't you, mother? You knew this was gonna happen."

"Nonsense," she yelled. "Now you go and do what I said. Everything's gonna be alright. Trust me."

He lifted Olivia and shuffled back to the house. There he took her to the bathroom where he wiped the blood off her face and arms with a wet washcloth before putting her to bed. "Now you try and get some sleep, okay," he said, tucking her in. "I'll be back later."

Back in the barn, the rest of the night was spent in silence, wrapping the body with an old carpet, and then loading it into the bed of his pickup. After it was secured, Nadine went back inside to wet down and then toss new straw onto the floor while he went back to the house to check on Olivia.

An empty bed confronted him as he walked inside the small bedroom. "Olivia? Olivia. Honey where are you?"

After a moment of silence he heard sounds like someone talking. He followed them to the closet and opened the door. There sat Olivia with her head between her legs rocking back and forth mumbling, "stop, don't stop, stop, don't stop_____

"Sweetheart, what're you doin' in there. Come on, we have to go meet your mommy. She's a waitin' for ya. We have to take her to the hospital now." He reached down and cradled her in his arms.

The little lids with the long eyelashes fluttered several times. When they opened, her eyes were filled with tears.

"Everything's gonna be alright. Now let's go see your mommy."

As Nadine stood on the threshold of the bedroom door, he passed by with Olivia in his arms and with his head hanging low, unable to look his mother in the eye.

"Don't forget the teddy bear. She won't give you any trouble as long as it's with her."

"Yes, mother, yes," he said out loud. "I won't forget."

The deputy, standing by the rear door, knocked on the window, taking him out of the old house. "Are you okay?"

Jack looked out the window just as the Coyote's howling waned and watched Cody and Billy return to the excavation site.


Cody scanned the potholed field of sparse, heat wilted grass behind the decaying farmhouse. It reminded him of his parent's fruitless battles against the increasing cost of feed, the constant maintenance of aging equipment, and the yearly droughts that had robbed the soil of its nutrients.

Once his parents realized their war was lost, they sold the homestead before the auction gavel had a chance to strike the first blow. And if it wasn't for the presence of the County Medical Examiner's vehicle, the task at hand could have easily been mistaken for an Archeological dig at a homestead that had succumbed to the same battles years ago.

"We've been at it for quite some time now," Billy said. "You know. This could turn out to be a waterhaul."

He couldn't help but wonder if perhaps Billy was right about the thing turning out to be a waste of time also, especially after having dug at six different locations without finding anything resembling human remains. But the word about a search for yet another victim spread throughout the county like an uncontrollable wildfire. Reporters from Fort Stockton and the surrounding area started gathering on the other side of the familiar yellow and black crime scene tape long before they even started digging. He had to go on. Not to further satisfy their appetite for sensationalism, but to bring closure to the decades old disappearance that had never been reported to the proper authorities.

Cody cradled his chin between the thumb and index finger of his left hand and took another look at the sketch. "According to this we should've found him by now."

"Maybe so. But you've gotta remember one thing."

"And what's that?"

"This so called map's been around for as long as he's been missing. Nothing stays the same. Not even the landscape."

"You're right. But it's too late to call it off now."

While they were talking, the jaw came down and took another bite at the same spot—only this time a little more careful and shallower. The last thing they needed was to have dirt trickle back down into the hole.

Within minutes, a deputy standing by the newly dug hole frantically waved his hands high above his head and yelled, "Hold it!" as he looked at the mound of dirt recently dumped onto the tarp.

Gears, belts, and hydraulic pistons ground to a halt as the operator cut the engine. The idle chatter, amplified by the sudden silence, quickly gave way to the buzzing of cedar flies, mosquitoes, and a host of other flying insects.

After looking into the hole where the dirt came out of, the deputy turned around and, with a waving hand, motioned to Cody.

He rushed over and dropped to one knee near the edge of the hole, unwittingly triggering what they had been trying to avoid.

The others came up behind him and gawked over his massive broad shoulders like back alley gamblers waiting to see the roll of the dice.

Billy's eyes widened as he knelt down next to him. "Well, whatd'ya know. We did find him."

"Let's just hope there's enough of him to give us a positive ID."

Billy looked up at the forest fire glow blanketing the western horizon and the shadows of the various plants and trees casting eastward. "Have you looked over there lately?"

"I'm afraid so." Cody glanced at his wristwatch. It was nearly

8:30 PM. "There's no telling how long this is gonna take. Go ahead and get the floodlights set up. I'll be right back." He stood up and walked away, leaving them to ogle the partially uncovered human skull at the bottom of the hole. He weaved his way through the small, murmuring crowd until he reached the backhoe. "You can take her back home now, Glen. We'll handle it from here. Much obliged."

"You bet, sheriff. Glad I could help."

"Sheriff, Johnson, over here," hollered a news reporter, who, like all the others, knew then that someone or something had been found.

"Did you find him?" asked another.

For the moment, he ignored the chorus of questions that followed and turned to those sifting through the dirt pile. "I want every piece exposed and photographed before taking them out." Then he turned back towards those struggling to stay behind the tapes. "I don't want to say anything just yet, boys," he hollered. "Be patient. In the meantime, how about letting the medical examiner by so he can do his job?"

Alerted by the commotion around him, Clinton worked his way through the contingent of volunteers, deputies, and reporters. When he reached the apparent gravesite, he nodded at Cody then gazed down at the remains.

"I have a feeling I'll be late getting home tonight," Clinton said.

"It looks that way."

"Have you told him yet?"

He looked back over his shoulder towards the Expedition. "I suppose now's as good a time as any." He left the grave site and, for the second time that day, headed towards the vehicle. When he got close to it, he nodded for the deputy standing near the rear door to open it. He stuck his head in. "We found him, Mr. Bauer. That old sketch your mother gave us finally paid off. Are you sure you want to do this?"

Jack swallowed hard. A tear threatened to expose a weakness forced upon him since childhood. But now questions long ignored were about to be answered. He hung his head. "Sure, why not."

Cody stepped back and motioned to the deputy. "Bring him out."

Still in pain from last month's ordeal in the barn, he winced as they took him out. Handcuffed and weak, he stumbled several times as the deputies on each side led him past the backhoe and on to the grave surrounded by the state's CSI unit.

At its edge, he looked down and gazed at the skull of his father, Carl. "She lied, didn't she?" he mumbled. "He never abandoned us. He never even had a chance."

"He tried," Cody said. "She found out he'd been having an affair with a woman who worked at the agriculture office. He was getting ready to file for divorce so they could start a new life together up in Colorado. As you can see that was something your mother wasn't about to let happen."

"So this is how she stopped him."

"I'm afraid so," Cody said, somberly.

"How'd she kill him?"

"Apparently he made the mistake of going back to the house to get some of his belongings. While he was in there, she snuck out and hid in the barn figuring he'd go in there also. Unfortunately for him, she was right. When he showed up, she came up from behind and hit him over the head several times with one of his hammers. After making sure he was dead, she went and got her sister to help drag his body out to bury him here."

"I kind'a figured Aunt Bev knew something all along."

"She did. But in the condition she's in now, there's no way she could testify against your mother."

"She killed Holly too, didn't she?"

"So you did know her?"

"Yea," he said, with a downcast look on his face. "I saw her at the gas station begging for money to fill up her car. While I was putting some in, she told me about running away from home with her boyfriend, and how he dumped her for another woman. She didn't have a place to stay so I brought her home. I thought sure she'd get a hold of her mother for some money. She never did."

"How long did she stay?"

"It's been so long ago…maybe a couple of days or so. I came home from delivering some stock and she was gone. Mother told me she packed up and left without saying a word…I ain't never really believed her."

"Your mother confessed to luring her into the barn for the purpose of getting rid of her."

"Why?"

"She wasn't about to let any woman influence or take you away from her, Mr. Bauer, especially one who she pegged for an immoral drug abuser."

"That's a lie!"

"Those were your mother's words, not mine. The sad part about it is she was right. In her mind she was protecting you, keeping other women from invading her territory, you might say." He paused and briefly glanced back over his shoulder towards the mountain just as the coyote howled again. "The only problem is," he continued, "she went about it in the wrong way."

"What about Holly's car? Her belongings? What did mother do with them?"

Cody turned his head back around. "She won't say. And the chances of finding them this late in time are slim to none. For now we have her signed confession. That's all we need to bring in an indictment on that case."

"What's gonna happen to me now?" he asked in a hushed voice.

"Aiding and abetting is a serious offense. The courts will have to decide your future now."

"All I did was help her get rid of Francis' body."

"Yes, I know. What I don't know is why. You claim you loved her. You thought she would be your ticket out of here. All you had to do was notify us. Why didn't you?"

"I guess I was afraid I'd lose mother too if I didn't do what she told me."

"Sheriff, we found it," hollered one of the deputies assisting the disinterment of the remains. He broke away from the others and walked towards Cody. In his outstretched gloved hand was the heavily rusted horseshoeing hammer mentioned in Nadine's confession.

He gave the hammer the once over as the deputy held it up by the tip of the handle, and then said, "Go ahead and turn it over to DPS. We'll let them process it for us. Find anything else?"

"This."

The deputy handed him a brown leather wallet that appeared to be in good shape considering most of its existence had been spent underground.

Cody opened it and carefully took out several photos. Although faded somewhat, he could still make out a young Carl Bauer with a small boy of about three years old sitting on his lap. He glanced at the tarp littered with fragments of bones and then the remains of an old boot, leather belt, and scraps of clothing that were set off to one side. He thanked the deputy then turned around and showed it to Jack.

Jack lifted his head. His eyes got as far as the photo in Cody's hand.

"So that's where she hid them."

"I'm afraid so. I'll see that you get them after the trial."

"I...I appreciate that, sheriff."

It looks like they've found just about all they're going to," Billy said. "Should we take him back to his cell?"

"Yes. We'll just finish this in the morning. At least he'll be able to get some sleep tonight."

# 52

The next day, Cody and Billy escorted Jack to the interrogation room to continue where he had left off back at the farm. Only this time, the DA was there, along with Jack's attorney, Rueben Schindler.

"What about the episode with Ben?" Cody asked, as memories of what Olivia had gone through in the past, and her reactions to it, came to mind. "He thought you were going to harm Olivia. Claims he tried to stop you. Is that true?"

"All I remember is a dark figure coming out of nowhere. I didn't know it was him at the time. When he came at me, I tried to knock his legs from under him with the shovel, but that didn't stop him. The raving maniac kept coming at me. I was lucky to get out of there alive."

"So Ben was telling the truth after all," Billy said.

"It sounds like it. Did you get all that?"

"Sure did. I'll have Martha add it to what we got last night."

"Wait. I'm not finished yet," Cody said. He removed his hat and gave Jack a close-up look at the scar on the side of his head. "Do you know anything about this?"

"What d'ya mean?"

"I got that up on the mountain just before our encounter with Ben. I have a funny feeling you had something to do with it. If I'm right, it'll be to your benefit to bring it out now and save us some valuable time. How about it?"

"That wasn't meant for you sheriff, I swear it. You came up just as I pulled the trigger. Honest."

"It was meant for Ben then," Cody said. "Just like the lieutenant here surmised."

"Yeah! I couldn't let mother find out he chased me off the mountain—that Olivia was still alive."

"You didn't tell her about what happened up there that night?"

"No. I planned to get rid of him before he was able to talk to anyone about it. I didn't know you guys were gonna be up there."

"Like I told you back on the highway. We're here to serve. It's our duty to respond to all citizens' concerns, including the sighting of a flashing light in the middle of a desert."

"Yeah, I remember."

"You're not only facing a possible aiding and abetting charge now, but obstruction of justice and attempted murder as well."

"What's gonna happen to mother?"

"That's up to the courts to decide," Cody said. "I'm sure she'll undergo mental evaluation before her trial, though. As for the verdict and sentence, that will depend on what the medical experts come up with. All you can do is hope for the best. The same thing goes for you too." He leaned back in his chair and nodded at Billy. "Now you can have Martha type it up."

"Yes, sir."

"Before I have them take you away, Mr. Bauer, there are a couple of things that need to be taken care of."

"Like what?"

"First of all, the teddy bear's taste for cocaine."

"What'ya talking about?"

"You didn't know Olivia had been cuddling over four hundred thousand dollars worth of stolen narcotics?"

"Are you serious?"

"I'm afraid so. It was stuffed inside his stomach. No telling how long it's been in there. You wouldn't believe all the lives it cost, or the heartaches for that matter. I suppose you don't know anything about the money either."

"What money?"

"I thought so. Apparently she didn't trust you enough to reveal much of her past, in particular the whereabouts of the money."

For a second, he wondered how a man could feel the way he did about a woman he knew nothing about. But then Susan came to mind.

"Are you through with him?" Rueben asked, after a long period of silence.

"Not exactly, counselor. There's a baggage *I* have to take care of."

Cody knew deep down inside there was no way of finding out for sure. No way of proving it was Jack veering towards him on that dark night of horror. Or that he may have been under the influence of alcohol that day or night. Even so, he had to try.

Billy cocked a knowing eye at him then glanced at the others who just shrugged their shoulders.

"Mr. Bauer. I want you to think carefully," Cody said. "Do you recall an incident that happened on highway 385 about a year ago?"

"Incident?"

"Yes. An automobile accident. It resulted in two fatalities—a woman and her daughter."

"No, sir, I sure don't."

"Do you spend a lot of time down in Marathon?"

"Yeah. I have friends down there, why?"

"Drinking buddies?"

"We tip the bottle once in a while. What's this all about?"

"Nothing. Forget it." He turned to Billy. "Let's just wrap this up and take him back to his cell."

He was certain now that all he could do was live with the knowledge that the man responsible for his loss had gotten away with leaving the scene of an accident. His only consolation was the future prison time awaiting Jack at the end of the current ordeal. That had to be enough, especially if he wanted Susan to be at the end of *his* ordeal.

# 53

"What about Carlos and Robert?"

"Carlos ran out of time, Susan. The organization he was working for got tired of waiting. As for Robert, DEA deferred their charges against him to the FBI."

"Now why would they do that?"

"I guess they just wanted to distance themselves from his personal actions and preserve their integrity."

"So you were right. He *was* operating on his own."

"He wasn't about to give up the lifestyle provided by his ex-wife. DEA had their suspicions about that and his activities for some time now. That's why they assisted the FBI in their investigation. That's also why the state's District Attorney here decided to postpone his case also. He felt the FBI had one that would result in a more severe punishment."

"And Ben?"

"Trauma Induced Amnesia. Cat scans revealed a previous head injury which may have been caused by a blow to the head during a mugging up in Buffalo. His wife is down here now helping with his therapy. From what I hear, he's starting to put some of the pieces of his past back together. Only time will tell, though, whether he'll be able to complete the puzzle or not. We'll just have to wait and see."

"I'm glad to hear that. Now what about us? How long will we have to wait and see?"

The void had been filled by a six year old angel by the name of Olivia. And he wasn't about to disappoint her. He put his arms around Susan's waist and drew her near, meeting her eyes then kissing her soft, moist lips. Eternity flashed by before he remembered something, forcing a parting he hated with a passion. "Does that answer your question?"

"You bet," she exclaimed, smiling.

He laughed then looked at his watch. "Will you excuse me for a minute? There's someone over in room seven I have to go see. I'll be right back."

"Yes, of course. I'll wait for them out here."

In her hands were all the necessary papers pertaining to the adoption. As she rifled through them, the front door of the county courthouse opened with a slight squeak. Upon hearing the tap, tap, tap sound of a women's high heel on the marble floor of the dimly lit hallway, she looked up. It was Peggy walking towards her with Olivia in hand and Jeremy by her side.

The expression on their faces was not what Susan had expected as she joyfully waved the papers at them.

The couple glanced at each other and then at Olivia as they approached. When they stopped in front of her, Jeremy took a deep breath and gave her the bad news. "Susan, we just don't know if we can go through with this."

"What do you mean?"

"The money," Peggy said. "We're just not sure we can afford all this. I mean, the court costs, attorney's fees, even the cost of raising her."

"You do love her, don't you?"

Their eyes answered for them as they smiled at Olivia. Even so, it wasn't hard to understand their reluctance. The procedure went faster than what was considered normal for the department; and perhaps faster than the couple had anticipated.

Nevertheless, Susan was determined, if at all possible, to bring about a perfect union between the have and have not.

"Why don't you let me worry about the court cost for now," She said. "We can get together later and take care of the other. There are government agencies and funds available that we can tap into."

"Well, now," Cody said, as he came out of room seven and approached them. "Why don't you just tap into this?"

He held up a cashier's check in front of Susan's wide opened eyes. She gasped. Not just because of the amount it was written for, but who signed it.

With a questioning look, Jeremy glanced at Peggy, shrugged, and then confronted Susan. "What's going on?"

"Here. See for yourself." She handed him the check Cody gave her.

Jeremy stared at it for what seemed to Peggy a lifetime before giving it to her in utter silence.

Cody wrapped his arm around Susan's waist as their eyes embraced. "That should help them take care of Olivia for a long time, don't you think?"

"I don't get it?" Jeremy shook his head. "After all he's been through. Why?"

Cody gestured towards the other end of the hallway where a man and a slender woman were walking away from them, heading towards the outer door of the courthouse "He's the only one who can answer that. If he sticks around long enough, that is."

"As you can see, you're not the only ones interested in Olivia's welfare," Susan said as she looked up at Cody. "Besides us, that is."

"That's not all," Cody said. "I have even better news."

"You do?" Susan asked.

"Yes. I've just been told there's a prominent attorney on his way here who's willing to take on the adoption case for free. No charge whatsoever. He's even going to pay the court costs."

Susan's eyes widened again. "What? Who?"

"I don't know. His secretary wouldn't give us his name. All Martha could tell me was that he was another New York resident, and that he's been keeping track of this case ever since it hit the airwaves."

"Why would he do that?"

"Maybe you should ask him yourself, Susan," Cody said, nodding towards the tall figure, whose face was half hidden by the dimness of the corridor. "I believe that's him coming right now."

The man had a proud, straight as an arrow posture. And when he stepped out of the shadows and into the light of an opened office door, Cody tilted his head slightly to one side and squinted with one brow slightly lower than the other. Then the creases on his forehead deepened even further as the man got closer to them.

"Good to see you again, Cody," the attorney said, as he got within two feet with his outstretched hand. "It's been a long time."

Cody's jaw dropped and his eyes widened when he noticed the prominent twitch of the attorney's left shoulder.

# About the Author

**Peter Chandler's** love of writing began with an op piece published by the Washington Post. Since then, he has been a member of a local writer's club and has taken classes in both fiction and none fiction writing at several Community Colleges and private venues.

To his credit he's had feature articles published in the American Fitness magazine, the Long Term Care magazine of Canada, the Plus family periodical, and several pieces for the local newspaper.

As a member of the Johnson County Writers Club, he has garnered first place awards for short stories sponsored by them and other writers clubs throughout Texas.

The 72 year old native Puerto Rican, who grew up in the streets of New York City, and who has served in the military during the Vietnam War, is now a retired Federal Government employee who loves gardening, traveling, and working out with weights at the local fitness center.

Peter Chandler

Peter Chandler